!Tention
A Story of Boy-Life during the Peninsular War

by

George Manville Fenn

Double 9
BOOKS

!Tention
A Story of Boy-Life during the Peninsular War
by George Manville Fenn

ISBN: 978-93-59956-69-5

Published by

DOUBLE 9 BOOKS

2/13-B, Ansari Road
Daryaganj, New Delhi – 110002
info@double9books.com
www.double9books.com
Tel. 011-40042856

ABOUT THE AUTHOR

George Manville Fenn was a very productive author of novels, a writer, an editor, and an educator from England. He was born on January 3, 1831, in Pimlico, London. He mostly learned on his own; he taught himself Italian, French, and German. During the years 1851-1854, he went to Battersea Training College for Teachers and then became the head of a state school in Alford, Lincolnshire. In the early 1850s, Fenn started to write short stories and pieces for newspapers and magazines. The Old Forest Ranger, his first book, came out in 1856. Afterward, he wrote more than 100 books, many of them for teenagers and young adults. He was one of the most famous writers of his time, and his books were well-liked and read by many people. I also worked as a reporter and writer for Fenn. Among the newspapers and magazines, he worked for was The Boy's Own Paper, which he ran from 1866 to 1874. He worked hard to make children's books better and was a strong supporter of education and reading. The Englishman Fenn passed away on August 26, 1909, in Isleworth.

CONTENTS

Chapter One
To save a Comrade

A sharp volley, which ran echoing along the ravine, then another, just as the faint bluish smoke from some hundred or two muskets floated up into the bright sunshine from amidst the scattered chestnuts and cork-trees that filled the lower part of the beautiful gorge, where, now hidden, now flashing out and scattering the rays of the sun, a torrent roared and foamed along its rocky course onward towards its junction with the great Spanish river whose destination was the sea.

Again another ragged volley; and this was followed by a few dull, heavy-sounding single shots, which came evidently from a skirmishing party which was working its way along the steep slope across the river.

There was no responsive platoon reply to the volley, but the skirmishing shots were answered directly by *crack! crack! crack*! the reports that sounded strangely different to those heavy, dull musket-shots which came from near at hand, and hardly needed glimpses of dark-green uniforms that dotted the hither slope of the mountain-side to proclaim that they were delivered by riflemen who a few minutes before were, almost in single line, making their way along a rugged mountain-path.

A second glance showed that they formed the rear-guard of a body of sharpshooters, beyond whom in the distance could be made out now and then glints of bright scarlet, which at times looked almost orange in the brilliant sunshine—orange flashed with silver, as the sun played upon musket-barrel and fixed bayonet more than shoulder-high.

The country Spain, amidst the towering Pyrenees; the scarlet that of a British column making its way along a rugged mule-path, from which those that traversed it looked down upon a scene of earthly beauty, and upwards at the celestial blue, beyond which towered the rugged peaks where here and there patches of the past winter's snow gleamed and sparkled in the sun.

Strategy had indicated retreat; and the black-green, tipped at collar and cuff with scarlet, of England's rifle-regiment was covering the retiring line, when the blue-coated columns of the French General's division had pressed on and delivered the wild volleys and scattered shots of the skirmishers which drew forth the sharp, vicious, snapping reply of the retreating rear-guard.

"At last!" said one of the riflemen, rising from where he had knelt on one knee to take cover behind a bush, and there stand driving down a cartridge with a peculiarly sharp, ringing sound of iron against iron, before finishing off with a few heavy thuds, returning the bright rod to its loops, and raising the pan of the lock to see that it was well primed with the coarse powder of the day.

"Yes—at last!" said his nearest comrade, who with a few more had halted at a subaltern's command to wait in cover for a shot or two at their pursuing foe. "Are we going to hold this place?"

"No," said the young officer. "Hear that, my man?" For a note or two of a bugle rang out sweet and clear in the beautiful valley, suggesting to one of the men a similar scene in an English dell; but he sighed to himself as it struck him that this was a different hunt, and that they, the men of the —th, the one rifle-regiment of the British Army, were the hunted, and that those who followed were the French.

A few more cracks from the rifles as the retreat was continued, and then the French musketry ceased; but the last of the sharpshooters obtained glimpses of the blue coats of the French coming quickly on.

"Have you sickened them, my lads?" said the young officer, as he led his men after the retreating main body of their friends.

"No, sir," said the young private addressed; "they seem to have lost touch of us. The mule-track has led right away to the left here."

"To be sure—yes. Then they will begin again directly. Keep your face well to the enemy, and take advantage of every bit of cover.—Here, bugler, keep close up to me."

The sturdy-looking boy addressed had just closed up to his officer's side when, as they were about to plunge into a low-growing patch of trees, there was another volley, the bullets pattering amongst the branches, twigs and leaves cut from above the men's heads falling thickly.

"Forward, my lads—double!" And the subaltern led his men through the trees to where the mountain-side opened out a little more; and, pointing with his sword to a dense patch a little farther on, he shouted, "Take cover there! We must hold that patch. — Here, bugler! — Where's that boy?"

No one answered, the men hurriedly following the speaker at the double; but the young private who had replied to the subaltern's questions, having fallen back to where he was running with a companion in the rear, looked over his shoulder, and then, startled by the feeling that the boy had not passed through the clump, he stopped short, his companion imitating his example and replying to the eager question addressed to him:

"I dunno, mate. I thought he was with his officer. Come on; we don't want to be prisoners."

He started again as he spoke, not hearing, or certainly not heeding, his comrade's angry words —

"He must be back there in the wood."

Carrying his rifle at the trail, he dashed back into the wood, hearing, as he ran, shouts as of orders being given by the enemy; but he ran on right through the clump of trees to where the mule-path meandered along by the edge of the precipice, and lay open before him to the next patch of woodland which screened the following enemy from view.

But the path was not unoccupied, for there, about fifty yards from him, he caught sight of his unfortunate young comrade, who, bugle in hand, was just struggling to his feet; and then, as he stood upright, he made a couple of steps forward, but only to stagger and reel for a moment; when, as his comrade uttered a cry, the boy tottered over the edge of the path, fell a few yards, and then rolled down the steep slope out of sight.

The young rifleman did not stop to think, but occupied the brief moments in running to his comrade's help; and, just as a volley came crashing from the open wood beyond the path, he dropped down over the side, striving hard to keep his feet and to check his downward progress to where he felt that the boy must have fallen. Catching vainly at branch and rock, he went on, down and down, till he was brought up short by a great mossy block of stone just as another volley was fired, apparently from the mule-track high above him; and half-unconsciously, in the confusion and excitement of the moment, he lay perfectly still, cowering amongst the sparse growth in the hope that he might not be seen from the shelf-like mule-track above, though expectant all the while that the next shot fired would be at him.

But, as it happened, that next shot was accompanied by many more; and as, fearing to move, he strained his eyes upward, he could see the grey smoke rising, and hear the sound of a bugle, followed by the rush of feet, and he knew that, so far, he had not been seen, but that the strong body of the enemy were hurrying along the mule-track in full pursuit of his friends.

"Just as if I had been running," muttered the young rifleman; and he stole his left hand slowly upwards, from where he was lying in a most awkward position, to rest it upon his breast as if to check the heavy beating of his heart.

"Ah!" he panted at last, as with strained eyes and ears he waited for some sign of his presence behind the advancing enemy being known. "Where's that boy?" he muttered hoarsely; and he tried to look about without moving, so as not to expose himself to any who might be passing along the rocky ledge.

The next minute the necessity for caution was emphasised, for there was a hoarse command from somewhere above, followed by the heavy tramp of feet which told only too plainly that he was being cut off from his regiment by another body of the enemy.

"I couldn't help it," he said. "I couldn't leave that poor fellow behind."

He had hardly uttered this thought when, apparently from just beyond the rugged mass of stone which had checked his descent, there came a low groan, followed by a few words, amongst which the listener made out, "The cowards!"

"That you, Punch?" whispered the young rifleman excitedly.

"Eh, who's that?" was the faint reply.

"Hist! Lie still. I'll try and get to you directly."

"That you, Private Gray?"

"Yes, yes," was whispered back, and the speaker felt his heart leap within his breast; "but lie still for a few moments."

"Oh, do come! I'm—I've got it bad."

The young private felt his heart sink again as he recalled the way in which the boy had staggered and fallen from the edge of the track above him. Then, in answer to the appeal for help, he passed his rifle over his body, and, wrenching himself round, he managed to lower himself beyond the mass of rock so as to get beneath and obtain its shelter from those passing along the ledge, but only to slip suddenly for a yard or two, with the result that the shrubs over which he had passed sprang up again and supplied the shelter which he sought.

"Punch! Punch! Where are you?" he whispered, as, satisfied now that he could not be seen from above, he raised his head a little and tried to make out him whom he sought.

But all was perfectly still about where he lay, while the sound of musketry came rolling and echoing along the narrow ravine; and above the trees, in the direction in which his friends must be, there was a rising and ever-thickening cloud of smoke.

Then for a few minutes the firing ceased, and in the midst of the intense silence there arose from the bushes just above the listener's head a quick twittering of premonitory notes, followed by the sharp, clear, ringing song of a bird, which thrilled the lad with a feeling of hope in the midst of what the moment before had been a silence that was awful.

Then from close at hand came a low, piteous groan, and a familiar voice muttered, "The cowards—to leave a comrade like this!"

Chapter Two
Poor Punch

Private Gray, of his Majesty's —th Rifles,—wrenched himself round once more, pressed aside a clump of heathery growth, crawled quickly about a couple of yards, and found himself lying face to face with the bugler of his company.

"Why, Punch, lad!" he said, "not hurt much, are you?"

"That you, Private Gray?"

"Yes. But tell me, are you wounded?"

"Yes!" half-groaned the boy; and then with a sudden access of excitement, "Here, I say, where's my bugle?"

"Oh, never mind your bugle. Where are you hurt?" cried the boy's comrade.

"In my bugle—I mean, somewhere in my back. But where's my instrument?"

"There it is, in the grass, hanging by the cord."

"Oh, that's better," groaned the boy. "I thought all our chaps had gone on and left me to die."

"And now you see that they hav'n't," said the boy's companion. "There, don't try to move. We mustn't be seen."

"Yes," almost babbled the boy, speaking piteously, "I thought they had all gone, and left me here. I did try to ketch up to them; but—oh, I am so faint and sick that it's all going round and round! Here, Private Gray, you are a good chap, shove the cord over my head, and take care the enemy don't get my bugle. Ah! Water—water, please! It's all going round and round."

Penton Gray made no effort now to look round for danger, but, unstopping his water-bottle, he crept closer to his companion in adversity, passed the strap of the boy's shako from under his chin, thrust his cap from his head to lie amongst the grass, and then opened the collar of his coatee and began to trickle a little water between the poor fellow's lips and sprinkled a little upon his temples.

"Ah!" sighed the boy, as he began to revive, "that's good! I don't mind now."

"But you are hurt. Where's your wound?" said the young private eagerly.

"Somewhere just under the shoulder," replied the boy. "'Tain't bleeding much, is it?"

"I don't know yet. — I won't hurt you more than I can help."

"Whatcher going to do?"

"Draw off your jacket so that I can see whether the hurt's bad."

"'Tain't very," said the boy, speaking feebly of body but stout of heart. "I don't mind, comrade. Soldiers don't mind a wound. — Oh, I say!" he cried, with more vigour than he had previously evinced.

"Did I hurt you?"

"Yes, you just did. Were you cutting it with your knife?"

"No," said his comrade with a half-laugh, as he drew his hand from where he had passed it under the boy's shoulder. "That's what cut you, Punch," and he held up a ragged-looking bullet which had dropped into his fingers as he manipulated the wound.

"Thought you was cutting me with your knife," said the boy, speaking with some energy now. "But, I say, don't you chuck that away; I want that. — What did they want to shoot me there for — the cowards! Just as if I was running away, when I was only obeying orders. If they had shot me in front I could have seen to it myself. — I say, does it bleed much?"

"No, my lad; but it's an ugly place."

"Well, who wants it to be handsome? I ain't a girl. Think you can stop it, private?"

"I think I can bind it up, Punch, and the bleeding will stop of itself."

"That's good. I say, though, private — sure to die after it, ain't I?"

"Yes, some day," said the young soldier, smiling encouragingly at the speaker; and then by the help of a shirt-sleeve and a bandage which he drew from his knapsack, the young soldier managed pretty deftly to bind up his comrade's wound, and then place him in a more comfortable position, lying upon his side.

"Thank ye!" said the boy with a sigh. "But, I say, you have give it me hot."

"I am very sorry, boy."

"Oh, never mind that. But just wipe my face; it's all as wet as wet, and the drops keep running together and tickling."

This little service was performed, and then the boy turned his head uneasily aside.

"What is it, Punch?"

"That there bullet—where is it?"

"I have got it safe."

"That's right. Now, where's my bugle?"

"There it is, quite safe too."

"Yes, that's right," said the boy faintly. "I don't want to lose that; but— Oh, I say, look at that there dent! What'll the colonel say when he sees that?"

"Shall I tell you, Punch?" said the young man, who bent over him, watching every change in his face.

"Yes—no. I know: 'Careless young whelp,' or something; and the sergeant—"

"Never mind the sergeant," said the young sharpshooter. "I want to tell you what the colonel will say, like the gentleman he is."

"Then, what'll he say?" said the wounded lad drowsily.

"That he has a very brave boy in his regiment, and— Poor chap, he has fainted again! My word, what a position to be in! Our fellows will never be able to get back, and if I shout for help it means hospital for him, prison for me. What shall I do?"

There was nothing to be done, as Pen Gray soon realised as he lay upon his side in the shade of the steep valley, watching his wounded comrade, who gradually sank into the sleep of exhaustion, while the private listened for every sound that might suggest the coming on or retreating of the French troops. His hopes rose once, for it seemed to him that the tide of war was ebbing and flowing lower down the valley, and his spirits rose as the mountain-breeze brought the sounds of firing apparently nearer and nearer, till he felt that the English troops had not only rallied, but were driving back the French over the ground by which they had come. But as the day wore on he found that his hopes were false; and, to make their position worse, fresh troops had come down the valley and were halted about a quarter of a mile from where he and his sleeping companion lay; while, lower down, the firing, which had grown fiercer and fiercer, gradually died out.

He was intently straining his ears, when to his surprise the afternoon sun began to flash upon the weapons of armed men, and once more his hopes revived in the belief that the French were being driven back; but to his astonishment and dismay, as they came more and more into sight, a halt seemed to have been called, and they too settled down into a bivouac, and communications by means of mounted men took place between them and the halted party higher up the valley; the young rifleman, by using great care, watching the going to and fro unseen.

Evening was coming on, and Pen Gray was still watching and wondering whether it would be possible to take advantage of the darkness, when it fell, to try and pass down the valley, circumvent the enemy, and overtake their friends, when the wounded boy's eyes unclosed, and he lay gazing wonderingly in his comrade's eyes.

"Better, Punch?" said Pen softly.

"What's the matter?" was the reply; and the boy gazed in his face in a dazed, half-stupid way.

"Don't you remember, lad?"

"No," was the reply. "Where's the ridgment?"

"Over yonder. Somewhere about the mouth of the valley, I expect."

"Oh, all right. What time is it?"

"I should think about five. Why?"

"Why?" said the boy. "Because there will be a row. Why are we here?"

"Waiting till you are better before trying to join our company."

"Better? Have we been resting, then, because my feet were so bad with the marching?"

Pen was silent as he half-knelt there, listening wonderingly to his comrade's half-delirious queries, and asking himself whether he had better tell the boy their real position.

"So much marching," continued the boy, "and those blisters. Ah, I remember! I say, private, didn't I get a bullet into me, and fall right down here? Yes, that's it. Here, Private Gray, what are you going to do?"

"Ah, what are we going to do?" said the young man sadly. "I was in hopes that you would be so much better, or rather I hoped you might, that we could creep along after dark and get back to our men; but I am afraid—"

"So'm I," said the boy bitterly, as he tried to move himself a little, and then sank back with a faint groan. "Couldn't do it, unless two of our fellows got me in a sergeant's sash and carried me."

"I'd try and carry you on my back," said Pen, "if you could bear it."

"Couldn't," said the boy abruptly. "I say, where do you think our lads are?"

"Beaten, perhaps taken prisoners," said Pen bitterly.

"Serve 'em right—cowards! To go and leave us behind like this!"

"Don't talk so much."

"Why?"

"It will make you feverish; and it's of no use to complain. They couldn't help leaving us. Besides, I was not left."

"Then how come you to be here?" said the boy sharply.

"I came after you, to help you."

"More old stupid you! Didn't you know when you were safe?"

Pen raised his brows a little and looked half-perplexed, half-amused at the irritable face of his comrade, who wrinkled up his forehead with pain, drew a hard breath, and then whispered softly, "I say, comrade, I oughtn't to have said that there, ought I?"

Pen was silent.

"You saw me go down, didn't you?"

Pen bowed his head.

"And you ran back to pick me up? Ah!" he ejaculated, drawing his breath hard.

"Wound hurt you much, my lad?"

"Ye–es," said the lad, wincing; "just as if some one was boring a hole through my shoulder with a red-hot ramrod."

"Punch, my lad, I don't think it's a bad wound, for while you were asleep I looked, and found that it had stopped bleeding."

"Stopped? That's a good job; ain't it, comrade?"

"Yes; and with a healthy young fellow like you a wound soon begins to heal up if the wounded man lies quiet."

"But I'm only a boy, private."

"Then the wound will heal all the more readily."

"I say, how do you know all this?" said the boy, looking at him curiously.

"By reading."

"Reading! Ah, I can't read—not much; only little words. Well, then, if you know that, I have got to lie still, then, till the hole's grown up. I say, have you got that bullet safe?"

"Oh yes."

"Don't you lose it, mind, because I mean to keep that to show people at home. Even if I am a boy I should like people to know that I have been in the wars. So I have got to lie still and get well? Won't be bad if you could get me a bundle or two of hay and a greatcoat to cover over me. The wind will come down pretty cold from the mountains; but I sha'n't mind that so long as the bears don't come too. I shall be all right, so you had better be off and get back to the regiment, and tell them where you have left me. I say, you will get promoted for it."

"Nonsense, Punch! What for?"

"Sticking to a comrade like this. I have been thinking about it, and I call it fine of you running back to help me, with the Frenchies coming on. Yes, I know. Don't make faces about it. The colonel will have you made corporal for trying to save me."

"Of course!" said Pen sarcastically. "Why, I'm not much older than you—the youngest private in the regiment; more likely to be in trouble for not keeping in the ranks, and shirking the enemy's fire."

"Don't you tell me," said the boy sharply. "I'll let the colonel and everybody know, if ever I get back to the ranks again."

"What's that?" said Pen sharply. "If ever you get back to the ranks again! Why, you are not going to set up a faint heart, are you?"

"'Tain't my heart's faint, but my head feels sick and swimmy. But, I say, do you think you ought to do any more about stopping up the hole so as to give a fellow a chance?"

"I'll do all I can, Punch," said Pen; "but you know I'm not a surgeon."

"Course I do," said the boy, laughing, but evidently fighting hard to hide his suffering. "You are better than a doctor."

"Better, eh?"

"Yes, ever so much, because you are here and the doctor isn't."

The boy lay silent for a few minutes, evidently thinking deeply.

"I say, private," he said at last, "I can't settle this all out about what's going to be done; but I think this will be best."

"What?"

"What I said before. You had better wait till night, and then creep off and follow our men's track. It will be awkward in the dark, but you ought to be able to find out somehow, because there's only one road all along by the side of this little river. You just keep along that while it's dark, and trust to luck when it's daytime again. Only, look here, my water-bottle's empty, so, as soon as you think it's dark enough, down you go to the river, fill it, and bring it back, and I shall be all right till our fellows fight their way back and pick me up."

"And if they are not able to—what then?" said Pen, smiling.

"Well, I shall wait till I get so hungry I can't wait any longer, and then I will cry *chy-ike* till the Frenchies come and pick me up. But, I say, they won't stick a bayonet through me, will they?"

"What, through a wounded boy!" said Pen angrily. "No, they are not so bad as that."

"Thank ye! I like that, private. I have often wished I was a man; but now I'm lying here, with a hole in my back, I'm rather glad that I am only a boy. Now then, catch hold of my water-bottle. It will soon be dark enough for you to get down to the river; and you mustn't lose any time. Oh, there's one thing more, though. You had better take my bugle; we mustn't let the enemy have that. I think as much of my bugle as Bony's chaps do of their eagles. You will take care of it, won't you?"

"Yes, when I carry it," said Pen quietly.

"Well, you are going to carry it now, aren't you?"

"No," said Pen quietly.

"Oh, you mean, not till you have fetched the water?"

Pen shook his head.

"What do you mean, then?"

"To do my duty, boy."

"Of course you do; but don't be so jolly fond of calling me boy. You said yourself a little while ago that you weren't much older than I am. But, I say, you had better go now; and I suppose I oughtn't to talk, for it makes my head turn swimmy, and we are wasting time; and—oh, Gray," the boy groaned, "I—I can't help it. I never felt so bad as this. There, do go now. Get the water, and if I am asleep when you come back, don't wake me so that I feel the pain again. But—but—shake hands first, and say good-bye."

The boy uttered a faint cry of agony as he tried to stretch out his hand, which only sank down helplessly by his side.

"Well, good-bye," he panted, as Pen's dropped slowly upon the quivering limb. "Well, why don't you go?"

"Because it isn't time yet," said Pen meaningly, as after a glance round he drew some of the overhanging twigs of the nearest shrub closer together, and then passed his hand across the boy's forehead, and afterwards held his wrist.

"Thank you, doctor," said the boy, smiling. "That seems to have done me good. Now then, aren't you going?"

"No," said Pen, with a sigh.

"I say—why?"

"You know as well as I do," replied Pen.

"You mean that you won't go and leave me here alone? That's what you mean."

"Yes, Punch; you are quite right. But look here. Suppose I was lying here wounded, would you go off and leave me at night on this cold mountain-side, knowing how those brutes of wolves hang about the rear of the army? You have heard them of a night, haven't you?"

"Yes," said the boy, shudderingly drawing his breath through his tightly closed teeth. "I say, comrade, what do you want to talk like that for?"

"Because I want you to answer my question: Would you go off and leave me here alone?"

"No, I'm blessed if I would," said the boy, speaking now in a voice full of animation. "I couldn't do it, comrade, and it wouldn't be like a soldier's son."

"But I am not a soldier's son, Punch."

"No," said the boy, "and that's what our lads say. They don't like you, and they say— There, I won't tell you what."

"Yes, tell me, Punch. I should like to know."

"They say that they have not got anything else against you, only you have no business here in the ranks."

"Why do they say that?"

"Because, when they are talking about it, they say you are a gentleman and a scholard."

"But I thought I was always friendly and sociable with them."

"So you are, Private Gray," cried the boy excitedly; "and if ever I get back to the ranks alive I'll tell them you are the best comrade in the regiment, and how you wouldn't leave me in the lurch."

"And I shall make you promise, Punch, that you never say a word."

"All right," said the boy, with a faint smile, "I'll promise. I won't say a word; but," he continued, with a shudder which did not conceal his smile, "they will be sure to find it out and get to like you as much as I do now."

"What's the matter, Punch?" said Pen shortly. "Cold?"

"Head's hot as fire, so's my shoulder; but everywhere else I am like ice. And there's that swimming coming in my head again.—I don't mind. It's all right, comrade; I shall be better soon, but just now—just now—"

The boy's voice trailed off into silence, and a few minutes later young Private Penton Gray, of his Majesty's newly raised —th Rifles, nearly all fresh bearers of the weapon which was to do so much to win the battles of the Peninsular War, prepared to keep his night-watch on the chilly mountain-side by stripping off his coatee and unrolling his carefully folded greatcoat to cover the wounded lad. And that night-watch was where he could hear the howling and answering howls of the loathsome beasts that seemed to him to say: "This way, comrades: here, and here, for men are lying wounded and slain; the watch-fires are distant, and there are none to hinder us where the banquet is spread. Come, brothers, come!"

Chapter Three
Where the Wolves howl

"Ugh!" A long, shivering shudder following upon the low, dismal howl of a wolf.

"Bah! How cold it is lying out here in this chilly wind which comes down from the mountain tops! I say, what an idiot I was to strip myself and turn my greatcoat into a counterpane! No, I won't be a humbug; that wasn't the cold. It was sheer fright—cowardice—and I should have felt just the same if I had had a blanket over me. The brutes! There is something so horrible about it. The very idea of their coming down from the mountains to follow the trail of the fighting, and hunt out the dead or the wounded who have been forgotten or have crawled somewhere for shelter."

Pen Gray lay thinking in the darkness, straining his ears the while to try and convince himself that the faint sound he heard was not a movement made by a prowling wolf scenting them out; and as he lay listening, he pictured to himself the gaunt, grisly beast creeping up to spring upon him.

"Only fancy!" he said sadly. "That wasn't the breathing of one of the beasts, only the wind again that comes sighing down from the mountains.—I wish I was more plucky."

He stretched out his hand and laid his rifle amongst the shrubs with its muzzle pointed in the direction from whence the sighing sound had come.

"I'll put an end to one of them," he muttered bitterly, "if I don't miss him in the dark. Pooh! They won't come here, or if they do I have only to jump up and the cowardly beasts will dash off at once; but it is horrid lying here in the darkness, so solitary and so strange. I wouldn't care so much if the stars would come out, but they won't to-night. To-night? Why, it must be nearly morning, for I have been lying here hours and hours. And how dark it is in this valley, with the mountains towering up on each side. I wish the day would come, but it always does seem ten times as long when you are waiting and expecting it. It is getting cold though. Seems to go right through to one's bones.—Poor boy," he continued, as he stretched out one hand and gently passed it beneath his companion's covering. "He's warm enough.

No—too hot; and I suppose that's fever from his wound. Poor chap! Such a boy too! But as brave as brave. He must be a couple of years younger than I am; but he's more of a man. Oh, I do wish it was morning, so that I could try and do something. There must be cottages somewhere—shepherds' or goat-herds'—where as soon as the people understand that we are not French they might give me some black-bread and an onion or two."

The young soldier laughed a soft, low, mocking kind of laugh.

"Black-bread and an onion! How queer it seems! Why, there was a time when I wouldn't have touched such stuff, while now it sounds like a feast. But let's see; let's think about what I have got to do. As soon as it's daylight I must find a cottage and try to make the people understand what's the matter, and get them to help me to carry poor Punch into shelter. Another night like this would kill him. I don't know, though. I always used to think that lying down in one's wet clothes, and perhaps rain coming in the night, would give me a cold; but it doesn't. I must get him into shelter, though, somehow. Oh, if morning would only come! The black darkness makes one feel so horribly lonely.—What nonsense! I have got poor Punch here. But he has the best of it; he can sleep, and here I haven't even closed my eyes. Being hungry, I suppose.—I wonder where our lads are. Gone right off perhaps. I hope we haven't lost many. But the firing was very sharp, and I suppose the French have kept up the pursuit, and they are all miles and miles away."

At that moment there was a sharp flash with the report of a musket, and its echoes seemed to be thrown back from the steep slope across the torrent, while almost simultaneously, as Gray raised himself upon his elbow, there was another report, and another, and another, followed by more, some of which seemed distant and the others close at hand; while, as the echoes zigzagged across the valley, and the lad stretched out his hand to draw himself up into a sitting position, oddly enough that hand touched something icy, and he snatched it back with a feeling of annoyance, for he realised that it was only the icy metal that formed his wounded companion's bugle, and he lay listening to the faint notes of another instrument calling upon the men to assemble.

"Why, it's a night attack," thought Pen excitedly, and unconsciously he began to breathe hard as he listened intently, while he fully grasped the fact that there were men of the French brigade dotted about in all directions.

"And there was I thinking that we were quite alone!" he said to himself.

Then by degrees his short experience of a few months of the British occupation on the borders of Portugal and Spain taught him that he had been listening to a night alarm, for from out of the darkness came the low buzz of voices, another bugle was sounded, distant orders rang out, and then by degrees the low murmur of voices died away, and once more all was still.

"I was in hopes," thought Gray, "that our fellows were making a night attack, giving the enemy a surprise. Why, there must be hundreds within reach. That puts an end to my going hunting about for help as soon as the day breaks, unless I mean us to be taken prisoners. Why, if I moved from here I should be seen.—Asleep, Punch?" he said softly.

There was no reply, and the speaker shuddered as he stretched out his hand to feel for his companion's forehead; but at the first touch there was an impatient movement, and a feeling of relief shot through the lad's breast, for imagination had been busy, and was ready to suggest that something horrible might have happened in the night.

"Oh, I do wish I wasn't such a coward," he muttered. "He's all right, only a bit feverish. What shall I do? Try and go to sleep till morning? What's the good of talking? I am sure I couldn't, even if I did try."

Then the weary hours slowly crept along, the watcher trying hard to settle in his own mind which was the east, but failing dismally, for the windings of the valley had been such that he could only guess at the direction where the dawn might appear.

There were no more of the dismal bowlings of the wolves, though, the scattered firing having effectually driven them away; but there were moments when it seemed to the young watcher that the night was being indefinitely prolonged, and he sighed again and again as he strained his eyes to pierce the darkness, and went on trying to form some plan as to his next movement.

"I wonder how long we could lie in hiding here," he said to himself, "without food. Poor Punch in his state wouldn't miss his ration; but by-and-by, if the French don't find us, this bitter cold will have passed away, and we shall be lying here in the scorching sunshine—for it can be hot in these stuffy valleys—and the poor boy will be raving for water—yes, water. Who was that chap who was tortured by having it close to him and not being able to reach it? Tantalus, of course! I am forgetting all my classics. Well, soldiers don't want cock-and-bull stories out of Lempriere. I wonder, though, whether I could crawl down among the bushes to the edge of the torrent and fill our water-bottles, and get back up here again without being seen. But perhaps, when the day comes, and if they don't see us, the French will move off, and then I need only wait patiently and try and find some cottage.—Yes, what is it?"

He raised himself upon his arm again, for Punch had begun to mutter; but there was no reply.

"Talking in his sleep," said Pen with a sigh. "Good for him that he can sleep! Oh, surely it must be near morning now!"

The lad sprang to his knees and placed one hand over his eyes as he strained himself round, for all at once he caught sight of a tiny speck as of glowing fire right overhead, and he stared in amazement.

"Why, that can't be daylight!" he thought. "It would appear, of course, low down in the east, just a faint streak of dawn. That must be some dull star peering through the clouds. Why, there are two of them," he said in a whisper; "no, three. Why, it is day coming!" And he uttered a faint cry of joy as he crouched low again and gazed, so to speak, with all his might at the wondrous scene of beauty formed by the myriad specks of orange light which began to spread overhead, and grow and grow till the mighty dome that seemed supported in a vast curve by the mountains on either side of the valley became one blaze of light.

"Punch," whispered Pen excitedly, "it's morning! Look, look! How stupid!" he muttered. "Why should I wake him to pain and misery? Yes, it is morning, sure enough," he muttered again, for a bugle rang out apparently close at hand, and was answered from first one direction and then another, the echoes taking up the notes softly and repeating them again and again till it seemed to the listener as if he must be lying with quite an army close at hand awakening to the day.

The light rapidly increased, and Pen began to look in various directions for danger, wondering the while whether some patch of forest would offer itself as an asylum somewhere close at hand; but he only uttered a sigh of relief as he grasped the fact that, while high above them the golden light was gleaming down from the sun-flecked clouds, the gorges were still full of purple gloom, and clouds of thick mist were slowly gathering in the valley-bottom and were being wafted along by the breath of morn and following the course of the river.

To his great relief too, as the minutes glided by, he found that great patches of the rolling smoke-like mist rose higher and higher till a soft, dank cloud enveloped them where they lay, and through it he could hear faintly uttered orders and the tramp of men apparently gathering and passing along the shelf-like mule-path.

"And I was longing for the sun to rise!" thought Pen.—"Ah, there's an officer;" for somewhere just overhead there was the sharp click of an iron-shod hoof among the rocks. "He must have seen us if it hadn't been for this mist," thought the lad. "Now if it will only last for half an hour we may be safe."

The mist did last for quite that space of time—in fact, until Pen Gray was realising that the east lay right away to his right—for a golden shaft of light suddenly shot horizontally from a gap in the mountains, turning the heavy mists it pierced into masses of opalescent hues; and, there before him, he suddenly caught sight of a cameo-like figure which stood out from where he knew that the shelf-like mule-path must run. The great bar of golden light enveloped both rider and horse, and flashed from the officer's raised sword and the horse's trappings.

Then the rolling cloud of mist swept on and blotted him from sight, and Pen crouched closer and closer to his sleeping comrade, and lay with bated breath listening to the tramp, tramp of the passing men not a hundred feet above his head, and praying now that the wreaths of mist might screen them, as they did till what seemed to him to be a strong brigade had gone on in the direction taken by his friends.

But he did not begin to breathe freely till the tramping of hoofs told to his experienced ears that a strong baggage-train of mules was on its way. Then came the tramp of men again.

"Rear-guard," he thought; and then his heart sank once more, for the tramping men swept by in the midst of a dense grey cloud, which looked like smoke as it rolled right onward, and as if by magic the sun burst out and filled the valley with a blaze of light.

"They must see us now," groaned Pen; and he closed his eyes in his despair.

Chapter Four
"Water, or I shall die!"

Pen's heart beat heavily as he lay listening to the tramping of feet upon the rocky shelf, and at last the sounds seemed so close that he drew himself together ready to spring to his feet and do what he could to protect his injured comrade. For in his strange position the idea was strong upon him that their first recognition by the enemy might be made with the presentation of a bayonet's point.

But his anticipations proved to be only the work of an excited brain; and, as he lay perfectly still once more, the heavy tramp, tramp, a good deal wanting in the regularity of the British troops, died out, and he relieved the oppression that bore down upon his breast with a deep sigh.

Nothing was visible as the sounds died out; and, waiting till he felt that he was safe, he changed his position slightly so as to try and make out whether the rear-guard of the enemy had quite disappeared.

In an instant he had shrunk down again amongst the bushes, for there, about a hundred yards away, at the point of an angle where the mule-path struck off suddenly to the left, and at a spot that had undoubtedly been chosen for its command of the road backward, he became aware of the presence of an outpost of seven or eight men.

This was startling, for it put a check upon any attempt at movement upon his own part.

Pen lay thinking for a few moments, during which he made sure that his comrade was still plunged in a deep, stupor-like sleep. Then, after a little investigation, he settled how he could move slightly without drawing the attention of the vedette; and, taking advantage thereof, crawled cautiously about a couple of yards with the greatest care. Then, looking back as he slowly raised his head, which he covered with a few leafy twigs, he was by no means surprised to see at the edge of the mule-path about a quarter of a mile away another vedette. This shut off any attempt at retreat in that direction, and he was about to move again when he was startled by a flash of light reflected from a musket-barrel whose bearer was one acting as the leader of a third vedette moving up the side of the valley across the river, and which soon came to a halt at about the same height above the stream as that which he occupied himself.

The lad could not control a movement of impatience as the little knot of infantry settled themselves exactly opposite to his own hiding-place, and in a position from which the French soldiers must be able to control one slope of the valley for a mile in each direction.

"It's maddening!" thought Pen. "I sha'n't be able to stir, and I dare say they'll have more vedettes stationed about. It means giving up, and nothing else."

Very slowly and cautiously he wrenched himself round, and then rolled over twice so as to bring himself alongside of his sleeping comrade; and then, as he resumed his reconnoitring, where he was just able to command the farther side of the valley away to his right and in a direction where he hoped to find the land clear, he started again.

"Why, they are everywhere!" said the lad half-aloud and with a faint groan of dismay; for there, higher up the opposite side, were a couple of sentries who seemed to be looking straight down upon him. "Why, they must have seen me!" he muttered; and for quite an hour now he lay without stirring, half in the expectation of seeing the low bushes in motion and a little party of the blue-coated enemy coming across to secure fresh prisoners.

But the time wore on, with the chill of the night dying out in the warm sunshine now beginning to search Pen's side of the valley with the bright shafts of light, which suggested to him the necessity for covering his well-kept rifle with the leafy twigs he was able to gather cautiously so as not to betray his presence.

He was in the act of doing this when, turning his head slightly, a flash of light began to play right into his eyes, and he stopped short once more to try and make out whether this had been seen by either of the enemy on duty, for he now awoke to the fact that poor Punch's bugle was lying quite exposed.

The fact was so startling that, instead of trying to reach its cord and draw the glistening instrument towards him, he lay perfectly still again, sweeping the sides of the valley as far as he could in search of danger, but searching in vain, till the thought occurred to him that he might achieve the object he had in view by cautiously taking out his knife and cutting twig after twig so that they might fall across the curving polished copper.

This he contrived to do, and then lay still once more, breathing freely in the full hope that if he gave up further attempt at movement he might escape detection.

"Besides," he said to himself, with a bitter smile playing upon his lips, "if they do make us out they may not trouble, for they will think we are dead."

He lay still then, waiting for Punch to awaken so that he could warn him to lie perfectly quiet.

The hours glided by, with the sun rising higher and setting the watcher thinking, in spite of his misery, weariness, and the pangs of hunger that attacked him, of what a wonderfully beautiful contrast there was between the night and the day. With nothing else that he could do, he recalled the horrors of the past hours, the alternating chills of cold and despair, and the howlings of the wolves; and he uttered more than one sigh of relief as his eyes swept the peaks away across the valley, which here and there sent forth flashes of light from a few scattered patches of melting snow, the beautiful violet shadows of the transverse gullies through which sparkling rivulets descended with many a fall to join the main stream, which dashed onward with the dull, musical roar which rose and fell, now quite loud, then almost dying completely away. The valley formed a very paradise to the unfortunate fugitive, and he muttered bitterly:

"How beautiful it would have been under other circumstances, when such a wondrous scene of peace was not disfigured by war! So bitterly cold last night," thought the young private impatiently, for he was fighting now against two assaults, both of which came upon him when he was trying hard to lie perfectly still and maintain his equanimity while the pangs of hunger and thirst were growing poignant. "It seems so easy," he muttered, "to lie still and keep silence, and here I am feeling that I must move and do something, and wanting so horribly to talk. It would be better if that poor boy would only awaken and speak to me. And there's that water, too," he continued, as the faint plashing, rippling sound rose to his ears from below. "Oh, how I could drink! I wish the wind would rise, so that I couldn't hear that dull plashing sound. How terribly hot the sun is; and it's getting worse!"

Then a horrible thought struck him, that Punch might suddenly wake up and begin to talk aloud, feverish and delirious from his sufferings; and then when Pen's troubles were at their very worst, and he could hardly contain himself and keep from creeping downwards to the water's edge, it seemed as if a cloud swept over him, and all was blank, for how long he could not tell, but his fingers closed sharply to clutch the twigs and grass amongst which he lay as he started into full consciousness.

"Why, I have been asleep!" he muttered. "I must have been;" and he stared wildly around. There was a great shadow there, and now the sun is beating down upon that little gully and lighting up the flashing waters of the fall. "Why, I must have been sleeping for hours, and it must be quite midday."

His eyes now sought the positions of the different vedettes, and all was so brilliant and clear that he saw where the men had stood up their muskets against bush or tree, noted the flash from bayonets and the duller gleam from musket-barrels. In one case, too, the men were sheltering themselves beneath a tree, and this sent an additional pang of suffering through the lad, as he felt for the first time that the sun was playing with burning force upon his neck.

"It's of no use," he said. "Even if they see me, I must move."

But he made the movement with the mental excuse that it was to see how his wounded companion fared.

It only meant seizing hold of a clump of wiry heather twice over and drawing himself to where his face was close to the sleeper. Then he resigned himself again with a sigh to try and bear his position.

"He's best off," he muttered, "bad as he is, for he can't feel what I do."

How the rest of that day of scorching sunshine and cruel thirst passed onward Pen Gray could not afterwards recall. For the most part it was like a feverish dream, till he awoke to the fact that the sun was sinking fast, and that from time to time a gentle breath of cool air was wafted down from the mountains.

Then the hunger began to torture him again, though at times the thirst was less. His brain was clearer, though, and he lay alternately watching the vedettes and noting that they had somewhat changed their positions, and trying to perfect his plans as to what he must do as soon as the shades of night should render it possible for him to move unseen.

Finally, the last sentry was completely blotted out by the gathering darkness; and, uttering the words aloud, "Now for it!" Pen tried to raise himself to his knees before proceeding to carry out his plan, when he sank back again with an ejaculation half of wonder, half of dread. For a feeling of utter numbness shot through him, paralysing every movement; while, prickling and stinging, every fibre of his frame literally quivered as he lay there in despair, feeling that all his planning had been in vain, and that now the time had arrived when he might carry out his attempt in safety the power of movement had absolutely gone.

How long he lay like this he could not tell, but it was until the night-breeze was coming down briskly from the mountains, and the sound of the plashing water far below sent a sudden feeling of excitement through his nerves.

"Water!" he muttered. "Water, or I shall die!"

Chapter Five
Hard Work

It was like coming back to life. In an instant Pen felt full of energy and excitement once more. The pangs of hunger supplemented those of thirst; and, almost raging against them now, he felt that he must fight, and he rose with an effort to his feet, with the tingling numbness feeling for the moment worse than ever, but only to prick and spur him into action.

"Ah!" he ejaculated, "it is like life coming back." Turning to where his comrade lay breathing heavily, he snatched off the leafy twigs with which he had sheltered him.

"Asleep, Punch?" he said; but he was only answered by a low sigh.

"Poor boy!" he muttered; "but I must."

He snatched off, full of energy now, his jacket and overcoat, and resumed them. Then, picking up his rifle, he slackened the sling and passed it over his shoulder. In doing this he kicked against the bugle, and slung the cord across the other shoulder. Then, tightening the strap of his shako beneath his chin, he drew a deep breath and looked first in the one direction and then in another in search of the vedettes; but all was darkness for a while, and he was beginning to feel the calm of certainty as regarded their being perfectly free from observation, when, from the nearest point where he had made out the watchers, he suddenly became aware of how close one party was by seeing the faint spark of light which the next minute deepened into a glow, and the wind wafted to his nostrils the odour of coarse, strong tobacco.

"Ah, nearer than I thought," said the lad to himself, and, looking round once more, he made out another faint glow of light; and then, bending over his comrade, he felt about for his hands and glided his own to the boy's wrists, which felt dank and cold, as he stood thinking for a moment or two of the poor fellow's condition.

"I can't help it. My only hope is that he is quite insensible to pain. He must be, or he couldn't sleep like this. It must be done."

Pen's plans had been carefully laid, and he had not anticipated any difficulty.

"It's only a matter of strength," he said to himself, "and I feel desperate and strong enough now to do anything."

But it meant several failures, and he was checked by groan after groan before he at last managed to seat himself with his back to the wounded boy, after propping him up against one of the gnarled little oak-trunks amongst which they had been lying.

Again and again he had been hindered by the rifle slung across his back. More than once, too, he had despairingly told himself that he must cast it aside, but only to feel that at any cost a soldier must hold to his arms. Then it was the cartouche-box; this, drawn round before him, he was troubled by the position of his haversack, and ready to rage with despair at the difficulties which he had to overcome.

At last, though, he sat there shivering, and listening to try and make out whether the poor boy's moanings had been heard, before drawing a deep breath and beginning to drag the poor fellow's wrists over his shoulders. Then, making one tremendous heave as he threw himself forward, he had Punch well upon his back and staggered up, finding himself plunging down the slope headlong as he struggled to keep his feet, but in vain; for his balance was gone, and a heavy fall was saved by his going head first into the tangled branches of a scrub oak, where he was brought up short with his shako driven down over his eyes.

Penton regained his balance and his breath—to stand listening for some sound of the enemy having taken the alarm, but all was quite still—and, freeing his rifle, he began to use it in the darkness as a staff of support, and to feel his way amongst the shrubs and stones downward always, the butt saving him from more than one fall, for he could not take a step without making sure of a safe place for his feet before he ventured farther.

It was a long and tedious task; but in the silence of the night the sound of the rushing water acted as a guide, and by slow degrees, and after many a rest, he felt at last that he must be getting nearer to the river.

But, unfortunately, the lower he plunged downwards the deeper grew the obscurity, while the moisture from the rushing stream made the tangled growth more dense. Consequently, he had several times over to stop and fight his way out of some thicket and make a fresh start.

At such times he took advantage more than once of some low-growing horizontal oak-boughs, which barred his way and afforded him a resting-place, across which he could lean and make the bough an easy support for his burden.

It had seemed but a short distance down to the stream from where he scrutinised his probable path overhead, and doubtless without burden and by the light of day half an hour would have been sufficient to carry him to the river's brink; but it was in all probability that nearer three hours had elapsed before his farther progress was checked by his finding himself in the midst of a perfect chaos of rocks, just beyond which the water was falling heavily; and, utterly exhausted, he was glad to lower his burden softly down upon a bed of loose shingle and dry sand.

"There's nothing for it but to wait for day," he said half-aloud, and then—after, as best he could in the darkness, placing the wounded boy in a comfortable position and again covering him with his outer garments—he began to feel his way cautiously onward till he found that every time and in whatever direction he thrust down the butt of his rifle it plashed into rushing water which came down so heavily that it splashed up again into his face, and in spite of the darkness he could feel that he was standing somewhere at the foot of a fall where a heavy volume of water was being dashed down from a considerable height.

Pen's first proceeding now was to go down upon his knees as close to the torrent as he could get, and there refill his water-bottle, before (after securing it) he leaned forward and lowered his face until his lips touched the flowing water, and he drank till his terrible thirst was assuaged.

This great desire satisfied, he rose again, to stand listening to the heavy rush and roar of the falls, which were evidently close at hand, and whose proximity produced a strange feeling of awe, suggestive, as it were, of a terrible danger which paralysed him for the time being and held him motionless lest at his next step he should be swept away.

The feeling passed off directly as the thought came that his comrade was insensible and dependent upon him for help; and it struck him now that he might not be able in that thick darkness to find the spot where he had left him.

This idea came upon him with such force as he made a step first in one direction and then in another that he began to lose nerve.

"Oh, it won't do to play the coward now," he muttered. "I must find him—I must! I must try till I do."

But there is something terribly confusing in thick darkness. It is as if a natural instinct is awakened that compels the one who is lost to go wrong; and before Pen Gray had correctly retraced his steps from where he had lain down to drink he had probably passed close to his insensible companion at least a score of times, while the sense of confusion, the nearness of danger and a terrible death, grew and grew till in utter despair and exhaustion he staggered a few steps and sank down almost breathless.

"It is no good," he groaned to himself. "I can do no more. I must wait till daylight."

As he lay stretched out upon his back, panting heavily from weakness, it seemed to him that the roar of the falling water had redoubled, and the fancy came upon him that there was a tone of mocking triumph over his helplessness. In fact, the exertion which he had been called upon to make, the want of sleep, and possibly the exposure during many hours to the burning sun, had slightly affected his brain, so that his wild imagination conjured up non-existent dangers till all was blank, for he sank into the deep sleep of exhaustion, and lay at last open-eyed, wondering, and asking himself whether the foaming water that was plunging down a few yards away was part of some dream, in which he was lying in a fairy-like glen gazing at a rainbow, a little iris that spanned in a bridge of beauty the sparkling water, coming and going as the soft breeze rose and fell, while the sun sent shafts of light through the dew-sprinkled leaves of the many shrubs and trees that overhung the flowing water and nearly filled the glen.

Sleep still held him in its slackening grasp, and he lay motionless, enjoying the pleasant sense of coolness and rest till his attention was caught by a black-and-white bird which suddenly came into sight by alighting upon a rock in the midst of the rushing stream.

It was one of many scattered here and there, and so nearly covered by the water that every now and then, as the black-and-white bird hurried here and there, its legs were nearly covered; but it seemed quite at home, and hurried away, wading easily and seldom using its wings, till all at once, as Pen watched, he saw the little creature take a step, give its tail a flick, and disappear, not diving but regularly walking into deep water, to reappear a few yards away, stepping on to another rock, running here and there for a few moments, and again disappearing in the most unaccountable way.

"It is all a dream," thought Pen. "Ducks dive, but no bird could walk under water like that. Why, it's swimming and using its wings like a fish's fins. I must be asleep."

At that moment the bird stepped on to another rock, to stand heel-deep; and as it was passing out of sight with a quick fluttering of its wings, which did not seem to be wetted in the least, Pen made an effort to raise himself on his elbow, felt a dull, aching sensation of strain, and lost sight of the object that had caught his attention. He found, however, that it was no dream, for across the little torrent and high up the steep, precipitous bank before him he could see a goat contentedly browsing upon the tender green twigs of the bushes; while, at his next movement, as he tried to raise himself a little more, there within touch, and half behind him, lay the companion whose very existence had been blotted out of his mind; and he uttered a cry of joy—or rather felt that he did, for the sound was covered by the roar of the falling water—and dragged himself painfully to where he could lay one hand upon the bugle-boy's breast.

"Why, Punch," he felt that he cried, as the events of the past hours came back with a rush, "I thought I'd lost you. No, I fancied—I— Here, am I going mad?"

He felt that he shouted that question aloud, and then, sending a pang through his strained shoulder, he clapped his hands to his forehead and looked down wildly at the still insensible boy.

"Here, Punch! Punch!" he repeated inaudibly. "Speak—answer! I—oh, how stupid!" he muttered—"I am awake, and it is the roar of that water that seems to sweep away every other sound. Yes, that must be it;" for just then he saw that the goat had raised its head as it gazed across at him, and stretched out its neck.

"Why, it's bleating," he said to himself, "and I can't hear a sound."

The efforts he had made seemed to enable him to think more clearly, and his next act was to rise to his knees stiffly and painfully, and then begin to work his joints a little before bending over his companion and shrinkingly laying his hand upon his breast.

This had the desired effect—one which sent a strange feeling of relief through the young private's breast—for the wondering, questioning eyes he now met looked bright and intelligent, making him bend lower till he could speak loudly in the boy's ear the simple question, "How are you?"

He could hardly hear the words himself, but that they had been heard by him for whom they were intended was evident, for Punch's lips moved in reply, and the next moment, to Pen's delight, he raised one hand to his parched lips and made a sign as of drinking.

"Ah, you are better!" cried Pen excitedly, and this time he felt that he almost heard his own words above the deep-toned, musical roar.

Chapter Six
Pen's Patient

Punch's appealing sign was sufficient to chase away the imaginative notions that had beset Pen's awakening. His hand went at once to the water-bottle slung to his side, and, as he held the mouth to his comrade's lips and forgot the pain he suffered in his strained and stiffening joints, he watched with a feeling of pleasure the avidity with which the boy drank; and as he saw the strange bird flit by once more he recalled having heard of such a bird living in the west country.

"Yes," he said to himself, "I remember now—the dipper. Busy after water-beetles and perhaps after tiny fish.—You are better, Punch, or you wouldn't drink like that;" and he carefully lowered the boy's head as he ceased drinking. "Yes, and though I can't hear you, you have come to your senses again, or you would not look at me like that.—Ah, I forgot all about them!" For a sound other than that produced by the falling waters came faintly to his ear. It was from somewhere far above, and echoed twice. "Yes, I had forgotten all about them."

He began looking anxiously about him, taking in the while that he was close to the river where it ran in a deep, precipitous gully; and as he looked up now to right and then to left, eagerly and searchingly, for the danger that he knew could not be far away, his eyes ranged through densely wooded slopes, lit up here and there by the morning sunshine, and always sweeping the sides of the valley in search of the vedettes, but without avail, not even the rugged mule-path that ran along the side being visible.

"They are not likely to see us here," Pen said to himself, "and they can't have seen me coming down. Oh, what a job it was! I feel as if I must have been walking in my sleep half the time, and I am so stiff I can hardly move. But I did it, and we must be safe if we can keep out of sight; and that ought to be easy, for they are not likely to come down here. Now, what's to be done?"

That was a hard question to answer; but growing once more full of energy now that he was satisfied that there was no immediate danger, Pen stepped back lamely, as if every muscle were strained, to his companion's side, to be greeted with a smile and a movement of the boy's lips.

"Now, let's see to your wound," he said, with his lips to the boy's ear; and he passed one hand under Punch's wounded shoulder to try and turn him over. This time, as Punch's lips parted and his face grew convulsed with pain, Pen's ears mastered the roar, and he heard the sufferer's cry.

"Hurt you too much?" he said, as he once more put his lips to the boy's ear.

The answer was a nod.

"Well," thought Pen, "he must be better, so I'll let him be; but we can't stop here. I must try and get him through the trees and away from this horrible noise. But I can't do it now. At least, I don't think I can. Then, what's next?"

The inaudible reply to the question came from somewhere inside, and he bent closer over Punch once more.

"Aren't you hungry?" he roared in his ear.

The boy shook his head.

"Well, I am," shouted Pen.—"Oh, how stupid! This is like telling the enemy where we are, if they are anywhere within hearing. Hullo, what does this mean?" For he suddenly caught sight of the goat springing from stone to stone low down the stream as if coming to their side of the rushing water; and with the thought filling his mind that a tame goat like this must have an owner who was more likely to be an enemy of strangers than a friend, Pen began searching the rugged slopes on both sides of the river, but in vain. The goat, which had crossed, was now coming slowly towards them, appearing to be quite alone, though soon proving itself to be quite accustomed to the presence of human beings, for it ended by trotting over the sand and shingle at the river's edge till it had approached them quite closely, to stand bleating at them, doubtless imploringly, though no sound was heard.

This lasted for a few minutes, and then the goat moved away, passing Punch, and disappearing upward through the dense growth, and apparently making its way up by the side of the great fall.

No sooner was it out of sight than a thought struck Pen; and, making a sign to his companion that meant "I won't be long," he shouldered his rifle and began to climb upwards in the direction taken by the goat.

He was beginning to regret now that he had not started sooner, for there was no sign of the little beast, and he was about to turn when, just to his right, he noted faint signs of what seemed to be a slightly used track which was easy to follow, and, stepping out, he observed the trees were more open, and at the end of a few minutes he found himself level with the top of the falls, where the river was gliding along in a deep, glassy sheet before making its plunge over the smooth, worn rocks into a basin below.

He had just grasped this when he saw that the faint track bore off to the right, and caught sight of the goat again moving amongst the trees, and for the next few minutes he had no difficulty in keeping it in sight, and, in addition, finding that it was making for what seemed to be the edge of another stream which issued from a patch of woodland on its way to the main torrent.

"I must get him here if I can," thought Pen, for the roar of the falling waters was subdued into a gentle murmur, and to his surprise he caught sight of a shed-like building amongst the trees, fenced in by piled-up pieces of stone evidently taken from the smaller stream which he approached; and it was plain that this was the spot for which the goat had been making.

The young rifleman stopped short, trying to make out whether the place was inhabited; but he could see no sign save that the goat was making for the stone fence, on to which the active beast leaped, balanced itself carefully for a few moments, and then sprang down on the other side, to be greeted by a burst of bleating that came from apparently two of its kind within.

Pen stood screened by the trees for a time, fully expecting to see some occupant of the hut make his appearance; but the bleating ceased directly, and, approaching carefully, the young private stood at last by the rough stone wall, looking down on a scene which fully explained the reason for the goat's visit.

She had returned to her kids; and after climbing the wall a very little search showed the visitor that the goat and her young ones were the sole occupants of the deserted place.

It was the rough home of a peasant who had apparently forsaken it upon the approach of the French soldiery. Everything was of the simplest kind; but situated as Pen Gray was it presented itself in a palatial guise, for there was everything that he could wish for at a time like that.

As before said, it was a shed-like structure; but there was bed and fireplace, a pile of wood outside the door, and, above all, a roof to cover those who sought shelter.

"Yes, I must bring him here somehow," thought Pen as he caught sight of a cleanly scrubbed pail and a tin or two hanging upon nails in the wall. But he saw far more than this, for his senses were sharpened by hunger; and with a smile of satisfaction he hurried out, noting as he passed them that the kids, keen of appetite, were satisfying their desire for food; and, hurrying onwards, he made his way back to where he had left his companion lying in the dry, sandy patch of shingle; and some hours of that forenoon were taken up in the painful task of bearing the wounded lad by slow degrees to where, after much painful effort, they could both look down upon the nearly hidden shed.

"How are you now, Punch?" asked Pen, turning his head upwards.

There was no reply.

"Why, Punch," cried Pen, "you are not asleep, are you?"

"Asleep!" said the boy bitterly; and then, in a faint whisper, "set me down."

Pen took a step forward to where he could take hold of a stunted oak-bough whose bark felt soft and strange; and, holding tightly with one hand, he held his burden with the other while he sank slowly, the branch bending the while till he was kneeling. Then he slid his load down amongst the undergrowth and quickly opened his water-bottle and held it to the boy's lips.

"Feel faint, lad?" he said.

Again there was no answer; but Punch swallowed a few mouthfuls.

"Ah, that's better," he said. "Head's swimming."

"Well, you shall lie still for a few minutes till you think you can bear it, and then I want you to get down to that hut."

Punch looked up at him with misty eyes, wonderingly.

"Hut!" he said faintly. "What hut?"

"The one I told you about. You will be able to see it when you are better. There's a rough bed there where you will be able to lie and rest till your wound heals."

"Hut!"

"Oh, never mind now. Will you have some more water?"

The boy shook his head.

"Not going to die, am I?" he said feebly.

"Die! No!" cried Pen, with his heart sinking. "A chap like you isn't going to die over a bit of a wound."

"Don't," said the boy faintly, but with a tone of protest in his words. "Don't gammon a fellow! I am not going to mind if I am. Our chaps don't make a fuss about it when their time comes."

"No," said Pen sharply; "but your time hasn't come yet."

The boy looked up at him with a peculiar smile.

"Saying that to comfort a fellow," he almost whispered; "only, I say, comrade, you did stick to me, and you won't—won't—"

"Won't what?" said Pen sharply. "Leave you now? Is it likely?"

"Not a bit yet," said the poor fellow faintly; "but I didn't mean that."

"Then what did you mean?" cried Pen wonderingly.

The poor lad made a snatch at his companion's arm, and tried to draw him down.

"What is it?" said Pen anxiously now, for he was startled by the look in the boy's eyes.

"Want to whisper," came in a broken voice.

"No; you can't have anything to whisper now," said Pen. "There, let me give you a little more water."

The boy shook his head.

"Want to whisper," he murmured in a harsh, low voice.

"Well, what is it? But you had better not. Shut your eyes and have a bit of a nap till you are rested and the faintness has gone. I shall be rested, too, then, and I can get you down into the hut, where I tell you there's a bed, and, better still, Punch, a draught of sweet warm milk."

"Gammon!" said the boy again; and he hung more heavily upon Pen's arm.—"Want to whisper."

"Well, what is it?" said Pen, trying hard to master the feeling of despair that was creeping over him.

"Them wolves!" whispered the boy. "Don't let them get me, comrade, when I'm gone."

"You shut your eyes and go to sleep," cried Pen angrily.

"No," said the boy, speaking more strongly now. "I aren't a baby, and I know what I'm saying. You tell me you won't let them have me, and then I will go to sleep; and then if I don't wake up no more—"

"What!" cried Pen, speaking with a simulated anger, "you won't be such a coward as to go and leave me all alone here?"

The boy started; his eyes brightened a little, and he gazed half-wonderingly in his companion's face.

"I—I didn't think of that, comrade," he faltered. "I was thinking I was going like some of our poor chaps; but I don't want to shirk. There, I'll try not."

"Of course you will," said Pen harshly. "Now then, try and have a nap."

The boy closed his eyes, and in less than a minute he was breathing steadily and well, but evidently suffering now and then in his sleep, for the hand that clasped Pen's gave a sudden jerk at intervals.

Quite an hour, during which the watcher did not stir, till there was a sharper twitch and the boy's eyes opened, to look wonderingly in his companion's as if he could not recall where he was.

"Have a little water now, Punch?"

"Drop," he said; but the drop proved to be a thirsty draught, and he spoke quite in his senses now as he put a brief question.

"Is it far?" he said.

"To the hut? No. Do you think you can bear me to get you on my back again?"

"Yes. Going to. Look sharp!"

But as soon as the boy felt his companion take hold of his hand after restopping the water-bottle, Punch whispered, "Stop!"

"What is it? Would you like to wait a little longer?"

"No. Give me a bullet out of a cartridge."

"A bullet? What for?"

"To bite," said the boy with a grim smile.

Pen hesitated for a moment in doubt, looking in the boy's smiling eyes the while. Then, as a flash of recollection of stories he had heard passed through his mind, he hastily drew a cartridge from his box, broke the little roll open, scattering the powder and setting the bullet free before passing it to his companion, who nodded in silence as he seized the piece of lead between his teeth. Then, nodding again, he raised one hand, which Pen took, and seizing one of the branches of the gnarled tree he bent it down till he got it close to his companion, and bade him hold on with all his might.

Punch's fingers closed tightly upon the bough, which acted like a spring and helped to raise its holder sufficiently high for Pen to get him once more upon his shoulders, which he had freed from straps thrown down beside his rifle.

"Try and bear it," he panted, as he heard the low, hissing breath from the poor fellow's lips, and felt him quiver and wince. "I know it's bad," he added encouragingly, "but it won't take me long."

He climbed over, . . . and staggered into the waiting shelter.

It did not, for in a very few minutes he had reached the rough stone wall, to which he shifted his burden, stood for a few moments panting, and then climbed over, took the sufferer in his arms, and staggered into the waiting shelter, where the next minute Punch was lying insensible upon the bed.

"Ha!" ejaculated Pen as he passed the back of his hand across his streaming forehead.

This suggested another action, but it was the palm of his hand that he laid across his companion's brow.

"All wet!" he muttered. "He can't be very feverish for the perspiration to come like that."

Then he started violently, for a shadow crossed the open door, and he involuntarily threw up one hand to draw his slung rifle from his shoulder, and then his teeth snapped together.

There was no rifle there. It was lying with his cartouche-box right away by the stunted oak, as he mentally called the cork-tree.

The next minute he was breathing freely, for the deep-toned bleat of the goat arose, and he looked out, to see that it was answerable for the shadow.

"Ah, you will have to pay for this," he muttered, as he started to run to where his weapon lay, his mind full now of thoughts that in his efforts over his comrade had been absent.

He was full of expectation that one or other of the vedettes might have caught sight of him bearing his load to the hut; and, with the full determination to get his rifle and hurry back to defend himself and his companion for as long as the cartridges held out, he started with a run up the slope, which proved to be only the stagger of one who was utterly exhausted, and degenerated almost into a crawl.

He was back at last, to find that Punch had not moved, but seemed to be sleeping heavily as he lay upon his sound shoulder; and, satisfied by this, Pen laid his rifle and belts across the foot of the bed and drew a deep breath.

"I can't help it," he nearly groaned. "It isn't selfish; but if I don't have something I can do no more."

Then, strangely enough, he uttered a mocking laugh as he stepped to a rough shelf and took a little pail-like vessel with one stave prolonged into a handle from the place where it had been left clean by the last occupant of the hut, and as he stepped with it to the open door something within it rattled.

He looked down at it in surprise and wonder, and it was some moments before he grasped the fact that the piece of what resembled blackened clay was hard, dry cake.

"Ah!" he half-shouted as he raised it to his lips and tried to bite off a piece, but only to break off what felt like wood, which refused to crumble but gradually began to soften.

Then, smiling grimly, he thrust the cake within his jacket and stepped out, forgetting his pain and stiffness, to find to his dismay that there was no sign of the goat.

"How stupid!" he muttered the next minute. "My head won't go. I can't think." And, recalling the goat's former visit to the rough shelter, he hurried to where he had been a witness of its object, and to his great delight found the animal standing with half-closed eyes nibbling at some of the plentiful herbage while one of its kids was partaking of its evening meal.

Pen advanced cautiously with the little wooden vessel, ready to seize the animal by one of its horns if it attempted to escape, as it turned sharply and stared at him in wonder; but it only sniffed as if in recognition at the little pail, and resumed its browsing. But the kid was disposed to resent the interruption of the stranger, and some little force had to be used to thrust it away, returning again and again to begin to make some pretence of butting at the intruder.

Pen laughed aloud at the absurdity of his task as he finally got rid of the little animal, and made his first essay at milking, finding to his great delight that he was successful, while the goat-mother took it all as a matter of course, and did not move while her new friend refreshed himself with a hearty draught of the contents of the little pail; and then, snatching at a happy thought, drew the hardened cake from his breast and placed it so that it could soak up the soft warm milk which flowed into the vessel.

"Ah!" sighed the young soldier, "who'd have thought that taking the king's shilling would bring a fellow to this? Now for poor Punch. Well, we sha'n't starve to-night."

Once more as he turned from the goat the thought assailed him that one of the vedettes might be in sight; but all was still and beautiful as he stepped back slowly, eating with avidity portions of the gradually softening black-bread, and feeling the while that life and hope and strength were gradually coming back.

"Now for poor Punch!" he muttered again; and, entering the rough shelter once more, he stood looking down upon the wounded boy, who was sleeping heavily, so soundly that Pen felt that it would be a cruelty to rouse him. So, partaking sparingly of his novel meal, he placed a part upon a stool within reach of the rough pallet.

"Wounded men don't want food," he muttered. "It's Nature's way of keeping off fever; and I must keep watch again, and give him a little milk when he wakes. Yes, when he wakes—when he wakes," he muttered, as he settled himself upon the earthen floor within touch of his sleeping comrade. "Mustn't close the door," he continued, with a little laugh, "for there doesn't seem to be one; and, besides, it would make the place dark. Why, there's a star peeping out over the shoulder of the mountain, and that soft, low, deep hum is the falling water. Why, that must be the star I used to see at home in the old days; and, oh, how beautiful and restful everything seems! But I mustn't go to sleep.—Are you asleep, Punch?" he whispered softly. "Poor fellow! That's right. Sleep and Nature will help you with your wound; but I must keep awake. It would never do for you to rouse up and find me fast. No," he half-sighed. "Poor lad, you mustn't go yet where so many other poor fellows have gone. A boy like you! Well! It's the—fortune—fortune—of war—and—and—"

Nature would take no denial. Pen Gray drew one long, deep, restful breath as if wide-awake, and then slowly and as if grudgingly respired.

Fast asleep.

Chapter Seven
More about him

It was bright daylight, and Pen Gray started up in alarm, his mind in a state of confusion consequent upon the heaviness of his sleep and the feeling of trouble that something—he knew not what—had happened.

For a few moments he was divided between the ideas that the enemy had come to arrest him and that his companion had passed away in his sleep. But these were only the ragged shadows of the night, for the boy was still sleeping soundly, the food remained untouched, and, upon cautiously looking outside, there was nothing to be seen but the beauties of a sunny morn.

Pen drew a deep breath as he returned to the hut, troubled with a sensation of weariness and strain, but still light-hearted and hopeful.

There was something invigorating in the mountain air even deep down there in the valley, and he was ready to smile at his position as his eyes lit upon the little pail.

"Oh, I say," he said to himself, "it is like temptation placed in one's way! How horribly hungry I am! Well, no wonder; but I must play fair."

Taking out his knife, he was about to divide the piece of cake, which had so swollen up in the milk that there seemed to be a goodly portion for two; but, setting his teeth hard, he shut the knife with a snap and pulled himself together.

"Come," he muttered, "I haven't gone through all this drilling for months to snatch the first chance to forget it. I will begin the day by waiting until poor Punch wakes."

He gave another look at his companion to make sure that he was still sleeping soundly and was no worse; and then, after glancing at the priming of his rifle, he stepped out to reconnoitre, keeping cautiously within shelter of the trees, but not obtaining a glimpse of any of the vedettes.

"Looks as if they have gone," he thought, and he stepped to the edge of another patch of woodland to again sweep the valley-sides as far as was possible.

This led him to the edge of the river, where, as soon as he appeared, he was conscious of the fact that scores of semi-transparent-looking fish had darted away from close to his feet, to take shelter beneath stones and the bank higher up the stream, which glided down towards the fall pure as crystal and sparkling in the sun.

"Trout!" he exclaimed. "Something to forage for; and then a fire. Doesn't look like starving."

Pen took another good look round, but nothing like a vedette or single sentry was in view; and after a few moments of hesitation he snatched at the opportunity.

Stepping back into the shelter of the woods, he hurriedly stripped, after hanging his rifle from a broken branch, and then dashing out into the sunshine he leaped at once into the beautiful, clear, sparkling water, which flashed up at his plunge. Then striking out, he swam with vigorous strokes right into the depths, and felt that he was being carried steadily downward towards the fall.

This was something to make him put forth his strength; and as he struck out upstream so as to reach the bank again there was something wondrously invigorating in the cool, crisp water which sent thrills of strength through his exhausted frame, making the lad laugh aloud as he fought against the pressure of the water, won, and waded ashore nearly a hundred yards below where he had plunged in.

"What a stream!" he exclaimed as he shook the streaming water from his tense muscles. "I must mind another time. How cold it was! But how hot the sun feels! Double!" he ejaculated, and he started along the bank in a military trot, reached the spot again where he had made his plunge, looked round, indulged in another run in the brilliant sunshine, and, pretty well half-dried by his efforts, stepped back into the wood and rapidly resumed his clothes.

"Why, it has pretty well taken the stiffness out of me," he muttered, "and I feel ready for anything, only I'm nearly famished. Here, I can't wait," he added, as he finished dressing, smartening himself up into soldierly trim, and giving his feet a stamp or two as he resumed his boots. "Now, how about poor Punch? He can't be worse, for he seemed to have slept so well. It seems hard, but I must wake him up."

To the lad's great satisfaction, as he reached the door of the rough cabin, he found that the wounded boy was just unclosing his eyes to look at him wonderingly as if unable to make out what it all meant.

"Gray," he said faintly.

"Yes. How are you, lad?"

"I—I don't quite know," was the reply, given in a faint voice.—"Oh, I recollect now. Yes. There, it stings—my wound."

"Yes, I'll bathe it and see to it soon," said Pen eagerly; "but you are no worse."

"Ain't I? I—I thought I was. I say, look here, Gray; what does this mean? I can't lift this arm at all. It hurts so."

"Yes. Stiff with your wound; but it will be better when I have done it up."

"Think so?"

"Yes."

"But look here."

"Yes, I am looking."

"This arm isn't wounded. Look at that."

"Yes, I see; you lifted it up and it fell down again."

"Yes. There's no strength in it. It ain't dead yet?"

"Didn't seem like it," said Pen, smiling cheerily. "You lifted it up."

"Yes, I know; but it fell back again. And what's the matter with my voice?"

"Nothing."

"Yes, there is," cried the boy peevishly. "It's all gone squeaky again, like it was before it changed and turned gruff. I say, Gray, am I going to be very bad, and never get well again?"

"Not you! What nonsense!"

"But I am so weak."

"Well, you have seen plenty of our poor fellows in hospital, haven't you?"

"Yes, some of them," said the boy feebly.

"Well, weren't they weak?"

"Yes, I forgot all that; but I wasn't so bad as this yesterday. It was yesterday, wasn't it?"

"Yes. Don't you remember?"

"No. How was it?"

"There, don't you bother your brains about that."

"But I want to know."

"And I want you to do all you can to get well."

"Course you do. 'Tisn't fever, is it?"

"Fever! No! Yes, you were feverish. Every one is after a wound. Now then," And he took out and opened his knife.

"Wound! Wound!" said the boy, watching him. "Whatcher going to do with your knife? Take your bay'net if you want to finish a fellow off."

"Well, I don't," said Pen, laughing.

"'Tain't anything to laugh at, comrade."

"Yes, it is, when you talk nonsense. Now then, breakfast."

"Don't gammon," said the poor fellow feebly. "My head isn't all swimmy now. Beginning to remember. Didn't you carry me down here?"

"To be sure, and precious heavy you were!"

"Good chap!" said the boy, sighing. "You always was a trump; but don't play with a poor fellow. There can't be no breakfast."

"Oh, can't there? I'll show you; and I want to begin. I say, Punch, I'm nearly starved."

"I'm not," said the poor fellow sadly. "I couldn't eat."

"Oh, well, you have got to, so look sharp, or I shall go mad."

"Whatcher mean?"

"I told you I'm starving. I have hardly touched anything for two days except water."

"Well, go on then. What is there for breakfast?"

"Bread."

"Ugh! Don't! Black dry bread! It makes me feel sick."

"Bread and milk."

"Where did you get the milk?"

"Never you mind," said Pen, plunging his knife into the dark sop which half-filled the little pail. "Now then, you have got to eat first."

"No, don't ask me; I can't touch it," and the boy closed his eyes against the piece of saturated bread that his companion held out to him on the knife.

"You must," said Pen; "so look sharp."

"I can't, I tell you."

"Well, then, I shall have to starve."

"No, no; go on."

"After you."

It took a good deal of pressure, but at last the truth of the French saying about its being only the first step that costs was proved, for after the first mouthful, of which the poor fellow shudderingly partook, the boy consented to open his mouth again, after holding out until his amateur surgeon and nurse had consented to share the meal, which proved refreshing to the patient, who partook of a little; while, bearing in mind that he could at all events restore the fluid food, Pen ate ravenously, his spirits rising with every mouthful.

"It will go hard," he said to himself, "if I can't forage something else. There are the trout, to begin with. I know I can catch some of them in the shallows, and that too without rod or line. That is," he added, "if we are not found out and marched off as prisoners."

"Whatcher thinking about?" said Punch drowsily.

"Catching fish, and making a fire to cook them."

"There's my flint and steel in my satchel, but where's your fish?"

"In the river."

"But you can't catch 'em."

"Oh, can't I, Punch?"

"Oh yes, I know," piped the boy. "They are trout. I saw some the other day when we crossed that stream. I saw some run under the stones, and wanted to creep up and tiddle one, only I couldn't leave the ranks."

"Ah, well, there are no ranks to leave now, Punch, and we shall have plenty of time to tiddle the trout, as you call it, for we shall have to stay here till you get well."

"I say, don't talk, please. Want to go to sleep."

"That's right," said Pen cheerfully. "Sleep away, and I won't bathe your wound till you wake again."

The boy made no answer, but dropped off at once.

"That's better," thought Pen, "and while he sleeps I will see whether I can't get some of the trout."

He waited until his companion was breathing heavily, and then he seated himself by the door and began to carefully clean his rifle and accoutrements, which soldierly task at an end, he stood over the sleeping boy a few minutes, and then stepped outside the dark hut to plunge into the sunshine; but, recollecting himself, he stepped in amongst the trees, and keeping close in their shelter moved from spot to spot spending nearly half an hour searching every eminence for signs of danger.

"The coast seems clear," he said to himself, "and the enemy may have moved on; but I must be careful. I want to join our fellows, of course; but if I'm made prisoner it will be the death of poor Punch, for they are not very careful about prisoners, and—"

Pen stopped short as he held on to the bough of one of the stunted trees growing in the rocky bottom and peered out to sweep the side of the valley where he felt that the mule-track ought to be.

He started back as if the bullet that had been fired from a musket had cut the leaves above his head and stood listening to the roll of echoes which followed the shot. Then there was another, and another, followed by scores, telling him that a sharp skirmish had begun; and after a while he could just make out a faint cloud of smoke above the trees, where the dim vapour was slowly rising.

"Yes," he said, "that's where I thought the mule-path must be. But what a height it is up! And what does it mean? Are our fellows coming back and driving the enemy before them, or is it the other way on?"

There was no telling; but when, about an hour later, the firing had grown nearer and then slowly become more and more distant till it died away, Pen had learned one thing, and that was the necessity for keeping carefully in hiding, for the enemy must be somewhere near.

He stepped back into the hut after silence once more reigned in the false scene of peace, and found that the peppering of the musketry had had no effect upon the sleeper, who did not stir when he leant over him and laid his hand upon the poor fellow's forehead, which was cool and moist.

"Ha!" sighed Pen, "he's not going to die; but he will be as weak as weak for a month to come, and I ought to have been with our fellows instead of hiding here, for I have no business to be doing ambulance work, and so they would tell me. Ah!" he ejaculated, as he started to the door again, for from somewhere much farther away there came the deep roll of a platoon of musketry, which was repeated again and again, but always more distant, though growing, while still more faintly, into the sounds of a sharp engagement, till it died quite away.

"I never thought of that. That first firing I heard must have been the enemy. I wonder I didn't think so before. I am sure now. There wasn't a single shot that I could have said was from a rifle. But it is impossible to say for certain which side is holding the valley. At any rate our fellows were not there."

Chapter Eight
The King's Shilling

"Ha, ha, ha, ha!" A bright, ringing specimen of a youth's laugh, given out by one who is healthy, strong, and fairly content, allowing for drawbacks, with the utterer's position in life.

"Whatcher laughing at?" followed in the querulous tones of one who was to a great extent at the opposite pole of life.

"You, Punch."

"I don't see nothing to laugh at, sick and weak as I am."

"Yes, you are weak enough, and don't know the difference as I do."

"Difference! There ain't no difference. I'm a regular invalid, as they calls them, and just as bad as some of our poor chaps who go back to live on the top of a wooden leg all the rest of their lives."

"Stuff and nonsense, Punch! You are getting better and stronger every day."

"I ain't. Look at that arm; it's as thin as a mop-stick."

"Well, it is thin, certainly; but a chap of your age, growing fast, generally is thin."

"Ya! Growing! How can a fellow grow with a hole in his back?"

"You haven't got a hole in your back. It's healing up fast."

"'Taint."

"Yes, it is. You haven't seen it, and I have every day. I say it's healing beautifully."

"Ah, you'll say next that I ain't weak."

"No, I shan't."

"Well, that's because you are always trying to make me think that I am better than I am."

"Well, what of that? I don't want to put you out of heart."

"No, but you needn't gammon me. I know I ain't as weak as a rat, because I am ten times weaker. I have got no wind at all; and I do wish you wouldn't be always wallacking me down to that big waterfall. I'm always pumped out before I get half-way there, and quite done up before I get back. What's the good of going there?"

"Beautiful place, Punchy, and the mountain air seems to come down with the water and fill you full of strength."

"Does you perhaps, but it don't do me no good. Beautiful place indeed! Ugly great hole!"

"'Tisn't; it's lovely. I don't believe we shall ever see a more beautiful spot in our lives."

"It makes me horrible. I feel sometimes as if I could jump in and put myself out of my misery. Just two steps, and a fellow would be washed away to nowhere."

"Why, you have regularly got the grumps to-day, Punch; just, too, when you were getting better than ever."

"I ain't, I tell you. I had a look at myself this morning while you were snoring, and I am as thin as a scarecrow. My poor old mother wouldn't know me again if ever I got back; and I sha'n't never see our old place no more."

"Yes, you will, Punch—grown up into a fine, manly-looking British rifleman, for you will be too big to blow your bugle then. You might believe me."

"Bugle! Yes, I didn't give it a rub yesterday. Just hand it off that peg."

Pen reached the bugle from where it hung by its green cord, and the lines in Punch's young forehead began to fade as he gave the instrument a touch with his sleeve, and then placed the mouthpiece to his lips, filled out his sadly pale, hollow cheeks, and looked as if he were going to blow with all his might, when he was checked by Pen clapping his hand over the glistening copper bell.

"Whatcher doing of?" cried the boy angrily.

"Stopping you. There, you see you are better. You couldn't have attempted that a while ago."

"Ya! Think I'm such a silly as to bring the enemy down upon us?"

"Well, I didn't know."

"Then you ought to. I should just like to give the call, though, to set our dear old lads going along the mountain-side there skirmishing and peppering the frog-eating warmints till they ran for their lives."

"Hurrah!" shouted Pen. "Who's trying to bring the enemy down upon us now, when we know there are some of them sneaking about in vedettes as they hold both ends of the valley. Now you say you are not better if you dare."

"Oh, I don't want to fall out," grumbled the invalid. "You think you know, but you ain't got a wound in your back to feel when a cold wind comes off the mountains. I think I ought to know best."

"But you don't, Punch. Those pains will die out in time, and you will go on growing, and keeping thin perhaps for a bit; but your muscles will fill out by-and-by, same as mine do in this beautiful air."

"Needn't be so precious proud of them," said the boy sourly.

"I'm not. There, have another fish."

"Sha'n't. I'm sick to death on them. They are only Spanish or Portuguee trout, and not half so good as roach and dace out of a good old English pond."

Pen laughed merrily again.

"Ah, grin away! I think I ought to know."

"Yes—better than to grumble when I have broiled the fish so nicely over the wood embers with sticks I cut for skewers. They were delicious, and I ate till I felt ashamed."

"So you ought to be."

"To enjoy myself so," continued Pen, "while you, with your mouth so out of taste and no appetite, could hardly eat a bit."

"Well, who's to have a happetite with a wound like mine? I shall never get no better till I get a mug of real old English beer."

"Never mind; you get plenty of milk."

"Ya! Nasty, sickly stuff! I'll never touch it again."

"Well then, beautiful sparkling water."

"Who wants sparkling water? 'Tain't like English. It's so thin and cold."

"Come, come; you must own that you are mending fast, Punch."

"Who wants to be mended," snarled the poor fellow, "and go through life like my old woman's cracked chayney plate with the rivet in it! I was a strong lad once, and could beat any drummer in the regiment in a race, while now I ought to be in horspital."

"No, you ought not. I'll tell you what you want, Punch."

"Oh, I know."

"No, you don't. You want to get just a little stronger, so as you can walk ten miles in a day."

"Ten miles! Why, I used to do twenty easy."

"So you will again, lad; but I mean in a night, for we shall have to lie up all day and march all night so as to keep clear of the enemy."

"Then you mean for us to try and get out of this wretched hole?"

"I mean for us to go on tramp as soon as you are quite strong enough; and then you will think it's a beautiful valley. Why, Punch, I have crept about here of a night while you have been asleep, so that I have got to know the place by heart, and I should like to have the chance of leading our fellows into places I know where they could hold it against ten times or twenty times their number of Frenchmen who might try to drive them out."

"You have got to know that?" said Punch with a show of animation that had grown strange to the poor fellow.

"Yes," cried Pen triumphantly.

"Well, then, all I have got to say is you waren't playing fair."

"Of course it wasn't. Seeing you were so weak you couldn't walk."

"There now, you are laughing at a fellow; but you don't play fair."

"Don't I? In what way?"

"Why, you promised while I have been so bad that you would read to me a bit."

"And I couldn't, Punch, because we have got nothing to read."

"And then you promised that you would tell me how it was you come to take the king's shilling."

"Well, yes, I did; but you don't want to know that."

"Yes, I do. I have been wanting to know ever since."

"Why, boy?"

"Because it seems so queer that a lad like you should join the ranks."

"Why queer? You are too young yet, but you will be in the ranks some day as a full private."

"Yes, some day; but then, you see, my father was a soldier. Yours warn't, was he?"

"No-o," said Pen, frowning and looking straight away before him out of the hut-door.

"Well, then, why don't you speak out?"

"Because I don't feel much disposed. It is rather a tender subject, Punch."

"There, I always knew there was something. Look here; you and me's friends and comrades, ain't we?"

"I think so, Punch. I have tried to be."

"So you have. Nobody could have been better. I have lain awake lots of times and thought about what you did. You haven't minded my saying such nasty things as I have sometimes?"

"Not I, Punch. Sick people are often irritable."

"Yes," said the boy eagerly, "that's it. I have said lots of things to you that I didn't mean; but it's when my back's been very bad, and it seemed to spur me on to be spiteful, and I have been very sorry sometimes, only I was ashamed to tell you. But you haven't done anything to be ashamed of?" Pen was silent for a few moments.

"Ashamed? No—yes."

"Well, you can't have been both," said the boy. "Whatcher mean by that?"

"There have been times, Punch, when I have felt ashamed of what I have done."

"Why, what have you done? I don't believe it was ever anything bad. You say what it was. I'll never tell."

"Enlisted for a soldier."

"What?" cried the boy. "Why, that ain't nothing to be ashamed of. What stuff! Why, that's something to be proud of, specially in our Rifles. In the other regiments we have got out here the lads are proud of being in scarlet. Let 'em. But I know better. There isn't one of them who wouldn't be proud to be in our dark-green, and to shoulder a rifle. Besides, we have got our bit of scarlet on the collar and cuffs, and that's quite enough. Why, you are laughing at me! You couldn't be ashamed of being in our regiment. I know what it was—you ran away from home?"

"It was no longer home to me, Punch."

"Why, didn't you live there?"

"Yes; but it didn't seem like home any longer. It was like this, Punch. My father and mother had died."

"Oh," said the boy softly, "that's bad. Very good uns, waren't they?"

Pen bowed his head.

"Then it waren't your home any longer?"

"Yes and no, Punch," said the lad gravely.

"There you go again! Don't aggravate a fellow when he is sick and weak. I ain't a scholar like you, and when you puts it into me with your 'yes and no' it makes my head ache. It can't be yes and no too."

"Well, Punch," said Pen, smiling, "it was mine by rights, but I was under age."

"What's under age?"

"Not twenty-one."

"Of course not. You told me months ago that you was only eighteen. Anybody could see that, because you ain't got no whiskers. But what has that got to do with it?"

"Well, I don't see why I should tell you all this, Punch, for it's all about law."

"But I want to know," said the boy, "because it's all about you."

"Well, it's like this: my father left my uncle to be executor and my trustee."

"Oh, I say, whatcher talking about? You said your father was a good un, didn't you?"

"I did."

"Well, then, he couldn't have left your uncle to be your executioner when you hadn't done nothing."

"Executor, Punch," said the lad, laughing.

"Well, that's what I said, didn't I?"

"No; that's a very different thing. An executor is one who executes."

"Well, I know that. Hangs people who ain't soldiers, and shoots them as is. Court-martial, you know."

"Punch, you are getting in a muddle."

"Glad of it," said the boy, "for I thought it was, and I don't like to hear you talk like that."

"Then let's put it right. An executor is one who executes the commands of a person who is dead."

"Oh, I see," said the boy. "Dead without being executed."

"Look here, Punch," said Pen, laughing, "you had better be still and listen, and I will try and make it plain to you. My uncle was my father's executor, who had to see that the property he left was rightfully distributed."

"Oh, I see," said Punch.

"And my father made him my trustee, to take charge of the money that was to be mine when I became twenty-one."

"All right; go on. I am getting it now."

"Then he had to see to my education, and advise me till I grew up."

"Well, that was all right, only if I had been your old man, seeing what a chap you are, I shouldn't have called in no uncle. I should have said, 'Young Penton Gray has got his head screwed on proper, and he will do what's right.' I suppose, then, your uncle didn't."

"I thought not, Punch."

"Then, of course, he didn't. What did he do, then?"

"Made me leave school," said Pen.

"Oh, well, that don't sound very bad. Made you leave school? Well, I never was at school but once, but I'd have given anything to be made to come away."

"Ah, perhaps you would, Punch. But then there are schools and schools."

"Well, I know that," said the boy irritably; "but don't tease a fellow, it makes me so wild now I'm all weak like."

"Well, then, let's say no more about it."

"What! Leave off telling of me?"

"Yes, while you are irritable."

"I ain't irritable; not a bit. It's only that I want to know."

"Very well, then, Punch; I will cut it short."

"No, you don't, so come now! You promised to tell me all about it, so play fair."

"Very well, then, you must listen patiently."

"That's what I'm a-doing of, only you will keep talking in riddles like about your executioners and trustees. I want you to tell me just in plain English."

"Very well, then, Punch. I was at a military school, and I didn't want to be fetched away."

"Oh, I see," cried the boy. "You mean one of them big schools where they makes young officers?"

"Yes."

"Like Woolwich and Addiscombe?"

"Yes."

"You were going to be a soldier, then—I mean, an officer?"

"An officer is a soldier, Punch."

"Of course he is. Oh, well, I don't wonder you didn't want to be fetched away. Learning to be an officer, eh? That's fine. Didn't your uncle want you to be a soldier, then?"

"No. He wanted me to go as a private pupil with a lawyer."

"What, and get to be a lawyer?" cried the boy excitedly. "Oh, I say, you weren't going to stand that?"

"No, Punch. Perhaps I should have obeyed him, only I knew that it had always been my father's wish that I should go into the army, and he had left the money for my education and to buy a commission when I left the military school."

"Here, I know," cried the boy excitedly; "you needn't tell me no more. I heard a story once about a wicked uncle. I know—your one bought the commission and kept it for himself."

"No, Punch; that wouldn't work out right. When I begged him to let me stay at the military school he mocked at me, and laughed, and said that my poor father must have been mad to think of throwing away money like that; and over and over again he insisted that I should go on with my studies of the law, and give up all notion of wearing a red coat, for he could see that that was all I thought about."

"Well?" said the boy.

"Well, Punch?"

"And then you punched his head, and ran away from home."

"No, I did not."

"Then you ought to have done. I would if anybody said my poor father was mad; and, besides, your uncle must have been a bad un to want to make you a lawyer. I suppose he was a lawyer too."

"Yes."

"There, if I didn't think so! But he must have been a bad un. Said you wanted to be a soldier so as to wear the uniform? Well, if you did want to, that's only nat'ral. A soldier's always proud of his uniform. I heard our colonel say that it was the king's livery and something to be proud on. I am proud of mine, even if it has got a bit raggy-taggy with sleeping out in it in all sorts of weather, and rooshing through bushes and mud, and crossing streams. But soldiers don't think of that sort of thing, and we shall all have new things served out by-and-by. Well, go on."

"Oh, that's about all, Punch."

"You get on. I know better. Tain't half all. I want you to come to the cutting off and taking the shilling."

"Oh, you want to hear that?"

"Why, of course I do. Why, it's all the juicy part. Don't hang fire. Let's have it with a rush now. Fix bayonets, and at them!"

"Why, Punch," said Pen, laughing, "don't you tell me again that you are not getting better!"

"I waren't going to now. This warms a fellow up a bit. I say, your uncle is a bad un, and no mistake. There, forward!"

"But I have nearly told all, Punch. Life got so miserable at home, and I was so sick of the law, that I led such a life with my uncle through begging him to let me go back to the school, that he, one day—"

"Well, whatcher stopping for?" cried the boy, whose cheeks were flushed and eyes sparkling with excitement.

"I don't like talking about it," replied Pen. "I suppose I was wrong, for my father had left all the management of my affairs in his brother-in-law's hands."

"Why, you said your uncle's hands just now!"

"Yes, Punch; in my mother's brother's hands, so he was my uncle."

"Well, go on."

"And I had been begging him to alter his plans."

"Yes, and let you go back to the school?"

"And I suppose he was tired out with what he called my obstinacy, and he told me that if ever I dared to mention the army again he would give me a sound flogging."

"And you up and said you would like to catch him at it?" cried Punch excitedly. "No, Punch; but I lost my temper."

"Enough to make you! Then you knocked him down?"

"No, Punch, but I told him he was forgetting the commands my father had given him, and that I would never go to the lawyer's office again."

"Well, and what then?"

"Then, Punch? Oh, I don't like to talk about it. It makes me feel hot all over even to think."

"Of course it does. It makes me hot too; but then, you see, I'm weak. But do go on. What happened then?"

"He knocked me down," said the lad hoarsely.

"Oh!" cried the boy, trying to spring up from his rough couch, but sinking back with the great beads of perspiration standing upon his brown forehead. "Don't you tell me you stood that!"

"No, Punch; I couldn't. That night I went right away from home, just as I stood, made my way to London, and the next day I went to King Street, Westminster, and saw where the recruiting sergeants were marching up and down."

"I know," cried the boy, "with their canes under their arms and their colours flying."

"Yes, Punch, and I picked out the one in the new regiment, the —th Rifles."

"Yes," cried Punch, "the Rifle green with the red collars and cuffs."

Pen, half-excited by his recollections, half-amused at the boy's intense interest, nodded again.

"And took the king's shilling," cried Punch; "and I know, but I want you to tell me—you joined ours just to show that uncle that you wanted to serve the king, and not for the sake of the scarlet coat."

"Yes, Punch, that was why; and that's all."

Chapter Nine
How to treat an Enemy

"Well, but is that all?" said Punch.

"Yes, and now you are tired and had better have a nap, and by the time you wake I will have some more milk for you."

"Bother the old milk! I'm sick of it; and I don't want to go to sleep. I feel sometimes as if I had nearly slept my head off. A fellow can't be always sleeping. Now, look here; I tell you what you have got to do some day. You must serve that uncle of yours out."

"Let him rest. You are tired and weak."

"No, I ain't. All that about you has done me good. I did not know that you had had such a lot of trouble, sir."

"Ah, what's that, Punch!" cried Pen sharply. "Don't you say 'sir' to me again!"

"Shall if I like. Ain't you a gentleman?"

"No, sir. Only Private Penton Gray, of the —th Rifles."

"Well, you are a-saying 'sir' to me."

"Yes, but I don't mean it as you do. While I am in the regiment we are equals."

"Oh yes, I like that!" said the boy with a faint laugh. "Wish we was. Only Private Penton Gray of the —th! Well, ain't that being a gentleman? Don't our chaps all carry rifles? They are not like the line regiments with their common Brown Besses. Sharpshooters, that's what we are. But they didn't shoot sharp enough the other day, or else we shouldn't be here. I have been thinking when I have been lying half-asleep that there were so many Frenchies that they got our lads between two fires and shot 'em all down."

"I hope not, Punch. What makes you think that?"

"Because if they had been all right they would have been after us before now to cut us out, and—and—I say, my head's beginning to swim again."

"Exactly, you are tired out and must go to sleep again."

"But I tell you I don't—"

The poor boy stopped short, to gaze appealingly in his companion's eyes as if asking for help, and the help Pen gave was to lay his hand gently on his eyelids and keep it there till he felt that the sufferer had sunk into a deep sleep.

The next day the poor fellow had quite a serious relapse, and lay looking so feeble that once more Pen in his alarm stood watching and blaming himself for rousing the boy into such a state of excitement that he seemed to have caused him serious harm.

But just as Punch seemed at the worst he brightened up again.

"Look here," he said, "I ain't bad. I know what it is."

"So do I," replied Pen. "You have been trying your strength too much."

"Wrong!" cried the boy faintly. "It was you give me too much to eat. You ought to have treated me like a doctor would, or as if I was a prisoner, and given me dry bread."

"Ah!" sighed Pen. "But where was the bread to come from?"

"Jusso," said Punch, with a faint little laugh; "and you can't make bread without flour, can you? But don't you think I'm going to die, because I am ever so much better to-day, and shall be all right soon. Now, go on talking to me again about your uncle."

"No," said Pen, "you have heard too much of my troubles already."

"Oh no, I ain't. I want to hear you talk about it."

"Then you will have to wait, Punch."

"All right, then. I shall lie and think till my head begins to go round and round, and I shall go on thinking about myself till I get all miserable and go backwards. You don't want that, do you?"

"You know I don't."

"Very well, then, let's have some more uncle. It's like doctor's stuff to me. I've been thinking that you might wait a bit, and then go and see that lawyer chap and punch his head, only that would be such a common sort of way. It would be all right if it was me, but it wouldn't do for you. This would be better. I have thought it out."

"Yes, you think too much, Punch," said Pen, laying his hand upon his companion's forehead.

"I wish you wouldn't do that," cried the boy pettishly. "It's nice and cool now."

"Yes, it is better now. That last sleep did you good."

"Not it, for I was thinking all the time."

"Nonsense! You were fast asleep."

"Yesterday," said the boy; "but I was only shamming to-day, so that I could think, and I have been thinking that this would do. You must wait till we have whopped the French and gone back to England, and got our new uniforms served out, and burnt all our rags. Then we must go and see your uncle, and—"

"That'll do, Punch. I want to see to your wound now."

"What for? It's going on all right. Here, whatcher doing of? You ain't going to cut up that other sleeve of your shirt, are you?"

"Yes; it is quite time that you had a fresh bandage."

"Ah, that's because you keep getting it into your head that I'm worse and that I'm going to die; and it's all wrong, for I am going to be all right. The Frenchies thought they'd done for me; but I won't die, out of spite. I am going to get strong again, and as soon as the colonel lets me carry a rifle I will let some of them have it, and— Oh, very well; if you must do it, I suppose I must lie still; only get it over. But—ya! I don't mean to die. What's the good of it, when there's so much for us to do in walloping the French? But when we do get back to the regiment you see how I will stick up for you, and what a lot I will make the chaps think of you!"

"Will you keep your tongue quiet, Punch?"

"No, I sha'n't," said the boy with a mocking laugh. "There, you needn't tie that so tight so as to make it hurt me, because I shall go on talking all the same—worse. You always begin to shy and kick out like one of those old mules when I begin talking to you like this. You hates to hear the truth. I shall tell the chaps every blessed thing."

But, all the same, Punch lay perfectly still now until the dressing of his wound was at an end; and then very faintly, almost in a whisper, he said, "Yes; our chaps never knew what a good chap—"

"Ah! Asleep again!" said Pen, with a sigh of relief. "There must be slight delirium, and I suppose I shall be doing no good by trying to stop him. Poor fellow! He doesn't know how he hurts me when he goes wandering on like this. I wish I could think out some way of getting a change of food. Plenty of milk, plenty of fish. I have been as far as I dared in every direction, but there isn't a trace of a cottage. I don't want much—only one of those black-bread cakes now and then. Any one would have thought that the people in a country like this would have kept plenty of fowls. Perhaps they do where there are any cottages. Ah, there's no shamming now. He's fast enough asleep, and perhaps when he awakes he will be more himself."

But poor Punch's sleep only lasted about half an hour, and then he woke up with his eyes glittering and with a strangely eager look in his countenance, as he stretched out the one hand that he could use.

"Yes," he said, "that's it. I know what you will have to do. Go to that uncle of yours—"

"Punch, lad," cried Pen, laying his hand softly upon the one that had closed upon his wrist, "don't talk now."

"I won't much, only it stops my head from going round. I just want to say—"

"Yes, I know; but I have been watching a deal while you slept."

"What for?" cried the boy.

"To make sure that the enemy did not surprise us."

"Ah, you are a good chap," said the boy, pressing his wrist.

"And I am very tired, and when you talk my head begins to go round too."

"Does it? Well, then, I won't say much; only I have got this into my head, and something seems to make me tell you."

"Leave it till to-morrow morning, then."

"No; it must come now, for fear I should forget it. What you have to do is to go to your uncle like an officer and a gentleman—"

"Punch, Punch!"

"All right; I have just done. Pistols like an officer—same as they uses when they fights duels. Then you walks straight up to him, with your head in the air, and you says to him, 'You don't desarve it, sir, but I won't take any dirty advantage of you; so there's the pistols,' you says. 'Which will you choose? For we are going to settle this little affair.' Then I'll tell you how it is. Old Pat Reilly—who was a corporal once, before he was put back into the ranks—I heerd him telling our chaps over their pipes how he went with the doctor of the regiment he was in to carry his tools to mend the one of them who was hurt. He called it—he was an Irishman, you know—a jool; and he said when you fight a jool, and marches so many paces, and somebody—not the doctor, but what they calls the second—only I think Pat made a mistake, because there can't be two seconds; one of them must be a first or a third—"

"There, Punch, tell me the rest to-morrow."

"No," said the boy obstinately; but his voice was growing weaker. "I have just done, and I shall be better then, for what I wanted to say will have left off worrying me. Let's see what it was. Oh, I know. You stands opposite to your uncle, turns sideways, raises your pistol, takes a good aim at him, and shoots him dead. Now then, what do you say to that?"

"That I don't want to shoot him dead, Punch."

"You don't?"

"No."

"Why, isn't he your enemy?"

"I don't know."

"Then I suppose that won't do."

"I'm afraid not, Punch."

"Then you must wait a little longer till you get promoted for bravery in the field. You will be Captain Gray then, and then you can go to him, and look him full in the face, and smile at him as if you felt that he was no better than a worm, and ask him what he thinks of that."

"What! Of my captain's uniform, Punch?"

"No, I mean you smiling down at him as if he wasn't worth your notice."

"Ah, that sounds better, Punch."

"Then, you think that will do?"

"Yes."

"Then, now I will go to sleep."

"Ah, and get better, Punch."

"Oh yes, I am going to get better now."

With a sigh of satisfaction, the boy closed his eyes, utterly exhausted, and lay breathing steadily and well, while Pen stood leaning over him waiting till he felt sure that the boy was asleep; and then, as he laid his hand lightly upon his patient's brow, a sense of hopefulness came over him on feeling that he was cool and calm.

"There are moments," he thought to himself, "when it seems as if I ought to give up as prisoners, for it is impossible to go on like this. Poor fellow, he wants suitable food, and think how I will I don't know what I could do to get him better food. I should be to blame if I stand by and see him die for want of proper nourishment." And it seemed to him that his depressing thoughts had affected his eyes, for the cabin had grown dull and gloomy, and his despair became more deep.

"Oh, it's no use to give way," he muttered. "There must be food of some kind to be found if I knew where to forage for it. Why not kill one of the kids?"

He stopped short in his planning and took a step forward, to pass round the rough heather pallet, thus bringing him out of the shadow into the light and face to face with a girl of about seventeen or eighteen, who was resting one hand upon the doorpost and peering in at the occupant of the rough bed, but who now uttered a faint cry and turned to run.

Chapter Ten
Talking in his Sleep

"No, no! Pray, pray, stop!" cried Pen, dashing out after his strange visitor, who was making for the edge of the nearest patch of wood.

The imploring tone of his words had its effect, though the tongue was foreign that fell upon the girl's ears, and she stopped slowly, to look back at him; and, then as it seemed to dawn upon her what her pursuer was, she slowly raised her hands imploringly towards him, the gesture seeming to speak of itself, and say, "Don't hurt me! I am only a helpless girl."

Then she looked up at him in wonder, for Pen raised his in turn, as he exclaimed, "Don't run away. I want your help."

The girl shook her head.

"*Inglés.*"

"*Si, si, Inglés, Inglés.* Don't go. I won't hurt you."

"*Si, si, Inglés,*" said the girl with some animation now.

"Ah, she understands that!" thought Pen; and then aloud, "Help! Wounded!" and he pointed at the open door.

The girl looked at him, then at the door, and then shook her head.

"Can you understand French?" cried Pen eagerly; and the girl shook her head again.

"How stupid to ask like that!" muttered Pen; and then aloud, "Help! Wounded."

The girl shook her head once more, and then started and struggled slightly as Pen caught her by the arm.

"Don't fight," he cried. "Help! help!" And he gesticulated towards the hut as he pointed through the door at the dimly seen bed, while the girl held back at arm's-length, gazing at him wildly, until a happy thought struck him, for he recalled the words that he had more than once heard used by the villagers while he and his fellows were foraging.

"*El pano,*" he cried; "*el pano*—bread, bread!" And he pointed to the dimly seen boy and then to his own mouth.

"*Si, el pano!*" cried the girl, ceasing her faint struggle.

"*Si, si!*" cried Pen again, and he joined his hands together for a moment before slowly beckoning their visitor to follow him into the cottage.

He stepped in, and then turned to look back, but only to find that the girl still held aloof, and then turned to look round again as if in search of help. As she once more glanced in his direction with eyes that were full of doubt, Pen walked round to the back of the rough pallet, placing the bed between them, and then beckoned to the girl to come nearer as he pointed downward at his sleeping patient.

Their visitor still held aloof, till Pen raised his hands towards her, joining them imploringly, and his heart leaped with satisfaction as she began slowly and cautiously to approach.

And now for his part he sank upon his knees, and as she watched him, looking ready to dart away at any moment, he placed one finger upon his lips and raised his left hand as if to ask for silence, while he uttered softly the one word, "Hush!"

To his great satisfaction the girl now approached till her shadow fell across the bed, and, supporting herself by one hand, she peered in.

"I'd give something if I could speak Spanish now," thought Pen. "What can I do to make her understand that he is wounded? She ought to be able to see. Ah, I know!"

He pointed quickly to his rifle, which was leaning against the bed, and then downward at where the last-applied bandage displayed one end. Then, pointing to poor Punch's face, he looked at the girl sadly and shook his head.

It was growing quite dusk inside the hut, but Pen was able to see the girl's face light up as, without a moment's hesitation now she stepped quickly through the rough portal and bent down so that she could lightly touch the sleeper's hand, which she took in hers as she bent lower and then rose slowly, to meet Pen's inquiring look; and as she shook her head at him sadly he saw that her eyes were filling with tears.

"Sick," he whispered; "dying. *El pano, el pano;*" and his next movement was telling though grotesque, for he opened his mouth and made signs of eating, before pointing downward at the boy.

"*Si, si,*" cried the girl quickly, and, turning to the door again, she passed through, signing to him to follow, but only to turn back, point to the little pail that stood upon the floor by the bed's head, and indicate that she wanted it.

Pen grasped her meaning, caught up the pail, handed it to her, and quite simply and naturally sank upon one knee and bent over to lightly kiss the girl's extended hand, which closed upon the edge of the little vessel.

She shrank quickly, and a look of half-dread, half-annoyance came upon her countenance; but, as Pen drew back, her face smoothed and she nodded quickly, pointed in the direction of the big fall, made two or three significant gestures that might or might not have meant, "I'll soon be back," and then whispered, "*El pano, el pano;*" and ran off over the rugged stones as swiftly as one of her own mountain goats.

"Ha!" said Pen softly, as he sighed with satisfaction, "*el pano* means bread, plain enough, and she must have understood that. Gone," he added, as the girl disappeared. "Then there must be another cottage somewhere in that direction, and I am going to hope that she will come back soon with something to eat. Who could have thought it?—But suppose she has gone to join some of the French who are about here, and comes back with a party to take us prisoners!—Oh, she wouldn't be so treacherous; she can't look upon us as enemies. We are not fighting against her people. But I don't know; they must look upon us as made up of enemies. No, no, she was only frightened, and no wonder, to find us in her hut, for it must be hers or her people's. Else she wouldn't have come here. No, a girl like that, a simple country girl, would only think of helping two poor lads in distress, and she will come back and bring us some bread."

As Pen stood watching the place where the girl had disappeared his hand went involuntarily to his pocket, where he jingled a few *pesetas* that he had left; and then, as he canvassed to himself the possibility of the girl's return before long, he went slowly back into the hut and stood looking down at the sleeper.

"Bread and milk," he said softly. "It will be like life to him. But how queer it seems that I should be worrying myself nearly to death, giving up my clothes to make him comfortable, playing doctor and nurse, and nearly starving myself, for a boy for whom I never cared a bit. I couldn't have done any more for him if he had been my brother. Why, when I used to hear him speak it jarred upon me, he seemed so coarse and common. It's human nature, I suppose, and I'm not going to doubt that poor girl again. She looks common and simple too—a Spanish peasant, I suppose, who had come to milk and see to the goats after perhaps being frightened away by the firing.

A girl of seventeen or eighteen, I should say. Well, Spanish girls would be just as tender-hearted as ours at home. Of course; and she did just the same as one of them would have done. She looked sorry for poor Punch, and I saw one tear trickle over and fall down.—There, Punch, boy; we shall be all right now if the French don't come."

Pen stepped out in the open and seated himself upon a piece of mossy rock where he could gaze in the direction where he had last seen his visitor. But it was all dull and misty now. There was the distant murmur of the great fall, the sharp, sibilant chirrup of crickets. The great planet which had seemed like a friend to him before had risen from behind the distant mountain, and there was a peculiar sweet, warm perfume in the air that made him feel drowsy and content.

"Ah," he sighed, "they say that when things are at their worst they begin to mend. They are mending now, and this valley never felt, never looked, so beautiful before. How one seems to breathe in the sweet, soft, dewy night-air! It's lovely. I don't think I ever felt so truly happy. There, it's of no use for me to watch that patch of wood, for I could not see our visitor unless she was coming with a lantern; and perhaps she has had miles to go. Well, watching the spot is doing no good, and if she's coming she will find her way, and she is more likely not to lose heart if I'm in the hut, for I might scare her away. Here, let's go in and see how poor old Punch is getting on! But I never thought—I never could have imagined—when I was getting up my 'lessons for to-morrow morning' that the time would come when I should be waiting and watching in a Spanish peasant's hut for some one to come and bring me in for a wounded comrade a cake of black-bread to keep us both alive."

Pen Gray walked softly in the direction of the dimly seen hut through heathery brush, rustling at every step and seeming to have the effect of making him walk on tiptoe for fear he should break the silence of the soft southern evening.

The lad stopped and listened eagerly, for there was a distant shout that suggested the hailing of a French soldier who had lost his way in the forest. Then it was repeated, "Ahoy-y-hoy-hoy-y-y!" and answered from far away, and it brought up a suggestion of watchful enemies searching for others in the darkened woods.

Then came another shout, and an ejaculation of impatience from the listener.

"I ought to have known it was an owl. Hallo! What's that? Has she come back by some other way?"

For the sound of a voice came to him from inside the rough hut, making him hurry over the short distance that separated him from the door, where he stood for a moment or two listening, and he heard distinctly, "Not me! I mean to make a big fight for it out of spite. Shoot me down—a boy—for obeying orders! Cowards! How would they like it themselves?"

"Why, Punch, lad," said Pen, stepping to the bedside and leaning over his comrade, "what's the matter? Talking in your sleep?"

There was no reply, but the muttering voice ceased, and Pen laid his hand upon the boy's forehead, as he said to himself, "Poor fellow! A good mess of bread-and-milk would save his life. I wonder how long she will be!"

Chapter Eleven
Punch's Commissariat

It was far longer than Pen anticipated, for the darkness grew deeper, the forest sounds fainter and fainter, and there were times when the watcher went out to listen and returned again and again to find Punch sleeping more restfully, while the very fact that the boy seemed so calm appeared to affect his comrade with a strange sense of drowsiness, out of which he kept on rousing himself, muttering the while with annoyance, "I can't have her come and find me asleep. It's so stupid. She must be here soon."

And after a trot up and down in the direction in which he had seen the girl pass, and back, he felt better.

"Sleep is queer," he said to himself. "I felt a few minutes ago as if I couldn't possibly keep awake."

He softly touched Punch's temples again, to find them now quite cool, and seating himself at the foot of the rough pallet he began to think hopefully of the future, and then with his back propped against the rough woodwork he stared wonderingly at the glowing orange disc of the sun, which was peering over the mountains and sending its level rays right through the open doorway of the hut.

Pen gazed at the soft, warm glow wonderingly, for everything seemed strange and incomprehensible.

There was the sun, and here was he lying back with his shoulders against the woodwork of the rough bed. But what did it all mean?

Then came the self-evolved answer, "Why, I have been asleep!"

Springing from the bed, he just glanced at his softly breathing companion as he ran out to look once more in the direction taken by the girl.

Then he stepped back again in the hope that she might have returned during the night and brought some bread; but all was still, and not a sign of anybody having been there.

Pen's heart sank.

"Grasping at shadows," he muttered. "Here have I been wasting time over sleep instead of hunting for food."

Ignorant for the time being of the cause of the wretched feeling of depression which now stole over him, and with no friendly voice at hand to say, "Heart sinking? Despondent? Why, of course you are ready to think anything is about to occur now that you are literally starving!" Pen had accepted the first ill thought that had occurred to him, and this was that his companion had turned worse in the night and was dying.

Bending over the poor fellow once more, he thrust a hand within the breast of his shirt, and his spirits sank lower, for there was no regular throbbing beat in response, for the simple reason that in his hurry and confusion of intellect he had not felt in the right place.

"Oh!" he gasped, and his own voice startled him with its husky, despairing tone, while he bent lower, and it seemed to him that he could not detect the boy's breath playing upon his cheek.

"Oh, what have I done?" he panted, and catching at the boy's shoulders he began to draw him up into a sitting position, with some wild idea that this would enable him to regain his breath.

But the next moment he had lowered him back upon the rough pallet, for a cry Punch uttered proved that he was very much alive.

"I say," he cried, "whatcher doing of? Don't! You hurt?"

"Oh, Punch," cried Pen, panting hard now, "how you frightened me!"

"Why, I never did nothink," cried the boy in an ill-used tone.

"No, no. Lie still. I only thought you were getting worse. You were so still, and I could not hear you breathe."

"But you shouldn't," grumbled the wounded boy surlily, as he screwed first one shoulder up to his ear and then the other. "Hff! You did hurt! What did you expect? Think I ought to be snoring? I say, though, give a fellow some more of that milk, will you? I'm thirsty. Couldn't you get some bread—not to eat, but to sop in it?"

"I don't think I could eat anything, but—" The boy stopped short as he lay passing his tongue over his fever-cracked lips, for the doorway of the miserable cabin was suddenly darkened, and Pen sprang round to find himself face to face with his visitor of the previous evening, who stood before him with the wooden vessel in one hand and a coarse-looking bread-cake in the other.

She looked searchingly and suspiciously at Pen for a few moments; and then, as if seeing no cause for fear, she stepped quickly in, placed the food she had brought upon the rough shelf, and then bent over Punch and laid one work-roughened hand upon the boy's forehead, while he stared up at her wonderingly.

The girl turned to look round at Pen, and uttered a few words hurriedly in her Spanish patois. Then, as if recollecting herself, she caught the bread-cake from where she had placed it, broke a piece off, and put it in the young rifleman's hand, speaking again quickly, every word being incomprehensible, though her movements were plain enough as she signed to him to eat.

"Yes, I know what you mean," said Pen smiling; "but I want the bread for him," and he pointed to the wounded boy.

The peasant-girl showed on the instant that though she could not understand the stranger's words his signs were clear enough. She broke off another piece of the bread and took down the little wooden-handled pail, which was half-full of warm milk. This she held up to Pen, and signed to him to drink; but he shook his head and pointed to Punch. This produced a quick, decisive nod of the head, as the girl wrinkled up her forehead and signed in an insistent way that Pen should drink first.

He obeyed, and then the girl seated herself upon the bed and began to sop pieces of the bread and hold them to Punch's lips.

"Thenkye," he said faintly, and for the first time for many days the boy showed his white teeth, as he smiled up in their visitor's face. "'Tis good," he said, and his lips parted to receive another fragment of the milk-softened bread, which was given in company with a bright girlish smile and a few more words.

"I say," said Punch, slowly turning his head from side to side, "I suppose you can't understand plain English, can you?"

The girl's voice sounded very pleasant, as she laughingly replied.

"Ah," said Punch, "and I can't understand plain Spanish. But I know what you mean, and I will try to eat.—'Tis good. Give us a bit more."

For the next ten minutes or so the peasant-girl remained seated upon the bedside attending to the wounded boy, breaking off the softer portions of the cake, soaking them in the warm milk, and placing them to the sufferer's lips, and more than once handing portions of the cake to Pen and giving him the clean wood vessel so that he might drink, while the sun lit up the interior of the hut and lent a peculiar brightness to the intently gazing eyes of its three occupants, till the rustic breakfast came to an end, this being when Punch kept his lips closed, gazed up straight in the girl's face, and smiled and shook his head.

"Good!" said the girl in her native tongue, and she nodded and laughed in satisfaction before playfully making believe to close the boy's eyes, and ending by keeping her hand across the lids so that he might understand that he was now to sleep.

To this Punch responded by taking the girl's hand in his and holding it for a few moments against his cheek before it was withdrawn, when the poor wounded lad turned his face away so that no one should see that a weak tear was stealing down his sun-browned cheek.

But the girl saw it, and her own eyes were wet as she turned quickly to Pen, pointed to the bread and milk, signed to him that he should go on eating, and then hurried out into the bright sunshine, Pen following, to see that she was making straight for the waterfall.

The next minute she had disappeared amongst the trees.

"Well, Punch," cried Pen, as he stepped back to the hut, "feel better for your breakfast?"

"Better? Yes, of course. But I say, she didn't see me snivelling, did she?"

"Yes, I think so; and it made her snivel too, as you call it. Of course she was sorry to see you so weak and bad."

"Ah!" said Punch, after a few moments' silence, during which he had lain with his eyes shut.

"What is it? Does your wound hurt you?"

"No; I forgot all about it. I say, I should like to give that girl something, because it was real kind of her; but I ain't got nothing but a sixpence with a hole in it, and she wouldn't care for that, because it's English."

"Well, I don't know, Punch. I dare say she would. A good-hearted girl like that wouldn't look upon its value, but would keep it out of remembrance of our meeting."

"Think so?" said Punch eagerly, and with his eyes sparkling. "Oh, don't I wish I could talk Spanish!"

"Oh, never mind that," said Pen. "Think about getting well. But, all the same, I wish I could make her understand so that she could guide me to where our fellows are."

"Eh?" cried the boy eagerly. "You ain't a-going to run away and leave me here, are you?"

"Is it likely, Punch?"

"Of course not," cried the boy. "Never you mind what I say. I get muddly and stupid in my head sometimes, and then I say things I don't mean."

"Of course you do; I understand. It's weakness," said Pen cheerily; "but you are getting better."

"Think so, comrade? You see, I ain't had no doctor."

"Yes, you have. Nature's a fine doctor; and if we can keep in hiding here a few days more, and that girl will keep on bringing us bread and milk, you will soon be in marching order; so we are not going to be in the dumps. We will find our fellows somehow."

"To be sure we will," said Punch cheerfully, as he wrenched himself a little over, wincing with pain the while.

"What is it, Punch? Wound hurt you again?"

"Yes; horrid," said the boy with a sigh.

"Then, why don't you lie still? You should tell me you wanted to move."

"Yes, all right; I will next time. It did give me a stinger. Sets a fellow thinking what some of our poor chaps must feel who get shot down and lie out in the mountains without a comrade to help them—a comrade like you. I shall never—"

"Look here, Punch," interrupted Pen, "I don't like butter."

"I do," said the boy, with his eyes dancing merrily. "Wished I had had some with that bread's morning."

"Now, you know what I mean," cried Pen; "and mind this, if you get talking like that to me again I will go off and leave you."

"Ha, ha!" said the boy softly, "don't believe you. All right then, I won't say any more if you don't like it; but I shall think about it all the more."

"There you go again," cried Pen. "What is it you want? What are you trying to get? You are hurting yourself again."

"Oh, I was only trying to get at that there sixpence," said the poor fellow, with a dismal look in his face. "I'm half-afraid it's lost.—No, it ain't! I just touched it then."

"Then don't touch it any more."

"But I want it."

"No, you don't, not till that girl comes; and you had better keep it till we say good-bye."

"Think so?" said Punch.

Pen nodded.

"You think she will come again, then?"

"She is sure to."

"Ah," said Punch, rather drowsily now, "I say, how nice it feels for any one to be kind to you when you are bad."

"Very," said Pen thoughtfully. "Pain gone off?"

"Yes; I am all right now. Think she will come back soon?"

"No, not for hours and hours."

"Oh, I say, Pen. Think it would be safe for me to go to sleep?"

"Yes, quite."

"Then I think I will, for I feel as if I could sleep for a week."

"Go to sleep then. It's the best thing you can do."

"Well, I will. Only, promise me one thing: if she comes while I'm asleep, I—I—want you—promise—promise—wake—"

"Poor fellow!" said Pen, "he's as weak as weak. But that breakfast has been like life to him. Well, there's some truth in what they say, that when things come to the worst they begin to mend."

A few minutes later, after noting that his poor wounded comrade had sunk into a deep sleep, Pen stole gently out among the trees, keeping a sharp lookout for danger as he swept the slopes of the valley in search of signs of the enemy, for he felt that it was too much to hope for the dark-green or scarlet of one of their own men.

But the valley now seemed thoroughly deserted, and a restful feeling began to steal through the lad's being, for everything looked peaceful and beautiful, and as if the horrors of war had never visited the land.

The sun was rising higher, and he was glad to take shelter beneath the rugged boughs of a gnarled old cork-tree, where he stood listening to the low, soft, musical murmur of the fall. And as he pictured the clear, bright, foaming water flashing back the sun's rays, and in imagination saw the shadowy forms of the trout darting here and there, he took a step or two outward, but checked himself directly and turned back to where he could command the door of the hut, for a feeling of doubt crossed his mind as to what might happen if he went away; and before long he stole back to the side of the rough pallet, where he found Punch sleeping heavily, feeling, as he seated himself upon a rough stool, that he could do nothing more but wait and watch. But it was with a feeling of hope, for there was something to look forward to in the coming of the peasant-girl.

"And that can't be for hours yet," thought the lad; and then his mind drifted off to England, and the various changes of his life, and the causes of his being there. And then, as he listened to the soft hum of insect-life that floated through the open door, his eyelids grew heavy as if he had caught the drowsy infection from his companion. Weak as he was from light feeding, he too dropped asleep, so that the long, weary time that he had been wondering how he should be able to pass was but as a minute, for the sun was setting when he next unclosed his eyes, to meet the mirthful gaze of Punch, who burst into a feeble laugh as he exclaimed, "Why, you have been asleep!"

Chapter Twelve
A Rustle among the Trees

"Asleep!" cried Pen, starting up and hurrying to the door.

"Yes; I have been watching ever so long. I woke up hours ago, all in a fright, thinking that gal had come back; and I seemed to see her come in at the door and look round, and then go again."

"Ah, you saw her!" said Pen, looking sharply to right and left as if in expectation of some trace of her coming.

"No," said Punch, "it's no use to look. I have done that lots of times. Hurt my shoulder, too, screwing myself round. She ain't been and left nothing."

"But you saw her?" cried Pen.

"Well," said Punch, in a hesitating way, "I did and I didn't, like as you may say. She seemed to come; not as I saw her at first—I only felt her, like. It was the same as I seemed to see things when I have been off my head a bit."

"Yes," said Pen, "I understand."

"Do you?" said Punch dreamily. "Well, I don't. I didn't see her, only it was like a shadow going out of the door; but I feel as sure as sure that she came and stood close to me for ever so long, and I think I saw her back as she went out; and then I quite woke up and lay and listened, hoping that she would come again."

"I hope it was only a dream, Punch," said Pen; "but I had no business to go to sleep like that."

"Why not? You waren't on sentry-go; and there was nothing to do."

"I ought to have kept awake."

"No, you oughtn't. I was jolly glad to see you sleep; and I lay here and thought of what a lot of times you must have kept awake and watched over me when I was so bad, and— Here, whatcher going to do?"

"Going away till you have done talking nonsense."

"Oh, all right. I won't say no more. You are such a touchy chap. Don't go away. Give us a drink."

"Ah, now you are talking sense," said Pen, as he made for the shelf upon which the little wooden vessel stood. "Here, Punch," he said, "you mustn't drink this. It has turned sour."

"Jolly glad of it. Chuck it away and fetch me a good drink of water. Only, I say, I'd give it a good rinse out first."

"Yes," said Pen dryly, "I think it would be as well. Now, you don't think that I should have given you water out of a dirty pail?"

"Well, how should I know?" said the boy querulously. "But, where are you going to get it from?"

"Out of the pool just below the waterfall."

"Ah, it will be nice and cool from there," said the boy, passing his tongue over his dry lips. "I was afraid that you might get it from where the sun had been on it all day."

"Were you?" said Pen, smiling.

"Here, I say, don't grin at a fellow like that," said the boy peevishly. "You do keep catching a chap up so. Oh, I am so thirsty! It's as if I had been eating charcoal cinders all day; and my wound's all as hot and dry as if it was being burnt."

"Yes, I had no business to have been asleep," said Pen. "I'll fetch the water, and when you have had a good drink I will bathe your wound."

"Ah, do; there's a good chap. But don't keep on in that aggravating way, saying you oughtn't to have gone to sleep. I wanted you to go to sleep; and it wasn't a dream about her coming and looking at me while I was asleep. I dessay my eyes were shut, but I felt somebody come, and it only aggravates me for you to say nobody did."

"Then I won't say it any more, Punch," cried Pen as he hurried out of the door. "But you dreamt it, all the same," he continued to himself as he hurried along the track in the direction of the fall, keeping a sharp lookout the while, partly in search of danger, partly in the faint hope that he might catch sight of their late compassionate visitor, who might be on the way bearing a fresh addition to their scanty store.

But he encountered no sign of either friend or enemy. One minute he was making his way amongst the gnarled cork-trees, the next he passed out to where the soft, deep, lulling, musical sound of the fall burst upon his ears; and soon after he was upon his knees drinking deeply of the fresh, cool water, before rinsing out and carefully filling the wooden *seau*, which he was in the act of raising from the pool when he started, for there was a movement amongst the bushes upon the steep slope on the other side of the falls.

Pen's heart beat heavily, for, fugitive as he was, the rustling leaves suggested an enemy bent upon taking aim at him or trapping him as a prisoner.

He turned to make his way back to the hut, and then as the water splashed from the little wooden pail, he paused.

"What a coward I am!" he muttered, and, sheltering himself among the trees, he began to thread his way between them towards where he could pass among the rocks that filled the bed of the stream below the falls so as to reach the other side and make sure of the cause of the movement amidst the low growth.

"I dare say it was only goats," he said. "Time enough to run when I see a Frenchman; but I wish I had brought my piece."

Keeping a sharp lookout for danger, he reached the other side of the little river, and then climbed up the rocky bank, gained the top in safety, and once more started violently, for he came suddenly upon a goat which was browsing amongst the bushes and sprang out in alarm.

"Yes, I am a coward!" muttered the lad with a forced laugh; and, stepping back directly, he lowered himself down the bank, recrossed the stream, filled the little pail, and made his way to where his wounded companion was waiting for him impatiently.

"Oh, I say, you have been a time!" grumbled the boy, "and I am so thirsty."

"Yes, Punch, I have been a while. I had rilled the pail, when there was a rustle among the trees, and I thought one of the Frenchies was about to pounce upon me."

"And was it?"

"No, only a goat amongst the bushes; and that made me longer. There, let me hold you up—no, no, don't try yourself. That's the way. Did it hurt you much?"

The boy drank with avidity, and then drew a long breath.

"Oh, 'tis good!" he said. "Nice and cool too. What, did it hurt? Yes, tidy; but I ain't going to howl about that. Good job it wasn't a Frenchy. Don't want them to find us now we are amongst friends. If that gal will only bring us a bit to eat for about another day I shall be all right then. Sha'n't I, comrade?"

"Better, I hope, Punch," said Pen, smiling; "but you won't be all right for some time yet."

"Gammon!" cried the boy. "I shall. It only wants plenty of pluck, and a wound soon gets well. I mean to be fit to go on again precious soon, and I will. I say, give us a bit more of that cake, and—I say—what's the Spanish for butter?"

Pen shook his head.

"Well, cheese, then? That will do. I want to ask her to bring us some. It's a good sign, ain't it, when a chap begins to get hungry?"

"Of course it is. All you have got to do is to lie still, and not worry your wound by trying to move."

"Yes, it is all very fine, but you ain't got a wound, and don't know how hard it is to lie still. I try and try, and I know how it hurts me if I do move, but I feel as if I must move all the same. I say, I wish we had got a book! I could keep quiet if you read to me."

"I wish I had one, Punch, but I must talk to you instead."

"Well, tell us a story."

"I can't, Punch."

"Yes, you can; you did tell me your story about how you came to take the shilling."

"Well, yes, I did tell you that."

"Of course you did, comrade. Well, that's right. Tell us again."

"Nonsense! You don't want to hear that again."

"Oh, don't I? But I do. I could listen to that a hundred times over. It sets me thinking about how I should like to punch somebody's head—your somebody, I mean. Tell us all about it again."

"No, no; don't ask me to do that, Punch," said Pen, wrinkling up his forehead.

"Why? It don't hurt your feelings, does it?"

"Well, yes, it does set me thinking about the past."

"All right, then; I won't ask you. Here, I know—give us my bugle and the bit of flannel and stuff out of the haversack. I want to give it a polish up again."

"Why, you made it quite bright last time, Punch. It doesn't want cleaning. You can't be always polishing it."

"Yes, I can. I want to keep on polishing till I have rubbed out that bruise in the side. It's coming better already. Give us hold on it."

Pen hesitated, but seeing how likely it was to quiet his patient's restlessness, he placed the bright instrument beside him, and with it the piece of cloth with which he scoured it, and the leather for a polisher, and then sat thoughtfully down to watch the satisfied look of intentness in the boy's countenance as he held the copper horn so close to his face that he could breathe upon it without moving his head, and then go on polish, polish, slowly, till by degrees the movement of his hand became more slow, his eyes gradually closed, his head fell sideways, and he sank to sleep.

"Poor fellow!" said Pen thoughtfully. "But he can't be worse, or he wouldn't sleep like that."

Pen rose carefully so as not to disturb the sleeper, and cautiously peered outside the hut-door, keeping well out of sight till he had assured himself that there was no enemy visible upon the slopes of the valley, and then, taking a few steps under the shelter of the trees, he scanned the valley again from another point of view, while he listened intently, trying to catch the sound of the tramping of feet or the voice of command such as would indicate the nearness of the enemy.

But all was still, all looked peaceful and beautiful; and after stepping back to peer through the hut-door again to see that Punch had not stirred, he passed round to the back, where he could gaze in the direction of the fall and of the track by which the peasant-girl had hurried away.

"I wonder whether she will come back again," thought Pen; and then feeling sure that they would have another visit from their new friend, he went slowly back to the hut and seated himself where he could watch the still-sleeping boy and think; for there was much to dwell upon in the solitude of that mountain valley—about home, and whether he should ever get back there and see England again, or be one of the unfortunates who were shot down and hastily laid beneath a foreign soil; about how long it would be before Punch was strong enough to tramp slowly by his side in search of their own corps or of some other regiment where they would be welcome enough until they could join their own.

These were not inspiriting thoughts, and he knew it must be weeks before the poor fellow's wound would be sufficiently healed. Then other mental suggestions came to worry him as to whether he was pursuing the right course; as a companion he felt that he was, but as a soldier he was in doubt about the way in which his conduct would be looked upon by his superiors.

"Can't help it," he muttered. "I didn't want to skulk. I couldn't leave the poor fellow alone—perhaps to the wolves."

The day went by very slowly. It was hot, and the air felt full of drowsiness, and the more Pen forced himself to be wakeful the more the silence seemed to press him down like a weight of sleep to which he was forced to yield from time to time, only to start awake again with a guilty look at his companion, followed by a feeling of relief on finding that Punch's eyes were still closed and not gazing at him mockingly.

Slow as it was, the evening began to approach at last, and with it the intense longing for the change that would be afforded by the sight of their visitor.

But the time glided on, and with it came doubts which were growing into feelings of surety which were clinched by a sudden movement on the part of the wounded boy, whose long afternoon-sleep was brought to an end with an impatient ejaculation.

"There! I knew how it would be," he said. "She won't come now."

"Never mind, Punch," said Pen, trying to speak cheerily. "There's a little more bread, and I will go now and see if I can find the goat, and try and get some milk."

"Not you," said the boy peevishly. "She will know you are a stranger, and won't let you try again. I know what them she-billy goats are. I have watched them over and over again. Leave the bread alone, and let's go to sleep. We shall want it for breakfast, and water will do. I mean to have one good long snooze ready for to-morrow, and then I am going to get up and march."

"Nonsense, Punch," cried Pen. "You can't."

"Can't I?" said the boy mockingly. "I must, and, besides, British soldiers don't know such a thing as can't."

"Ah!" cried Pen excitedly, as he started up and made for the door, for there was the rustling sound of feet amongst the bushes; and directly after, hot and panting with exertion, the peasant-girl appeared at the opening that was growing dim in the failing light.

Chapter Thirteen
"Look out, Comrade!"

"Hooray!" cried Punch, wrenching his head round and stretching one hand towards their visitor, who stepped in, put the basket she carried upon the bed, and placed her hand upon her side, breathing hard as if she were in pain.

"Why, you have been running," cried Punch, looking at her reproachfully. "It was all right on you, and you are a good little lass to come, but you shouldn't have run so fast. 'Tain't good."

As the girl began to recover her breath she showed her white teeth and nodded merrily at the wounded boy; and then, as if she had grasped his meaning, she turned to Pen, caught up the basket, and began rapidly to take out its contents, which consisted first of bunches of grapes, a few oranges, and from beneath them a piece of thin cheese and another cake, which lay at the bottom in company with a rough-looking drinking-mug.

These were all arranged upon the bed close beside Punch, while the girl, as she emptied her basket, kept on talking to Pen in a hurried way, which he took to mean as an apology for her present being so common and simple.

Upon this base Pen made what he considered a suitable reply, thanking the girl warmly for her compassion and kindness to two unfortunate strangers.

"I wish I could make you understand," he said; "but we are both most grateful and we shall never forget it, and— What's the matter?"

For all at once, as the girl was listening eagerly to his words and trying to understand them, nodding smilingly at him the while, a sudden change came over her countenance as she gazed fixedly past the young soldier at the little square opening in the hut-wall behind him which served as a window, and then turned to snatch her basket from the bed.

"What is it?" cried Pen.

"Look out, comrade—the window behind," said Punch.

Pen turned on the instant, but the dim window gave no enlightenment, and he looked back now at the girl, who was about to pass through the door, but darted back again to run round the foot of the bed, so as to place it between her and the swarthy-looking Spanish peasant-lad who suddenly appeared to block the doorway, a fierce look of savage triumph in his eyes, as he planted his hands upon his hips and burst out into an angry tirade which made the girl shrink back against the wall.

Not a word was intelligible to the lookers-on, but all the same the scene told its own tale. Punch's lips parted, his face turned white, and he lay back helpless, with his fingers clenched, while Pen's chest began to heave and he stood there irresolute, breathing hard as if he had been running, knowing well as he did what the young Spaniard's words must mean.

What followed passed very quickly, for the young Spaniard stepped quickly into the hut, thrust Pen aside, stepped round to the foot of the bed, and caught the shrinking girl savagely by the wrist.

She shrank from him, but he uttered what sounded more like a snarl than words, and began to drag her back round the foot of the bed towards the door.

Pen felt as if something were burning in his chest, and he breathed harder, for there was a twofold struggle taking place therein between the desire to interfere and the feeling of prudence that told him he had no right to meddle under the circumstances in which he was placed.

Prudence meant well, and there was something very frank and brave in her suggestions; but she had the worst of it, for the girl began to resist and retort upon her assailant angrily, her eyes flashing as she struggled bravely to drag her wrist away; but she was almost helpless against the strong muscles of the man, and the next moment she turned upon Pen an appealing look, as she uttered one word which could only mean "Help!"

Pen took that to be the meaning, and the hot feeling in his young English breast burst, metaphorically, into flame.

Springing at the young Spaniard, he literally wrested the girl from his grasp; and as she sprang now to catch at Punch's extended hand, Pen closed with her assailant, there was a brief struggle, and the Spaniard was driven here and there for a few moments before he caught his heel against the rough sill at the bottom of the doorway and went down heavily outside, but only to spring up again with his teeth bared like those of some wild beast as he sprang at Pen.

A piercing shriek came from the girl's lips, and she tried to free herself from Punch's detaining hand; but the boy held fast, checking the girl in her brave effort to throw herself between the contending pair, while Punch uttered the warning cry, "Look out! Mind, comrade! Knife! Knife!"

The next instant there was a dull thud, and the Spaniard fell heavily in the doorway, while Pen stood breathing hard, shaking his now open hand, which was rapidly growing discoloured.

"Has he cut you, comrade?" cried Punch in a husky voice.

"No. All right!" panted Pen with a half-laugh. "It's only the skin off—his teeth. I hit first," But he muttered to himself, "Cowardly brute! It was very near.—No, no, my girl," he said now, aloud, as the girl stripped a little handkerchief from her neck and came up to him timidly, as if to bind up his bleeding knuckles. "I will go down to the stream. That will soon stop;" and he brushed past her, to again face the Spaniard, who was approaching him cautiously now, knife in hand, apparently about to spring.

"Oh, that's it, is it?" said Pen sternly, and still facing the Spaniard he took a couple of steps backward towards the wall of the hut.

His assailant did not read his intention, and uttered a snarl of triumph as he continued his cautious tactics and went on advancing, swinging himself from side to side as if about to spring; and a dull gleam of light flashed from the knife he held in his hand.

Throwing forward horizontally the rifle Pen had caught from where it stood in the corner of the hut.

But the hand Pen had thrust out behind him had not been idle; and Punch, who lay helplessly upon the bed, uttered a sigh of satisfaction, for with one quick movement Pen threw forward his right again to where it came closely in contact with his left, which joined on in throwing forward horizontally the rifle Pen had caught from where it stood in the corner of the hut, the muzzle delivering a dull blow in the Spaniard's chest. There was a sharp click, click, and Pen thundered out, "Drop that knife and run, before it's—fire!"

The man could not understand a word of English, but he plainly comprehended the young soldier's meaning, for his right hand relinquished its grasp, the knife fell with a dull sound upon the earthen floor, and its owner turned and dashed away, while the girl stood with her hands clasped as she uttered a low sigh full of relief, and then sank down in a heap upon the floor, sobbing as if her heart would break.

"One for him, comrade," cried Punch hoarsely. "How would it be to spend a cartridge over his head? Make him run the faster."

"No need, Punch. This is a bad bit of luck."

"Bad luck!" said Punch. "I call it fine. Only I couldn't come and help. Yes, fine! Teach him what British soldier means. Oh, can't you say something to tell that poor girl not to cry like that? Say, old man," said the boy, dropping into a whisper, "didn't see it before. Why, he must be her chap!"

Chapter Fourteen
Punch will talk

"Yes, I suppose you are right, Punch," said Pen, frowning. "Thick-headed idiot. I have quite taken the skin off my knuckles. Poor girl," he continued, "she has been cruelly punished for doing a womanly action."

"Yes; but he's got it too, and serve him right. Oh, didn't I want to help! But, my word, he will never forget what a British fist is. Yours will soon be all right. Oh, I wish she wouldn't go on crying like that! Do say something to her and tell her we are very sorry she got into a scrape."

"No, you say something," said Pen quietly. But there was no need, for the girl suddenly sprang up, hurriedly dashing away her tears, her eyes flashing as if she were ashamed of being seen crying; and, looking sharply from one to the other, she frowned, stamped her little foot upon the earthen floor, and pointed through the open door.

"*Juan malo!*" she cried, and, springing to where the knife lay, she caught it up, ran outside, and sent it flying in amongst the trees. Then coming back, she approached Pen.

"*Juan malo!*" she cried. "*Malo—malo!*"

"*Mal*—bad," said Pen, smiling. "That's Latin as well as Spanish. *Si,*" he continued, to the girl, "*Juan mal—malo.*"

The girl nodded quickly and pointed to his hand. "*Navajo?*" she said.

"What does that mean?" said Pen. "Knife?" And he shook his head. "No, no, no, no," he said, and to give effect to his words he energetically struck the injured hand into its fellow-palm, and then held up the knuckles, which had begun to bleed again.

The girl smiled and nodded, and she made again to take the handkerchief from her neck to bind it up.

"No, no, no!" cried Pen, laughing and shaking his head.

The girl looked a little annoyed, and smiled again, and pointed to the provisions she had brought.

"*Queso, pano,*" she said. "*Las uvas;*" and she caught up one of the bunches of grapes, picked off a few, and placed them in Punch's hand. Then turning quickly to the door, she stopped to look round. "*Juan malo!*" she cried; and the next minute she was out of sight.

"Ah!" said Punch with a sigh, "wish I was a Spaniel and could tell her what a good little lass she is, or that I was a scholar like you are; I'd know how you do it. Why, you quite began to talk her lingo at once. Think that chap's waiting to begin bullying her again?"

"I hope not, Punch."

"So do I. Perhaps he won't for fear that she should tell you, and him have to run up against your fist again."

"It's a bad job, Punch, and I want to go down to the stream to bathe my hand. I dare say I should see him if he were hanging about, for the girl came from that way."

"But you needn't say it's a bad job," said Punch. "There's nothing to mind."

"I hope not," said Pen thoughtfully. "Perhaps there's nothing to mind. It would have been a deal worse if the French had found out that we were here."

"Yes, ever so much," said Punch. "Here, have some of these grapes; they are fine. Do you know, that bit of a spurt did me good. I feel better now as long as I lie quite still. Just as if I had been shamming, and ought to get up, and—and—oh, no I don't," said the poor fellow softly, as he made an effort to change his position, the slight movement bringing forth an ejaculation of pain. "Just like a red-hot bayonet."

"Poor old chap!" said Pen, gently altering the injured lad's position. "You must be careful, and wait."

"But I don't want to wait," cried the boy peevishly. "It has made me feel as weak as a great gal. I don't believe that one would have made so much fuss as I do."

"There, there, don't worry about it. Go on eating the grapes."

"No," said the boy piteously. "Don't feel to want them now. The shoot that went through me turned me quite sick. I say, comrade, I sha'n't want to get up and go on to-morrow. I suppose I must wait another day."

"Yes, Punch," said Pen, laying his uninjured hand upon the boy's forehead, which felt cold and dank with the perspiration produced by the pain.

"But, I say, do have some of these grapes."

"Yes, if you will," said Pen, picking up the little bunch that the wounded boy had let fall upon the bed. "Try. They will take off the feeling of sickness. Can you eat some of the bread too?"

"No," said Punch, shaking his head; but he did, and by degrees the pain died out, and he began to chat about the encounter, and how eager he felt to get out into the open country again.

"I say, comrade," he said at last, "I never liked to tell you before, but when it's been dark I have been an awful coward and lain coming out wet with scare, thinking I was going to die and that you would have to scrape a hole for me somewhere and cover me up with stones. I didn't like to tell you before, because I knew you would laugh at me and tell me it was all nonsense for being such a coward. D'ye see, that bullet made a hole in my back and let all the pluck out of me. But your set-to with that chap seemed to tell me that it hadn't all gone, for I felt ready for anything again, and that there was nothing the matter with me, only being as weak as a rat."

"To be sure!" cried Pen, laying his hand upon the boy's shoulder. "That is all that's the matter with you. You have got to wait till your strength comes back again, and then, Punch, you and I are going to see if we can't join the regiment again."

"That's right," cried the boy, with his dull eyes brightening; "and if we don't find them we will go on our travels till we do. Why, it will be fine, won't it, as soon as I get over being such a cripple. We shall have 'ventures, sha'n't we?"

"To be sure," replied Pen; "and you want to get strong, don't you?"

"Oh, don't I just! I should just like to be strong enough to meet that brown Spaniel chap and chuck my cap at him."

"What for?"

"What for? Set his monkey up and make him come at me. I should just like it. I have licked chaps as big as he is before now—our chaps, and one of the Noughty-fourths who was always bragging about and crowing over me. I don't mind telling you now, I was a bit afraid of him till one day when he gave me one on the nose and made it bleed. That made me so savage I forgot all about his being big and stronger, and I went in at him hot and strong, and the next thing I knew was Corporal Grady was patting me on the back, and there was quite a crowd of our chaps standing laughing, and the corporal says, 'Bedad, Punchard, boy, ye licked him foine! Yes, *foine*,' he said, just like that. 'Now, go and wash your face, and be proud of it,' just like that. And then I remember—"

"Yes, but remember that another time," said Pen quietly. "You are talking too much," And he laid his hand on the boy's forehead again.

"Oh, but I just want to tell you this."

"Tell me to-morrow, Punch. You are growing excited and feverish."

"How do you know? You ain't a doctor."

"No; but I know that your forehead was cold and wet a few minutes ago, and that it is hot and burning now."

"Well, that only means that it's getting dry."

"No; it means doing yourself harm when you want to get well."

"Well, I must talk," pleaded the boy.

"Yes, a little."

"What am I to do? I can't be always going to sleep."

"No; but go as much as you can, and you will get well the quicker."

"All right," said Punch sadly. "'Bey orders; so here goes. But I do wish that the chap as gave me this bullet had got it hisself. I say, comrade," added the boy, after lying silent for a few minutes.

"What is it? What do you want?"

"Just unhook that there cord and hang my bugle on that other peg. Ah, that's better; I can see it now. Stop a minute—give us hold."

The boy's eyes brightened as Pen handed him the instrument, and he looked at it with pride, while directly after, obeying the impulse that seized him, he placed the mouthpiece to his lips, drew a deep breath, and with expanding cheeks was about to give forth a blast when Pen snatched it from his hands.

"Whatcher doing of?" cried the boy angrily. "Stopping you from bringing the French down upon us," cried Pen sharply. "What were you thinking about?"

"I wasn't thinking at all," said the boy slowly, as his brow wrinkled up in a puzzled way. "Well, I was a fool! Got a sort of idea in my head that some of our fellows might hear it and come down and find us."

"I wish they would," said Pen sadly; "but I don't think there's a doubt of it, Punch, we are surrounded by the French. There, I'm sorry I was so rough with you, only you were going to make a mistake."

"Sarve me jolly well right," said the boy. "I must have been quite off my chump. There, hang it up. I won't do it again."

It was quite dark now, and in the silence Pen soon after heard a low, deep breathing which told him that his wounded companion had once more sunk asleep, while on his part a busy brain and a smarting hand tended to reproduce the evening scene, and with it a series of mental questions as to what would be the result; and so startling were some of the suggestions that came to trouble the watcher that he placed himself by the side of the bed farthest from the door and laid his rifle across the foot ready to hand, as he half-expected to see the dim, oblong square of the open doorway darkened by an approaching enemy stealing upon them, knife-armed and silent, ready to take revenge for the blow, urged thereto by a feeling of jealous hatred against one who had never meant him the slightest harm.

That night Pen never closed his eyes, and it was with a sigh of relief that he saw the first pale light of day stealing down into the rocky vale.

Chapter Fifteen
Juan's Revenge

"Oh, you have come back again, then," grumbled Punch, as Pen met his weary eyes and the dismal face that was turned sideways to watch the door of the hut. "Thought you had gone for good and forgotten all about a poor fellow."

"No, you didn't, Punch," said Pen, slowly standing his rifle up in a corner close at hand, as he sank utterly exhausted upon the foot of the bed.

"Yes, I did. I expected that you had come across some place where there was plenty to eat, and some one was giving you bottles of Spanish wine, and that you had forgotten all about your poor comrade lying here."

"There, I am too tired to argue with you, Punch," said Pen with a sigh. "You have drunk all the water, then?"

"Course I have, hours ago, and eat the last of the bread, and I should have eat that bit of hard, dry cheese, only I let it slip out of my fingers and it bounced like a bit of wood under the bed. Well, whatcher brought for us to eat?"

"Nothing, I am sorry to say."

"Well, but what are we going to do? We can't starve."

"I am afraid we can, Punch, if things are going on like this."

"But they ain't to go on like this. I won't lie here and starve. Nice thing for a poor fellow tied up here so bad that he couldn't pick up a bit of wittles again as had tumbled down, and you gone off roaming about where you liked, leaving your poor wounded comrade to die! Oh, I do call it a shame!" cried the lad piteously.

"Yes, it does seem a shame, Punch," said Pen gently; "but I can fetch some water. Are you very thirsty?"

"Thirsty? Course I am! Burnt up! It has been like an oven here all day."

Pen caught up the wooden *seau* and hurried out through the wood, to return in a few minutes with the vessel brimful of cold, clear water, which he set down ready, and then after carefully raising the poor boy into a sitting position he lifted the well-filled drinking-cup to his lips and replenished it again twice before the poor fellow would give up.

"Ah!" he sighed, "that's better! Which way did you go this time?"

"Out there to the west, where the sun goes down, Punch."

"Well, didn't you find no farmhouses nor cottages where they'd give you a bit of something to eat?"

"Not one; only rough mountain-land, with a goat here and there."

"Well, why didn't you catch one, or drive your bayonet into it? If we couldn't cook it we could have eaten it raw."

"I tried to, Punch, but the two or three I saw had been hunted by the enemy till they were perfectly wild, and I never got near one."

"But you didn't see no enemy this time, did you?"

"Yes; they are dotted about everywhere, and I have been crawling about all day through the woods so as not to be seen. It's worse there than in any direction I have been this week. The French are holding the country wherever I have been."

"Oh, I do call this a nice game," groaned the wounded boy. "Here, give us another cup of water. It does fill one up, and I have been feeling as hollow as a drum."

Pen handed him the cup once more, and Punch drank with as much avidity as if it were his first.

"Yes," he sighed, "I do call it a nice game! I say, though, comrade, don't you think if you'd waited till it was dark, and then tried, you could have got through their lines to some place and have begged a bit of bread?"

"Perhaps, Punch, if I had not been taken."

"Well, then, why didn't you try?"

"Well, we have had that over times enough," said Pen quietly, "and I think you know."

"Course I do," said the boy, changing his tone; "only this wound, and being so hungry, do make me such a beast. If it had been you going on like this, lying wounded here, and it was me waiting on you, and feeding you, and tying you up, I should have been sick of it a week ago, and left you to take your chance."

"No, you wouldn't, Punch, old chap; it isn't in you," said Pen, "so we won't argue about that. I only want you to feel that I have done everything I could."

"'Cept cutting off and leaving me to take my chance. You haven't done that."

"No, I haven't done that, Punch."

"And I suppose you ain't going to," said the boy, "and I ought to tell you you are a fool for your pains."

"But you are not going to do that, Punch."

"No, I suppose not; and I wish I wasn't such a beast—such an ungrateful brute. It is all that sore place; and it don't get no better. But, I say, why don't you go out straight and find the first lot of Frenchies you can, and say to them like a man, 'Here, I give myself up as a prisoner'?"

"I told you, Punch, what I believe," replied Pen.

"Yes; you said you were afraid that they wouldn't have me carried away on account of my wound."

"Well, that's what I do believe, Punch. I don't want to be hard on the French, but they are a very rough lot here in this wild mountain-land, and I don't believe they would burden themselves with wounded."

"Well, it wouldn't matter," said the boy dismally.

"Of course they wouldn't carry me about; but they would put me out of my misery, and a good job too."

Pen said nothing, but his face wrinkled up with lines which made him look ten years older, as he laid his hand upon his comrade's fevered brow.

"Ha!" sighed Punch, "that does a fellow good. I don't believe any poor chap ever had such a comrade as you are; and I lie here sometimes wondering how you can do so much for such an—"

"Will you be quiet, Punch?" cried Pen, snatching away his hand.

"Yes, yes—please don't take it away."

"Then be quiet. You know how I hate you to talk like this."

"Yes, all right; I have done. But, I say, do you think it's likely that gal will come again? She must know that what she brought wouldn't last."

"I think, poor lass, she must have got into such trouble with her people that she daren't come again."

"Her people!" cried the boy. "It's that ugly black-looking nigger of a sweetheart of hers. You had a good sight of him that night when you took aim with your rifle. Why didn't you pull the trigger? A chap like that's no good in the world."

"Just the same as you would if you had had hold of the rifle yourself, Punch—eh?"

"There you go again," said the boy sulkily. "What a chap you are! You are always pitching it at me like that. Why, of course I should have shot him like a man."

"Would you?" said Pen, smiling.

"Oh, well, I don't know. Perhaps I shouldn't. Such a chap as that makes you feel as you couldn't be too hard on him. But it wouldn't be quite the right thing, I suppose. There, don't bother. It makes my sore place ache. But, oh, shouldn't I like to tell him what I think of him! I say, don't you think she may come to-night?"

"No, Punch; I have almost ceased to hope. Besides, I don't want to depend on people's charity, though I like to see it I want to be able to do something for ourselves. No, I don't think she will come any more."

"I do," said the boy confidently. "I am beginning to think that she will come after all. She is sure to. She must know how jolly hungry I should be. She looked so kind. A gal like that wouldn't leave us to starve. She is a nice, soft-hearted one, she is, though she is Spanish. I wouldn't take no notice, but I see the tears come in her eyes, and one of them dropped on my hand when she leaned over me and looked so sorry because I was in pain. It's a pity she ain't English and lived somewhere at home where one might expect to see her again. It is very sad and shocking to have to live in a country like this."

"Do you feel so hungry now, Punch?"

"Yes, horrid. Give us a bit of that cheese to nibble. Then I must have another drink, and try and go to sleep. Feel as though I could now you have come back. I was afraid I was never going to see you again."

"I don't believe you thought I had forsaken you, Punch."

"Not me! You couldn't have done it. 'Tain't in you, comrade, I know. But I tell you what I did think: that the Frenchies had got hold of you and made you prisoner. Then I lay here feeling that I could not move myself, and trying to work it out as to what you'd do—whether you would try and make them come and fetch me to be a prisoner too, or whether you would think it wouldn't be safe, and you would be afraid to speak for fear they should come and bayonet me. And so I went on. Oh, I say, comrade, it does make a chap feel queer to lie here without being able to help hisself. I got to think at last that I wished I was dead and out of my misery."

"Yes, Punch, lad, I know. It was very hard to bear, but I couldn't help being so long. I was working for you—for both of us—all the time."

"Course you was, comrade! I know. And now you've come back, and it's all right again. Give us another drink of water. It's better than nothing— ever so much better, because there's plenty of it—and I shall go to sleep and do as I did last night when I was so hungry—get dreaming away about there being plenty of good things to eat. I seemed to see a regular feast— roast-meat and fruit and beautiful white bread; only it was as rum as rum. I kept on eating all the time, only nothing seemed to have any taste in it. And, hooray! What did I say! There she is! But," the boy added, his eager tones of delight seeming to die away in despair, "she ain't brought no basket!"

For, eager and panting with her exertions, her eyes bright with excitement, the peasant-girl suddenly dashed in through the open door, caught Pen by the breast with one hand, and pointed with the other in the direction from which she had come, as she whispered excitedly, "*Los Francéses!*"

Then, loosening her grasp, she turned quickly to the boy and passed one hand beneath his neck, signing to Pen to help her raise the wounded lad from the bed, while Pen hurried to the door to look out.

"Yes," he whispered quickly, as he turned back, "she means the enemy are coming, and wants me to carry you to a place of safety.—All right, my lass; I understand.—Here, Punch, I won't hurt you more than I can help. Clasp your hands round my neck, and I will carry you.—Here, girl, take my rifle!"

He held out the piece, and the girl caught it in her hand, while Pen drew his companion into a sitting position, stooped down, and turned his back to the bed.

"All right; I won't squeak, comrade. Up with me. For'ard!"

But the boy could not control his muscles, the contractions in his face showing plainly enough the agony he felt as with one quick movement Pen raised himself, pressing the clinging hands to his breast, and swung the poor fellow upon his back.

The girl nodded sharply, as, rifle in hand, she made for the door, beckoning to Pen to follow quickly; and then, with a look of despair, she stopped short, her actions showing plainly enough what she must be saying, for there was a quick rush among the trees outside, and the young Spaniard dashed to the front of the hut, made a snatch at the rifle the girl was bearing, and tore it from her grasp as he drove her back into the hut and barred the way, uttering a loud hail the while.

"Too late! We are too late, Punch," said Pen bitterly. "Here they are! Prisoners, my lad. I can do no more."

For, as he spoke, about a dozen of the enemy doubled up to the front of the hut, and the young Spaniard who had betrayed the two lads stood before Pen, showing his white teeth in a malignant grin of triumph, as he held the girl by the wrist.

Chapter Sixteen
Prisoners

"Are you in much pain, Punch?" said Pen, as, with his wrists tied tightly behind him he knelt beside his comrade, who lay now just outside the door of the hut, a couple of French chasseurs on guard.

The officer in command of the little party had taken possession of the hut for temporary bivouac, and his men had lighted a fire, whose flames picturesquely lit up the surrounding trees, beneath which the new-comers had stretched themselves and were now partaking of bread, grapes, and the water a couple of their party had fetched from the stream.

The young Spaniard was seated aloof from the girl, whose back was half-turned from him as she sat there seeming to have lost all interest in the scene and those whom she had tried to warn of the danger they were in.

From time to time the Spanish lad spoke to her, but she only jerked her head away from him, looking more indifferent than ever.

"Are you in much pain, Punch?" asked Pen again; for the boy had not replied, and Pen leaned more towards him, to gaze in his face searchingly.

"Oh, pretty tidy," replied the boy at last; "but it's better now. You seemed to wake up my wound, but it's going to sleep again. I say, though, I didn't show nothing, did I?"

"No, you bore it bravely."

"Did I? That's right. I was afraid, though, that I should have to howl; but I am all right now. And I say, comrade, look here; some chaps miche— you know, sham bad—so as to get into hospital to be fed up and get off duty, and they do it too, you know."

"Yes, I know," said Pen, watching the lad anxiously. "But don't talk so much."

"Must; I want to tell you, I am going to miche—sham, you know—the other way on."

"What do you mean?" said Pen.

"Why, make-believe I'm all right. Make these froggies think my wound's only a scratch. Then perhaps they will march me off along with you as a prisoner. I don't want them to—you know."

"March you off!" said Pen bitterly. "Why, you know you can't stand."

"Can't! I've got to. You'll let me hold tight of your arm. I've got to, comrade, and I will. It means setting one's teeth pretty hard. Only wish I had got a bullet to bite. It would come easy then. Look here, wait a bit, and then you back up a bit closer to me. Haven't tied my hands like yours. Just you edge close so as I can slip my fingers into your box. I want to get out one cartridge for the sake of the bullet."

"You can't, Punch. Didn't you see they slipped off the belt, and that young Spaniard's got it along with my rifle?"

"So he has! I didn't know. Now then, wasn't I right when I said you ought to have fired at him and brought him down? Well, I must have a bullet somehow. I know. I will try and get the girl to get hold of the case; only I don't know how it's to be done without knowing what to say. Can't you put me up to it, comrade?"

"No, Punch."

"But you might give a fellow a bit of advice."

"My advice is to lie still and wait."

"Well, that's pretty advice, that is, comrade. Wait till they comes and makes an end of a fellow if he breaks down, for I am beginning to think that I sha'n't be able to go through with it."

"Let's wait and see what happens, Punch. We have done our best, and we can do no more."

Just then Pen's attention was taken up by the young officer, who came to the door of the hut, yawned, and stood looking about at his men before slowly sauntering round the bivouac as if to see that all was right, the sentries drawing themselves up stiffly as he passed on, till he caught sight of the Spanish girl and the lad seated together in the full light cast by the fire.

Then turning sharply to one of his men, the young officer pointed at the Spaniard and gave an order in a low, imperious tone.

Two of his men advanced to the lit-up group, and one of them gave the lad a sharp clap on the shoulder which made him spring up angrily, while the other chasseur snatched the English rifle from his hand, the first chasseur seizing the cartridge-belt and case.

There was a brief struggle, but it was two to one, and the Spaniard, as Pen watched the encounter eagerly, was sent staggering back, catching his heel in a bush and falling heavily, but only to rebound on the instant, springing up knife now in hand and making at the nearest soldier.

"Ha!" gasped Punch excitedly, as he saw the gleam of the knife; and then he drew in his breath with a hiss, for it was almost momentary: one of the two French soldiers who had approached him to obey his officer's orders and disarm the informer just raised his musket and made a drive with the butt at the knife-armed Spaniard, who received the metal plate of the stock full in his temple and rolled over, half-stunned, amongst the bushes.

Another order rang out from the officer, and before the young Spaniard could recover himself a couple more of the soldiers had pounced upon him, and a minute later he was firmly bound, as helpless a prisoner as the young rifleman who watched the scene.

"Say, comrade," whispered Punch, "that's done me good. But do you see that?"

"See it? Why, of course I saw it. That's not what he bargained for when he led the Frenchmen here."

"No, I don't mean that," whispered Punch impatiently. "I meant the gal."

"The girl?" said Pen. "What about her?"

"Where is she?" whispered Punch.

"Why, she was—"

"Yes, *was*," whispered Punch again; "but where is she now? She went off like a shot into the woods."

"Ah!" exclaimed Pen, with a look of relief in his eyes.

"Yes, she's gone; and now I want to know what's going to be next. Here comes the officer. What'll be his first order? To shoot us, and that young Spaniel too?"

"No," said Pen. "But don't talk; he's close here."

The officer approached his prisoners now, closely followed by one of his men, whose *galons* showed that he was a sergeant.

"Badly wounded, eh?" said the officer in French.

"Yes, sir; too bad to stand."

"The worse for him," said the officer. "Well, we can't take wounded men with us; we have enough of our own."

"Yes, sir," said the sergeant; and Pen felt the blood seem to run cold through his veins.

And then curiously enough there was a feeling of relief in the knowledge that his wounded comrade could not understand the words he had grasped at once.

"We shall go back to camp in half an hour," continued the officer; and then running his eye over Pen as he sat up by Punch's side, "This fellow all right?"

"Yes, sir."

"See to his fastenings. I leave him to you."

"But surely, sir," cried Pen, in very good French, "you are not going to have my poor companion shot in cold blood because he has the misfortune to be wounded?"

"Eh, do you understand French?"

"Yes, sir; every word you have said."

"But you are not an officer?"

"I have my feelings, sir, and I appeal to you as an officer and a gentleman to save that poor fellow. It would be murder, and not the act of a soldier."

"Humph!" grunted the officer. "You boys should have stayed at home.—Here, sergeant, carry the lad into camp. Find room for him in the ambulance.—There, sir, are you satisfied now?" he continued to Pen.

"Yes, sir," replied Pen quickly; "satisfied that I am in the presence of a brave French officer. God bless you for this!"

The officer nodded and turned away, the sergeant stopping by the prisoners.

"Here, I say," whispered Punch, "what was all that talking about?"

"Only arranging about how you were to be carried into camp, Punch," replied Pen.

"Gammon! Don't you try and gull me. I know," panted the boy excitedly. "I could not understand the lingo; but you were begging him not to have me shot, and he gave orders to this 'ere sergeant to carry out what he said. You are trying to hide it from me so as I shouldn't know. But you needn't. I should like to have gone out like our other chaps have—shot fair in the field; but if it's to be shot as a prisoner, well, I mean to take it like a man."

The boy's voice faltered for a few moments as he uttered the last words, and then he added almost in a whisper, "I mean, if I can, for I'm awful weak just now. But you'll stand by me, comrade, and I think I will go through it as I ought. And you will tell the lads when you get back that I didn't show the white feather, but went out just like a fellow ought?"

"That won't be now, Punch," said Pen, leaning over him. "I am not deceiving you. I appealed to the officer, and he gave orders at once that you were to be carried by the men to their camp and placed in one of the ambulance wagons."

"Honour?" cried Punch excitedly. "Honour bright," replied Pen. "But that means taking me away from you," cried the boy, with his voice breaking.

"Yes; but to go into hospital and be well treated."

"Oh, but I don't want to go like that," cried the boy wildly. "Can't you ask the officer—can't you tell him that—oh, here—you—we two mustn't—mustn't be—" For the sergeant now joined them with a couple of men carrying a rough litter; and as Punch, almost speechless now, caught at his wrist and clung to him tightly, he looked down in the prisoner's wildly appealing eyes.

"Why, what's the matter with the boy?" growled the sergeant roughly. "Does he think he's going to be shot?"

"He's badly hurt, sir," said Pen quietly, "and can't bear being separated from me."

"Oh, that's it, is it, sir?" said the sergeant. "My faith, but you speak good French! Tell him that I'll see that he's all right. What's his hurt—bayonet?"

"No," said Pen, smiling. "A French bullet—one of your men aimed too well."

"Ha, ha! Yes, we know how to shoot. Poor fellow! Why, I have just such a boy as he.—Lift him up gently, lads.—Humph! He has fainted."

For poor Punch had held out bravely to the last; but nature was too strong even for his British pluck.

Chapter Seventeen
In Misery

"I say, Pen, are you there?"

"Yes, I'm here. What do you want?"

"Want you to turn me round so as I can look out of the door. What made you put me like this?"

"It wasn't my doing. You were put so that you might be more comfortable."

"But I am not more comfortable, and it's so jolly dark. I like to be able to look out of the door if I wake in the night."

"Hush! Don't talk so loudly."

"Why not? There's nobody to hear. But just turn me over first."

"Hush! There are three or four other people to hear," whispered Pen. "You are half-asleep yet. Don't you understand, Punch?"

"Understand—understand what?" said the poor fellow, subduing his voice in obedience to his companion's words.

"I must tell you, I suppose."

"Tell me? Why, of course! Oh, I begin to understand now. Have I been off my head a bit?"

"Yes; you were very much upset when the French officer was with us, and fainted away."

"Phee-ew!" whistled the boy softly. "Oh, it's all coming back now. The French came, and knocked over that Spanish chap, and I thought that they were going to take me away and shoot me. Why, they didn't, then! That's all right. Yes, I remember now. My head was all in a muddledum. I got thinking I was never going to see you any more. When was it—just now?"

"No, Punch, it was two nights ago, and the doctor thought—"

"The doctor? Why, you have been my doctor. I say—"

"Don't get excited. Lie quite still, and I will tell you."

"Ah, do. I am all in a muddle still; only you might turn me round, so that I can look straight out of the door, and I could breathe the fresh air then. I am being quite stuffercated like this."

"Yes, the hut is dreadfully hot," said Pen with a sigh. "There are six other poor wounded fellows lying here."

"Six other wounded fellows lying here! Whatcher talking about?"

"Only this, Punch," said Pen, with his lips close to the boy's ear. "You were carried to the little camp where those French came from that made us prisoners, and there you were put in an ambulance wagon with six more poor fellows, and the mules dragged us right away to a village where a detachment of the French army was in occupation. Do you understand?"

"I think so. But you said something about doctors."

"Yes. There are several surgeons in this village, and wounded men in every hut. There has been fighting going on, and a good many more wounded men were brought in yesterday."

"Halt!" said Punch in a quick, short whisper. "Steady! Did we win?"

"I don't know, but I think not. I've seen nothing but wounded men and the doctors and the French orderlies. The French officer was very nice, and let me stay with you in the ambulance; and when we came to a halt and I helped to carry you and the other wounded into this hut, one of the doctors ordered me to stop and help, so that I have been able to attend to you as well as the others."

"Good chap! That was lucky. Then this ain't our hut at all?"

"No."

"What's become of that gal, then?"

"She escaped somewhere in the darkness," replied Pen.

"And what about that Spanish beggar? Ah, I recollect that now. He brought the French to take us prisoners."

"I haven't seen any more of him, Punch, since they led him away."

"Serve him right! And so I've been lying here in this hut ever since?"

"Yes, quite insensible, and I don't think you even knew when the French surgeon dressed your wound and took out a ragged bit of the cartridge."

"Took out what?"

"A piece of the wad that was driven in, and kept the wound from healing."

"Well, you have been carrying on nice games without me knowing of it!" said the boy. "And it hasn't done me a bit of good."

"The doctor says it has. He told me yesterday evening that you would soon get right now."

"And shall I?"

"Yes, I hope so."

"So do I. But it does seem rum that all this should be done without my knowing of it."

"Well, you have been quite insensible."

"I suppose so. But where are we now, then?"

"I don't know, Punch, except that this is a little Spanish village which the French have been occupying as a sort of hospital."

"But where's all the fighting?"

"I don't know, Punch, much more than you do. There was some firing last night. I heard a good deal of tramping close at hand, as if some more men were marching in, and then more and more came through the night, and I heard firing again about a couple of hours ago; but it seemed to be miles away."

"And you don't know who's beat?"

"I know nothing, I tell you, only that everything has been very quiet for the last hour or so."

"Perhaps because you have been asleep," said Punch.

"No; I have been quite awake, fetching water from a mountain-stream here for the poor fellows who keep asking for more and more."

"Do they know we are English?"

"I don't think so. Poor fellows! their wounds keep them from thinking about such a thing as that; and, besides, I am just able to understand what they say, and to say a few words when they ask for drink or to be moved a little."

"Oh," said Punch, "that comes of being able to talk French. Wish I could. Here, I say, you said the doctor had been doing up my wound again. Think I could walk now?"

"I am sure you couldn't."

"I ain't," said the boy. "Perhaps I could if I tried."

"But why do you ask?" said Pen. "Because it's so jolly nice and dark; and, besides, it's all so quiet. Couldn't we slip off and find the way to our troops?"

"That's what I've been thinking, Punch, ever since you have been lying here."

"Of course you would," said the boy in an eager whisper. "And why not? I think I could manage it, and I'm game."

"You must wait, Punch, and with me think ourselves lucky that we are still together. Wait and get strong enough, and then we will try."

"Oh, all right. I shall do what you tell me. But I say, what's become of your rifle and belt?"

"I don't know. I saw them once. They were with some muskets and bayonets laid in the mule-wagon under the straw on one side. But I haven't seen them since."

"That's a pity," sighed the boy faintly; and soon after Pen found, when he whispered to him, that he was breathing softly and regularly, while his head felt fairly cool in spite of the stifling air of the crowded hut.

Punch did not stir till long after sunrise, and when he did it was to see that, utterly exhausted, his companion had sunk into a deep sleep, for the rest of that terrible night had been spent in trying to assuage the agony of first one and then another of the most badly wounded who were lying around. Every now and then there had been a piteous appeal for water to slake the burning thirst, and twice over the lad had to pass through the terrible experience of holding the hand of some poor fellow who in the darkness had whispered his last few words as he passed away.

Later on a couple more wounded men had been borne in by the light of a lantern, by whose aid a place was found for them in the already too crowded hut, and it became Pen's duty to hold the dim open lantern and cast the light so that a busy surgeon, who was already exhausted by his long and terrible duties, could do his best to bandage and stop some wound.

It was just at daylight, in the midst of the terrible silence which had now fallen around, that Pen's head had sunk slowly down till it rested upon Punch's shoulder; and when the sun rose at last its horizontal rays lit up the dismal scene, with the elder lad's pallid and besmirched face, consequent upon the help he had been called upon to render, giving him the appearance of being one of the wounded men.

Chapter Eighteen
War's Horrors

But the morning brought not only the horizontal rays of the great sun which lit up the hut with its sad tale of death and suffering, but likewise a renewal of the fight of the previous day, and this time the tide of battle swept much nearer to the encampment of the wounded.

Punch started out of a state of dreamy calm, and wondered why the noise he heard had not roused up his sleeping comrade, for from apparently quite near at hand came the boom of artillery, a sound which for the moment drowned all others, even the hoarse, harshly uttered words of command, as large bodies of men swung past the doorway of the hut, and the fitful bugle-calls which a minute before had fallen on his ear.

"Ah," he muttered, "it's a big fight going on out there. I wonder if those are our guns;" and once more the air was rent by the dull, angry roar of artillery. "Pen! Pen! Oh, I can't let him sleep! Why doesn't he wake up? Here, I say, comrade!"

"Eh, what is it?" And Pen opened his eyes, to gaze wonderingly at Punch's excited face.

"Don't you hear?"

"Hear? Yes, yes," And the dreamy look vanished from the other's eyes.

The two lads waited, listening, and then Punch put his lips close to Pen's ear.

"I am sure we are winning," he said. "Hear that?"

"How can I help hearing it?"

"Well, it's English guns, I know."

"Think so?"

"Yes, and they will be here soon."

Pen shook his head.

"Afraid not," he said; "and— Ah, all right.—Punch, lad, I'm wanted." For just then a man came hurriedly into the hut and made him a sign.

"What does he want?" grumbled Punch.

"It's the surgeon," said Pen, and he hurried away.

For some hours—long, hot, weary hours—Punch saw little of his fellow-prisoner, the morning wearing on and the atmosphere of the hovel becoming unbearably close, while all the time outside in the brilliant sunshine, evidently just on the other side of a stretch of purple hilly land, a battle was in progress, the rattle of musketry breaking into the heavy volume of sound made by the field-guns, while every now and again on the sun-baked, dusty stretch which lay beyond the doorway, where the shadows were dark, a mounted man galloped past.

"Wish my comrade would come back," he muttered; and it was long ere his wish was fulfilled. But the time came at last, and Pen was standing there before him, holding in his hands a tin drinking-cup and a piece of bread.

"Take hold," he said hoarsely, looking away.

"Where you been?" said Punch.

"Working in the ambulance. I—I—" And Pen staggered, and sat down suddenly on the ground.

"What's the matter? Not hit?"

"No, no."

"Had anything yourself?"

"Bother!" said Pen. "Make haste. Toss off that water. I want the cup."

"Had anything yourself?" repeated Punch firmly.

"Well, no."

"Then I sha'n't touch a drop until you have half and take some of that bread."

"But—"

"It's no good, Pen. I sha'n't and I won't—so there!"

Pen hesitated.

"Very well," he said; "half." And he drank some of the water. "It's very good—makes one feel better," and he ate a morsel or two of bread. "I had a job to get it."

"What did that fellow want?" asked Punch as he attacked his share.

"Me to help with the wounded," said Pen huskily. "So you thought me long?"

"Course I did. But the wounded—are there many?"

"Heaps," said Pen. "But don't talk so loudly."

"Poor chaps," said Punch, "they can't hear what we say. How are things going? There, they are at it again."

"I think the French are giving ground," said Pen in a whisper.

"Hooray!"

"Hush!"

"What, mayn't I say hooray?"

"No, you mayn't. I have picked up a little since I went away. I fancy our men have been coming on to try and take this village, but I couldn't make out much for the smoke; and, besides, I have been with that surgeon nearly all the time."

"Yes," said Punch. "Well, will they do it?"

Pen shook his head.

"Don't think so," he said. "They have tried it twice. I heard what was being done. Our people were driven back, and—"

He said no more, but turned to the door; and Punch strained his eyes in the same direction, as from away to the right, beyond a group of cottages, came a bugle-call, shrill, piercing, then again and again, while Punch started upright with a cry, catching Pen's arm.

"I say, hear that? That's our charge. Don't you hear? They are coming on again!"

The effort Punch had made caused a pain so intense that he fell back with a groan.

"You can leave me, Pen, old chap," he said.

"Don't mind me; don't look. But—but it's the English charge. Go to them. They are coming—they are, I tell you. Don't look like that, and—and— There, listen!"

The two lads were not the only ones in that hut to listen then and to note that the conflict was drawing nearer and nearer.

Punch, indeed, was right, and a short time after Pen crouched down closer to his companion, for now, quite close at hand, came volley after volley, the *zip, zip* of the ricochetting bullets seeming to clear the way for the charge.

Then more volleys.

The dust was ploughed up, and Punch started as a bullet came with a soft *plug* in the hut-wall, and Pen's heart felt ready to stop beating as there was a hoarse command outside, and half-a-dozen French infantry dashed into the building, to fill the doorway, two lying down and their comrades kneeling and standing.

"Don't speak," whispered Pen, for the boy had wrenched himself round and was gazing intently at the backs of the soldiers. "Don't speak."

Silence, before a grim happening. Then a roar from outside, exultant and fierce, and in the wide-open space beyond the hut-door the two lads saw a large body of the enemy in retreat before the serried ranks of British infantry who came on at the double, their bayonets flashing in the sun's rays, and cheering as they swept onward.

The muskets in the doorway flashed, and the hut was filled with smoke.

"Pen, I must whisper it—Hooroar!"

There was a long interval then, with distant shouting and scattered firing, and it was long ere the cloud of smoke was dissipated sufficiently for the two lads to make out that now the doorway was untenanted except by a French chasseur who lay athwart the threshold on his back, his hand still clutching at the sling of his piece.

"Think we have won?" whispered Punch, looking away.

"Don't know," muttered Pen; but the knowledge that was wanted came soon enough, for an hour later it became evident that the gallant attempt of the British commander to take the village had been foiled.

The British cheer they had heard still echoed in their ears, but it was not repeated, and it was speedily apparent that the fight had swept away to their left; and from scraps of information dropped by the members of the bearer-party who brought more wounded into the already crowded hut, and took away the silent figure lying prone in the entrance, Pen made out that the French had made a stand and had finally succeeded in driving back their foes.

In obedience to an order from the grim-featured surgeon, he left Punch's side again soon after, and it was dark ere he returned, to find the boy fast asleep. He sank down and listened, feeling now but little fatigue, starting up, however, once more, every sense on the alert, as there came a series of sharp commands at the hut-door, and he realised that he must have dropped off, for it was late in the evening, and outside the soft moonlight was making the scene look weird and strange.

Chapter Nineteen
Another Breakdown

Punch heard the voices too, and he reached out and felt for his comrade's hand.

"What is it?" he whispered. "Have they won? Not going to shoot me, are they?"

"No, no," said Pen, "but" — and he dropped his voice — "I think we are all going on."

He was quite right, and all through that night the slow business of setting a division on the march was under way, and the long, long train of baggage wagons drawn by the little wiry mules of the country began to move.

The ambulance train followed, with its terrible burden heavily increased with the results of the late engagement, while as before — thanks to the service he had been able to render — Pen was able to accompany the heavily laden wagon in which Punch lay.

"So we were beaten," said the boy sadly — as the wheels of the lumbering vehicle creaked loudly, for the route was rough and stony — and Pen nodded.

"Beaten. Yes," And his voice was graver than before at the thought of what he had seen since they had been prisoners.

On, on, on, through the dark hours, with Punch falling off every now and again into a fitful sleep — a sleep broken by sudden intervals of half-consciousness, when Pen's heart was wrung by the broken words uttered by his companion: "Not going to shoot me, are they? Don't let them do that, comrade." While, as the weary procession continued its way on to the next village, where they were about to halt, Pen had another distraction, for as he trudged painfully on by the side of the creaking wagon a hand was suddenly placed on his arm.

He turned sharply.

"Eh, what?" he cried.

"Well?" said a half-familiar voice, and in the dim light he recognised the features of the young French captain who had listened to his appeal to save the bugler's life.

"Rough work, sir," said Pen.

"Yes. Your fellows played a bold game in trying to dislodge us. Nearly succeeded, *ma foi*! But we drove them back."

"Yes," said Pen.

"How's your friend?" asked the captain.

"Better."

"That's well. And now tell me, where did you learn to speak French so well?"

"From my tutor," answered Pen.

"Your tutor! And you a simple soldier! Well, well! You English are full of surprises."

Pen laughed.

"I suppose so," he said; "but we are not alone in that."

The French captain chatted a little longer, and then once more Pen was alone—alone but for the strange accompaniment of sounds incident to the night march: the neighing of horses, the scraps of quick talking which fell on his ear, along with that never-ceasing creak, rumble, and jolt of the wagons, a creaking and jolting which seemed to the tired brain as though they would go on for ever and ever.

He was aroused out of a strange waking dream, in which the past and the present were weirdly blended, by a voice which called him by name, and he tried to shake himself free from the tangle of confused thought which hemmed him in.

"Aren't you there?" came the voice again.

"Yes, Punch, yes. What is it?"

"Ah, that's all right! I wanted to tell you that I feel such a lot better."

"Glad to hear it, Punch."

"Yes, I feel as if I could get out of this now."

"You had better not try," said Pen with a forced laugh. "I think—I think—" And then the confusion came again.

"What do you think?" said Punch.

"Think?" cried the other. "I—what do you mean?"

In the darkness of the heavy vehicle, Punch's face betrayed a feeling of alarm, and he tried to figure it out. Something in Pen's voice frightened him.

"He is not the same," he muttered; and his impression was substantiated when a halt was called just about the time of dawn, for Pen dropped like a log by the wagon-side; and when Punch, with great pain to himself, struggled into a sitting position, and then clambered down to his comrade, he found to his horror that his worst fears were realised.

Pen's forehead was burning, and the poor lad was muttering incoherently, and not in a condition to pay heed to the words of his companion.

"Gray, Gray! Can't you hear? What's wrong?"

The village which was the new headquarters was higher up in the mountains; and whether it was the fresher air operating beneficially, or whether the period of natural recovery had arrived, certain it was that Punch found himself able to move about again; and during the days and weeks that followed he it was who took the post of nurse and attended to the wants of Pen—wants, alas! too few, for the sufferer was a victim to something worse than a mere shot-wound susceptible to efficient dressing, for the most dangerous, perhaps, of all fevers had laid him low.

The period passed as in a long dream, and the thought of rejoining the British column had for a time ceased to animate Punch's brain.

But youth and a strong constitution rose superior in Pen's case to all the evils of circumstance and environment, and one afternoon the old clear look came back to his eyes.

"Ah, Punch," he said, "better?"

"Better?" said the boy. "I—I am well; but you—how are you now?"

"I—have I been ill?"

"Ill!" cried Punch, and he turned and looked at an orderly who was hurrying past. "He asks if he has been ill!—Why, Pen, you have had a fever which has lasted for weeks."

Pen tried to sit up, and he would have dismally failed in the attempt had not Punch encircled him with his arm.

"Why—why," he said faintly, "I am as weak as weak!"

"Yes, that you are."

"But, Punch, what has been happening?"

"I don't know. I can't understand what all these people say; but they let me fetch water for them and attend to you; and to-day there has been a lot going on—troops marching past."

"Yes," said Pen; "that means there has been another fight."

"No, I don't think so."

"Why not?"

"Because I have heard no firing. But hadn't you better go to sleep again?"

Pen smiled, but he took the advice and lay back.

"Perhaps I had," he said faintly; and as Punch watched him he fell into a restful doze.

So it was during the days that followed, each one bringing back more strength to the invalid, and likewise each day a further contingent of the wounded in the battle of a month before being passed as fit for service again and drafted to the front; while each day, too, Pen found that the strength that used to be his was returning little by little, and he listened eagerly one night when Punch bent over him and whispered something in his ear.

"You know I have been talking about it to you," said the boy, "for several nights past; and when I wasn't talking about it I was thinking of it. But now—now I think the time has come."

"To escape?" cried Pen eagerly. "You mean it?"

"Yes; I have been watching what has gone on. We are almost alone here, with only wounded and surgeons. The rest have gone; and—and behind this village there is a forest of those scrubby-barked oak-trees."

"Cork-trees," said Pen.

"Oh, that's it!" And the boy drew himself up. "But do you think you are strong enough yet?"

"Strong enough? Of course." And Pen rose, to stand at his companion's side. "Do you know the way?"

"Yes," And Punch felt for and took his companion's hand, trying to see his face in the pitchy darkness. "It is to the right of the camp."

"Then let's go."

"Wait," said Punch, and he glided off into the blackness, leaving Pen standing there alone.

But it was not for long. In a minute or two the boy was back once more, and this time he held something in his arms.

"Ready?" he asked in a whisper.

"Yes. What for?"

"Stoop.—That's it. I watched, and took them—not English ones, but they will shoot, I expect," And softly he slipped the sling of a musket over Pen's shoulders, following that by handing him a cartouche-box and belt. "I have got a gun for myself too. Better than a bugle. There!" And in the darkness there was the sound of a belt being tightly drawn through a buckle. "Are you ready?"

"Yes," said Pen.

"Where's your hand?"

"Here."

"Right!" And the younger lad gripped his friend's extended palm. "Now, it's this way. I planned it all when you were so ill, and said to myself that it would be the way when you got better. Come along."

Softly and silently the two slipped off in the darkness, making for the belt of forest where the gloomy leafage made only a slight blur against the black velvet sky.

Chapter Twenty
Hunted

"What's the matter, Punch? Wound beginning to hurt you again?"

"No," said the boy surlily.

"What is it, then? What are you thinking about?"

"Thinking about you being so grumpy."

"Grumpy! Well, isn't it enough to make a fellow feel low-spirited when he has been ill for weeks, wandering about here on these mountain-sides, hunted as if we were wild beasts, almost starving, and afraid to go near any of the people?"

"No," replied Punch with quite a snarl. "If you had had a bullet in your back like I did there's something to grumble about. I don't believe you ever knew how it hurt."

"Oh yes, I did, Punch," said Pen quietly, "for many a time I have felt for you when I have seen you wincing and your face twitching with pain."

"Of course you did. I know. You couldn't have been nicer than you were. But what have you got to grumble about now you're better?"

"Our bad luck in not getting back to some of our people."

"Well, I should like that too, only I don't much mind. You see, I can't help feeling as jolly as a sand-boy."

"I don't know that sand-boys have anything much to be jolly about, Punch," said Pen, brightening up.

"More do I—but it's what people say," said Punch; "only, I do feel jolly. To be out here in the sunshine—and the moonshine, too, of a night—and having a sort of feeling that I can sit down now without my back aching and smarting, and feeling that I want to run and jump and shout. You know what it is to feel better, now, as well as I do. This ain't home, of course; but everything looks wonderful nice, and every morning I wake up it all seems to me as if I was having a regular long holiday. I say, do say you are enjoying yourself too."

"I can't, Punch. There are too many drawbacks."

"Oh, never mind them."

"But I can't help it. You know I have been dreadfully weak."

"But you shouldn't worry about that. I don't mind a bit now you are getting well."

"What, not when we are faint with hunger?"

"No, not a bit. It makes me laugh. It seems such a jolly game to think we have got to hunt for our victuals. Oh, I think we are having a regular fine time. It's a splendid place! Come on."

"No, no; we had better rest a little more."

"Not me! Let's get some chestnuts. Ain't it a shame to grumble when you get plenty of them as you can eat raw or make a fire and roast them? Starve, indeed! Then look at the grapes we have had; and you never know what we shall find next. Why, it was only yesterday that woman gave us some bread, and pointed to the onions, and told us to take more; leastways she jabbered and kept on pointing again. Of course, we haven't done as well as we did in the hut, when the girl brought us bread and cheese and milk; but I couldn't enjoy it then with all that stinging in my back. And everything's good now except when you look so grumpy."

"Well, Punch, most of my grumpiness has been on your account, and I will cheer up now. If I could only meet some one to talk to and understand us, so that we could find out where our people are, I wouldn't care."

"Well, never mind all that, and don't care. I don't. Here we are having a big holiday in the country. We have got away from the French, and we are not prisoners. I am all alive and kicking again, and I feel more than ever that I don't care for anything now you are getting more and more well. There's only one thing as would make me as grumpy as you are."

"What's that, Punch?"

"To feel that my wound was getting bad again. I say, you don't think it will, do you?"

"No; why should I? It's all healing up beautifully."

"Then I don't care for anything," cried the boy joyously. "Yes, I do. I feel horrid wild sometimes to think they took away my bugle; leastways, I suppose they did. I never saw it no more; and it don't seem natural not to have that to polish up. I have got a musket, though; and, I say, why don't we have a day's shooting, and knock over a kid or a pig?"

"Because it would be somebody's kid or pig, and we should be hunted down worse than ever, for, instead of the French being after us for escaped prisoners, we should rouse the people against us for killing their property."

"Yes, that would be bad," said Punch; "but it would only be because we are hungry."

"Yes, but the people wouldn't study that."

"Think they would knife us for it?" said the boy thoughtfully.

"I hope not; but they would treat us as enemies, and it would go bad with us, I feel sure."

"Well, we are rested now," said Punch. "Let's get on again a bit."

"Which way shall we go?" said Pen.

"I dunno; anywhere so's not to run against the French. I have had enough of them. Let's chance it."

Pen laughed merrily, his comrade's easy-going, reckless way having its humorous side, and cheering him up at a time when their helpless condition made him ready to despair.

"Well," he said, "if we are to chance it, Punch, let's get out of this wood and try to go downhill."

"What for?"

"Easier travelling," said Pen. "We may reach another pleasant valley, and find a village where the people will let us beg some bread and fruit."

"Yes, of course," said Punch, frowning; "but it don't seem nice—begging."

"Well, we have no money to buy. What are we to do?"

"Grab," said Punch laconically.

"What—steal?" cried Pen.

"Steal! Gammon! Aren't we soldiers? Soldiers forage. 'Tain't stealing. We must live in an enemy's country."

"But the Spaniards are not our enemies."

"There, now you are harguing, and I hate to hargue when you are hungry. What I say is, we are soldiers and in a strange country, and that we must take what we want. It's only foraging; so come on."

"Come along then, Punch," said Pen good-humouredly. "But you are spoiling my morals, and—"

"Pst!" whispered Punch. "Lie down."

He set the example, throwing himself prone amongst the rough growth that sprang up along the mountain-slope; and Pen followed his example.

"What can you see?" he whispered, as he crept closer to his comrade's side, noting the while that as he lay upon his chest the boy had made ready his musket and prepared to take aim. "You had better not shoot."

"Then tell them that too," whispered Punch.

"Them! Who?"

"Didn't you see?"

"I saw nothing."

"I did—bayonets, just below yonder. Soldiers marching."

"Soldiers?" whispered Pen joyfully. "They may be some of our men."

"That they are not. They are French."

French they undoubtedly were; for as the lads peered cautiously from their hiding-place, and listened to the rustling and tramp of many feet, an order rang out which betrayed the nationality of what seemed to be a large body of men coming in their direction.

"Keep snug," whispered Punch, "and they won't see us. It's too close here."

Pen gripped his companion's arm, and lay trying to catch sight of the marching men for some minutes with a satisfied feeling that the troops were bearing away from them. But his heart sank directly after; a bugle-call rang out, the men again changed their direction, the line extended, and it became plain that they would pass right over the ground where the two lads lay.

"I am afraid they will see us, Punch," whispered Pen. "What's to be done?"

"Run for it. Look here, make straight for that wood up the slope," whispered Punch. "You go first, and I will follow."

"But that's uphill," whispered Pen.

"Bad for them as for us," replied the boy. "Up with you; right for the wood. Once there, we are safe."

Punch had said he hated to argue, and it was no time for argument then as to the best course.

Pen gazed in the direction of the approaching party, but they were invisible; and, turning to his comrade, "Now then," he said, "off!"

Springing up, he started at a quick run in and out amongst the bushes and rocks in the direction of the forest indicated by his companion, conscious the next minute, as he glanced back in turning a block of stone, that Punch was imitating his tactics, carrying his musket at the trail and bending low as he ran.

"Keep your head down, Punch," he said softly, as the boy raced up alongside. "We can't see them, so they can't see us."

"Don't talk—run," whispered Punch. "That's right—round to your left. Don't mind me if I hang back a bit. I am short-winded yet. I shall follow you."

For answer, Pen slackened pace, and let Punch pass him.

"Whatcher doing?" whispered the boy.

"You go first," replied Pen, "just as fast as you can. I will keep close behind you."

Punch uttered a low growl, but he did not stop to argue, and they ran on and on, getting out of breath but lighter hearted, as they both felt that every minute carried them nearer to safety, for the risky part where the slope was all stone and low bush was nearly passed, the dense patch of forest nearer at hand offering to them shelter so thick that, once there, their enemies would have hard work to judge which direction had been taken; and then all at once, when all danger seemed to be past, there came a shout from behind, and then a shot.

"Stoop! Stoop, Punch! More to the left!"

"All right. Come on," was whispered back; and, as Punch bore in the direction indicated by his comrade, there came shout after shout, shot after shot, and the next minute, as the fugitives tore on heedless of everything but their effort to reach the shelter in advance, it was perfectly evident to them that the bullets fired were whizzing in their direction.

There came a scattered volley, and both lads went down heavily.

Twigs were cut and fell; there was the loud *spat, spat* of the bullets striking the rocks; and then, when they were almost within touch of the dark shadows spread by the trees, there came a scattered volley, and both lads went down heavily, disappearing from the sight of their pursuers, who sent up a yell of triumph.

"Punch," panted Pen, "not hurt?"

The answer was a hoarse utterance, as the boy struggled to his feet and then dropped again on all-fours.

"No, no," he gasped. "Come on! come on! We are close there."

Pen was breathing hard as he too followed his comrade's movements just as if forced thereto by the natural instinct that prompted imitation; but the moment he reached his feet he dropped down again heavily, and then began to crawl awkwardly forward so that he might from time to time catch a glimpse of Punch's retiring form.

"Come on, come on!" kept reaching his ears; and then he felt dizzy and sick at heart.

It seemed to be growing dark all at once, but he set it down to the closing-in of the overshadowing trees. And then minutes passed of confusion, exertion, and a feeling as of suffocation consequent upon the difficulty of catching his breath.

Then at last—he could not tell how long after—Punch was whispering in his ear as they lay side by side so close together that the boy's breath came hot upon his cheek.

"Oh, how slow you have been! But this 'ere will do—must do, for we can get no farther. Why, you were worse than me. Hurt yourself when you went down?"

Pen was about to reply, when a French voice shouted, "Forward! Right through the forest!"

There was the trampling of feet, the crackling of dead twigs, and Punch's hand gripped his companion's arm with painful force, as the two lads lay breathless, with their faces buried in the thick covering of past years' dead leaves, till the trampling died away and the fugitives dared to raise their faces a little in the fight for breath.

Chapter Twenty One
Hide-and-Seek

"Oh, I say," whispered Punch, in a half-suffocated tone, "my word! Talk about near as a toucher! It's all right, comrade; but if I had held my breath half a jiffy longer I should have gone off pop. Don't you call this a game? Hide-and-seek and whoop is nothing to it! Garn with you, you thick-headed old frog-soup eaters! Wait till I get my breath. I want to laugh.—Can't hear 'em now; can you?"

"No," said Pen faintly. "Will they come back?"

"Not they," replied Punch chuckling. "Couldn't find the way again if they tried. But we shall have to stay here now till it's dark. It don't matter. I want to cool down and get my wind. I say, though, catch your foot on a stone?"

"No," replied Pen, breathing hard.

"Thought you did. You did go down—quelch! What you breathing like that for? You did get out of breath! Turn over on your back. There's nobody to see us now. I say, isn't it nice and shady! Talk about a hiding-place! Look at the beautiful great, long green leaves. Hooray! Chestnuts. We have dropped just into the right place for foraging. Wait a bit and we will creep right into the forest and make a little fire, and have a roast. What? Oh, it's all right. They have gone straight on and can't hear me. Here! I say: why, comrade, you did hurt yourself when you went down. Here, what is it? Oh, I am sorry! Ain't broke anything, have you?"

"My leg, Punch—my leg," said Pen faintly.

"Broke your leg, comrade?" cried the boy.

"No, no," said Pen faintly; "not so bad as that. One of the bullets, I think, scraped my leg when they fired."

"Shot!" cried Punch in an excited voice full of agony. "Oh, comrade, not you! Don't say that!"

The lad talked fast, but he was acting all the time. Leaving his musket amongst the leaves, he had crept to Pen's side, and was eagerly examining his comrade's now helpless leg.

"Can't help it," he whispered, as he searched for and drew out his knife. "I will rip it down the seam, and we will sew it up again some time." And then muttering to himself, "Scraped! It's a bad wound! We must get the bullet out. No—no bullet here." And then, making use of the little knowledge he had picked up, Punch tore off strips of cotton from his own and his companion's garments, and tightly bandaged the bleeding wound.

"It's a bad job, comrade," he said cheerily; "but it might have been worse if the Frenchies could shoot. There's no bones broke, and you are not going to grumble; but I'd have given anything if it hadn't been your turn now. Hurt much."

"Quite enough, Punch," said Pen with a rather piteous smile. "It's quite right; my turn now; but don't stop. You've stopped the bleeding, so get on."

"What say?"

"Go on now," said Pen, "while there's a chance to escape. Those fellows will be sure to come back this way, and you will lose your opportunity if you wait."

"Poor chap!" said Punch, as if speaking to himself, and he laid a hand on Pen's wet forehead. "Look at that now! I have made a nasty mark; but I couldn't help it, for there was no water here for a wash. But, poor chap, he won't know. He's worse than I thought, though; talking like that—quite off his head."

"I am not, Punch, but you will send me off it if you go on like that. Do as I tell you, boy. Escape while there's a chance."

"He's quite queer," said Punch, "and getting worse; but I suppose I can't do anything more."

"No; you can do no more, so don't waste your chance of escape. It will be horrible for you to be made prisoner again, so off with you while the coast's clear. Do you hear me?"

"Hear you! Yes, you needn't shout and tell the Johnnies that we are hiding here."

"No, no, of course not; it was very foolish, but the pain of the wound and your obstinacy made me excited. Now then, shake hands, and, there's a good fellow, go."

"Likely!" said Punch, wiping the pain-drops from Pen's face.

"What do you mean by that?" said Pen angrily.

"What do I mean by what? You are a bit cracked like, or else you wouldn't talk like this."

"Not tell you to run while there's a chance?"

"Not tell me to run like this when there's a chance!" replied Punch. "Jigger the chance! So you just hold your tongue and lie quiet. Sha'n't go! There."

"But, Punch, don't be foolish, there's a good fellow."

"No, I won't; and don't you be foolish. Pst! Hear that? They are coming back."

"There's time still," said Pen, lowering his voice.

"Oh, is there? You just look here. Here they are, coming nearer and nearer. Do you want them to come and take us both?"

"No, no, no," whispered Pen.

"Then just you hold your tongue," said Punch, nestling down close to his comrade's side, for the rustle and tramp of many feet began to grow nearer again; and as Punch lay upon his back with his eyes turned in the direction of the approaching sound he soon after caught a glimpse or two of sunlight flashed from the barrels of muskets far down the forest aisles, as their bearers seemed to be coming right for where they lay.

"Look here," said Punch softly, "they look as if they are coming straight here; but there's a chance for us yet, so let's take it, and if they don't find us— Mind, I didn't want you to be hit; but as you are, and I suppose was to be, I am jolly glad of it, for it gives a fellow a chance. And what's the good of me talking?" said the boy to himself now. "He's gone right off, swoonded, as they call it. Poor old chap! It does seem queer. But it might have been worse, as I said before. Wanted me to run away, did you? Likely, wasn't it? Why, if I had run it would have served me jolly well right if somebody had shot me down again. Not likely, comrade! I mayn't be a man, but my father was a British soldier, and that's what's the matter with me."

Punch lay talking to himself, but not loudly enough to startle a bird which came flitting from tree to tree in advance of the approaching soldiers, and checked its flight in one of the low branches of a great overhanging chestnut, and then kept on changing its position as it peered down at the two recumbent figures, its movements startling the bugler, who now began in a whisper to address the bird.

"Here," he said, "what game do you call that? You don't mean to say you have come here like this to show the Johnny Crapauds where we are, so that they may take us prisoners? No, I thought not. It wouldn't be fair, and I don't suppose they have even seen you; but it did look like it. Here they come, though, and in another minute they will see us, and— Oh, poor Gray! It will be bad for him, poor chap; and— No, they don't. They are wheeling off to the left; but if they look this way they must see us, and if they had been English lads that's just what they would have done. Why, they couldn't help seeing us—a set of bat-eyed bull-frogs; that's what I call them. Yah! Go on home! I don't think much of you. Now then, they are not coming here, and I don't care where they go as long as they don't find us. Now, what's next to be done? What I want is another goat-herd's hut, so as I can carry my poor old comrade into shelter. Now, where is it to be found? I don't know, but it's got to be done; and ain't it rum that my poor old mate here should have his dose, and me have to play the nurse twice over!"

Chapter Twenty Two
"Unlucky Beggars"

"If one wasn't in such trouble," said Punch to himself, as he lay in the growing darkness beneath the great chestnut-tree, "one would have time to think what a beautiful country this is. But of all the unlucky beggars that ever lived, Private Pen Gray and Bugler Bob Punchard is about the two worst. Only think of it: we had just got out of all that trouble with my wound and Gray's fever, then he gets hit and I got to nurse him all over again. Well, that's all clear enough.—How are you now, comrade?" he said aloud, as after cautiously gazing round in search of danger, he raised his head and bent over his wounded companion.

There was no reply, and Punch went on softly, "It's my turn now to say what you said to me. Sleepy, are you? Well, go on, and have plenty of it. It's the best thing for you. What did you say? Nature sets to work to mend you again? No, he didn't. I forget now, but that's what he meant. Now, I wonder whether it's safe for me to go away and leave him. No, of course it isn't, for I may tumble up against the French, who will make me a prisoner, and I sha'n't be able to make them understand that my comrade is lying wounded under this tree, and if I could I don't want to. That's one thing. Another is that if I start off and leave him here I sha'n't be able to find him again. Then, what am I going for? To try and find water, for my throat's like sand, and something to eat better than these chestnuts, for I don't believe they are anything like ripe. Oh dear! This is a rum start altogether. I don't know what to do. This is coming to the wars, and no mistake! There never was really such unlucky chaps as we are. It will be dark before long. Then I shall seem to be quite alone. To be all alone here in a great wood like this is enough to make any fellow feel scared. It's just the sort of place where the wolves will be. Well, if they do come, we have got two muskets, and if it isn't too dark I will have two wolves, and that will keep the others off as long as they have got the ones I shot to eat.—Did you speak, comrade?" he whispered, as he once more bent over Pen. "No, he's fast asleep. Wish I was, so as to forget all about it, for the sun's quite down now, and I don't know how I am to get through such a night as this. However, here goes to try. Ugh! How cold it is turning!"

The boy shivered as the wind that came down from the mountains seemed bitterly cold to one who had been drenched in perspiration by the exertion and excitement that he had passed through.

"Poor old Private Gray!" he muttered. "He will be feeling it worse than me if he don't turn feverish."

The boy hesitated for a few moments, and then, stripping off his jacket, he crept as close to his wounded companion as he could, and then carefully spread the ragged uniform coat over their breasts.

"Ought to have got his off too," he muttered, "but I mustn't. Must make the best of it and try and go to sleep, keeping him warm. But no fellow could go to sleep at a time like this."

It was a rash assertion, for many minutes had not passed before the boy was sleeping soundly the sleep of utter weariness and exhaustion; and the next time he unclosed his eyes as he lay there upon his back, not having moved since he lay down, it was to gaze wonderingly at the beautiful play of morning light upon the long, glossy, dark-green leaves over his head; for the sun had just risen and was bronzing the leaves with ruddy gold.

The birds were singing somewhere at the edge of the forest, and all seemed so wonderful and strange that the boy muttered to himself as he asked the question, "Where am I?"

So deep had been his sleep that it seemed to be one great puzzle.

He knew it was cold, and he wondered at that, for now and then he felt a faint glow of warm sunshine. Then, like a flash, recollection came back, and he turned his head to gaze at his companion, but only to wrench himself away and roll over and over a yard or two, before sitting up quickly, trembling violently. For he was chilled with horror by the thought that his companion had passed away during the night.

It was some minutes before he dared speak. "Pen!" he whispered, at last. "Gray!" He waited, with the horror deepening, for there his companion lay upon his back motionless, and though he strained his neck towards him he could detect no movement of his breath, while his own staring eyes began to grow dim, and the outstretched figure before him looked misty and strange.

"He's dead! He's dead!" groaned the poor fellow. "And me lying sleeping there, never taking any notice of him when he called for help—for he must have called—and me pretending to be his comrade all the time! 'Tain't how he treated me. Oh, Pen! Pen Gray, old chap! Speak to me, if it's only just one word! Oh, if I had not laid down! I ought to have stood up and watched him; but I did think it was to keep him warm. No, you didn't!" he cried angrily, addressing himself. "You did it to warm yourself."

At last, recovering his nerve somewhat, the boy began to crawl on hands and knees towards the motionless figure, till he was near enough to lay his hand upon his companion's breast. Then twice over he stretched it out slowly and cautiously, but only to snatch it back, till a feeling of rage at his cowardice ran through him, and he softly lowered it down, let it rest there for a few moments, and then with a thrill of joy he exclaimed, "Why, it's all fancy! He is alive."

"Yes, what? Who spoke?"

"I did," cried Punch, springing to his feet. "Hooray, comrade! It's all right. I woke up, and began to think— Pst! pst!" he whispered, as he dropped down upon hands and knees again. For there was a rush of feet, and a patch of undergrowth a short distance beyond the spread of the great chestnut boughs was violently agitated.

"Why, it's only goats," muttered Punch angrily. "I scared them by jumping up. Wish I had got one of their young uns here."

"What is it? Who's that? You, Punch?"

"Yes, comrade; it's all right. But how are you? All right?"

"Yes—no. I have been asleep and dreaming. What does it all mean, Punch? What's the matter with my leg?"

"Can't you recollect, comrade?"

Pen was silent for a few moments, and then: "Yes," he said softly, "I understand now. I was hurt. Why, it's morning! I haven't been to sleep all the night, have I?"

"Yes, comrade, and," —Punch hesitated for a moment, and then with an effort—"so have I."

"I am glad of it," sighed Pen.

Then he winced, for he had made an effort to rise, but sank back again, feeling faint.

"Help me, Punch," he said.

"Whatcher want?"

"To sit up with my back against the tree."

Punch hesitated, and then obeyed.

"Ah, that's better," sighed Pen. "I am not much hurt."

"Oh yes, you are," said Punch, shaking his head.

"Nonsense! I recollect all about it now. Can you get me some water?"

"I'll try," was the reply; "but can you really sit up like that?"

"Yes, of course. We shall be able to go on again soon."

"Wha-at!" cried Punch. "Oh yes, I dare say! You can't go on. But I know what I am going to do. If the French are gone I am going to hunt round till I find one of them cottages. There must be one somewhere about, because I just started some goats. And look there! Why, of course there must be some people living near here." And the boy pointed to a dozen or so of pigs busily rooting about amongst the dead leaves of the forest, evidently searching for chestnuts and last year's acorns shed by the evergreen oaks.

"Now, look here," continued the boy. "Soon as I am sure that you can sit up and wait, I am just off to look out for some place where I can carry you."

"I can sit up," replied Pen. "I have got a nasty wound that will take some time to heal; but it's nothing to mind, Punch, for it's the sort of thing that will get well without a doctor. But you must find shelter or beg shelter for us till I can tramp again."

"But I can carry yer, comrade."

"A little way perhaps. There, don't stop to talk. Go and do the best you can."

"But is it safe to leave you?" protested Punch.

"Yes; there is nothing to mind, unless some of the French fellows find me."

"That does it, then," said Punch sturdily. "I sha'n't go."

"You must, I tell you."

"I don't care; I ain't going to leave you."

"Do you want me to starve, or perish with cold in the night."

"Course I don't!"

"Then do as I tell you."

"But suppose the French come?"

"Well, if they do we must chance it; but if you are careful in going and coming I don't think they will find me; and I don't suppose you will be long."

"That I won't," cried the boy confidently. "Here goes, then—I am to do it?"

"Yes."

"Then here's off."

"No, don't do that," cried Pen.

"Why not? Hadn't I better take the muskets?"

"No. You are more likely to get help for me if you go without arms; and, besides, Punch," added Pen, with a faint smile, "I might want the muskets to defend myself against the wolves."

"All right," replied the boy, replacing the two clumsy French pieces by his comrade's side. "Keep up your spirits, old chap; I won't be long."

The next minute the boy had plunged into the thicket-like outskirts of the forest, where he stopped short to look back and mentally mark the great chestnut-tree.

"I shall know that," he said, "from ever so far off. It is easy to 'member by the trunk, which goes up twisted like a screw. Now then, which way had I better go?"

Punch had a look round as far as the density of the foliage would allow him, and then gave his head a scratch.

"Oh dear!" he muttered, "who's to know which way to go? It's regular blind-man's buff. How many horses has your father got? Shut your eyes, comrade. Now then. Three! What colour? Black, white, and grey. Turn round three times and catch who you may."

The boy, with his eyes tightly closed and his arms spread out on either side, turned round the three times of the game, and then opened his eyes and strode right away.

"There can't be no better way than chancing it," he said. "But hold hard! Where's my tree?"

He was standing close to a beautifully shaped ilex, and for a few moments he could not make out the great spiral-barked chestnut, till, just as he began to fancy that he had lost his way at once, he caught sight of its glossy bronzed leaves behind the greyish green ilex.

"That's all right," he said. "Now then, here's luck."

It was a bitter fight with grim giant despair as the boy tramped on, and time after time, faint with hunger, suffering from misery, he was about to throw himself down upon the earth, utterly broken in spirit, but he fought on bravely.

"I never saw such a country!" he muttered. "There ought to be plenty of towns and villages and people, but it's all desert and stones and scrubby trees. Any one would think that you couldn't walk anywhere without finding something to eat, and there's nothing but the goats and pigs, and as soon as they catch sight of you away they go."

Over and over again he climbed hillsides to reach spots where he could look down, in the full expectation of seeing some village or cluster of huts. But it was all the same, there was nothing to be seen; till, growing alarmed lest he should find that he had lost touch with his landmarks, he began to retrace his steps in utter despair, but only to drop down on his knees at last and bury his face in his hands, to give way to the emotion that for a few moments he could not master.

"There," he muttered, recovering himself, "I could not help it, but there was no one to see. Just like a silly great gal. It is being hungry, I suppose, and weak with my wound; and, my word, it does sting! But there's some one at last!"

The boy looked sharply round.

"Why, you idgit!" he gasped, "you've lost him again. No, it's all right," he cried, and he started off at a trot in the direction of a short, plump-looking figure in rusty black, who, bent of head and book in hand, was slowly descending a slope away to his right.

Chapter Twenty Three
The Use of Latin

"There! Ahoy!" shouted Punch, and the black figure slowly raised his head and began to look round till he was gazing in quite the opposite direction to where the boy was hurrying towards him, and Punch had a full view of the stranger's back and a ruddy-brown roll of fat flesh which seemed to be supporting a curious old hat, looking like a rusty old stove-pipe, perched horizontally upon the wearer's head.

"Hi! Not that way! Look this!" cried Punch as he closed up. "Here, I say, where's the nearest village?"

The stove-pipe turned slowly round, and Punch found himself face to face with a plump-looking little man who slowly closed the book he carried and tucked it inside his shabby gown.

"Morning!" said Punch.

The little man bowed slowly and with some show of dignity, and then gazed sternly in the boy's face and waited.

"I said good-morning, sir," said the boy; and then to himself, "what a rum-looking little chap!—Can you tell me—"

Punch got no further, for the little stranger shook his head, frowned more sternly, and shrugged his shoulders as he made as if to take out his book again.

"I ain't a beggar, sir," cried the boy. "I only want you to— Oh, he can't understand me!" he groaned. "Look here, can you understand this?" And he commenced in dumb motions to give the stranger a difficult problem to solve.

But it proved to be not too difficult, for the little man smiled, nodded his head, and imitated Punch's suggestive pantomime of eating and drinking. Then, laying one hand upon the boy's shoulder, he pointed with the other down the slope and tried to guide him in that direction.

"All right," said Punch, nodding, "I understand. That's where you live; but not yet. Come this way." And, catching the little stranger by the arm,

Punch pointed towards the forest and tried to draw his companion in that direction.

The plump little man shook his head and suggested that they should go in the other direction.

"Oh, a mercy me!" cried Punch excitedly. "Why, don't you understand? Look here, sir, I can see what you are. You are a priest. I have seen folks like you more than once. Now, just look here."

The little man shrugged his shoulders again, shook his head, and then looked compassionately at the boy.

"That's better," said Punch. "Now, sir, do try and understand, there's a good fellow. Just look here!"

The boy tapped him on the shoulder now, and pointed towards the wood.

"Now, look here, sir; it's like this."

Punch made-believe to present a musket, after giving a sharp *click, click* with his tongue in imitation of the cocking of the piece, cried *Bang*! and then gave a jump, clapped his hand to his right leg, staggered, threw himself down, and then struggled up into a sitting position, to sit up nursing his leg, which he made-believe to bind up with a bandage. Then, holding out his hand to the little priest, he caught hold of him, dragged himself up, but let himself fall back, rolled over, and lay looking at him helplessly.

"Understand that?" he cried, as he sprang to his feet again. "You must be jolly stupid if you can't. Now then, look here, sir," he continued, pointing and gesticulating with great energy, "my poor comrade is lying over yonder under a tree, wounded and starving. Come and help me to fetch him, there's a.good old chap."

The priest looked at him fixedly, and then, taking his cue from the boy, he pointed in the direction Punch had indicated, nodded, clapped the boy on the shoulder, and began to walk by his side.

"There, I thought I could make you understand," cried Punch eagerly. "But you might say something. Ain't deaf and dumb, are you?"

The little priest shook his head, muttered to himself, and then, bending down, he tapped his own leg, and looking questioningly in his would-be guide's face, he began to limp.

"Yes, yes, yes!" cried Punch excitedly. And, imitating his companion, he bent down, tapped his own leg, then limped as if walking with the greatest of difficulty and made-believe to sink down helplessly.

"Good! I understand," said the little priest in Spanish. "Wounded. Lead on."

Punch held out his hand, which the little stranger took, and suffered himself to be led in the direction of the great chestnut, shaking his head and looking questioningly more than once at the boy, as Punch hesitated and seemed to be in doubt, and ran here and there trying to make out his bearings, successfully as it happened, for he caught sight at last of the object of his search, hurried back to the little priest's side, to stand panting and faint, passing his hand over his dripping face, utterly exhausted.

"Can't help it, sir," he said piteously. "I have been wounded. Just let me get my breath, and then we will go on again. I am sure now. Oh, I do wish I could make you understand better!" added the boy piteously. "There's my poor comrade yonder, perhaps dying by this time, and me turning like this!"

For just then he reeled and would have fallen if the little priest had not caught him by the arms and lowered him slowly down.

"Thank you, sir," said Punch, with a sob half-choking his utterance. "It's all on account of my wound, sir. There, I'm better now. Come on."

He tried to struggle up, but the little priest shook his head and pressed him back.

"Thank you, sir. It's very good of you; but I want to get on. He's getting tired of waiting, you know." And Punch pointed excitedly in the direction of the tree.

The journey was continued soon after, with Punch's arm locked in that of his new-found friend; and in due time Punch staggered through the trees to where Pen lay, now meeting his gaze with a wild look of misery and despair.

"It's all right, comrade," cried Punch. "I have found somebody at last. He must live somewhere near here, but I can't make him understand anything, only that you were lying wounded. Did you think I had forgotten you?"

"No," said Pen faintly, "I never thought that."

"Look here," said Punch, "say something to him in French. Tell him I want to get you to a cottage, and say we are starving."

Pen obeyed, and faintly muttered a few words in French; but the priest shook his head.

"*Francés?*" he said.

"No, no," replied Pen. "*Inglés.*"

"Ah, *Inglés!*" said the priest, smiling; and he went down on one knee to softly touch the rough bandage that was about the wounded leg.

Then, to the surprise of both boys, he carefully raised Pen into a sitting position, signed to Punch to hold him up, and then taking off his curiously fashioned hat and hanging it upon a broken branch of the tree, the boys saw that Nature had furnished him with the tonsure of the priest without the barber's aid, and they had the opportunity now of seeing that it was a pleasantly wrinkled rosy face, with a pair of good-humoured-looking eyes that gazed up in theirs.

"What's he going to do?" said Punch in a whisper.

He comprehended the next minute, and eagerly lent his aid, for the little priest, twisting up his gown and securing it round his waist, began to prove himself a worthy descendant of the Good Samaritan, though wanting in the ability to set the wounded traveller upon his own ass.

Going down, though, upon one knee, he took hold of first one hand and then the other, and, with Punch's assistance to his own natural strength, he got Pen upon his back, hitching him up a little, and then a little more, till he had drawn the wounded lad's arms across his chest.

This done, he knelt there on one knee, panting, before drawing a deep breath prior to rising with his burden. Then he tried to stand up, but without success.

He waited, then tried again; but once more without success, for the weight was greater than he had anticipated.

"Can't you manage it, sir?" said Punch. "Here, let me try."

The little priest shook his head, but released one of Pen's hands and caught hold of Punch by the shoulder.

"Yes, I know, sir," cried Punch, and after waiting till their new friend was ready, the boy brought his strength to bear as well, and the little priest stood up, gave his load a hitch or two to balance it well upon his shoulders, and then looked sharply at Punch and then at his hat.

"Carry your hat, sir?" cried Punch excitedly, "of course I will. It will be all right."

The priest shook his head.

"What? Oh, you mean stick it on, sir? All right, sir; I understand. What, is that wrong? Oh, t'other side first! There you are, then, sir. Will that do?"

The priest shook his head, bent a little forward so as to well balance his load, and then, setting one hand at liberty, he put his hat on correctly, grasped both Pen's hands once more, and then began to march out of the forest.

"I'm blessed!" muttered Punch. "Didn't know they carried pickaback in Spain. The little chap's as strong as a horse—pony, I mean.—Does it hurt you much, comrade?"

"Not much, Punch. Don't talk to me, though; only, thank goodness that we have found a friend!" The little priest trudged sturdily on with his load, taking a direction along the edge of the forest, which Punch noted was different from any that he had traversed during his search, while at the same time it became plain to him that their new friend was finding his load rather hard work to carry, for first a little dew began to appear; this dew gradually grew into tiny beads, the tiny beads ran into drops, and the drops gathered together till they began to trickle and run.

At this point the little priest stopped short by the side of a rugged, gnarled tree, and, bending a little lower, rested his hands upon a horizontal branch.

"Look here, sir," said Punch, "let me have a try now. I ain't up to it much, but it would give you a rest."

The priest shook his head, drew a deep breath, and trudged on again, proving his strength to be greater than could have been imagined to exist in such a little, plump, almost dwarf-like form, for with an occasional rest he tramped on for the best part of an hour, till at last he paused just at the edge of a deep slope, and struck off a little way to his left to where a beaten track led to a good-sized cottage.

"Why couldn't I find all this?" thought Punch, as he gazed down into a valley dotted with huts, evidently a village fairly well inhabited. "Why, it was as easy as easy, only I didn't know the way."

"Ah!" ejaculated the priest, as he thrust open the door, stepped into a very humbly furnished room, crossed at once to a rough pallet, and gently lowered his burden upon the simple bed. "The saints be praised!" he said in Latin; and the words and the new position had such a reviving effect upon the wounded rifleman that he caught at one of the priest's hands and held to it firmly.

"God bless you for this!" he said, for unconsciously the priest's words had been the opening of the door of communication between him and those he had brought to his home; for though the words possessed a pronunciation that was unfamiliar, the old Latin tongue recalled to Pen years of study in the past, and he snatched at the opportunity of saying a few words that the old man could understand.

A pleasant smile beamed on the utterly wearied out old fellow's countenance as he bent over Pen and patted him gently on the shoulder.

"Good, good!" he said in Latin; and he set himself about the task of supplying them with food.

This was simple enough, consisting as it did of bread and herbs—just such a repast as might have been expected from some ascetic holy man dwelling in the mountains; but the herbs in this case were silvery-brown skinned Spanish onions with salt.

Then taking up a small earthen jar, he passed out of the dark room into the sunshine; and as soon as the boys were alone Punch turned eagerly to his companion.

"Not worse, are you, comrade?" he said anxiously.

"No, Punch, not worse. But has he gone to fetch water?"

"Yes, I think so. But just you tell me: does your leg hurt you much?"

"Quite enough," replied Pen, breaking off a portion of the bread and placing a few fragments between his lips. "But don't talk to me now. I am starving."

"Yes, I know that," cried Punch; "and call this 'ere bread! It's all solid crust, when it ought to be crumb for a chap like you. Look here, you could eat one of these onions, couldn't you?"

"No, no; not now. Go on; never mind me."

"But I do mind you," cried the boy. "And how can I go on eating without you? I say, though, what a chap you are! What was that you said to him?"

"Bless you for this!"

"Yes, I guessed that was it; but how did you say it so as to make him understand? I talked to him enough, but he couldn't make out a word of what I said. Was that there Spanish?"

"No, Punch; Latin."

"Ah, you seem to know everything."

At that moment a shadow fell athwart the door, and the speaker made a dash at one of the muskets he had stood up against the wall on entering the priest's cottage.

"Oh, I beg your pardon, sir!" he cried hastily. "I didn't know it was you."

The old man smiled, and entered with the dripping jar which he had just filled from a neighbouring spring, and held it towards the boy.

"Me drink, sir? Thank ye, sir," cried Punch; and, taking the jar, he was raising it towards his parched mouth, but before it was half-way there he recollected himself, and carried it to the priest's pallet, where he went down on his knees and held it to Pen's lips, so that the poor fellow, who was burning with feverish pain, was able to drink long and deeply.

Pen was still drinking when Punch started and spilt a few drops of the water as he turned hastily to look up at their host, who had laid a soft brown hand upon his head, and was looking down at him with a pleasant smile.

"What did he do that for, comrade?"

"I don't know," said Pen, drawing a deep breath, as he withdrew his lips from the water. "Yes, I do," he added quickly. "He meant that he was pleased because you let me drink first."

"Course I did. I don't see anything to be pleased about in that. But have a drop more, comrade. Quick, look sharp, before I go mad and snatches it away from you, for I never felt like this before."

"Go on then now, Punch."

"But—"

"Go on then now; I can wait."

"Ah, then!" ejaculated the boy, with a deep sigh that was almost a groan; and with trembling hands he held the jar to his lips and drank, and recovered his breath and drank again as if it was impossible to satisfy his burning thirst.

Then recovering himself, he held the jar against Pen's lips.

"Talk about wine," he said; "why, it ain't in it! I don't wonder that he looks so fat and happy, though he is dressed up like an old scarecrow. Fancy living here with a pump of water like this close at hand!—Had enough now?—That's right. Now you go on breaking off bits of that bread and dipping it in the water while I cuts up one of these."

He took his knife from his pocket and began to peel one of the onions, when their host placed the little vessel of salt close to his hand.

"Thank you, sir," cried Punch. "You are a real gentleman."

The priest smiled and nodded, and watched the two lads as Pen took an earthenware bowl that their host placed close to his hand after half-filling it with water so that he could steep the bread, while Punch deftly peeled one of the onions, not scrupling about littering the floor, and then proceeded to quarter it and then divide the segments again, dipping one in the salt and placing it between his wounded companion's lips.

"Good! good!" said the priest again, smiling with satisfaction, and laying his hand once more upon Punch's head. "*Bonum! bonum!*"

"Bone 'em!" said Punch. "Why, he give it to me!"

"He means it was good, Punch," said Pen, smiling.

"Good! Yes," cried the boy, crunching up one of the savoury pieces of vegetable. "That's what he means, is it? Thought he meant I had stolen it.— *Bonum*, eh, sir? I should just think it is! Wants a bit more salt; but my word, it's fine! Have a bit more, comrade. You eat while there's a chance. Never mind me. I can keep both of us going. Talk about a dinner or a supper; I could keep on till dark! Only wish, though, I'd got one of their Spanish shillings to pay for it; but those French beggars took care of them for me. I can give him my knife, though; and I will too, as soon as I have done with it. How do you feel now, comrade?"

"Better, Punch, better," replied Pen. "Thank you," he continued, as his companion broke off more bread for him and then began to peel another onion. "But you are paying more attention to me than you are to yourself."

"Course I am, comrade. Didn't you pay more attention to me when I was wounded?"

Then turning to the priest, he pointed to the bread with his knife, and then tapped the onion he had begun to quarter with the blade.

"Splendid, sir," he said, smiling. "*Bonum! bonum!*"

The priest nodded, and then rose from where he had been seated watching the boys and walked through the open door, to stand just outside sweeping the scattered houses of the little village with his eyes, and remaining there, so as to leave his two guests to themselves.

"You are beginning to get a bit better, comrade?" asked Punch anxiously.

"Yes, Punch, yes," was the reply.

"So am I. Feel as if I am growing as strong as a horse again. Why, comrade, it was worth getting as hungry, thirsty, and tired as that, so as to enjoy such a meal. I don't mean speaking for you, because I know you must be feeling that gnaw, gnaw, grinding pain in your wound. But do go on eating, and when you have had enough you shut-up shop and go off to sleep. Then I will ask that old chap to give me a bit of rag and let me wash and tie up your wound. I say, comrade, I hope he didn't see me laugh at him. Did you?"

"See you laugh at him? No. Did you?"

"Yes; couldn't help it, when he was carrying you, bent down like he was, with that queer shako of his. When I was behind he looked something like a bear, and I couldn't help having a good grin. Mum, though; here he comes."

The old priest now came slowly in and stood watching the two lads, who hurriedly finished their meal.

"Stand up, Punch," said Pen.

"What for? I was just going to clear away."

"Stand up, I tell you!"

"All right;" and the boy rose immediately, staring hard at his companion, as Pen, with a quiver of emotion in his utterance, laid his hand over the remains of the black-bread, and said, gazing hard at the old priest the while, "*Benedictus, benedicat.* Amen."

"Ah!" said the priest, with a long-drawn breath of satisfaction; "*Benedictus, benedicat* Amen."

Then, taking a step towards them, he laid his hand upon the heads of his two guests in turn and said a few words in an undertone. Next, pointing to the rough pallet-bed, he signed to Punch that he should lie down beside his companion.

"What, take a snooze there, sir?" said Punch. "Thank you, sir. But not yet.—You tell him in your Latin stuff, comrade, that I want to do a bit of doctoring first."

"I'll try," said Pen wearily, already half-asleep; when, to the surprise of both, the old man went outside and returned with a little wooden tub of water which he brought to the bedside, and then, in spite of a half-hearted protestation on the part of Punch, he proceeded to carefully attend to the wound.

"Well, it's very good of you, sir," said the boy at last, after doing his best to help, "and I wish I could make you understand what I say. But you have done it a deal better than I could have done, and I am sure if my comrade could have kept himself awake he would be ready enough to say something in Latin that would mean you are a trump, and he's very much obliged. But, you see, all I know, sir, about Latin—"

"Latin!" said the old priest, beaming upon him with wondering eyes.

"Yes, sir—Latin, sir, as I learnt of him;" and then, pointing to the carefully bandaged limb, "*bonum*, sir; *bonum!*"

The priest nodded, as he pointed to the pallet, where there was room for Punch to lie down by his sleeping companion; but the boy shook his head.

"No, sir," he said, "that's your roost; I do know that," And, before his host could interfere, the boy placed one musket within reach of Pen's hand, the other beside the door, across which he stretched himself.

It was now nearly dark, and after placing his little home in something like order, the old man turned to where Punch had been resting upon one arm a few minutes before, watching his movements, but was now prone upon the beaten-earth floor fast asleep, with a look of restfulness upon his young, sunburnt countenance.

The old man stepped carefully across him, to stand outside peering through the evening gloom down into the silent village before, satisfied and content, he turned back into the hut, closing the door carefully after him, placing across it a heavy oaken bar, before stepping back across Punch, to stand in the middle of the floor deep in thought.

Then his hand began to move, from force of habit, searching for and bringing out from beneath his gown a little, worn snuff-box, which squeaked faintly as he turned the lid and refreshed himself with two pinches of its brown contents.

This was done very slowly and deliberately in the semi-darkness, and finally the box was replaced and a few grains of the dust flicked away.

"Ah!" ejaculated the old man with a long-drawn sigh, as he looked from one to the other of his guests. "English," he muttered. "Soldiers, but friends and defenders against the French. English—heretics! But," he added softly, as if recalling something that had passed, "*Benedictus, benedicat.* Amen!"

Then, crossing softly to one corner of the room, he drew open what seemed to be the door of a cupboard; but it was too dark to show that in place of staircase there was a broad step-ladder.

This the old man ascended, and directly after the ill-fitting boards which formed the ceiling of his humble living-room creaked as he stepped upon them, and then there was a faint rustling as if he were removing leaves and stems of the Indian corn that was laid in company with other stores in what was undoubtedly a little loft, whose air was heavy with various odours suggesting the presence of vegetables and fruit.

The oaken boards creaked once more as if the old man was stretching himself upon them with a sigh of weariness and satisfaction.

"Amen!" he said softly, and directly after a ray of light shot across the place, coming through the wooden bars in the gable of the sloping roof, for the moon had just risen over the shoulder of the mountain to light up the valley beneath, where the priest's hut clung to its rocky wall; to light up, too, the little loft and its contents, and, above all, the features of the sleeping man, gentle-looking in their repose. And could the lads he had befriended have gazed upon him then they would have seen nothing that appeared grotesque.

Chapter Twenty Four
Through a Knot-Hole

"Yes, what is it?" cried Pen, starting up on the bed at a touch from his companion, who had laid his hand gently on the sleeping lad's forehead, and then sinking back again with a faint ejaculation of pain.

"Don't be scared, comrade; it's only me. Does it hurt you?"

"Yes, my leg's horribly stiff and painful."

"Poor chap! Never mind. I will bathe it and dress it by-and-by if that old priest don't do it. When you jumped up like that I thought you fancied it was the French coming."

"I did, Punch," said Pen with a faint smile. "I seem to have been dreaming all night that they were after us, and I could not get away because my leg hurt me so."

"Then lie down again," said Punch. "Things ain't so bad as that. But, I say, comrade, I can't help it; I am as bad as ever again."

"Bad! Your wound?"

"No, no; that's getting all right. But that old chap seems to have shut us up here and gone. Didn't happen to see, did you, where he put the bread and onions? I am quite hollow inside."

"No, Punch. I fell asleep, and I can't recollect how or when."

"That's a pity, 'cause I know we should be welcome, and I can't make out where he put the forage when he cleared away."

It was the sunrise of a bright morning, and the sounds of bleating goats came plainly to the listeners' ears as the nimble animals were making their way up the valley-side to their pasture.

Then all at once came the sharp creak of a board, and Punch dashed at his musket, caught it up, cocked it, and stood ready to use it in defence of his companion.

There was another creak or two, evidently from overhead, and as Punch stood there on the alert, his brows knit and teeth clenched, Pen softly stole his hand in the direction of his own musket and raised himself up on the bed ready to help.

Again there came a creak or two, a rustling in the corner of the room as of some one descending from above, and, though invisible, the muzzles of the two pieces were slowly lowered in the direction of the noise, till with a crack the door in the corner was thrust inward and the little old priest stood looking wonderingly from one to the other as he raised his hand.

It was as if this were a signal to disarm, when the two muskets were hurriedly replaced, and Punch advanced towards the corner of the room, offering to shake hands.

The priest smiled, took the boy's fingers, and then, thrusting to the door, he crossed to the bed, felt Pen's forehead, and afterwards pointed to the wounded leg.

The next minute he went to the door, removed the great bar, and admitted the bright light and fresh air of the morning in company with the louder bleating of the goats, which animals evidently came trotting up to the old man as he stepped back to look searchingly round. Then, after speaking kindly to them, he drove them away, returned into the room directly after with water, and proceeded to busily attend to Pen's wound.

"That's good of him," said Punch petulantly, "and I am glad to see him do it, comrade; but I wish he'd thought to attend to my wound too—I mean, give me the chance to dress it myself with bread and onion poultice. I don't know when I felt so hollow inside."

But he had not long to wait, for, evidently well satisfied with the state of Pen's injury, the priest finished attending to him as tenderly as if his touch were that of a woman, and then Punch was at rest, for the old man placed the last night's simple fare before them, signed to them to eat, and, leaving them to themselves, went outside again, to sweep the valley below with a long and scrutinising gaze.

Twice over during the next two days Pen made an effort to rise, telling his companion when they were alone that if he had a stick he thought he could manage to limp along a short distance at a time, for it was very evident that the old man, their host, was uneasy in his own mind about their presence.

"He evidently wants to get rid of us, Punch."

"Think so?" said the boy.

"Yes. See how he keeps fidgeting in and out to go on looking round to see if anybody's coming."

"Yes, I have noticed that," said Punch. "He thinks the French are coming after us, and that he will get into trouble for keeping us here."

"Yes; it's plain enough, so let's go."

"But you can't, comrade."

"Yes, I can."

"Not without making your wound worse. That's what you would have said to me."

"Then I must make it worse," said Pen angrily. "Next time he comes in I'll try to make him explain which way we ought to go to find some of our people."

"Well, we can only try," replied Punch, "for 'tain't nice living on anybody when you can't pay, and I do feel ashamed to eat as I do without being able to find money for it. 'Tain't as if he was an enemy. I'd let him see then."

"Go and open the door, Punch, and let the fresh air in. The sun does make this place so hot!"

"Can't, comrade."

"Why not?"

"I did try while you was asleep; but he's locked us in."

"Nonsense! He fastens the door with that big bar, and there it is standing up by the side."

"Yes, but there's another one outside somewhere, for I tried, and the door won't move. I think he's gone to tell somebody we are here, and he has shut us up so that we sha'n't get away while he's gone."

"No, no," said Pen impatiently. "The old man means well to us; I am sure of that."

"That's what I keep thinking, comrade; but then I keep thinking, too, that he's going to get something given him for taking two prisoners to give up to the French."

"Nonsense! It is cowardly and ungenerous to think so."

"Then what's he been gone such a long time for? It's hours since he went away and shut us in."

"Hours?"

"Yes; you don't know, because you sleep so much."

"Well, I don't believe he'd betray us. The old man's too good and generous for that."

"Then, why has he made prisoners of us?" said Punch sourly. "Why has he shut us up?"

"To keep anybody else from coming in," said Pen decisively. "What time can it be now?"

"Getting on towards sunset. Pst! Here he comes—or somebody else."

All doubts as to who it was were put an end to the next minute, for the familiar step of the old priest approached the door. They plainly heard what seemed to be another bar removed, and the old man stood before them with a big basket on his arm, and remained looking back as if to see whether he had been followed.

Then, apparently satisfied, he came in, closed the door, and smilingly placed the contents of the basket before them.

He had evidently been some distance, and looked hot and weary; but he was quite ready to listen to Pen's lame efforts to make known his desires that they should now say good-bye, and, with his help as to direction, continue their journey.

The little man stood up smiling before Pen, listening patiently to the lad's blundering Latin, probably not understanding half, and only replying with a word or two from time to time, these words from their pronunciation puzzling Pen in turn; but it was evident to Punch, the listener, that on the whole a mutual understanding was arrived at, for all at once the priest offered Pen his arm, and as the lad took it he helped him to walk across the room and back to the pallet, where he pressed him back so that he sat down in spite of himself, when the old man patted him on the shoulder, smiling gently, and then going down on one knee passed his hand softly over the wound, and, looking up, shook his head sadly.

"What does he mean by that, Punch?" said Pen excitedly, as he sat, looking pinched of face and half-wild with excitement.

"It means, comrade, that you ain't fit to go on the march. That's what he means; I can make him out. He is saying as you must give it up, and I don't think now as he means any harm.—I say, you don't, do you, old chap?" he continued, turning sharply on the priest.

It seemed as if their host comprehended the boy's words, for he patted Punch on the shoulder, smiling, and pointed to the basket, which he opened and displayed its contents.

Punch only caught a glimpse thereof; but he saw that there were bread and onions and goat's-milk cheese before he turned sharply round, startled by a quick tapping at the closed door.

It was not only he who was startled, for the priest turned sharply and hurried to the door.

"Oh, comrade," cried Punch in an excited whisper, "don't say that he's against us after all!"

But with the sturdy boy it was a word and a blow, for he made for his loaded musket and caught it up.

"Hist!" ejaculated the priest, turning upon him and raising one hand.

"Oh, I don't care for that," whispered Punch, "and I don't mind what you are. If you sold us to the enemy you shall have the first shot."

The priest shook his hand at him as if to bid him be silent; and then, placing his lips close to the door, he said something in Spanish, and listened to a reply that came in a hurried voice.

"Ah!" ejaculated the priest; and then he whispered again.

The next minute he was busy barring the closed door; and this done, he turned to the boys, to cross the room and open wide the cupboard-like door in the corner. Then, returning to Pen, he helped him to rise again, guided his halting steps, and half-carrying him to the step-like ladder urged him with a word or two to climb up.

"What does he mean, comrade?" whispered Punch.

"He means there's somebody coming, and we are to go upstairs."

"Let's stop here, comrade, and fight it out."

"No, he means well," replied Pen; and, making a brave effort, he began to climb the ladder, pulling himself up, but panting heavily the while and drawing his breath with pain.

As soon as the old man saw that he was being obeyed he turned to Punch, caught up Pen's musket, and signed to the boy to follow him.

"Well, you can't mean to give us up," said Punch excitedly, "or you wouldn't want me to keep my gun and his."

Disposition to resist passed away the next moment, for the old man pressed the second musket into his hand and urged him towards the door.

"Can you get up, comrade?" whispered Punch, who was now all excited action.

"Yes," came in a hoarse whisper, and a loud creak came from the ceiling.

"Ketch hold of these guns then. He wants me to bring the forage-basket.—Got 'em?" he continued, as he placed the two pieces together and held them up against the ladder.

"*Bonum!*" ejaculated the priest, who stood close up, as the two muskets were drawn upwards and disappeared.

"Right, sir," said Punch in answer, and he took hold of the basket, raised it above his head, took a step or two, then whispered, "Basket! Got it, comrade?"

"Yes," And it was drawn up after the muskets, the boards overhead creaking loudly the while.

"Anything else, master?—What, take this 'ere jar of water? Right! Of course! Here, comrade, you must look out now. Lean down and catch hold of the jar; and take care as you don't slop it over."

"*Presto!*" whispered the priest.

"Hi, presto!" muttered Punch. "That's what the conjuror said," he continued to himself, "and it means, 'Look sharp!' Got it, comrade?"

"Yes," came in Pen's eager whisper.

"Oh, I say," muttered Punch, "I don't want my face washed!"

"*Bonum! Presto!*" whispered the priest, as Punch shrank back with his face dripping; and, pressing the boy into the opening, he closed the door upon him and then hurried to the cottage entrance, took down the bar, throw the door wide, and then began slowly to strike a light, after placing a lamp upon the rough table.

By this time Punch had reached the little loft-like chamber, where Pen was lying beside the water-vessel.

"What game's this, comrade?" he whispered, breathless with his exertions.

"Hist! Hist!" came from below.

"It's all very fine," muttered Punch to himself; and he changed his position, with the result that the boards upon which he knelt creaked once more.

"Hist! Hist!" came again from below.

"Oh, all right then. I hear you," muttered the boy; and he cautiously drew himself to where he could place his eye to a large hole from which a knot in the plank had fallen out, so that he could now see what was going on below.

"Here, this caps me," he said to himself. "I don't want to think he's a bad un, but he's took down the bar and shoved the door wide-open. It don't mean, do it, that he's sent for some one to come and take us? No, or he wouldn't have given us our guns."

Nick, nick, nick, nick, went the flint against the steel; and the boy watched the sparks flying till one of them seemed to settle lightly in the priest's tinder-box, and the next minute that single spark began to glow as the old man deliberately breathed upon it till the tinder grew plain before the watcher's eyes, and the shape of the old man's bald head, with its roll of fat across the back of the neck, stood out like a silhouette.

Then there was a rustling sound, and the boy saw the point of a match applied, and marked that that point was formed of pale yellow brimstone, which began to turn of a lambent blue as it melted and quivered, and anon grew a flame-colour as the burning mineral fired the match.

A deep, heavy breath as of relief rose now through the floor as the old man applied the burning match to the wick of his oil-lamp, and Punch drew back from the knot-hole, for the loft was dimly lit up by the rays which came through the cracks of the badly laid floor, so that it seemed to him as if this could be no hiding-place, for any one in the room below must for certain be aware of the presence of any one in the loft.

In spite of himself, Punch started and extended his hand to catch at his comrade's arm, for he could see him plainly, though dimly, lying with the muskets on one side, the basket and jar of water upon the other, while half-behind him, where he himself lay, there was the black trap-like opening through which he had climbed.

The boy's was a very slight movement, but it was sufficient to make a board creak, and a warning "Hist!" came once more from below; while, as he looked downward, the boy found that he could see what the old man was doing, as he drew his lamp across the rough table and bent over a little open book, while he began muttering softly, half-aloud, as he read from his Book of Hours.

Punch softly pressed his comrade's arm, and then there was a slight movement and the pressure was returned.

"Wonder whether he can see too," thought Punch; and then in spite of himself he started, and his breath seemed to come thick and short, for plainly from a short distance off came the unmistakable tramp of marching men.

"Then he has sold us after all," thought the boy, and by slow degrees he strained himself over so that he could look through the knot-hole again. To his great surprise the priest had not stirred, but was bending over his book, and his muttered words rose softly to the boy's ear, while the old man seemed to be in profound ignorance of the approaching steps.

Chapter Twenty Five
In the Night

Nearer and nearer came the sound of marching, and it was all Punch could do to keep from rising to his knees and changing his position; but he mastered himself into a state of content by sending and receiving signals with his companion, each giving and taking a long, firm pressure, as at last the invisible body of approaching men reached the cottage door, and an authoritative voice uttered the sharp command, "*Halte!*"

Punch's eye was now glued to the hole. He felt that if anybody looked up he would be sure to see it glittering in the lamplight; but the fascination to learn what was to be their fate was too strong to be resisted.

From his coign of vantage he could command the doorway and the legs of a small detachment of men, two of whom separated themselves and came full into sight, one being an officer, from the sword he bore, the other a rough, clumsy-looking peasant. And now for the first time the little priest appeared to be aware of the presence of strangers, for he slowly lowered the hand which held the book, raised his head, and seemed to be looking wonderingly at his visitors.

"Ah!" he said, as if just awakened from his studies; and he uttered some words, which sounded like a question, to the peasant, who made a rough obeisance and replied in apologetic tones, as if making an excuse for his presence there.

And now the officer uttered an impatient ejaculation and took another step into the room, saying in French, "I am sorry to interrupt your devotions, father; but this fellow tells me that he saw a couple of our English prisoners take refuge here."

"I do not speak French, my son," replied the old man calmly.

"Bah! I forgot," ejaculated the officer; and then in a halting way he stumbled through the same sentence in a very bad translation as he rendered it into Spanish.

"Ah!" said the old man, rising slowly; and Punch saw him look as if wonderingly at the rough peasant, who seemed to shrink back, half-startled, from the priest's stern gaze.

There was a few moments' silence, during which the two fugitives clutched each other's hands so tightly that Punch's nerves literally quivered as he listened for the sharp cracking of the boards, which he seemed to know must betray them to their pursuers.

But no sound came; and, as the perspiration stood out in big drops upon his face in the close heat of the little loft, both he and his companion could feel the horrible tickling sensation of the beads joining together and trickling down their necks.

Then after what seemed to be quite an interval, the old man's voice arose in deep, stern tones, as he exclaimed, "What lie is this, my son, that you have uttered to these strangers?"

"I—I, father—" faltered the man, shrinking back a step and dropping the soft cap he was turning in his hands upon the beaten floor, and then stooping hastily to snatch it up again—"I—father—I—"

"I say, what lie is this you have told these strangers for the sake of gaining a few accursed pieces of silver? Go, before I— Ah!" For there was a quick movement on the part of the peasant, and he dashed out of the door.

"*Halte!*" yelled the French officer, following the peasant outside; and then, giving a sharp command, the scattered reports of some half-dozen muskets rang out on the night-air, the two fugitives starting as at each shot the flash of the musket lit up the loft where they lay. Then a short question or two, and their replies came through the open doorway, and it became evident to the listeners that the peasant had escaped.

"Bah!" ejaculated the officer, as Punch saw him stride through the doorway into the room again. "Look here, father," he said in his bad Spanish, "I paid this scoundrel to guide me to the place where he said two Englishmen were in hiding; but he did not tell me it was with his priest. As he has brought us here I must search."

"For the escaped prisoners?" the old man said, drawing himself up with dignity. "I do not speak your language, sir, but I think that is what you mean. Can you repeat your words in Latin? You might make your wishes more plain."

"Latin? No, I have forgotten all that," said the officer impatiently in more clumsy Spanish than before. "The English prisoners—my men must search," And the fugitives, unable though they were to comprehend the words, naturally grasped their meaning and held their breath till they felt they must draw it again with a sound that would betray their presence.

Then, with a slight laugh, the old priest laid his book upon the table and took up the smoky oil-lamp. As he did so, Punch could see his face plainly, for it was lit up by the lamp, and the boy could perceive the mocking mirth in his eyes as he raised it above his head with his left hand, and walked slowly towards the door which covered the ladder-like staircase; and then as Punch felt that all was over, the old man slowly passed the light across and moved to the rough fireplace, and so on all round the room, before raising the light above his head once more, and with a comprehensive movement waving his right hand slowly round the place as if to say, "You see there are no prisoners here."

"Bah!" ejaculated the French officer, and, turning angrily, he marched out through the open doorway.

Punch was beginning to breathe again, but to his horror the officer marched back into the room, for he had recollected himself. He was the French gentleman still.

"*Pardon, mon père!*" he said sharply, keeping now to his own tongue. "*Bon soir!*"

Then, marching out again, he gave a short command, and, from where Punch's eye was still glued to the opening, he saw the soldiers turn rightabout face, disappear through the open doorway, and then, *beat, beat, beat*, the sound of marching began again, this time to die slowly away, and he looked and listened till the pressure of Pen's hand upon his arm grew almost painful. But he did not wince, till a movement on the part of the priest drew his attention to what was passing beneath; and he saw him set down the lamp and cross to the door, which he closed and barred, and then dropped upon his knees, as his head sank down upon his clasped-together hands.

Chapter Twenty Six
Contrabandistas

"Think they have gone, comrade?" whispered Punch, after they had listened for some minutes, and the tramp of the French soldiers had quite died away.

"Yes; but speak low. He will come and tell us when he thinks it is safe."

"All right, I'll whisper; but I must talk. I can't bear it any longer, I do feel so savage with myself."

"Why, what about?"

"To think about that old chap. I wanted to trust him, but I kept on feeling that he was going to sell us; and all the time he's been doing everything he could for us. But, I say, it was comic to see him carrying you. Here, I mustn't talk about it, or I shall be bursting out laughing."

"Hush! Don't!" whispered Pen.

"All right. But, I say, don't you think we might have a go at the prog? There's all sorts of good things in that basket; and I want a drink of water too. But you needn't have poured a lot of it down my back. I know you couldn't help it, but it was horrid wet all the same."

"Don't touch anything, Punch; and be quiet. He will be coming up soon, I dare say."

"Wish he'd come, then," said the boy wearily. "I say, how's your leg?"

"Hurts," said Pen curtly.

"Poor old chap! Can't you turn yourself round?"

"No. It's worse when I try to move it."

"That's bad; but, I say, you see now we couldn't have gone away unless I carried you."

"But it seems so unfair to be staying here," said Pen bitterly. "I believe now I could limp along very slowly."

"I don't," said Punch. "You see, those Frenchies have made up their minds to catch us, and I believe if they caught sight of us creeping along now they would let go at us again; and as we have had a bullet apiece, we don't want any more."

"Hist!" whispered Pen; "they think we are here still, and they are coming back."

"Nonsense! Fancy!"

"Listen."

"Oh, murder!" whispered Punch. "This is hard!" For he could distinctly hear hurried steps approaching the cottage, and he placed his eye to the knot-hole again to see what effect it was having upon the old man. But he was so still as he crouched there in the lamplight that it seemed as if he had dropped asleep, worn out by his efforts, till all at once the footsteps ceased and there was a sharp tapping on the door, given in a peculiar way, first a rap, then a pause, then two raps close together, another pause, and then *rap, rap, rap,* quickly.

The old man sprang to his feet, unbarred the door, and seized it to throw it open.

"It's all over, comrade," whispered Punch. "Well, let's fill our pockets with the prog. I don't want to starve any more."

He placed his eye to the knot-hole again, and then turned his head to whisper to his companion.

"'Tain't the Frenchmen," he said. "It's one of the Spanish chaps with a red handkercher tied round his head, and him and the old priest is friends, for they are a hugging one another. This chap has got a short gun, and now he's lighting a cigarette at the lamp. Can you hear me?"

"Yes; go on."

"There's four more of them outside the door, and they have all got short guns. One of them's holding one of them horse-donkeys. Oh, I say, comrade!" continued the boy, as a quick whispering went on and the aromatic, pungent odour of tobacco floated up between the boards.

"What is it, Punch? Oh, go on—tell me! You can see, and I'm lying here on my back and can make out nothing. What does it all mean?"

"Well, I don't like to tell you, comrade?" whispered the boy huskily.

"Oh yes; tell me. I can bear it."

"Well, it seems to me, comrade, as we have got out of the frying-pan into the fire."

"Why, what do you mean?"

"That we thought the old chap was going to sell us to the French when all the time it was to some of those Spanish thieves, and it's them as has come now to take us away.—Here, wait a minute."

"I can't, Punch. I can't bear it."

"I'm afraid you will have to, comrade—both on us—like Englishmen. But if we are to be shot for furriners I should like it to have been as soldiers, and by soldiers who know how to use their guns, and not by Spanish what-do-you-call-'ems—robbers and thieves—with little short blunderbusters."

There was a few moments' pause, during which hurried talking went on. Then a couple more fierce-looking Spaniards came in, saluted the priest, lit cigarettes at the lamp, and propped the short carbines they carried against the cottage-wall before joining in the conversation.

"What are they doing now, Punch?"

"Talking about shooting or something," whispered the boy, "and that old ruffian's laughing and pointing up at the ceiling to tell them he has got us safe. Oh, murder in Irish!" continued the boy. "He's took up the lamp and he's showing them the way. Here, Private Gray, try and pull yourself together and let's make a fight for it, if we only have a shot apiece. They are coming up to fetch us now."

Pen stretched out his hand in the dim loft to seize his musket, but he could not reach it, while in his excitement the boy did not notice his comrade's helplessness, but seized his own weapon and stood up ready as the light and shadows danced in the gloomy loft, and prepared to give the armed strangers a warm reception.

And now the door at the foot of the ladder creaked and the light of the lamp struck up as the old man began to ascend the few steps till he could reach up, thrusting the lamp he carried before him, and placing it upon the floor, pushing it farther along towards the two boys; and then, drawing himself up, he lifted the light and held it so that those who followed him could see their way.

At that moment he caught sight of Punch's attitude, and a smile broke out across his face.

"No, no!" he said eagerly. "*Amigos! Contrabandistas.*"

"No, no!" he said eagerly. "*Amigos! Contrabandistas.*"

"What does he mean by that, Pen?"

"That they are friends."

And the head of the first friend now appeared above the trap in the shape of the first-comer, a handsome, swarthy-looking Spaniard, whose dark eyes flashed as his face was lit up by the priest's lamp, which shot the scarlet silk handkerchief about his head with hues of orange.

"*Buenos Inglés, amigos,*" he cried, as he noted the presented musket; and then volubly he asked if either of them spoke French.

"Yes," cried Pen eagerly; and the rest was easy, for the man went on in that tongue:

"My friend the priest tells me that you have had a narrow escape from the French soldiers who had shot you down. But you are safe now. We are friends to the English. Do you want to join your people?"

"Yes, yes," cried Pen eagerly. "Can you help us? Are any of our regiments near?"

"Not very," replied the Spanish smuggler, "for the French are holding nearly all the passes; but we will help you and get you up into the mountains, where you will be safe with us. But our good friend the *padre* tells me that one of you is badly hurt, and he wants me to look at your wound."

"Oh, it's not very bad," said Pen warmly.

"Ah, I must see," said the man, who had seated himself at the edge of the opening up which he had come, and proceeded to light a fresh cigarette.

The next moment, as he began puffing away, he seemed to recollect himself, and drew out a cigar, which he offered with a polite gesture to the old priest.

The old man set down the lamp which he had held for his visitor to light his cigarette, and smiled as he shook his head. Then, thrusting a hand into his gown, he took out his snuff-box, made the lid squeak loudly, and proceeded to help himself to a bounteous pinch.

"It is you who have the wound," continued the smuggler. "You are, I suppose, an officer and a gentleman?"

"No," said Pen, "only a common English soldier."

"But you speak French like a gentleman. Ah, well, no matter. You are wounded—fighting for my country against the brigand French, and we are friends and brothers. I have had many a fight with them, my friend, and I know what their bullets do, so that I perhaps can dress your wound better than the *padre*—brave old man! He can cure our souls—eh, father?" he added, in Spanish—"but I can cure bodies better than he, sometimes, when the French bullets have not been too bad.—Now, father," he added, "hold the lamp and let us see."

The priest nodded as he took up the lamp again in answer to the request made to him in his own tongue; and he now spoke a few words to the smuggler which resulted in the picturesque-looking man shaking his head.

"The good father," he said to Pen, "asks me if I think the French soldiers will come back; but I think not. If they do we shall have warning from my men, who are watching them, for we are expecting friends to meet us here—friends who may come to-night, perhaps many nights hence—for us to guide them through the passes."

Then, drawing up his legs, he stepped into the loft and called down the stairway to the men below.

There was a short reply, and steps were heard as if the two men had stepped out into the open.

"Now, my friend," said the smuggler, as he went down on one knee and leaned over Pen, whose hand he took, afterwards feeling his temples and looking keenly into his eyes as the priest threw the light full in the wounded lad's face.

"Why," he said, "you are suffering from something else besides your wound. My men will bring some wine. I see you have water here. You are faint. There, let me place you more comfortably.—That's better. I'll see to your wound soon.—And you, my friend," he continued, turning to Punch, who started and shook his head.

"No parly Frenchy," he said.

"Never mind," continued the smuggler. "Your friend can.—Tell him to eat some of the bread and fruit, and I will give him some of our grape medicine as soon as my men bring the skin.—A good hearty draught would do you good too, father," he added, turning to the old man and laying his hand with an affectionate gesture upon the priest's arm. "You have been working too hard, and must have had quite a scare. I am very glad we have come."

A deep-toned voice came now from the room below, the smuggler replied, and there was a sound of ascending steps; then another of the smugglers appeared at the opening in the floor, thrusting something so peculiar and strange through the aperture that, as it subsided upon the edge in the full light cast by the smoky lamp, Punch whispered:

"Why, it's a raw kid, comrade, and I don't believe it's dead!"

Pen laughed, and Punch's eyes dilated as he saw the smuggler, who was standing with his head and shoulders in the opening, take what looked like a drinking-horn from his breast and place it upon the floor; and then it seemed to the boy that he untied a thong that was about one of the kid's legs, and the next moment it appeared as if the animal had begun to bleed, its vital juice trickling softly into the horn cup, for it was his first acquaintance with a skin of rich Spanish wine.

"There, my friend," said the smuggler, taking up the half-filled cup, "they say this is bad for fever, but I never knew it do harm to a man whose lifeblood had been drained. Drink: it will put some spirit in you before I perhaps put you to a good deal of pain." And the next moment he was holding the wine-cup to the wounded lad's lips.

"There," said the smuggler at last, as he finished his self-imposed task, "I think you have borne it bravely."

"Oh, nonsense," said Pen quietly. "Surely a soldier should be able to bear a little pain."

"I suppose so," said his new surgeon; "but I am afraid that some of my countrymen would have shouted aloud at what I have done to you. I know some of my men have when I have tied them up after they have been unlucky enough to get one of the French Guards' bullets in them. There now, the best thing you can do is to go to sleep;" and, having improvised a pillow for him with one of his follower's cloaks, the Spaniard descended to the priest's room, where several of his men were assembled; and after the priest had seen that Punch had been supplied from the basket, he followed his friend to where the men were gathered, leaving the boys in the semi-darkness, for he took down the lamp, whose rays once more shone up through the knot-hole and between the ill-fitting boards.

"Feel better, comrade?" asked Punch. But there was no reply. "I say, you aren't gone to sleep already, are you?"

Still no answer, and, creeping closer, Punch passed his hand gently over Pen's arm and touched his face; but this evoked no movement, only the drawing and expiration of a deep breath which came warmly to the boy's hand as he whispered:

"Well, he must be better or he wouldn't have gone to sleep like that. Don't think I could. And, my word, that chap did serve him out!"

The low sound of voices from below now attracted the boy's attention; and, turning to the knot-hole, he looked down into the priest's room to see that it was nearly full of the dark, fierce-looking Spaniards, who were listening to the old padre, whose face shone with animation, lit up as it was by the lamp, while he talked earnestly to those who bent forward to listen to his words.

It was a picturesque scene, for the moon was now shining brightly, its rays striking in through the open door and throwing up the figures of several of the *contrabandistas* for whom there was no room within the cottage, but who pressed forward as if to listen to the priest's words.

"Why, he must be preaching to them," said Punch to himself at last, "but I can't understand a word. This Spanish seems queer stuff. What does *el rey* mean, I wonder. Dunno," he muttered, as he yawned drowsily. "Seems queer that eating and drinking should make you sleepy. Well, I ain't obliged to listen to what that old fellow says. Wonder whether Private Gray knows what *el rey* means? Better not ask him, though, now he's asleep. Phew! It is hot up here! *Buzz, buzz, buzz!* What is he talking about? Seems to make me sleepier to listen to him.—I say, not awake, are you, comrade?"

There was no reply, and soon after Punch's heavy breathing was heard in addition to the low murmur of the priest's voice, for the boy too, worn out with what he had gone through during the past hours, was fast asleep.

Chapter Twenty Seven
The new Friend

Punch woke up with a start to find that it was broad daylight, for the sun was up, the goats on the valley-side were bleating, and a loud musical bell was giving forth its constantly iterated sounds.

Punch looked down the knot-hole through which the bright morning rays were streaming up as well as between the ill-fitting boards; but as far as he could make out there was no one below, and he remained peering down for some minutes, recalling all that had taken place overnight, till, turning slightly, he caught sight of the basket of provisions.

"It makes one feel hungry again," muttered the boy, and his hand was stretched out to draw the basket to his side. "No, no," he continued, pulling back his hand; "let's have fair-play.—Awake, comrade?—Fast asleep. That looks well. My word, how I slept after that supper! Wish he would wake up, though. Be no harm in filling up with water," And, creeping softly to where the jar had been placed for safety, he took a long, deep draught. "Ah!" he ejaculated, "that will keep the hungries quiet for a bit;" and then he chuckled to himself as his eye wandered about the loft, and he noted how the priest used it for a storeroom, one of his chief stores being onions. "And so the French are holding the country everywhere, are they? And we are to lie snug here for a bit, and then that Spanish chap is going to show us the way to get to our regiment again. Well, we have tumbled among friends at last; but I hope we sha'n't have to lie here till all the fighting's done, for my comrade and me owe the Frenchies something, and we should both like to get a chance to pay it.—Here, I say, Private Gray, you might wake up now. Water's only water, after all, and I want my breakfast. I shouldn't mind if there was none, but it's aggravating to your inside to see it lying there.— Hallo! There's somebody coming," for he heard voices from somewhere outside. "That's the old father," muttered the boy. "Yes, and that's that big Spanish chap. Didn't he look fine with his silk handkercher round his head and his pistols in his scarf? I suppose he's captain of the band. What did

Gray say they were—smugglers? Why, they couldn't be. Smugglers have vessels by the seaside. I do know that. There's no seaside here up in the mountains. What have they got to smuggle?"

"Punch, you there?" came in a sharp whisper.

"Yes," whispered back the boy. "All right. Wake up. Here's your doctor coming to see to your wound."

The next minute the voices sounded from the room below, and the smuggler's voice was raised and he called up in French:

"Are you awake there, my friends?" And upon receiving an answer in the affirmative he began to ascend the step-ladder cautiously, and apparently quite at home. As soon as he stood stooping in the loft he drew back a rough shutter and admitted a little of the sunshine.

"Good-morning!" he said. "How's the wound? Kept you awake all night?"

Pen explained that he had only just woke up.

"Well, that means you are getting better," said the smuggler; and the boys scanned the speaker's handsome, manly-looking face.

Just then fresh steps were heard upon the ladder, and the pleasant-countenanced priest appeared, carefully bearing a large bowl of water, and with a long strip of coarse linen hanging over his arm.

He smilingly nodded at the two lads, and then knelt by the side of the bowl and watched attentively while Pen's wound was dressed and carefully bandaged with the coarse strip of linen, after which a few words passed in Spanish between the priest and the smuggler, who directly after addressed Pen.

"He was asking me about getting you down to breakfast, but I tell him that you will be better if you lie quite still for a bit, perhaps for a few days, I don't think the French will come here again. They are more likely to forget all about you, for they are always on the move; but you could do no good if you came down, and I shall not stir for some days yet, unless my friends come, and I don't expect they will. It would be too risky. So you lie here patiently and give your wound a chance to get well before I try to take you through the pass. Besides, your friends are a long way off, and they will be sure to come nearer before long. You can make yourself very comfortable here, can't you, and eat and drink and sleep?"

"But it is not fair to the father," said Pen, "and we have no money to pay him for our lodging."

"You Englishmen are brave fellows," said the smuggler with a merry laugh. "You like to pay your way, while those French thieves plunder and steal and ill-use every one they come near. Don't you make yourself uncomfortable about that, my lad. As you hinted just now, the holy father is poor, and it may seem to you hard that you should live upon him; but you English are our friends, and so is the father. Make yourselves quite comfortable. You are very welcome, and we are glad to have you as our guests.—Eh, *padre mio!*" he continued, relapsing into his own tongue. "They are quite welcome, are they not?"

The priest nodded and smiled as he bent down and patted both the lads on the shoulder, Punch contenting himself with what he did not understand, for it seemed very friendly, while Pen took the hand that rested on his shoulder and raised it to his lips.

Then the old man slowly descended, and the smuggler turned and continued talking pleasantly to Pen.

"I have told him," he said, "that I am going to have breakfast with you here, as my men have gone up to the mountains with the mules, and I don't want to show myself and get a shot sent after me, for some of the Frenchmen are down in the village still. Be quiet for a day or two, and if my friends come before you are able to march we will get you on one of my mules. Hallo!" he added, "the father's making a fire to cook us some breakfast. I shouldn't wonder if he bakes us a cake and makes us a cup of good fragrant coffee. He generally contents himself with bread and herbs and a glass of water; but he knows my weaknesses—and I know his," added the smuggler, laughing. "He never objects to a glass of good wine."

The smuggler's surmises were right, for before very long the old man paid several visits to the loft, and ended by seating himself with the others and partaking of a roughly prepared but excellent breakfast, which included newly made cake, fried bacon and eggs, with a capital bowl of coffee and goat's-milk.

"Well, my friend," said the smuggler, turning to Punch, "have you made a good meal?"

Punch looked uncomfortable, gave his head a scratch, and frowned.

"Tell him, comrade, I can't jabber French," he said.

"He asks if you have made a good breakfast, Punch."

"Tell him it's splendid."

The wounded lad interpreted between them; while the smuggler now addressed himself to his patient.

"And you?" he said. "I suppose I may tell the father that his breakfast was capital, and that you can make yourself happy here till you get better?"

"Yes; and tell him, please, that our only regret is that we cannot show our gratitude more."

"Tut, tut! There is no need. The father has helped you because you are brave young Englishmen who are over here risking your lives for our countrymen in trying to drive out the French invaders who have come down like a swarm of locusts upon our land. You understand very well, I suppose," — continued the Spaniard, rolling up a cigarette and offering it to Pen, who took it and waited while the smuggler rolled up another for Punch and again another for himself before turning and taking a smouldering brand of wood from the priest, who had fetched it from the hearth below — "you understand very well why the French are here?"

"Not very well," said Pen. "I am an English soldier here with my people to fight against the French, who have placed a French king in your country."

"Yes," said the Spaniard, frowning, as he sent a curl of fragrant smoke eddying towards the shutter-opening in the sloping roof, where as it rose soft and grey it began to glow with gold as it reached the sunshine that streamed across the little square; "they have thrust upon us another of the usurper's kin, and this Napoleon has imprisoned our lawful ruler in Valençay."

"I didn't know all this," replied Pen; "but I like to hear."

"Good!" said the smuggler, nodding and speaking eagerly. "And you are an Englishman and fighting on our side. I know all this, and that your Wellesley is a brave general who is only waiting his time to sweep our enemies back to their own country. You are a friend who has suffered in our cause, and I can confide in you. You will be glad to hear that the prisoner has escaped."

"Yes," said Pen, forgetting the pain of his wound for the time in the interest of what he heard, while Punch yawned and did not seem happy with his cigarette. "But what prisoner?"

"The King, Ferdinand."

Pen had never heard of any Ferdinand except one that he had read of in Shakespeare; but he said softly, "I am glad."

"Yes," said the smuggler, "and I and my friends are glad — glad that, poor smugglers though we are, and no soldiers, we can be of service to his Majesty. He has escaped from the French prison and is on his way to the Pyrenees, where we can help him onward to Madrid. For we as *contrabandistas* know all the passes through the frontier; and I and my followers are waiting till he reaches the appointed spot, where some of our brothers will bring him on to meet us, who will be ready to guide him and his friends farther on their way to the capital, or place them in safety in one of our hiding-places, our stores, of which we have many here in the mountains. He is long in coming, but he is on his way, and the last news I heard is that he is hidden by my friends at one of our *caches* a score or so of leagues away. He may be here to-night if the pass seems clear. It may be many nights; but he will come, and if the French arrive — well, they will have to fight," said the smuggler, with a smile; and he lightly tapped the butt of one of his pistols. "It is hard for a king to have to steal away and hide; but every league he passes through the mountains here he will find more friends; and we shall try, some of us, to guide your English generals to where they can strike at our French foes. Yes, my young friend," continued the captain, rolling up a fresh cigarette, "and we shall serve our King well in all this, and if some of us fall — well, it will be in a good cause, and better than spending our lives in carrying smuggled goods — silks and laces, *eau de vie*, cigars and tobacco duty free across these hills. There, we are *contrabandistas*, and we are used to risking our lives, for on either side of the mountains the Governments shoot us down. But we are patriots all the same, and we are risking our lives for our King just as if we were of the best. So get well, you two brave soldier lads. I see you have your guns, and maybe, as we have helped you, we may ask you to help us. You need not mind, for you will be fighting against your enemies the French. Come, light up your cigarette again. You must be tired of my long story."

"Tired! No," said Pen. "I am glad to hear it, for I have often thought and wondered why we English had come here to fight, and all I knew was that Napoleon was conquering everywhere and trying to master the world."

"Which he will never do," said the smuggler, laughing. "Strong as he is, and masterful, he will never succeed, and you know why?"

"No, I can't say that," replied Pen, wincing.

"Then I will tell you. Because the more he conquers the more enemies he makes, and nowhere friends. There, you are growing weary."

"Oh no," cried Pen. "I shrank because I felt my wound a little more. I am glad to hear all this."

"But your friend—no?" said the *contrabandista*.

"That's because he cannot understand what you say; but I shall tell him all that you have said when we are alone, and then he will be as much your friend as I am, and quite as ready to fight in your cause, though he is a boy."

"Good!" said the Spaniard. "And some day I shall put you both to the proof."

Chapter Twenty Eight
Punch proves sturdy

"Thank you," said Punch. "I didn't want to bother you, you know, comrade, only you see I ain't like you—I don't know a dozen languages, French and Latin, and all the rest of them; and when you get on talking to that *contrabando* chap it worries me. Seems as if you are saying all sorts of things about me. He will keep looking at me all the time he's talking. I've got to know a bit now that it's meant for you, but he will keep fixing his eyes like a pair of gimlets, and screwing them into me; and then he goes on talking, and it makes you feel uncomfortable like. Now, you see, there was the other day, a week—no, it was nine days—ago, when you said when he was telling you all about the Spanish King coming here—"

"Nine days ago, Punch! Nonsense! We can't have been here nine days."

"Oh yes, we can. It's ten, because there was the day before, when he came first and doctored your leg."

"Well, you seem very sure about it; but I think you are wrong."

"I ain't," said Punch sturdily. "Lookye here," and he thrust his hand into his pocket and brought it out again full of little pebbles.

"Well, what have they got to do with it?"

"Everything. I puts a fresh one into my pocket every day we stops."

"What for?"

"To count up with. Each of those means two shillings that we owe the old gentleman for our prog. Knowing what a gentleman you are in your ideas, I says to myself you will want to pay him some day—a shilling apiece a day; that's what I put it at, and that means we owe him a pound; and if we are going to stop here much longer I must try another dodge, especially if we are going on the march, for I don't want to go tramping along with half a hundredweight of stones in my pocket."

"You're a rum fellow, Punch," said Pen, smiling.

"That's what my mother used to say; and I am glad of it. It does a fellow good to see you burst out laughing. Why, I haven't seen you grin like that not since the day when I went down with the bullet in my back. Here, I know what I'll do. I'll chuck all these stones, and make a scratch for every day on the stock of my musket. 'Tain't as if it was a Bri'sh rifle and the sergeant coming round and giving you hooroar for not keeping your arms in order. That would be a good way, wouldn't it, because the musket-stock wouldn't weigh any heavier when you had done than when you had begun."

"Well, are you satisfied now, Punch, that he isn't talking about you?"

"Well, you say he ain't, and that's enough; but I want to know, all the same, why that there Spanish King don't come."

"So does he. You saw how earnest he was yesterday when he came and talked to me, after seeing to my leg, and telling me that he shouldn't do any more to it."

"Telled you that, did he? I am glad. And that means it's nearly well."

"It means it's so far well that I am to exercise it all I can."

"Glad of it. But you ought to have telled me. That is good news. But how are you going to exercise it if we are under orders not to go outside this place for fear of the people seeing us and splitting upon the father?"

"Yes, that is awkward, Punch."

"Awkward! I call it more than awkward, for we did nearly get the poor old chap into a bad scrape that first night. Tell you what, though. You ask Mr Contrabando to come some night and show us the way."

"Show us the way where?"

"Anywhere. Up into the passes, as he calls them, right up in the mountains, so that we shall know which way to go when we want to join the Bri'sh army."

"It would be hardly fair to him, Punch," said Pen.

"Never mind that. It would be fair to us, and it would be exercising your leg. Pretty muddle we should be in when the order comes to march and your poor old leg won't go."

"Ah, well, we shall see, Punch," said Pen.

"Ah, I would; and soon. It strikes me sometimes that he's getting rather tired of his job, him and all his chaps too. I've watched them when they come here of an evening to ask questions of the father and lay their heads together; and I can't understand their jibber-jabber, but it's plain enough to see that they are grumpy and don't like it, and the way they goes on screwing up those bits of paper and lighting up and smoking away is enough to make you ill to watch them. 'Tain't as if they were good honest pipes. Why, they must smoke as much paper as they do 'bacco. Think their captain is going to give it up as a bad job?"

"No, Punch."

"Well, anyhow, I think you might ask him to take us out with him a bit. If you don't like to do it on account of yourself, because, as you say, he might think it ungrateful, you put it all on to me. Look here. You says, if you can put it into French, as you wouldn't mind it a bit. You says as it's your comrade as wants to stretch his legs awful bad. Yes, and you tell him this too, that I keeps on worrying you about having pins and needles in my back."

"Stuff, Punch!"

"That it ain't, honour bright. It's lying on my back so much up there in that there cock-loft. It all goes dead-like where the bullet went in. It's just as if it lay there still, and swelled up nearly as big as a cannon ball, and that lump goes all dead and dumb in needles and pins like for ever so long. There, you try it on him that way. You say I'm so sick of it as never was."

"And it was only yesterday, Punch, you told me that you were thoroughly happy and contented here, and the country was so beautiful and we were living so well that you didn't mind if we stayed here for months."

"'Twaren't yesterday. It was the day before the day before that. You have got all the time mixed up. I don't know where you would have been if I hadn't counted up."

"Well, never mind when it was. You can't deny that you said something like that."

"Ah, but I wasn't so tired then. I am all right again now, and so are you, and I want to be at it. Who's going to be contented shut-up here like a prisoner?"

"Not bad sort of imprisonment, Punch."

"Oh no, that's all right enough, comrade; but I want to get back to our chaps. They'll be crossing us off as killed and wounded, and your people at home will be thinking you are dead. I want to get back to the fighting again. Why, if we go on like this, one of these days they will be sarving out the promotions, and then where do we come in? I say, the captain didn't come to see us last week. Think he will to-night?"

"I hope so, and bring us news."

"So do I. But isn't it about time that Mr Padre came back?"

"Must be very near," said Pen.

"Quite," said Punch. "He gets all the fun, going out for his walks, a-roving up and down amongst the trees with his book in his hand. Here, if he don't volunteer to take us for a walk—something more than a bit of a tramp up and down in the darkness—I shall vote that we run away. There, if you don't talk to him I shall."

"Don't, Punch."

"Why not?"

"Because I don't want us to seem ungrateful."

"Oh, all right then.—I say, here he comes!" cried Punch the next minute; and the old man trudged up to the door with the basket he had taken away empty evidently well-filled again.

The priest looked tired as he came in, and according to his custom looked questioningly at the boys, who could only respond with a shake of the head; and this made the old man sigh.

"*Paz!*" he said sadly; and, smiling cheerfully, he displayed the contents of his basket, stored the provisions he had brought in, and then according to his wont proceeded to set out the evening meal up in the loft.

This meal seemed to have lost its zest to the weary fugitives, and quite late in the evening, when the lads, after sitting talking together in whispers so as not to awaken the priest, who, evidently tired out by his afternoon expedition, had lain down upon the pallet and was sleeping heavily, were about to follow his example for want of something better to do, he suddenly sprang up, ascended to the loft, and told Punch that he was going out again on the watch to see if the friends expected were coming along the pass, and ended by telling them that they had better lie down to rest.

"That's settled it for me," said Punch, as the old man went out and closed the door. "I can't sleep now. I want to follow him and stretch my legs."

"But you can't do that, Punch."

"Ho! Couldn't I? Why, I could set off and run like I haven't done since I was shot down."

"But you can't, Punch," said Pen gravely. "It's quite possible that the captain may come and ask where the father is. I think we ought to stay."

"Oh, very well, then, we will stop; but I don't call this half living. I want to go and attack somebody or have them attack us. Why, it's like being dead, going on this round—yes, dead, and just as if they had forgot to bury us because they've got too much to do. Are you going to lie down to sleep?"

"No," said Pen, "I feel as wakeful as you are."

"I say, look at that now! Of course we can't go to sleep. Well, we might have a walk up and down outside in the dark. No one could see us, and it would make us sleepy again."

"Very well; only we mustn't go out of sight of the door, in case the captain should come."

"Yah! He won't come," grumbled Punch; and he descended to the lower room, scraped the faintly glowing wood-ashes together, and then went to the door, peered out, and listened, and afterwards, followed by his comrade, he began to tramp up and down the shelf-like ledge upon which the priest's cottage was built.

It was very dark, for the sky was so overcast that not a star was visible; and, as if feeling depressed by the silence, neither was disposed for talk, and the consequence was that at the end of about half an hour Pen caught his companion by the arm and stopped short. His reason was plain enough, for Punch uttered a faint "Hist!" and led the way to the cottage door, where they both stopped and listened to a sound which had grown plainer—that of steps coming swiftly towards them. They hardly had time to softly close the door and climb up to the loft before the door was thrown open, there was a quick step below, and a soft whistle which they well knew now was uttered at the foot of the steps.

Pen replied in the way he had learned, and directly after came the question, "Where's the father?"

"He went out an hour ago," Pen replied.

"Which way?"

"By the upper pass," replied Pen.

There was a sharp ejaculation, expressive of impatience, the steps crossed the room again, the door creaked as it was shut to, and then the steps died away.

"There, Punch, you see I was right," said Pen.

"Who's to see anybody's right when it's as black as your hat?" replied the boy impatiently.

"Well, I think it's right if you don't. What shall we do—go to sleep now?"

"Go to sleep?" growled the boy irritably. "Go to wake you mean! I tell you what I am just fit for."

"Well, what?" said Pen good-humouredly.

"Sentry-go. No fear of anybody catching me asleep who came on his rounds. I used to think that was the very worst part of being a soldier, but I could just enjoy it now. 'Tis miserable work, though, isn't it?"

"No," replied Pen thoughtfully.

"But you get very sleepy over it, don't you?"

"I never did," said Pen gravely, as they both settled themselves upon the floor of the loft, and the bundles of straw and dried-fern litter which the priest had added for their comfort rustled loudly while they placed themselves in restful postures. "I used to find it a capital time to think, Punch."

"What about?"

"The old days when I was a boy at school, and the troubles I had had. Then I used to question myself."

"How did you do that?"

"How did I do that? Why, I used to ask myself questions as to whether I hadn't done a very foolish thing in enlisting for a soldier."

"And then of course you used to say no," cried Punch. "Anybody could answer that question. Why didn't you ask yourself some good tough questions that you couldn't answer—regular puzzlers?"

"I always found that puzzle enough, Punch," said Pen gravely; "and I have never been able to answer it yet."

"Well, that's a rum un," said Punch, with a sort of laugh. "You have often called me a queer fellow. You do puzzle me. Why, of course you did right. You are not down-hearted because we have had a bit of a venture or two? It's all experience, and you like it as much as I do, even if I do grumble a bit sometimes because it's so dull. Something's sure to turn up before long, and— What did you do that for?"

"Pst!" whispered Pen; and Punch was silence itself, for he too caught the hurrying of many feet, and low voices in eager converse coming nearer and nearer; and the next minute there was the heavy thump as of a fist upon the door, which was thrust open so roughly that it banged against the wall.

And then midst the sounds of heavy breathing and the scuffling of feet as of men bearing in a heavy burden, the room below seemed to be rapidly filling up, and the door was closed and barred.

Chapter Twenty Nine
The Royal Visitor

The two lads grasped hands as they listened in the intense darkness to what seemed to be a scene of extreme excitement, the actors in it having evidently been hurrying to reach the cottage, which they had gained in a state of exhaustion; for those who spoke gave utterance to their words as if panting and breathless with their exertions, while from their whispering it seemed evident that they were afraid of being overheard.

The two listeners dared not stir, for the least movement would have betrayed them to those below, and before many minutes had elapsed they felt certain that the present invaders of the cottage were strangers.

All at once some one gave vent to a piteous sigh and an ejaculation or two as if of pain; and this was followed by what sounded to be words that were full of pity and compassion, mingled with great deference, towards the sufferer.

Pen could make out nothing more in the hurried and whispered conversation than that it was in Spanish, and for the time being he felt somewhat dazed as to who the new-comers were. He was too much startled to try and puzzle out matters calmly, and for a while he devoted himself to the preservation of utter silence.

At last, though, a few more utterances below, spoken in a deferential tone, followed by a sharp, angry command or two, sent a flash through his brain, and he pressed Punch's arm with greater energy in an effort to try and convey to his companion the thought that he knew who the fresh-comers must be.

"If they would only strike a light," he thought to himself, "I might get a peep through the knot-hole"—which was always carefully kept clear for inspection of what took place below—"and I could see then at a glance whether this was the expected King with his followers."

But the darkness remained profound.

"If it is the escaped Spanish King," he said to himself, "it will be plain to see. It must be, and they have been pursued by the French, or they wouldn't be afraid to speak aloud."

Then he began to doubt again, for the Spanish King and his followers, who needed a guide to lead them through the intricate passes of the mountains, would not have known their way to the cottage.

"Nonsense!" he thought to himself, as fresh doubts arose. "The old priest or the captain must have met them and brought them here."

Then all was silent for a time, till it was evident that some one was moving by the fireplace; and then there was the sound of some one blowing.

This was followed by a faint glow of light; the blowing sound increased, and it was evident that the wood-ashes possessed sufficient life to be fanned into flame, which increased as the embers were evidently being drawn together by a piece of metal; and before another minute had elapsed Pen made out through the knot-hole that the instrument used for reviving the fire was the blade of a sword.

Then some one sighed deeply and uttered a few words in an imperious tone whose effect was to set some one fanning the fire with more energy, when the cracks in the boarded floor began to show, and the watcher above began to get glimpses of those below him.

A few minutes later the embers began to crackle, the members of the party below grew more visible, and some one uttered a few words in an eager tone—words which evoked an ejaculation or two of satisfaction, followed by an eager conversation that sounded like a dispute.

This was followed by an angry, imperious command, and this again by what sounded to Pen like a word or two of protest. Then the sharp, commanding voice beat down the respectful objection, one of the flaming brands seemed to rise from the hearth, and directly after the smoky wick of the *padre's* lamp flamed up.

Now Pen had a view of the crowded room.

And now Pen had a view of the crowded room which completely dashed his belief in the party being the Spanish King and his followers, for he was looking down upon the heads of a gathering of rough-looking, unshorn, peasant-like men, for the most part in cloaks. Some wore the regular handkerchief tied round their heads and had their sombrero hats held in hand or laid by their sides. All, too, were well armed, wearing swords and rough scarves or belts which contained pistols.

This scene was enough to sweep away all thought of this being a king and his courtiers, for nothing could have been less suggestive thereof, and the lad looked in vain for one of them who might have been wounded or so wearied out that he had been carried in.

Then for a moment Pen let his thoughts run in another direction, but only for a few moments. These were evidently not any of the smuggler's men. He had seen too many of them during his sojourn at the priest's hut not to know what they were like—that is to say, men accustomed to the mountains; for they were all in their way jaunty of mien. Their arms, too, were different, and once more the thought began to gain entrance that his former surmise was right, and that these bearers of swords who had spoken in such deferential tones to one of their party were after all faithful followers or courtiers who had assumed disguises that would enable them to pass over the mountains unnoticed. Which then was the King?

"If some of them would speak," said Pen to himself, "it would be easier to tell."

But the silence, save for a faint crack or two from the burning wood, remained profound.

At last the watcher was beginning to come to a conclusion and settle in his own mind that one of the party who was bending forward towards the fire with his cloak drawn about his face might be the King; and his belief grew stronger as a flickering flame from the tiny fire played upon this man's high boots, one of which displayed a rusty spur.

The next minute all doubt was at an end, for one of the men nearest the door uttered a sharp ejaculation which resulted in the occupants of the *padre's* dwelling springing to their feet. Swords leapt from their scabbards, and some of the men drew their cloaks about their left arms, while others snatched pistols from their belts, and there followed the sharp clicking of their locks.

It was evident they were on the alert for anticipated danger, and Pen's eyes glistened, for he could hear no sound. But he noted one thing, and that was that the booted and spurred individual in the cloak did not stir from where he was seated upon the priest's stool by the fire.

Then, with a gesture of impatience, Pen saw him throw back his cloak and put his hand to his belt to draw forth a pistol which refused to come. Then with an angry word he gave a fierce tug, with the result that the weapon came out so suddenly that its holder's arm flew up, the pistol exploded with a loud crash, the bullet with which it was loaded passed upward through the boarded ceiling, and Pen started and made a snatch at the spot where his musket was propped up against the wall, while Punch leaped from where he had crouched and came down again upon the ill-fitting boards, which cracked loudly as if the boy were going through.

Chapter Thirty
An awkward Position

There was a burst of excitement, hurried ejaculations, and half-a-dozen pistols were rapidly discharged by their holders at the ceiling; while directly after, in obedience to a command uttered by one of the party, a dash was made for the corner door, which was dragged open, and, sword in hand, several of the men climbed to the loft. The boards creaked, there was a hurried scuffle, and first Punch and then Pen were compelled to descend into the room below, dragged before the leader, forced upon their knees, and surrounded by a circle of sword-points, whose bearers gazed at their leader, awaiting his command to strike.

The leader sank back in his seat, nursing the pistol he had accidentally discharged. Then with his eyes half-closed he slowly raised it to take aim at Pen, who gazed at him firmly and without seeming to blench, while Punch uttered a low, growling ejaculation full of rage as he made a struggle to escape, but was forced back upon his knees, to start and wince as he felt the point of a sword touch his neck. Then he cried aloud, "Never mind, comrade! Let 'em see we are Bri'sh soldiers and mean to die game."

Pen did not withdraw his eyes from the man who held his life in hand, and reached out behind him to grasp Punch's arm; but his effort was vain.

Just then the seated man seemed to recollect himself, for he threw the empty pistol upon the floor and tugged another from his belt, cocked it, and then swung himself round, directing the pistol at the door, which was dashed open by the old priest, who ran in and stood, panting hard, between the prisoners and the holder of the pistol.

He was too breathless to speak, but he gesticulated violently before grasping Pen's shoulder with one hand and waving the other round as if to drive back those who held the prisoners upon their knees.

He tried to speak, but the words would not come; and then there was another diversion, for a fresh-comer dashed in through the open door, and, regardless of the swords directed at him, forced his way to where the prisoners were awaiting their fate.

He, too, was breathless with running, for he sank quickly on one knee, caught at the hand which held the pistol and raised it quickly to his lips, as he exclaimed in French:

"No, no, your Majesty! Not that!"

"They are spies," shouted the tired-looking Spaniard who had given the command which had sent his followers to make the seizure in the loft.

"No spies," cried the *contrabandista*. "Our and his Majesty's friends— wounded English soldiers who had been fighting upon our side."

There was a burst of ejaculations; swords were sheathed, and the dethroned Spanish monarch uncocked his pistol and thrust it back into his belt.

"They have had a narrow escape," he said bitterly. "Why were you not here with the friends you promised?"

"They are outside awaiting my orders, your Majesty," said the smuggler bluntly. "May I remind you that you are not to your time, neither have you come by the pass I promised you to watch."

"Bah! How could I, when I was driven by these wretched French, who are ten times our number? We had to reach the trysting-place how we could, and it was natural that these boys should be looked upon as spies. Now then, where are you going to take us? The French soldiers cannot be far behind."

"No, sire; they are very near."

"And your men—where are they?"

"Out yonder, sire, between you and your pursuers."

"Then are we to continue our flight to-night?"

"I cannot tell yet, sire. Not if my men can hold the enemy at bay. It may be that they will fall back here, but I cannot say yet. I did intend to lead you through the forest and along a path I know by the mountain-side; but it is possible that the French are there before us."

"And are these your plans of which you boasted?" cried the King bitterly.

"No, sire," replied the *contrabandista* bluntly. "Your Majesty's delay has upset all those."

The King made an angry gesticulation.

"How could I help it?" he said bitterly. "Man, we have been hemmed in on all sides. There, I spoke hastily. You are a tried friend. Act as you think best. You must not withdraw your help."

"Your Majesty trusts me, then, again?"

"Trust you? Of course," said the King, holding out his hand, which the smuggler took reverently and raised to his lips.

Then dropping it he turned sharply to the priest and the two prisoners.

"All a mistake, my friends. There," he added, with a smile, "I see you are not afraid;" and noting Punch's questioning look, he patted him on the shoulder before turning to Pen again. "Where are your guns?" he said.

Pen pointed up to the loft.

"Get them, then, quickly. We shall have to leave here now."

He had hardly spoken before a murmur arose and swords were drawn, for there was a quick step outside, a voice cried "*El rey!*" and one of the smuggler's followers pressed through to whisper a few words.

"Ah!" cried the recipient, who turned and said a few words in Spanish to the King, who rose to his feet, drew his rough cloak around him, and stood as if prepared for anything that might come.

Just then Pen's voice was heard, and, quite free now, Punch stepped to the door and took the two muskets that were passed down to him. Then Pen descended with the cartouche-boxes and belts, and handed one to Punch in exchange for a musket, and the two lads stood ready.

The smuggler smiled approval as he saw his young friends' prompt action, and nodded his head.

"Can you walk?" he said.

Pen nodded.

"And can you fire a few shots on our behalf?"

"Try us," replied Pen. "But it rather goes against the grain after what we have received. You only came in time."

"Yes, I know," replied the smuggler. "But there are many mistakes in war, and we are all friends now."

The *contrabandista* turned from him sharply and hurried to the door, where another of his followers appeared, who whispered a few words to him, received an order, and stepped back, while his leader turned to the father and said something, which resulted in the old man joining the two lads and pressing their hands, looking at them sadly.

The next minute the smuggler signed to them to join his follower who was waiting by the door, while he stepped to the King, spoke to him firmly for a few minutes, and then led the way out into the darkness, with the two English lads, who were conscious that they were being followed by the royal fugitive and his men, out along the shelf in the direction of the forest-path, which they had just gained when a distant shot rang out, to be repeated by the echoes and followed by another and another, ample indication that there was danger very near at hand.

The captain said a few words to his follower, and then turned to Pen.

"Keep with this man," he said, "when I am not here. I must go back and see what is going on."

The lads heard his steps for a minute amongst the crackling husks of the past year's chestnuts and parched twigs. Then they were merged with those of the party following.

"I say," whispered Punch, "how's your leg?"

"I had almost forgotten it," replied Pen in a whisper.

"That's good, comrade. But, I say, all that set a fellow thinking."

"Yes; don't talk about it," replied Pen.

"All right. But I say, isn't this lovely—on the march again with a loaded gun over your shoulder? If I had got my bugle back, and one's officer alongside, I should be just happy. Think we shall have a chance of a shot or two?"

The smuggler, who was leading the way, stopped short and turned upon Punch with a deep, low growl.

"Eh?" replied Punch. "It's no good, comrade; I can't understand a word."

The man growled again, and laid his hand sharply upon the boy's lips.

"Here, don't do that!" cried Punch. "How do I know when you washed that last?"

"Be quiet, Punch. The man means we may be nearing the enemy."

"Why don't he say so, then?" grumbled Punch; and their guide grunted as if satisfied with the effect of Pen's words, and led on again in and out a rugged, winding path, sometimes ascending, sometimes descending, but never at fault in spite of the darkness.

Sometimes he stopped short to listen as if to find out how near the King's party were behind, and when satisfied he led on again, giving the two lads a friendly tap or two upon the shoulder after finding that any attempt at other communication was in vain.

At last after what must have been about a couple of hours' tramp along the extremely rugged path, made profoundly dark by the overhanging low, gnarled trees, he stopped short again and laid his hand in turn upon the lips of the boys, and then touched Pen's musket, which he made him ground, took hold of his hands in turn and laid them on the muzzle, and then stood still.

"What's he up to now?" whispered Punch, with his lips close to his comrade's ear.

"I think he means we are to halt and keep guard."

"Oh, that's it, is it?" muttered Punch; and he stood fast, while the smuggler patted him on the shoulder and went off quickly, leaving the boys alone, with Punch muttering and fuming in his intense desire to speak. But he mastered himself and stood firm, listening as the steps of the party behind came nearer and nearer till they were close at hand. This was too much for Punch.

"Lookye here," he whispered; "they will be ready to march over us directly. How are we going to tell them to halt?"

"Be silent. Perhaps they will have the sense to see that they ought to stop. Most likely there are some amongst them who understand French."

Pen proved to be right in his surmise, for directly after a portion of the following party were close to them, and the foremost asked a question in Spanish. "*Halte!*" said Pen sharply, and at a venture; but it proved sufficient. And as he stood in the dim, shadowy, overhung path the word was passed along to the rear, and the dull sound of footsteps died out. "Bravo!" whispered Punch. "They are beginning to understand English after all. I say, ain't that our chaps coming back?"

Pen heard nothing for a few moments. Then there was the faint crack of a twig breaking beneath some one's feet, and the smuggler who was acting as their guide rejoined them.

"*Los Francéses*," said the man, in a whisper; and he dropped the carbine he carried with its butt upon the stony earth, rested his hands upon the muzzle, and stood in silence gazing right away, and evidently listening and keenly on the alert, for he turned sharply upon Punch, who could not keep his tongue quiet.

"Oh, bother! All right," growled the boy. "Here, comrade," he whispered to Pen; "aren't these 'ere cork-trees?"

"Perhaps. I'm not sure," whispered his companion impatiently. "Why do you ask? What does it matter now?"

"Lots. Just you cut one of them. Cut a good big bung off and stuff it into my mouth; for I can't help it, I feel as if I must talk."

"Urrrrrr!" growled the guide; and then, "Hist! hist!" for there was a whispering behind, and directly after the *contrabandista* captain joined them, to ask a low question in Spanish.

"The enemy are in front. They are before us," said the smuggler in French to Pen.

Then he spoke to his follower, who immediately began to retrace his steps, while the leader followed him with the two lads, who were led back to where the King was waiting in the midst of his followers; and now a short colloquy took place which resulted in all facing round and following the two smugglers, who retraced their path for the next half-hour, and then suddenly struck off along a rugged track whose difficulty was such that it was quite plain to the two lads that they were striking off right up into the mountains.

It was a wearisome route that was only followed with great difficulty, and now it was that Pen's wounded leg began to give him such intense pain that there were moments when he felt that he must break down.

But it came to an end at last, just before daybreak, in the midst of what seemed to be an amphitheatre of stones, or what might have been some quarry or place where prospecting had taken place in search of some one or other of the minerals which abounded in parts of the sterile land.

And now a halt was made, the smuggler picking out a spot which was rough with bushes; and here he signed to the two lads to lie down and rest, a silent command so welcome that Pen sank at full length at once, the rugged couch seeming to him so welcome that it felt to him like down.

A few specks of orange light high up in the sky told that sunrise was very near at hand, and for a few minutes Pen gazed upwards, rapt in wonder by the beauty of the sight. But as he lay and listened to the low murmur of voices, these gradually grew fainter and apparently more distant, while the ruddy specks of light paled and there seemed to be nothing more, for pain and exhaustion had had their way. Thoughts of Spaniards, officers and men, and the *contrabandistas* with their arms of knife and carbine, were quite as naught, danger non-existent, and for the time being sleep was lord of all.

Chapter Thirty One
A Dream of a Ramrod

It seemed to Pen to be a dream, and then by some kind of mental change it appeared to be all reality. In the first instance he felt that he was lying in the loft over the priest's room, trying to sleep, but he could not get himself into a comfortable position because Punch had gone down below to clean his musket and wanted him to come down too and submit his weapon to the same process. But it had happened that he wanted to go to sleep horribly, and he had refused to go down; with the consequence that as he lay just over the knot-hole Punch kept on poking his ramrod through the opening to waken him up, and the hard rod was being forced through the dry leaves of the Indian corn to reach his leg exactly where the bullet had ploughed, while in the most aggravating way Punch would keep on sawing the ramrod to and fro and giving him the most acute pain.

Then the boy seemed to leave off in a tiff and tell him that he might sleep for a month for aught he cared, and that he would not try to waken him any more.

Then somehow, as the pain ceased, he did not go to sleep, but went right off up the mountain-side in the darkness, guiding the King and his followers into a place of safety; still it was not so safe but that he could hear the French coming and firing at them now and then.

However, he went on and on, feeling puzzled all the time that he should know the way through the mountains so well, and he took the King to rest under the great chestnut-tree, and then on again to where the French were firing, and one of them brought him down with the bullet that ploughed his leg.

But that did not seem to matter, for, as if he knew every bit of the country by heart, he led the King to the goat-herd's cottage, and advised him to lie down and have a good rest on the rough bed, because the peasant-girl would be there before long with a basket of food.

The King said that he did not care to sleep because he was so dreadfully thirsty, and what he wanted was a bowl of goat's-milk. Then somehow he went to where the goat was waiting to be milked, and for a long time the milk would not come, but when it did and he was trying to fill the little wooden *seau* it was all full of beautiful cold water from the foot of the falls where the trout were rushing about.

Then somehow Punch kept on sawing his ramrod to and fro along the wound in his leg, and the more he tried to catch hold of the iron rod the more Punch kept on snatching it away; and they were going through the darkness again, with the King and his followers close behind, on the way to safety; while Pen felt that he was quite happy now, because he had saved the King, who was so pleased that he made him Sir Arthur Wellesley and gave him command of the British army.

Whereupon Punch exclaimed, "I never saw such a fellow as you are to sleep! Do wake up. Here's Mr Contrabando waiting to speak to you, and he looks as if he wanted to go away."

"Punch!" exclaimed Pen, starting up.

"Punch it is. Are you awake now?"

"Awake? Yes. Have I been dreaming?"

"I d'know whether you have been dreaming or not, but you have been snoring till I was ashamed of you, and the more I stirred you up the more you would keep on saying, 'Ramrod.'"

"Bah! Nonsense!"

"That's what I thought, comrade. But steady! Here he is again."

"Ah, my young friend!" said the *contrabandista*, holding out his hand. "Better after your long sleep?"

"Better? Yes," replied Pen eagerly. "Leg's very stiff; but I am ready to go on. Are we to march again?"

"Well, no, there's not much chance of that, for we are pretty well surrounded by the enemy, and here we shall have to stay unless we can beat them off."

"Where are we? What place is this?" asked Pen rather confusedly.

"One of our hiding-places, my friend, where we store up our goods and stable the mules when the pass near here is blocked up by snow or the frontier guards. Well, how do you feel now? Ready to go into hiding where you will be safe, or are you ready to help us against your enemies the French?"

"Will there be fighting?" asked Pen eagerly.

"You may be pretty sure of that; but I don't want to force you two wounded young fellows into taking part therein unless you are willing."

"I am willing," said Pen decisively; "but it's only fair that I should ask my comrade, who is only one of the buglers of my regiment."

"Oh, of course," said the smuggler captain, "a non-combatant. He carries a musket, I see, like yourself."

"Yes," replied Pen, with a smile, "but it is only a French piece. We belong to a rifle-regiment by rights."

"Yes; I have heard of it," said the smuggler.

"Well, I will ask him," said Pen, "for he doesn't understand a word we are saying.—Punch," he continued, addressing the boy, "the *contrabandista* wants to know whether we will fire a few shots against the French who are trying to take the Spanish King."

"Where do they want to take him?" cried the boy eagerly.

"Back to prison."

"Why, of course we will," said the boy sharply. "What do you want to ask that for?"

"Because he knows that you are not a private soldier, but a bugle-boy."

"Well, I can't help that, can I? I am a-growing, and I dare say I could hit a haystack as well as a good many of our chaps. They ain't all of them so clever because they are a bit older than I am."

"Well, don't get into a tiff, Punch. This isn't a time to show your temper."

"Who's a-showing temper? I can't help being a boy. What does he want to chuck that in a fellow's teeth for?"

"Quiet! Quiet!" said Pen, smiling. "Then I am to tell him that you are ready to have a shot or two at the enemy?"

"Well, I do call you a pretty comrade!" said the boy indignantly. "I should have thought you would have said yes at once, instead of parlyvooing about it like that.—Right, sir!" cried the boy, catching up his musket, giving it two or three military slaps, and drawing himself up as if he had just heard the command, "Present arms!"

"*Bon!*" said the smuggler, smiling; and he gave the boy a friendly slap on the shoulder.

"Ah!" ejaculated Punch, "that's better," as the smuggler now turned away to speak to a group of his men who were standing keeping watch behind some rocks a short distance away.—"I say, comrade—you did tell me once, but I forgetted it—what does *bong* mean?"

"Good."

"Ho! All right. *Bong*! I shall remember that next time. Fire a few shots! I am game to go on shooting as long as the cartridges last; and my box is full. How's yours?"

"Only half," replied Pen.

"Oh, well, fair-play's a jewel; share and share alike. Here, catch hold. That looks like fair measure. We don't want to count them, do we?"

"Oh no, that's quite near enough."

"Will we fire a few shots at the French?" continued Punch eagerly. "I should just think we will! Father always said to me, 'Pay your debts, my boy, as long as the money lasts;' and though it ain't silver and copper here, it's cartridges and— There! Ain't it rum, comrade? Now, I wonder whether you feel the same. The very thought of paying has made the pain in my back come again. I say, how's your leg?"

Chapter Thirty Two
A cavernous Breakfast

"I say, comrade," whispered Punch; "are we going to begin soon?"

The boys were seated upon a huge block of stone watching the coming and going of the *contrabandistas*, several of whom formed a group in a nook of the natural amphitheatre-like chasm in which they had made their halt.

This seemed to be the entrance to a gully, down which, as they waited, the lads had seen the smuggler-leader pass to and fro several times over, and as far as they could make out away to their left lay the track by which they had approached during the night; but they could not be sure.

That which had led them to this idea was the fact that it seemed as if sentries had been stationed somewhere down there, one of whom had come hurriedly into the amphitheatre as if in search of his chief.

"I say, comrade," said Punch, repeating his question rather impatiently, "aren't we going to begin soon? I feel just like old O'Grady."

"How's that, Punch?"

"What he calls 'spoiling for a fight, me boy.'"

"Oh, you needn't feel like that, Punch," said Pen, smiling.

"Well, don't you?"

"No. I never do. I never want to kill anybody."

"You don't? That ain't being a good soldier."

"I can't help that, Punch. Of course, when one's in for it I fire away like the rest; but when I'm cool I somehow don't like the feeling that one has killed or wounded some brave man."

"Oh, get out," cried the boy, "with your 'killed or wounded some brave man!' They ain't brave men—only Frenchies."

"Why, Punch, there are as brave men amongst the French as amongst the English."

"Get out! I don't believe that," said the boy. "There can't be. If there were, how could our General with his little bit of an army drive the big army of Frenchies about as he does? Ask any of our fellows, and they will tell you that one Englishman is worth a dozen Frenchies. Why, you must have heard them say so."

"Oh yes, I have, Punch," said Pen, laughing, as he nursed his leg, which reminded him of his wound from time to time. "But I don't believe it. It's only bluster and brag, of which I think our fellows ought to be ashamed. Why, you've more than once seen the French soldiers drive our men back."

"Well, yes," said Punch grudgingly. "But that's when there have been more of them."

"Not always, Punch."

"Why is it, then?"

"Oh, when they have had better positions and our officers have been outflanked."

"Now you are dodging away from what we were talking about," said Punch. "You were saying that you didn't like shooting the men."

"Well, I don't."

"That's because you don't understand things," cried the boy triumphantly. "You see, although I am only a boy, and younger than you are, I am an older soldier."

"Are you, Punch?" said Pen, smiling.

"Course I am! Why, you've only been about a year in the regiment."

"Yes, about a year."

"Well," cried the boy triumphantly, "I was born in it, so I'm just as old a soldier as I am years old. You needn't mind shooting as many of them as you can. They are the King's enemies, and it is your duty to. Don't the song say, 'God save the King?' Well, every British soldier has got to help and kill as many enemies as he can. But I say, we are going to fight for the Spanish King, then? Well, all right; he's our King's friend. But where is he now? I haven't seen anything of him this morning. I hope he hasn't run away and left us to do the fighting."

"Oh no," said Pen, "I don't think so. Our smuggler friend said we were surrounded by the French."

"Surrounded, eh?" cried Punch. "So much the better! Won't matter which way we fire then, we shall be sure to bring some one down. Glad you think the Spanish King ain't run away though. If I was a king I know what I should do, comrade," continued Punch, nursing his musket and giving it an affectionate rub and pat here and there. "Leg hurt you, comrade?"

"No, only now and then," said Pen, smiling. "But what would you do if you were a king?"

"Lead my army like a man."

"Nonsense! What are the generals for?"

"Oh, you would want your generals, of course, and the more brave generals the King has—like Sir Arthur Wellesley—the better. I say, he's an Irishman, isn't he?"

"Yes, I believe so," replied Pen.

"Yes," continued Punch after a minute. "They are splendid fellows to fight. I wonder whether he's spoiling for one now. Old O'Grady would say he was. You should hear him sometimes when he's on the talk. How he let go, my boy, about the Oirish! Well, they are good soldiers, and I wish, my boy, old O was here to help. O, O, and it's O with me, I am so hungry! Ain't they going to give us anything to eat?"

"Perhaps not, Punch, for it's very doubtful whether our friends keep their provisions here."

"Oh, I say!" cried the boy, with his face resembling that of the brave man in *Chevy Chase* who was in doleful dump, "that's a thing I'd see to if I was a king and led my army. I would have my men get a good feed before they advanced. They would fight ever so much better. Yes, if I was a king I'd lead my own men. They'd like seeing him, and fight for him all the better. Of course I wouldn't have him do all the dirty work, but— Look there, comrade; there's Mr Contrabando making signals to you. We are going to begin. Come on!"

The boy sprang to his feet, and the companions marched sharply towards the opening where the group of smugglers were gathered.

"Bah!" ejaculated Punch contemptuously. "What a pity it is! I don't believe that they will do much good with dumpy tools like them;" and the boy literally glared at the short carbines the smugglers had slung across their shoulders. "Of course a rifle would be best, but a good musket and bayonet is worth a dozen of those blunderbusters. What do they call them? Bell-mouthed? Why, they are just like so many trumpet-things out of the band stuck upon a stick. Why, it stands to reason that they can't go bang. It will only be a sort of a *pooh!*" And the boy pursed up his lips and held his hand to his mouth as if it were his lost bugle, and emitted a soft, low note—*poooooh!*

"*Déjeuner, mes amis!*" said the smuggler, as the boys advanced; and he led the way past a group of his followers along the narrow passage-like opening to where it became a hewn-out tunnel which showed the marks of picks, and on into a rock-chamber of great extent, in one corner of which a fire was blazing cheerfully, with the smoke rising to an outlet in the roof. Directly after the aromatic scent of hot coffee smote the nostrils of the hungry lads, as well as the aroma of newly fried ham, while away at one side to the right they caught sight of the strangers of the past night, Pen recognising at once the now uncloaked leader who had presented a pistol at his head.

"Here, I say," whispered Punch excitedly, "hold me up, comrade, or I shall faint."

"What's the matter?" said Pen anxiously. "You feel that dreadful pain again? Is it your wound?"

"Pain? Yes," whispered Punch; "but it ain't there;" and he thrust his hand into his pocket to feel for his knife.

It was a rough meal, roughly served, but so abundant that it was evident that the smugglers were adepts in looking after the commissariat department. In one part of the cavern-like place the King and his followers were being amply supplied, while right on the other side—partly hidden by a couple of stacks piled-up in the centre of the great chamber, and formed in the one case of spirit-kegs, in the other of carefully bound up bales that might have been of silk or velvet—were grouped together near the fire some scores of the *contrabandistas* who seemed to be always coming and going— coming to receive portions of food, and going to make place for others of the band.

And it was beyond these stacks of smuggled goods that their *contrabandista* friend signed to the lads to seat themselves. One of the men brought them coffee and freshly fried ham and cake, which the captain shared with them and joined heartily in the meal.

"I say, Pen," whispered Punch, "do tell him in 'parlyvoo' that I say he's a trump! Fight for him and the King! I should just think we will! D'ye 'ear? Tell him."

"No," said Pen. "Let him know what we feel towards him by what we do, Punch, not what we say."

"All right. Have it your own way," said the boy. "But, I say, I do like this ham. I suppose it's made of some of them little pigs we see running about in the woods. Talk about that goat's mutton! Why, 'tain't half so good as ours made of sheep, even though they do serve it out and call it kid. Why, when we have had it sometimes for rations, you couldn't get your teeth into it. Kid, indeed! Grandfather kid! I'm sure of that. I say, pass the coffee, comrade. Only fancy! Milk and sugar too! Oh no, go on; drink first. Age before honesty. I wonder whether this was smuggled.—What's the matter now?"

For in answer to a shrill whistle that rang loudly in echoes from the roof, every *contrabandista* in the place sprang up and seized his carbine, their captain setting the example.

"No, no," he said, turning to the two lads. "Finish your breakfast, and eat well, boys. It may be a long time before you get another chance. There's plenty of time before the firing begins, and I will come back for you and station you where you can fight for Spain."

He walked quickly across to where the King's followers had started up and stood sword in hand, their chief remaining seated upon an upturned keg, looking calm and stern; but at the same time his eyes wandered proudly over the roughly disguised devoted little band who were ready to defend him to the last.

Pen watched the *contrabandista* as he advanced and saluted the dethroned monarch without a trace of anything servile; the Spanish gentleman spoke as he addressed his sovereign in a low tone, but his words were not audible to the young rifleman. Still the latter could interpret them to himself by the Spaniard's gestures.

"What's he a-saying of?" whispered Punch; and as he spoke the boy surreptitiously cut open a cake, turned it into a sandwich, and thrust it into his haversack.

"I can't hear, Punch," replied Pen; "and if I could I shouldn't understand, for he's speaking in Spanish. But he's evidently telling him that his people may finish their breakfast in peace, for, like us, they are not wanted yet."

As Pen spoke the officers sheathed their swords, and two or three of them replaced pistols in their sashes. Then the *contrabandista* turned and walked sharply across the cavern-like chamber to overtake his men, and as he disappeared, distant but sharp and echoing *rap, rap, rap*, came the reports of firearms, and Punch looked sharply at his companion.

"Muskets, ain't they?" he said excitedly.

"I think so," replied Pen.

"Must be, comrade. Those blunderbusters—*trabookoos* don't they call them?—couldn't go off with a bang like that. All right; we are ready. But, I say, a soldier should always make his hay when the sun shines. Fill your pockets and haversack, comrade.—There they go again! I am glad. It's like the old days once more. It will be 'Forward!' directly—a skirmishing advance. Oh, bad luck, as old O'Grady says, to the spalpeen who stole my bugle! The game's begun."

Chapter Thirty Three
At Bay

The King's party remained perfectly still during the first few shots, and then, unable to contain themselves, they seemed to the lads to be preparing for immediate action. The tall, stern-looking Spaniard who had seemed to be their leader the previous night, and who had given the orders which resulted in the boys being dragged down into the priest's room, now with a due show of deference approached the King, who remained seated, and seemed to be begging his Sovereign to go in the direction he pointed, where a dark passage evidently led onward right into the inner portions of the cavern or deserted mine.

The conversation, which was carried on in Spanish, would not have been comprehended by the two lads even if they had understood that tongue; but in spite of the Spaniard going even so far as to follow up his request and persuasion by catching at the King's arm and trying to draw him in the direction he indicated, that refugee shook his head violently, wrested his wrist away, drew his sword, placed himself in front of his followers, and signed to them to advance towards the entrance.

"Well done!" whispered Punch. "He is something like a king after all. He means fighting, he does!"

"Hush," whispered back Pen, "or you will be heard."

"Not us," replied Punch, who began busying himself most unnecessarily with his musket, placing the butt between his feet, pulling out the ramrod and running it down the barrel to tap the end of the cartridge as if to make sure that it was well driven home.

Satisfied with this, he drew the iron rod again, thrust it into the loops, threw the piece muzzle forward, opened the pan to see that it was full of powder, shut it down again, and made a careful examination of the flint. For these were the days long prior to the birth of the copper percussion-cap, and plenty of preliminaries had to be gone through before the musket could be fired.

Satisfied now that everything possible had been done, he whispered a suggestion to his companion that he too should make an examination.

"I did," replied Pen, "a few minutes ago."

"But hadn't you better look again?" whispered Punch.

"No, no," cried his companion impatiently. "Look at them; they are all advancing to the entrance, and we oughtn't to be left behind."

"We ain't a-going to be," said the boy through his set teeth. "Come on."

"No," replied Pen.

"Come on, I say," cried the boy again. "We have only got muskets, but we are riflemen all the same, and our dooty is to go right in front skirmishing to clear the way."

"Our orders were," said Pen, "to wait here till our captain fetched us to the front and did what he told us."

"But he ain't come," protested Punch.

"Not yet," replied Pen. "Do you want him to come and find that we have broken faith with him and are not here?"

"Course I don't," cried the boy, speaking now excitedly. "But suppose he ain't coming? How do we know that he aren't got a bullet in him and has gone down? He can't come then." Pen was silent.

"And look here," continued Punch; "when he gave us those orders he told that other lot—the Spaniel reserve, you may call them—to stop yonder till he come. Well, that's the King, ain't it? He's ordered an advance, and he's leading it hisself. Where's his cloud of riflemen feeling the way for him? Are we to stop in the rear? I thought you did know better than that, comrade. I do. This comes of you only being a year in the regiment and me going on learning for years and years. I say our place is in the front; so come on."

"Yes, Punch; you must be right," said Pen unwillingly, "Forwards then. Double!"

"That's your sort!" And falling into step and carrying their muskets at the trail, the two lads ran forward, their steps drowned for the moment by the heavy firing going on away beyond the entrance; and they were nearly close up to the little Spanish party before their advance was observed, and then one of the Spaniards shouted a command which resulted in his fellows of the King's bodyguard of friends turning suddenly upon them to form a *chevaux-de-frise* of sword-blades for the protection of their Sovereign.

For the moment, in the excitement, the two lads' lives were in peril; but Pen did not flinch, and, though suffering acute pain from his wound, ran on, his left arm almost brushing the little hedge of sword-points, and only slackening his speed when he was a dozen yards in front and came right upon the smuggler-leader, pistol in one hand, long Spanish knife in the other.

Instead of angrily denouncing them for their disobedience to his order, he signed to them to stop, and ran on to meet the King's party, holding up his hand; and then, taking the lead, he turned off a little way to his left toward a huge pile of stones and mine-refuse, where he placed them, as it were, behind a bank which would act as a defence if a rush upon them were made from the front.

The two lads watched him, panting the while with excitement, listening as they watched to the fierce burst of firing that was now being sustained.

The King gave way at once to the smuggler's orders, planting himself with his followers ready for an anticipated assault; and, apparently satisfied, the smuggler waved the hand that grasped his knife and ran forward again with the two young Englishmen.

This time it was the pistol that he waved to them as if bidding them follow, and he ran on some forty or fifty yards to where the entrance widened out and another heap of mine-rubbish offered itself upon the other side as a rough earthwork for defence, and where the two lads could find a temporary parapet which commanded the entry for nearly a hundred yards.

Here he bade the two lads kneel where, perfectly safe themselves, they could do something to protect their Spanish friends behind on their left.

"Do your best," he said hoarsely. "They are driving my men back fast; but if you can keep up a steady fire, little as it will be, it will act as a surprise and maybe check their advance. But take care and mind not to injure any of my men."

He said no more, but ran forward again along the still unoccupied way, till a curve of the great rift hid him from their sight.

"What did he say?" whispered Punch excitedly, as Pen now looked round and diagonally across the way to the great chamber, and could see the other rough stonework, above which appeared a little line of swords.

"Said we were to be careful not to hurt him and his friends if they were beaten back."

"No fear," said Punch; "we can tell them by their red handkerchiefs round their heads and their little footy guns. We've got nothing to do, then, yet."

"For a while, Punch; but they are coming on fast. Hark at them!" For the firing grew louder and louder, and was evidently coming nearer.

"And only two of us as a covering-party!" muttered Punch. "Oh, don't I wish all our chaps were here!"

"Or half of them," said Pen.

"Yes, or half of them, comrade. Why, I'd say thank ye if it was only old O'Grady, me boy. He can load and fire faster than any chap in our company. Here, look at that!" For the sunlight shone plainly upon the red silk handkerchief of a Spaniard who suddenly ran into sight, stopped short, and turned to discharge his carbine as if at some invisible pursuers, and then dropped his piece, threw up his hands, and fell heavily across the way, which was now tenanted by a Spanish defender of the King.

"Only wounded perhaps," panted Punch; and Pen watched the fallen man hopefully in the expectation of seeing him make an effort to crawl out of the line of fire; but the two lads now became fully conscious of the fact that bullets were pattering faster and faster right into the gully-like passage and striking the walls, some to bury themselves, others to flatten and fall down, bringing with them fragments of stone and dust.

The musketry of the attacking party and the replies of pistol and carbine blended now in a regular roll, but it was evident that the defenders were stubbornly holding their own; while the muskets that rested on the stones in front of the two lads remained silent, and Punch uttered an impatient ejaculation as he looked sharply round at Pen.

"Oh, do give us a chance," he cried. "Here, comrade, oughtn't we two to run to cover a little way in advance?"

"No," said Pen excitedly. "Now then, look out! Here they come!"

As the words left his lips, first one and then another, and directly after three more, of the *contrabandistas* ran round the curve well into sight and divided, some to one side, some to the other, seeking the shelter of the rocky wall, and fired back apparently at their pursuing enemy before beginning to reload.

They were nearly a hundred yards from the two boys, who crouched, trembling with excitement, waiting impatiently to afford the little help they could by bringing their muskets to bear. Then, as the firing went on, there was another little rush of retiring men, half-a-dozen coming one by one into sight, to turn, seek the cover of the wall, and fire back as if in the hope of checking pursuit. But a couple of these went down, and it soon became evident from the firing that the advance was steadily continued.

Another ten minutes of wild excitement followed, and then there was a rush of the Spaniards, who continued their predecessors' tactics, firing back and sheltering themselves; but the enemy were still hidden from the two lads.

"Let's—oh, do let's cross over to the other side," cried Punch. "There's two places there where we could get shelter;" and he pointed to a couple of heaps of stone that diagonally were about forty yards in advance.

But as he spoke there was another rush of their friends round the curve, with the same tactics, while those who had come before now dashed across the great passage and occupied the two rough stoneworks themselves.

"Too late!" muttered Punch amidst the roar of musketry which now seemed to have increased in a vast degree, multiplied as the shots were by echoing repetitions as they crossed and recrossed from wall to wall.

"No!" shouted Pen. "Fire!" For half-a-dozen French chasseurs suddenly came running into sight in pursuit of the last little party of the Spaniards, dropped upon one knee, and, rapidly taking aim, fired at and brought down a couple more of the retreating men.

There was a sharp flash from Punch's piece, and a report from Pen's which sounded like an echo from the first, and two of the half-dozen chasseurs rolled over in the dust, while their comrades turned on the instant and ran back out of sight, followed by a tremendous yell of triumph from the Spaniards, who had now manned the two heaps of stones on the other side.

There was another yell, and another which seemed to fill the entry to the old mine with a hundred echoes, while as the boys were busily reloading a figure they did not recognise came running towards their coign of vantage at the top of his speed.

"Quick, Punch! An enemy! Bayonets!" cried Pen.

"Tain't," grumbled Punch. "Nearly ready. It's Contrabando."

The next minute the Spaniard was behind them, slapping each on the back.

"Bravo! Bravissimo!" he shouted, making his voice heard above the enemy's firing, for his men now were making no reply. "*Continuez! Continuez!*" he cried, and then dashed off forward again and, heedless of the flying bullets, crossed to where his men were lying down behind the two farther heaps of stones, evidently encouraging some of them to occupy better places ready for the enemy when they made their attack in force.

Chapter Thirty Four
Keeping the Bridge

Slight as was the check—two shots only—the sight of a couple of their men going down was sufficient to stop the advance of the attacking party for a few minutes; but the firing continued in the blind, unreasoning way of excited soldiery until the leaders had forced it upon the notice of their eager men that they were firing down a wide gully-like spot where, consequent on the curve, none of those they sought to shoot down were in sight.

But this state of excitement lasted only a few minutes, and then, headed by an officer, about a dozen of the enemy dashed into view.

"Now then," whispered Punch; but it was not necessary, for the two muskets the lads had laid ready went off almost as one, and a couple of the French chasseurs stumbled forward and fell headlong almost within touch of their dead or wounded comrades.

Once more that was enough to make the others turn tail and dash back, leaving their leader behind shaking his sword after them as they ran; and then, in contempt and rage, he stopped short and bent down over each of the poor fellows who had fallen.

Pen could see him lay his hand upon their breasts before coolly sheathing his sword and stopping in bravado to take out a cigarette, light it, and then, calmly smoking, turn his back upon his enemies and walk round the curve and disappear.

"There, Punch," said Pen, finishing the loading of his musket; "don't you tell me again that the French have no brave men amongst them."

"Well," said the boy slowly, "after that I won't. Do you know, it made me feel queer."

"It made me feel I don't know how," said Pen—"half-choking in the throat."

"Oh, it didn't make me feel like that," said Punch thoughtfully. "I had finished reloading before he had felt all his fellows to see if they were dead, and I could have brought him down as easy as kiss my hand, but somehow

I felt as if it would be a shame, like hitting a chap when he's down, and so I didn't fire. Then I looked at you, and I could see you hadn't opened your pan through looking at him. You don't think I ought to have fired, do you?"

"You know I don't, Punch," said Pen shortly. "It would have been cowardly to have fired at a man like that."

"But I say," said Punch, "wasn't it cheek! It was as good as telling us that he didn't care a button for us."

"I don't believe he does," said Pen thoughtfully; "but, I say, Punch, I shouldn't like to be one of his men."

"What, them two as we brought down? Of course not!"

"No, no; I mean those who ran away and left him in the lurch. He's just the sort of captain who would be ready to lay about him with the flat of his sword."

"And serve the cowardly beggars right," cried Punch. "Think they will come on again?"

"Come on again, with such a prize as the Spanish King to be made a prisoner? Yes, and before long too. There, be ready. There'll be another rush directly."

There was, and almost before the words were out of Pen's lips. This time, though, another officer, as far as the lads could make out, was leading the little detachment, which was about twice as strong as the last, and the lads fired once more, with the result that two of the attacking party went down; but instead of the rest turning tail in panic and rushing back, they followed their officer a dozen yards farther. Then they began to waver, checked their pace, and stood hesitating; while, in spite of their officer excitedly shouting and waving his sword to make them advance, they came to a stand, with the brave fellow some distance in front, where the lads could hear him shout and rage before making a dash back at the leading files, evidently with the intention of flogging them into following him.

But, damped by the fate of their fellows, it only wanted the appearance of flight, as they judged the officer's movement, to set them in motion, and they began to run back in panic, followed by the jeering yells of the *contrabandistas*, who hurried their pace by sending a scattered volley from their carbines, not a bullet from which took effect.

"Look at that, Punch; there's another brave fellow!"

"Yes," cried the boy, finishing loading. "There, go on, load away, I don't want you to shoot him. Yes, he's another plucky un. But, my word, look at him! He must be a-cussing and a-swearing like hooray. But I call that stupid. He needn't have done that. My word, ain't he in a jolly rage!"

Much to the surprise of Pen, the officer did not imitate his fellow who paused to light a cigarette, but took the point of his sword in his left hand, stooped down with his back to his enemies, broke the blade in half across his knee, dashed the pieces to the ground, and then slowly walked back.

"Poor fellow!" said Pen thoughtfully.

"Yes, and poor sword," said Punch. "I suppose he will have to pay for that out of his own pocket, or have it stopped out of his pay. Oh no; he's an officer, and finds his own swords. But he was a stupid. Won't he be sorry for it when he cools down!"

They were not long kept in suspense as to what would occur next, for just before he disappeared the lookers-on saw the officer suddenly turn aside to close up to the natural wail of the little ravine, giving place to the passage of the stronger party still who came on cheering and yelling as if to disconcert the sharpshooters who were committing such havoc in their little detachments. But their effort was in vain, for at a short interval the two young riflemen once more fired at the dense little party, which it was impossible to miss. Two men in the front went down, three or four of their fellows leaped over their prostrate forms, and then several of those who followed stumbled and fell, panic ensued, and once more the company was in full flight, followed slowly by a couple of despondent-looking officers, one of whom turned while the carbine bullets were flying around him to shake his sword at his enemies, his fellow taking his cue from this act to contemptuously raise his *képi* in a mocking salute.

"Here, I won't say anything about the Frenchmen any more," said Punch. "Why, those officers are splendid! They are just laughing at the contra-what-you-may-call-'ems, and telling them they can't shoot a bit. It's just what I thought," he continued, finishing his loading; "those little dumpy blunderbuss things are no good at all. I suppose that will about sicken them, won't it?"

Pen shook his head as he closed the pan of his musket with a sharp click.

"The officers will not be satisfied till they have put a stop to our shooting, Punch."

"Oh, but they can't," said the boy, with a laugh. "But, I say, I never thought I could shoot so well as this. Ain't it easy!"

"No," said Pen quietly. "I think we shot well at first, but here with our muskets resting steady on the stones in front, and with so many men to shoot at, we can't help hitting some of them. Hallo! Here comes our friend."

For now that the little gorge before them lay open the *contrabandista* joined them, to begin addressing his words of eulogy to Pen.

"Tell your comrade too," he continued, "how proud I am of the way in which you are holding the enemy in check. I have just come from the King, and he sends a message to you—a message, he says, to the two brave young Englishmen, and he wants to know how he can reward you for all that you have done."

"Oh, we don't want rewarding," said Pen quietly. "But tell me, is there any way by which the enemy can take us in the rear?"

"No," said the smuggler quietly. "But it would be bad for you—and us—if they could climb up to the top there and throw pieces of rock down. But they would want ladders to do that. I am afraid, though—no," he added; "there's nothing to be afraid of—that they will be coming on again, and you must keep up your firing till they are so sick of their losses that they will not be able to get any more of their men to advance."

"And what then?" said Pen.

"Why, then," said the smuggler, "we shall have to wait till it's dark and see if we can't steal by them and thread our way through the lower pass, leaving them to watch our empty *cache*."

Quite a quarter of an hour passed now, and it seemed as if the spirits of the French chasseurs were too much damped for their officers to get them to advance again.

Then there was another rush, with much the same result as before, and again another and another, and this was kept up at intervals for hours, till Pen grew faint and heart-sick, his comrade dull and stubborn; and both were faint too, for the sun had been beating down with torrid violence so that the heated rocks grew too hot to touch, and the burning thirst caused by the want of air made the ravine seem to swim before Pen's eyes.

But they kept on, and with terrible repetition the scenes of the morning followed, until, as the two lads reloaded, they rested the hot musket-barrels before them upon the heated rock and looked full in each other's eyes.

"Well, Punch," said Pen hoarsely, "what are you thinking?"

The boy was silent for a few moments, and then in the horrible stillness which was repeated between each attack he said slowly, "Just the same as you are, comrade."

"That your old wound throbs and burns just the same as mine does?"

"Oh, it does," said Punch, "and has for ever so long; but I wasn't thinking that."

"Then you were thinking, the same as I was, that you were glad that this horrible business was nearly over, and that these Spanish fellows, who have done nothing to help us, must now finish it themselves?"

"Well, not azackly," replied the boy. "What I was thinking was that it's all over now—as soon as we have had another shot apiece."

"Yes," said Pen; "one more shot apiece, and we have fired our last cartridges."

"But look here," said Punch, "couldn't we manage with powder and shot from their blunderbusters?"

"I don't know," said Pen wearily. "I only know this, that I shall be too heart-sick and tired out to try."

Chapter Thirty Five
For the King

As the evening drew near, it was to the two young riflemen as if Nature had joined hands with the enemy and had seemed to bid them stand back and rest while she took up their work and finished it to the bitter end.

"It's just as if Nature were fighting against us," said Pen.

"Nature! Who's she? What's she got to do with it?" grumbled Punch. "Phew! Just feel here! The sun's as low down as that, and here's my musket-barrel so hot you can hardly touch it. But I don't know what you mean."

"Well, it doesn't matter," said Pen bitterly. "I only meant that, now the enemy are not coming on, it's growing hotter and hotter, and one's so thirsty one feels ready to choke."

"Oh, I see now. It's just the same here. But why don't they come on. Must be half an hour since they made their last charge, and if they don't come soon my gun will go off all of itself, and then if they come I sha'n't have a shot for them. Think they will come now?"

"Yes," said Pen; "but I believe they are waiting till it's dark and we sha'n't be able to see to shoot."

"Why, the cowards!" cried Punch angrily. "The cowardly, mean beggars! Perhaps you are right; but, I say, comrade, they wouldn't stop till it's dark if they knew that we had only got one cartridge apiece, and that we were so stupid and giddy that I am sure I couldn't hit. Why, last time when they came on they seemed to me to be swimming round and round."

"Yes, it was horrible," said Pen thoughtfully, as he tried to recollect the varied incidents of the last charge, and gave up in despair. "I wish it was all over, Punch!"

"Well, don't be in such a hurry about that," said the boy. "I wish the fighting was over, but to wish it was *all* over sounds ugly. You see, they must be precious savage with us for shooting as we have, and if they charge home, as you call it, and find that we haven't got a shot, I want to know what we are going to do then."

"I don't feel as if it matters now," said Pen despondently.

"Oh, don't you! But I do, comrade. It's bad enough to be wounded and a prisoner; that's all in the regular work; but these Frenchies must be horribly wild now, and when we can't help ourselves it seems to me that we sha'n't be safe. You are tired, and your wound bothers you, and no wonder. It's that makes you talk so grumpy. But it seems to me as if it does matter. Course soldiers have to take their chance, even if they are only buglers, and I took mine, and got it. Now my wound's better, I don't feel like giving up. I feel as if I hadn't half had my innings. I haven't even got to be what you are—full private. But, I say, it ain't getting dark yet, is it?"

"No, Punch. But I feel so giddy I can hardly see."

"Look out, then!" cried the boy excitedly. "Here they come; and you are all wrong."

For the boy had caught sight of another rush being made, with the enemy scattered wildly; and catching up his musket, Punch fired, while it was as if mechanically and hardly knowing what he was about that Pen raised his piece and followed his companion's example.

What ensued seemed to be part of a nightmare-like dream, during which Pen once more followed his comrade's example; and, grasping his musket by the heated barrel he clubbed it and struck out wildly for a few minutes before he felt that he was borne down, trampled upon, and then lay half-conscious of what was going on.

He was in no pain, but felt as if he were listening to something that was taking place at a distance. There were defiant shouts, there was the rushing of feet, there was firing. Orders were being given in French; but what it all meant he could not grasp, till all at once it seemed to him that it was very dark, and a hot, wet hand was laid upon his forehead.

Then a voice came—a familiar voice; but this too seemed to be from far away, and it did not seem natural that he should be feeling the touch upon his forehead while the voice came from a distance.

"I say, they haven't done for you, have they, comrade? Oh, do try to speak. Tell me where it hurts."

"Hurts! That you, Punch?"

"Course it is. Hooray! Where's your wound? Speak up, or I can't make it out in all this row. Where have you got it?"

"Got what?"

"Why, I told you. The wound."

"My wound?" said Pen dreamily. Why, you know—in my leg. But it's better now. So am I. But what does it all mean? Did something hit me on the head?

"I didn't half see; but you went down a horrid kelch, and must have hit your head against the rocks."

"Yes, yes, I am beginning to understand now. But where are we? What's going on? Fighting?"

"Fighting? I should just think there is! Can't you hear?"

"I can hear the shouting, but I don't quite understand yet."

"Never mind, then. I was afraid you were done for."

"Done for! What, killed?"

"Something of the kind," grumbled Punch; "but don't bother about it now."

"I must," said Pen, with what was passing around seeming to lighten up. "Here, tell me, are my arms fastened behind me?"

"Yes, and mine too. But I just wriggled one hand out so as to feel for you. We are prisoners, lad, and the Frenchies have chivied right back to where the King and his men have been making a bit of a stand. I can't tell you all azackly, but that's something like it, and I think they are fighting now—bad luck to them, as O'Grady would say!—right in yonder where we had our braxfas'. I say, it's better than I thought, comrade."

"In what way, Punch?"

"Why, I had made up my mind, though I didn't like to tell you, that they'd give us both the bay'net. But they haven't. Perhaps, though, they are keeping us to shoot through the head because they caught us along with the smugglers. That's what they always do with them."

"Well,"—began Pen drearily.

"No, 'tain't. 'Tain't well, nor anything like it."

The boy ceased speaking, for the fight that had been raging in the interior of the cavern seemed to be growing fiercer; in fact, it soon became plain to the listeners that the tide of warfare was setting in their direction; the French, who had been driving the *contrabandista's* followers backward into the cavern, and apparently carrying all before them, had met with a sudden check. For a fairly brief space they had felt that the day was their own, and eager to make up for the long check they had suffered, principally through the keen firing of the two boys, they had pressed on recklessly, while the undrilled *contrabandistas*, losing heart in turn, were beginning, in spite of the daring of their leader, who seemed to be in every part of their front at once, to drop back into the cavern, giving way more and more, till at last they had shrunk some distance into the old mine, bearing back with them the royal party, who had struggled to restrain them in vain.

The part of the old workings to which they had retreated was almost in utter darkness, and just when the French were having their own way and the Spanish party were giving up in despair, their enemies came to a stand, the French officers hesitating to continue the pursuit, fearing a trap, or that they might be led into so dangerous a position that they might meet with another reverse.

They felt that where they were they thoroughly commanded the exit, and after a brief colloquy it was decided to give their men breathing-time while a party went back into the great cave, where the fire was still burning, and did what they could to contrive a supply of firebrands or torches before they made another advance.

Fortunately for the Spanish party, the cessation of the attack on the part of the French gave the former breathing-time as well; and, wearied out though he was, and rather badly wounded, the *contrabandista* hurriedly gathered his men together, and though ready to upbraid them bitterly for the way in which they had yielded to the French attack, he busied himself instead in trying to prepare them for a more stubborn resistance when the encounter was resumed.

He had the advantage of his enemies in this, that they were all thoroughly well acquainted with the ramifications of the old mine, and it would be in his power, he felt, to lead the enemy on by giving way strategically and guiding them where, while they were meeting with great difficulties in tracing their flying foes, these latter would be able to escape through one of the old adits and carry with them the King and his followers.

The *contrabandista*, too, had this further advantage—that he could easily refresh his exhausted men, who were now suffering cruelly from hunger and thirst. To this end he gave his orders quickly to several, who hurried away, to return at the end of a short time bearing a couple of skins of wine and bread from their regular store. These refreshments were hurriedly distributed, the King and his party not being forgotten; and after all partook most hastily, the men's leader busied himself in seeing to the worst of the wounded, sending several of these latter into hiding in a long vault where the mules of the party were stabled ready to resume their loads when the next raid was made across the passes.

"Now, my lads," he said, addressing his men, "I am not going to upbraid you with the want of courage you have shown, only to tell you that when the French come on again it will most likely be with lights. Those are what I believe they are waiting for. The poor fools think that torches will enable them to see us and shoot us down, but they will be to our advantage. We shall be in the darkness; they will be in the light; and I am going to lead you in such an attack that I feel sure if you follow out my instructions we can make them flee. Once get them on the run, it will be your duty to scatter them and not let them stop. Yes," he added, turning sharply in the darkness to some one who had touched him on the shoulder; "who is it?"

"It is I," said the officer who had taken the lead in the King's flight, and to whom the whole of the monarch's followers looked for direction. "His Majesty wants to speak with you."

"I'll come," replied the *contrabandista*. "Do you know why he wants me?"

"Yes," replied the officer briefly.

"I suppose it is to find fault with me for our want of success."

"I believe that is the case," said the officer coldly.

"Ha!" ejaculated the *contrabandista*. "I have as good a right to blame his Majesty for the meagreness of the help his followers have afforded me."

"I have done my best," said the officer gravely, "and so have the rest. But this is no time for recriminations. I believe you, sir, are a faithful friend to his Majesty; and I believe you think the same of me."

"I do," replied the smuggler, "and his Majesty is not to blame for thinking hard of one who has brought him into such a position as this."

"Be brief, please," said the officer, "and be frank with me before you join the King. He feels with me that we are completely trapped, and but a short time back he went so far as to ask me whether the time had not come for us all to make a desperate charge upon the enemy, and die like men."

The smuggler uttered an ejaculation which the officer misconstrued.

"I meant for us, sir," he said bitterly, "for I suppose it is possible that you and your men are sufficiently at home in these noisome passages to find hiding-places, and finally escape."

The smuggler laughed scornfully.

"You speak, sir," he said, "as if you believe that my men would leave his Majesty to his fate."

"Their acts to-day have not inspired him with much confidence in them," said the officer coldly.

"Well, no," said the smuggler; "but you must consider that my men, who are perfect in their own pursuits and able enough to carry on a guerilla-like fight against the Civil Guards in the mountains, have for the first time in their lives been brought face to face with a body of well-drilled soldiers ten times their number, and armed with weapons far superior to ours."

"That is true," said the officer quietly; "but I expected to have seen them do more to-day, and, with this strong place to hold, not so ready to give up as they were."

"You take it, then," said the smuggler, "that we are beaten?"

"His Majesty has been the judge, and it is his opinion."

"His Majesty is a great and good king, then," said the smuggler, "but a bad judge. We are not beaten. We certainly have the worst of it, and my poor fellows have been a good deal disheartened, and matters would have gone far worse with us if it had not been for the clever marksmanship of those two boys."

"Ah!" exclaimed the officer, "I may as well come to that. His Majesty speaks bitterly in the extreme about what he calls the cowardice which resulted in those two poor lads being mastered and taken prisoners, perhaps slain, before his eyes."

"Indeed!" said the smuggler sharply. "But I did not see that his Majesty's followers did more to save them than my men."

"There, we had better cease this unfruitful conversation. But before I take you to his Majesty, who is waiting for us, tell me as man to man, perhaps face to face with death, what is really our position? You are beaten, and unable to do more to save the King?"

The smuggler was silent for a few moments, busily tightening a bandage round his arm.

"One moment, sir," he said. "Would you mind tying this?"

"A wound!" said the officer, starting.

"Yes, and it bleeds more freely than I could wish, for I want every drop of blood to spend in his Majesty's service."

The officer sheathed his sword quickly, bent forward, and, in spite of the darkness, carefully tightened the bandage.

"I beg your pardon, Señor el Contrabandista. I trust you more than ever," he said. "But we are beaten, are we not?"

"Thanks, señor.—Beaten? No! When my fellows have finished their bread and wine they will be more full of fight than ever. We smugglers have plenty of the fox in our nature, and we should not treasure up our rich contraband stores in a cave that has not two holes."

"Ha! You put life into me," cried the officer.

"I wish to," said the smuggler. "Tell his Majesty that in a short time he will see the Frenchmen coming on lighting their way with torches, and that he and his followers will show a good front; but do as we do—keep on retreating farther and farther through the black passages of this old copper-mine."

"But retreating?" said the officer.

"Yes; they will keep pressing us on, driving us back, as they think, till they can make a rush and capture us to a man—King, noble, and simple smuggler; and when at last they make their final rush they will capture nothing but the darkness, for we shall have doubled round by one of the side-passages and be making our way back into the passes to find liberty and life."

"But one moment," said a stern voice from the deeper darkness behind. "What of the entrance to this great cavern-mine? Do you think these French officers are such poor tacticians that they will leave the entrance unguarded by a body of troops?"

"One entrance, sire," said the smuggler deferentially.

"Your Majesty!" said the officer, "I did not know that you were within hearing."

"I had grown weary of waiting, Count," said the King. "I came on, and I have heard all that I wished. Señor Contrabandista, I, your King, ask your pardon. I ask it as a bitterly stricken, hunted man who has been driven by his misfortunes to see enemies on every hand, and who has grown accustomed to lead a weary life, halting ever between doubt and despair."

"Your Majesty trusts me then," said the smuggler, sinking upon one knee to seize the hand that was extended to him and pressing it to his lips.

"Ha!" ejaculated the monarch. "Your plans are those of a general; but there is one thing presses hard upon me. For hours I was watching the way in which those two boys held the enemy at bay, fighting in my poor cause like heroes; and again and again as I stood watching, my fingers tingled to grasp my sword and lead my few brave fellows to lend them aid. But it was ever the same: I was hemmed in by those who were ready to give their lives in my defence, and I was forced to yield to their assurances that such an advance would be not merely to throw their lives away and my own, but giving life to the usurper, death to Spain."

"They spoke the truth, sire," said the smuggler gravely.

"But tell me," cried the King with a piteous sigh, "can nothing be done? Your men, you say, will be refreshed. My friends here are as ready as I am. Before you commence the retreat, can we not, say, by a bold dash, drive them past where those two young Englishmen lie prisoners at the back of the little stonework they defended so bravely till the last cartridge was fired away? You do not answer," said the King.

"Your Majesty stung me to the heart," said the *contrabandista*, "in thinking that I played a coward's part in not rescuing those two lads."

"I hoped I had condoned all that," said the King quickly.

"You have, sire, and perhaps it is the weakness and vanity in my nature that makes me say in my defence, I and half-a-dozen of my men made as brave an effort as we could, twice over, when the French made their final rush, and each time my poor fellows helped me back with a bayonet-wound.—Ah! what I expected!" he exclaimed hastily, for there was a flickering light away in front, followed by another and another, and the sound of hurrying feet, accompanied by the clicking of gun and pistol lock as the *contrabandistas* gathered together, rested and refreshed, and ready for action once again.

Chapter Thirty Six
In the Rout

It is one thing—or two things—to make plans mentally or upon paper, and another thing to carry them out. A general lays down his plan of campaign, but a dozen hazards of the war may tend to baffle and spoil courses which seem as they are laid down sure ways leading to success.

The *contrabandista* chief had made his arrangements in a way that when he explained them made his hearers believe that nothing could be better. His reluctant silence respecting the position of the two lads had impressed the Spanish King with the belief that he considered the young riflemen's situation to be hopeless, and that he felt that he had done everything possible.

In fact, he doubted their being alive, and the possibility, even if they still breathed where they were struck down, of forcing his way through the strong force of French that occupied the mine, and reaching their side. Above all, he felt that he would not be justified in risking the lives of many men for the sake of two.

And now the flickering lights in the distance told that the French had somehow contrived the means for making their way through the darkness easier. They had evidently been busy breaking up case and keg, starting the brands thoroughly in the fire, and keeping them well alight by their bearers brandishing them to and fro as they advanced, with the full intent of driving the Spaniards into some cul-de-sac among the ancient workings of the mine, and there bayoneting them or forcing them to lay down their arms.

All this was in accordance with the orders given by the French officers, and the chasseurs advanced perfect in their parts and with a bold front. But the *contrabandista's* followers and those of the King were also as perfect in what they would do, and they knew exactly that they were to fire and bring down their adversaries as they had an opportunity given them by their exposure in the light, and after firing they were to lead the untouched on by an orderly retreat, thus tempting the enemy farther and farther into the winding intricacies of the old workings.

Those advancing and those in retreat began to carry out their orders with exactitude; the chasseurs cheered and advanced in about equal numbers, torch-bearers and musketeers with fixed bayonets, the former waving their burning brands, and all cheering loudly as in the distance they caught sight of those in retreat; but it was only to find as the rattle and echoing roll of carbine and pistol rang out and smoke began to rise, that they were forming excellent marks for those who fired, and before they had advanced, almost at a run, fifty yards, the mine-floor was becoming dotted with those who were wounded and fell.

The distance between the advancing and retreating lines remained about the same, but the pace began to slacken, the run soon became a walk, and a very short time afterwards a stand on the part of those who attacked, and the smoke of the pieces began to grow more dense as the firing increased.

Orders kept on ringing out as the French officers shouted "Forward!" but in vain, and the light that, as they ran, had flashed brilliantly, as they stood began to pale, and the well-drilled men who now saw a dense black curtain of smoke before them, riven here and there by flashes of light, began to hesitate, then to fall back, slowly at first, and before many paces to the rear had been taken they found the light begin to increase again and more men fell.

That pause had been the turning-point, for from a slow falling back the pace grew swifter, the waving and tossing lights burned more brightly, and those who fired sent ragged volley after volley in amongst the now clearly seen chasseurs; while the Spaniards, forgetful now of the commands they had received, kept on advancing, in fact, pursuers in their turn, firing more eagerly as each few steps took them clear of the cloud of smoke which they left behind.

It was a completely unexpected change of position. The French officers shouted their commands, and the *contrabandista* captain gave forth his, but in both cases it was in vain, for almost before he could realise the fact a panic had seized upon chasseur and torch-bearer alike, and soon all were in flight—a strangely weird medley of men whose way was lit up by the lights that were borne and blazed fiercely on their side, while their pace was hastened by the firing in their rear.

It was only a matter of some few minutes before the French officers found that all their attempts to check the rout were in vain.

The hurry of the flight increased till the darkness of the mine-passage was left behind and all raced onward through the great store-cavern and out into the narrow gully, now faint in the evening light, and on past the rough stone-piled defences, where the officers once more tried to check the headlong flight.

Here their orders began to have some effect, for there were dead and wounded lying in the way, and some from breathlessness, some from shame, now slackened their pace and stooped to form litters of their muskets, on which some poor wretch who was crying for help with extended hands was placed and carried onward.

And somehow, in the confusion of the flight, as the fallen wounded were snatched up in the semi-darkness from where they lay, the last burning brand having been tossed aside as useless by those who could now see their way, two of the wounded who lay with their arms secured behind them with straps were lifted and borne onward, for those who were now obeying their officers' orders were too hurried and confused, hastened as they were in their movements by the rattle and crash of firearms in their rear, to scrutinise who the wounded were. It was sufficient for them that they were not wearers of the rough *contrabandista's* garb; and so it was that the dark-green uniform of the bandaged wounded was enough, and the two young riflemen became prisoners and participators in the chasseurs' rout.

Chapter Thirty Seven
After "Wiggling"

"Where do you suppose we are, Punch?"

"Don't quite know," was the reply. "Chap can't think with his arms strapped behind him and his wrists aching sometimes as if they were sawn off and at other times being all pins and needles. Can you think?"

"Not very clearly; and it has been too dark to see much. But where should you say we are? Quite in a new part of the country?"

"No; I think we came nearly over the same ground as we were going after we left that good old chap's cottage; and if we waited till it was quite daylight, and we could start off, I think I could find my way back to where we left the old man."

"So do I," said Pen eagerly. "That must be the mountain that the *contrabandista* captain took us up in the darkness."

"Why, that's what I was thinking," said Punch; "and if we had gone on a little farther I think we should have got to the place where the Frenchies attacked us. Of course I ain't sure, because it was all in the darkness. But, I say, Mr Contrabando and his fellows have given up the pursuit. I haven't heard anything of them for hours now."

"No," said Pen; "we may be sure that they have given it up, else we shouldn't be halted here. I fancy, Punch—but, like you, I can't be sure—that the Frenchmen have been making for the place where they surprised us after being driven down the mountain pass."

"That's it," said Punch; "and our friends, after beating off the enemy, have gone back to their what-you-may-call-it quarters—mine, didn't they call it?"

"Yes."

"Well, then, that's what we have got to do—get away from here and go back and join Mr Contrabando again."

"Impossible, Punch, even if we were free."

"Not it! Why, I could do it in the dark if I could only get rid of these straps, now that the Frenchies are beaten."

"Not beaten, Punch; only driven back, and I feel pretty sure in thinking it out that they have come to a halt here in what I dare say is a good, strong place where they can defend themselves and wait for reinforcements before attacking again."

"Oh, they won't do that," said Punch roughly. "They had such a sickener last night."

"Well, I can't be sure," said Pen; "but as far as I can make out they have a lot of wounded men lying about here in this bit of a valley, and there are hundreds of them camped down about the fires. They wouldn't have lit those fires if it hadn't been a strong place."

"I suppose not," said Punch. "I never thought of that. Because they would have been afraid to show the smugglers where they were, and it sounded when they were talking as if there were hundreds and hundreds of them—regiments, I think. One couldn't see in the night, but while I was lying awake I thought there were thousands of them."

"Say hundreds, Punch. Well, I haven't spoken to you much lately, for I thought you were asleep."

"Asleep! Not me! That's what I thought about you; and I hoped you was, so that you could forget what a muddle we got into. Well, I don't know how you feel now, but what I want to do is to get away from here."

"Don't talk so loud," said Pen; "there are those fellows on sentry, and they keep on coming very near now and then."

"That don't matter," said Punch, "they can't understand what we talk about. What do you say to having a go at getting our arms loose?"

"They would find it out, and only bind us up again."

"Yes, if we stopped to let 'em see."

"Then you think we could get away, Punch?"

"To be sure I do; only we should have to crawl. And the sooner the better, for once it gets light the sentries will have a shot at us, and we have had enough of that. I say, though, didn't they pick us up because they thought we were wounded?"

"The men did; and then one of the officers saw our uniforms and that we were the two who had been taken prisoners when they made their rush."

"Oh, that was it, was it?" said Punch. "Well, what do you say? Hadn't we better make a start?"

"How?" said Pen. "I have been trying again and again to get my arms loose, and I am growing more helpless than ever."

Punch gave a low grunt, raised his head a little, and tried to look round and pierce the darkness, seeing very little though but the fact that they were surrounded by wounded men, for the most part asleep, though here and there was one who kept trying to move himself into an easier position, but only to utter a low moan and relapse into a state of semi-insensibility.

About a dozen paces away, though, he could just make out one of the sentries leaning upon his musket and with his back to them. Satisfied with his scrutiny, Punch shifted his position a little, drawing himself into a position where he could get his lips close to his companion's ear.

"Look here," he said, "can you bite?"

"Bite! Nonsense! Who could think of eating now?"

"Tchah!" whispered Punch, "who wants to eat? I have been wiggling myself about quietly ever since they set me down, and I have got my hands a bit loose. Now, I am just going to squirm myself a bit farther and turn over when I have got my hands about opposite your mouth, and I want you to set-to with your teeth and try hard to draw the tongue of the strap out of the buckle, for it's so loose now that I think you could do it."

"Ah! I'll try, Punch," whispered Pen.

"Then if you try," said the boy, "you'll do it. I know what you are."

"Don't talk, then," replied Pen excitedly, "but turn over at once. Why didn't you think of this before? We might have tried at once, and had a better chance, for it will be light before long."

"Didn't think of it. My arms hurt so that they made me stupid."

Giving himself a wrench, the boy managed to move forward a little, turned over, and then worked himself so that he placed his bandaged wrists close to his comrade's mouth, and then lay perfectly still, for the sentry turned suddenly as if he had heard the movement.

Apparently satisfied, though, that all was well, he changed his position again, and then, to the great satisfaction of the two prisoners, he shouldered his musket and began to pace up and down, coming and going, and halting at last at the far end of his beat.

Then, full of doubt but eager to make an effort, Pen set to work, felt for the buckle, and after several tries got hold of the strap in his teeth, tugging at it fiercely and with his heart sinking more and more at every effort, for he seemed to make no progress.

Twice over, after tremendous efforts that he half-fancied loosened his teeth, he gave up what seemed to be an impossibility; but he was roused upon each occasion by an impatient movement on the part of Punch.

With one final drag he jerked his head back.

"It's of no use," he thought. "I am only punishing myself more and more;" and, fixing his teeth firmly once more in the leather, he gave one shake and tug such as a wild beast might have done in worrying an enemy. With one final drag he jerked his head back and lay still with his jaws throbbing and the sensation upon him that he had injured himself so that several of his teeth had given way.

"It's no good. It's of no use, Punch," he said to himself; for the boy shook his wrists sharply as if to urge him to begin again. "I can't do it, and I won't try;" when to his astonishment he felt that his comrade was moving and had forced himself back with a low, dull, rustling sound so that he could place his lips to his ear again; and to Pen's surprise the boy whispered, "That last did it, and I got the strap quite loose. My! How my wrists do ache! Just wait a bit, and then I will pull you over on to your face and have a turn at yours."

Pen felt too much confused to believe that his companion had succeeded, but he lay perfectly still, with his teeth still aching violently, till all at once he felt Punch's hands busy about him, and he was jerked over upon his face.

Then he felt that the boy had raised himself up a little as if to take an observation of their surroundings before busying himself with the straps that bound his numbed wrists.

"Lie still," was whispered, "don't flinch; but I have got my knife out, and I am going to shove it under the strap. Don't holloa if it hurts."

Pen set his aching teeth hard, and the next minute he felt the point of the long Spanish clasp-knife which his comrade carried being thrust beneath one of the straps.

"He will cut me," thought Pen, for he knew that the pressure of the strap had made his flesh swell so that the leather was half-bedded in his arm; but setting his teeth harder—the pain he felt there was more intense—while, when the knife-blade was being forced under the strap he only suffered a dull sensation, and then grew conscious that as the knife was being thrust beneath the strap it steadily divided the bond, so that directly after there was a dull sound and the blade had forced its way so thoroughly that the severed portions fell apart; sensation was so much dulled in the numbed limbs that he was hardly conscious of what had been done, but he knew that one extremely tight ligature had ceased its duty, though he could hardly grasp the idea that one of his bonds was cut.

Then a peculiar throbbing sensation came on, so painful that it diverted the lad's attention from the continuation of Punch's task, and before he could thoroughly grasp it Pen found that the sharp blade had been thrust under another strap, dividing it so that the leather fell apart, and he was free.

But upon his making an effort to put this to the proof it seemed as if his arms were like two senseless pieces of wood; but only for a few minutes, till they began to prove themselves limbs which were bearers of the most intense agony.

Click! went Punch's closing knife-blade; and then he whispered, "That's done it! Now, when you are ready, lead off right between those sleeping chaps. Creep, you know, in case the sentry looks round."

"A minute first," whispered Pen; "my arms are like lead."

"So's mine. I say, don't they ache?"

Pen made no reply, but lay breathing hard for a time; and then, raising his head a little so as to make sure of the safest direction to take, he turned towards his comrade and whispered, "Now then: off!"

Chapter Thirty Eight
"Hear that?"

It was still dark, but there were faint suggestions of the coming day when Pen began to creep in the direction of a black patch which he felt must be forest.

This promised shelter; but he had first to thread his way amongst the wounded who lay sleeping around, and his difficulty was to avoid touching them, for they apparently lay thickest in the direction he had chosen.

Before he was aware of what he was doing he had laid his inert right hand upon an outstretched arm, which was drawn back with a sharp wince, and its owner uttered a groan. Bearing to the left and whispering to Punch to take care, Pen crept on, to find himself almost in contact with another sufferer, who said something incoherently; and then a whisper from Punch checked his companion.

"Come on," said Pen hastily, "or they will give the alarm."

"Not they, poor chaps! They are too bad. That sentry isn't coming, is he?"

Pen glanced in the man's direction, but he was not visible, for some low bushes intervened.

"I can't see him," said Pen.

"Then look here, comrade; now's our time. It's all fair in war. Every man for himself."

"What do you mean? Don't stop to talk, but come on."

"All right; but just this," came back in a whisper. "They can't help themselves, and won't take any notice whatever we do, unless they think we are going to kill them. Help yourself, comrade, the same as I do."

Pen hesitated for a moment. Then, as he saw Punch busily taking possession of musket and cartouche-belt, he followed his example.

"It's for life, perhaps," he thought.

He had no difficulty in furnishing himself with the required arms from a pile, and that too without any of the wounded seeming to pay the slightest attention.

"Ready?" whispered Punch. "Got a full box?"

"Yes," was the answer.

"Sling your musket then. Look sharp, for it's getting light fast."

Directly after the two lads were crawling onward painfully upon hands and knees, for every yard sent a pang through Pen's wrists, and he thoroughly appreciated his comrade's advice, for there were moments when he felt that had he been carrying the musket he would certainly have left it behind.

He did not breathe freely till he had entered the dark patch of woodland, where it was fairly open, and they had pressed on but a short distance in the direction of the mountain, which high up began to look lighter against the sky, when he started violently, for the clear notes of a bugle rang out from somewhere beyond the spot where the wounded lay, to be answered away to left and right over and over again, teaching plainly enough that it was the reveille, and also that they were in close proximity to a very large body of troops.

"Just in time, comrade," said Punch coolly, as he rose to his feet.

"Take care!" cried Pen. "It isn't safe to stand up yet."

"Think not? Oh, we shall be all right," replied the boy. "Lead on. Didn't you know? The reveille was going right behind and off to the left and right; so there's no troops in front, and all we have got to do is to get on as fast as we can up the mountain yonder. And it's no good; I must walk. My wristies are so bad that if I try to crawl any more on my hands they will drop off. Ain't yours bad?"

"Terribly," replied Pen.

"Come on, then; we must risk it. There, right incline. Can't you see? There's a bit of a track yonder."

"I didn't see it, Punch," said Pen, as they bore off to their right, where the way was more open, and they increased their pace now to a steady walk, a glance back showing them that they were apparently well screened by the low growth of trees which flourished in the bottom slopes of the mountains that they could now see more clearly rising in front.

"We've done it, comrade," said Punch cheerily, "and I call this a bit of luck."

"Don't talk so loudly."

"Oh, it don't matter," replied the boy. "They're making too much noise themselves to hear us. Hark at them! Listen to the buzz! Why, it's just as if there's thousands of them down there, just as you thought; and we've hit on the right way, for those Frenchies wouldn't come through here unless it was skirmishing with the enemy in front. Their enemy's all behind, and they'll be thinking about making their way back to the mine."

"To see if they can't make up for yesterday's reverses. I'm afraid, Punch, it's all over with the poor King and his followers."

"Yes," said Punch thoughtfully, as he trudged on as close as he could get to his companion. "It's a bad lookout for them, comrade; but somehow I seem to think more of Mr Contrabando. I liked him. Good luck to the poor chap! And when we get a bit farther on we will pitch upon a snug spot where there's water, and make a bit of breakfast."

"Breakfast! How?" said Pen, smiling; but, wearied out and faint with his sufferings, it was a very poor exhibition of mirth—a sort of smile and water, like that of a sun-gleam upon a drizzly day. "Breakfast!" he said, half-scornfully, "You are always thinking of eating, Punch."

"That I ain't, only at bugle-time, when one blows 'soup and tater' for breakfast or dinner. I say, do you know what the cavalry chaps say the trumpet call is for stables?"

"No," said Pen quietly; and then to humour his companion he tried to smile again, as the boy said, "Oh, I know lots of them! This is what the trumpet says for the morning call:—

"Ye lads that are able
Now come to the stable,
And give all your horses some water and hay–y–y–y!"

And the boy put his half-crippled fist to his lips and softly rang out the cavalry call.

"Punch!" whispered Pen angrily, "how can you be such a fool?"

"Tchah! Nobody can hear us. I wanted to cheer you up a bit. Well, it has stirred you up. There: all right, comrade. For'ard! We are safe enough here. But, I say, what made you jump upon me and tell me I was always thinking about eating when I said breakfast?"

"Because this is no time to think of eating and drinking."

"Oh my! Ain't it?" chuckled the boy. "Why, when you are on the march in the enemy's country you ought to be always on the forage, and it's the time to think of breakfast whenever you get the chance."

"Of course," said Pen.

"Well, ain't we got the chance? We was too busy to think of eating all yesterday, and while we were lying tied up there like a couple of calves in a farmer's cart."

"Well, are we much better off now, Punch?"

"Much better—much better off! I should think we are! It was talking about poor Mr Contrabando that made me think of it. Poor chap! I hope he will be able to repulse, as you call it, the Frenchies at the next attack. He is well provisioned; that's one comfort. And didn't he provision us? My haversack's all right with what I helped myself to at breakfast yesterday. Ain't yours?"

Pen clapped his hand to his side. "No," he said. "The band was torn off, and it's gone."

"What a pity! Never mind, comrade. Mine's all right, and regular bulgy; and, as they say, what's enough for one is enough for two; so that will be all right. I say, ain't it getting against the collar?"

"Yes, we are on the mountain-slope, Punch."

"Think we are not getting up the same mountain where the old mine is?"

"No, Punch. That must be off more to the right, I think."

"Yes, I suppose so. But of course we ain't sure; and I suppose we are not going anywhere near the old *padre's* place?"

"No, Punch; that lies farther away still to the right."

"Yes. But, I say, how you seem to get it into your head where all the places lie! I can't. It seems to me as if you could make a map."

"No, no. But I suppose if I wandered about here for long enough I should be able to make out some of the roads and tracks."

"Then I suppose you haven't been here long enough," said the boy banteringly. "If you had, you would be able to tell where the British army is, and lead right on to it at once."

"That would be rather a hard job, Punch, when troops are perhaps changing their quarters every day."

"I say, hear that?" said the boy excitedly, as a distant call rang out.

"Yes, plain enough to hear," replied Pen.

"Then we ought to turn back, oughtn't we?"

"No. Why?"

"Some of the Frenchies in front. That was just before us, half a mile away."

Pen shook his head, and the boy looked at him wonderingly.

"There! There it is again! Let's get into hiding somewhere, or we shall be running right into them."

For another clear bugle-note rang out as if in answer to the first.

"That's nothing to mind, Punch," said Pen. "These notes came from behind, and were echoed from the mountain in front."

"Why, of course! But I can't help it. Father always said that I had got the thickest head he ever see. I got thinking that we were going to run right into some French regiment. Then it's all right, and we shall be able to divide our rations somewhere up yonder where the echoes are playing that game. I say, what a mistake might be made if some officer took an echo like that for the real thing!"

"Yes," said Pen thoughtfully; and the two lads stopped and listened to different repetitions of the calls, which seemed fainter and fainter as the time went on; and the sun was well up, brightening as lovely a landscape of mountain, glen, and green slope as ever met human eye.

But it was blurred to Pen by the desolation and wildness of a country that was being ravaged by invasion and its train of the horrors of war.

As the lads tramped on, seeing no sign of human habitation, not even a goat-herd's hut on the mountain-slopes, the sun grew hotter and the way more weary, till all at once Punch pointed to a few goats just visible where the country was growing more rugged and wild.

"See that, comrade?" he cried.

"Yes, goats," said Pen wearily; and he stopped short, to throw himself down upon a heathery patch, and removed his cap to wipe his perspiring forehead.

"No, no; don't sit down. Don't stop yet," cried Punch. "I didn't mean those old goats. Look away to the left in that hollow. Can't you see it sparkling?" And the boy pointed to the place where a little rivulet was trickling down the mountain-side to form a fall, the water making a bright leap into a fair-sized pool. "Let's get up yonder first and sit down and see what I have got in my haversack. Then a good drink of water, and we shall be able to go on, and perhaps find where our fellows are before night."

"Yes, Punch—or march right into the lines of the French," said Pen bitterly.

"Oh, well, we must take our chance of that, comrade. One's as likely as the other. There's the French troops about, and there's our English lads—the lads in red as well as the boys in green. No, it's no use to be down in the mouth. We are just as likely to find one as the other. I wonder how they are getting on up there in the old mine. Shall we be near enough to hear if there's any fighting going on?"

"Perhaps," said Pen, springing up. "But let's make for that water."

But it was farther off than it had at first appeared, and it was nearly half an hour after they had startled the browsing goats when the two weary lads threw themselves down with a sigh of content beside the mountain pool, which supplied them with delicious draughts of clear cold water as an accompaniment to the contents of the haversack which Punch's foresight had provided.

"Ah!" sighed the boy. "'Lishus, wasn't it?"

"Yes, delicious," said Pen.

"Only one thing agin it," said Punch.

"One thing against it," said Pen, looking up, "Why, it could not have been better."

"Yes," said the boy sadly. "It waren't half enough."

"Hark! Listen!" said Pen, holding up his hand.

"Guns firing!" exclaimed Punch in a whisper. "Think that's in the little valley that leads up to the old mine?"

"It's impossible to say," replied Pen. "It's firing, sure enough, and a long way off; but I can't tell whether it's being replied to or whether we are only listening to the echoes."

"Anyhow," said Punch, "it's marching orders, and I suppose we ought to get farther away."

"Yes," replied Pen with a sigh. "But how do you feel? Ready to go on now?"

"No, not a bit. I feel as if I want to take off my coat and bathe my arms in the water here, for they ache like hooray."

"Do it, then," said Pen wearily, "and I must do the same to my wound as well; and then, Punch, there's only one thing I can do more."

"What's that, comrade?"

"Get in the shade under that grey-looking old olive, and have a few hours' sleep."

"Splendour!" said Punch, taking off his coat. "Hark at the firing!"

"Yes," said Pen wearily, as he followed his comrade's example. "They may fire, but I am so done up that they can't keep me awake."

The water proved to be a delicious balm for the bruised limbs and the wound—a balm so restful and calming to the nerves that somehow the sun had long set, and the evening star was shining brilliantly in the soft grey evening sky when the two sleepers, who had lain utterly unconscious for hours, started awake together, wondering what it all meant, and then prepared themselves to face the darkness of the coming night, not knowing what fate might bring; but Pen felt a strange chill run through his breast with a shiver as Punch exclaimed in a low, warning whisper, "I say, comrade, hear that? Wolves?"

Chapter Thirty Nine
Strung-Up

"Or dogs," said Pen angrily. "What a fellow you are, Punch! Don't you think we had enough to make us low-spirited and miserable without you imagining that the first howl you hear comes from one of those horrible brutes?"

"It's all very well," said Punch with a shudder. "I have heard dogs enough in my time. Why, I used to be once close to the kennel where they kept the foxhounds, and they used to set-to and sing sometimes all at once. Then I have heard shut-up dogs howl all night, and other sorts begin to howl when it was moonlight; but I never heard a dog make a noise like that. I am sure it's wolves."

"Well, perhaps you are right, Punch; but I suppose they never attack people except in the winter-time when they are starving and the ground's covered with snow; and this is summer, and they have no reason for coming down from the mountains."

"Oh, I say," exclaimed the boy, "haven't they just!"

"Will you hold your tongue, Punch!" cried Pen angrily. "This is a nice way to prepare ourselves for a tramp over the mountains, isn't it?"

"Are we going to tramp over the mountains in the night?" said the boy rather dolefully.

"Yes, and be glad of the opportunity to get farther away from the French before morning."

"But won't it be very bad for your leg, comrade?"

"No worse than it will be for your back, Punch."

"But wouldn't it be better if we had a good rest to-night?"

"Where?" said Pen bluntly.

"In some goat-keeper's cottage. We saw goats before we came here, and there must be people who keep them."

"Perhaps so," said Pen; "but I have seen no cottages."

"We ain't looked," said Punch.

"No, and I don't think it would be very wise to look for them in the dark. Come, Punch, don't be a coward."

"I ain't one; but I can't stand going tramping about in these mountains with those horrid beasts hunting you, smelling you out and following you wherever you go."

"I don't believe they would dare to come near us if we shouted at them," said Pen firmly; "and we needn't be satisfied with that, for if they came near and we fired at them they would never come near us again."

"Yes, we have got the guns," said the boy; and he unslung the one he carried and began to try the charge with the ramrod. "Hadn't you better see if yours is all right too?" he said.

"Perhaps I had," was the reply, "for we might have to use them for business that had nothing to do with wolves."

As he spoke, Pen followed his comrade's example, driving the cartridge and bullet well home, and then feeling whether the powder was up in the pan.

"Oh, I say," cried the boy huskily, "there they go again! They're coming down from high up the mountains. Hadn't we better go lower down and try and find some cottage?"

"I don't think so," said Pen sturdily.

"But we might find one, you know—an empty one, just the same as we did before, when my back was so bad. Then we could shut ourselves in and laugh at the wolves if they came."

"We don't want to laugh at the wolves," said Pen jocularly. "And it might make them savage. I know I used to have a dog and I could always put him in a rage by laughing at him and calling him names."

"And now you are laughing at me. I can't help it. I am ashamed perhaps; but, knowing what I do about the wolves, and what our chaps have seen— Ugh! It's horrid! There they go again. Let's get lower down."

"To where the French are lying in camp, so that they may get hold of us again? Nonsense, Punch! What was the good of our slipping away if it was only to give ourselves up?"

"But we didn't know then that we should run up against these wolves."

"We are not going to run up against them, Punch, but they are going to run away from us if we behave like men."

"But, don't you see, I can't behave like a man when I'm only a boy? Oh, there they go again!" half-whispered the poor fellow, who seemed thoroughly unnerved. "Come along, there's a good chap."

"No," said Pen firmly. "You can't behave like a man, but you can behave like a brave boy, and that's what you are going to do. If we ever get back to our company you wouldn't like me to tell the lads that you were so frightened by the howling of the wolves that you let me go on alone to face them, and—"

"Here, I say," cried Punch excitedly, "you don't mean to say that you would go on alone!"

"I mean to say I would," said Pen firmly; "but I shall not have to, because you are coming on along with me."

"No, I ain't," said the boy stubbornly.

"Yes, you are."

"You don't know," continued the boy, through his set teeth. "Hanged if I do—so there!"

Pen laughed bitterly.

"Well, you are a queer fellow, Punch," he said. "You stood by me yesterday and faced dozens of those French chasseurs, and fought till we had fired off our last cartridge, and then set-to to keep them off with the butt of your musket, though you were quite sure they would come on again and again."

"Perhaps I did," said the boy huskily, "because I felt I ought to as a soldier, and it was dooty; but 'tain't a soldier's dooty to get torn to pieces by wolves. Ugh! It's horrid, and I can't bear it."

"Come on, Punch. I am going."

"No, don't! I say, pray don't, comrade!" cried the boy passionately; and he caught at Pen's arm and clung to it with all his might. "I tell you I'd shoulder arms, keep touch with you, and keep step and march straight up to a regiment of the French, with the bullets flying all about our ears. I wouldn't show the white once till I dropped. You know I'd be game if it was obeying orders, and all our fellows coming on behind. I tell you I would, as true as true!"

"What!" said Pen, turning upon him firmly, "you would do that if you were ordered?"

"That I would, and I wouldn't flinch a bit. You know I never did," cried the boy passionately. "Didn't I always double beside my company-leader, and give the calls whenever I was told?"

"Yes; and now I am going to be your company-leader to-night. Now then, my lad, forward!"

Pen jerked his arm free and stepped off at once, while his comrade staggered with the violence of the thrust he had received. Then, recovering himself, he stood fast, struggling with the stubborn rage that filled his young breast, till Pen was a dozen paces in front, marching sturdily on in the direction of the howls that they had heard, and without once looking back.

Then from out of the silence came the boy's voice.

"You'll be sorry for this," he shouted.

Pen made no reply.

"Oh, it's too bad of him," muttered Punch. "I say," he shouted, "you will be sorry for this, comrade. D'ye 'ear?"

Tramp, tramp, tramp went Pen's feet over the stony ground.

"Oh, I say, comrade, this is too bad!" whimpered the boy; and then, giving his musket one or two angry slaps as if in an exaggerated salute, he shouldered the piece and marched steadily after his leader.

Pen halted till the boy closed up, and then started again.

"There, Punch," he said quietly, "I knew you better than you know yourself."

The boy made no reply, but marched forward with his teeth set; and evidently now thoroughly strung-up to meet anything that was in store, he stared straight before him into the darkness and paid no heed to the distant howls that floated to them upon the night-air from time to time.

Chapter Forty
Friends or Foes?

"This is rather hard work, Punch, lad," said Pen, after a long silence; but the boy took no notice. "The ground's so rugged that I've nearly gone down half-a-dozen times. Well, haven't you anything to say?"

The boy kept his teeth firmly pressed together and marched on in silence; and the night tramp went on for quite a couple of hours, till, growing wearied out by the boy's determination, Pen began again to try and break the icy reserve between them.

"What a country this is!" he said. "To think of our going on hour after hour never once seeing a sign of any one's dwelling-place. Ah, look at that!" he exclaimed excitedly. "Do you see that light?"

"Yes," said Punch sulkily, "a wolf's eye staring at us."

"Then he's got one shut," said Pen, laughing softly. "I can only see one. Why, you are thinking of nothing else but wolves. It's a little watch-fire far away."

Punch lowered his piece quickly and cocked it.

"Look out, comrade," he said, "some one will challenge directly. Drop down together, don't us, if he does?"

"I don't think they will be sentries right up here," said Pen.

"What then?"

"Shepherds," replied Pen abruptly.

He was about to add, "to keep off the wolves," but he checked himself in time, as he half-laughed and thought that it would scare his companion again.

Punch remained silent and marched on, keeping step, till they were getting very close to a tiny scrap of a smouldering fire; and then there was a rush of feet as if about a couple of dozen goats had been startled, to spring up and scatter away, with their horny hoofs pattering amongst the stones; and at the same moment the two lads became aware of the fact that after their habit the sturdy little animals had been sleeping around a couple of fierce-looking, goatskin-clothed, half-savage Spanish goat-herds, one of whom kicked at the fire, making it burst into a temporary blaze which lit up their swarthy features and flashed in their eyes, and, what was more startling still, on the blades of the two long knives which they snatched from their belts.

"*Amigos, amigos!*" cried Pen, and he grounded arms, Punch following his example.

"*Amigos! No, Francéses,*" shouted one of the men, as the fire burnt up more brightly; and he pointed at Pen's musket.

"*No,*" cried Pen, "*Ingléses.*" And laying down his piece near the fire, he coolly seated himself and began to warm his hands. "Come on, Punch," he said, "sit down; and give me your haversack."

The boy obeyed, and as the two men looked at them doubtingly Pen took the haversack, held it out, thrust his hand within two or three times, and shook his head before pointing to his lips and making signs as if he wanted to eat.

"*El pano, agua,*" he said.

The men turned to gaze into each other's eyes as if in doubt, and then began slowly to thrust their long, sharp knives into their belts; and it proved directly afterwards that Pen's pantomime had been sufficiently good, for one of them strode away into the darkness, where the lads could make out a sort of wind-shade of piled-up stones, from which he returned directly afterwards with what proved to be a goatskin-bag, which he carried to his companion, and then went off again, to return from somewhere behind the stones, carrying a peculiar-looking earthen jar, which proved to be filled with water.

Just then Punch drew the two muskets a little farther from the fire, and to Pen's surprise took off his jacket and carefully covered their locks.

"Afraid of the damp," muttered Pen to himself; and then he smiled up in the face of the fiercer-looking of the two goat-herds as the man placed a cake of coarse-looking bread in his hands and afterwards turned out from the bag a couple of large onions, to which he added a small bullock's horn whose opening was stopped with a ball of goatskin.

"*Bueno, bueno!*" said Pen, taking the food which was offered to him with the grave courtesy of a gentleman; and, not to be outdone, he took the hand that gave and lightly raised it to his lips. The act of courtesy seemed to melt all chilling reserve, and the two men hurried to throw some heather-like twigs upon the fire, which began to burn up brightly, emitting a pleasant aromatic smoke. Then, seating themselves, the more fierce-looking of the pair pointed to the bread and held up the jar so that they could drink.

"*Amigos, amigos!*" he said softly; and he took the jar in turn, drank to the lads, and gravely set it down between them; and then as Pen broke bread Punch started violently, for each of the men drew out his knife, and the boy's hand was stretched out towards the muskets, but withdrawn directly as he realised the meaning of the unsheathed knives, each of the goat-herds snatching up one of the onions and beginning to peel it for the guests, before hastening to stick the point of his knife into the vegetable and hand both to their visitors.

"They scared me," said Punch. "I say, don't the onions smell good! Want a bit of salt, though."

He had hardly said the word before the taller of the two men caught up the horn, drew out the ball-like wad which closed it up, and revealed within a reddish-looking powder which glistened in the light of the fire and proved to be rock-salt.

It was a very rough and humble meal, but Punch expressed his companion's feelings when he said it was 'lishus.

"Worth coming for—eh, Punch?" said Pen, "and risking the wolves."

"Here, I say, drop that, comrade. Don't be hard on a fellow. One can't help having one's feelings. But I say, you looked half-scared too when these two Spaniards whipped out their knives."

"I was more than half, Punch. But it was the same with them; they looked startled enough when we came upon them suddenly with our muskets and woke them out of sleep."

"Yes; they thought we was Frenchies till you showed them we was friends."

It was a rough but savoury meal, and wonderfully picturesque too, for the fire burned up briskly, shedding a bright light upon their hosts in their rough goatskin clothes, as they sat looking on as if pleased and amused at Punch's voracity, while now the herd of goats that had scampered away into the darkness recovered from their panic and came slowly back one by one, to form a circle round the fire, where they stood, long-horned, shaggy, and full-bearded, looking in the half-light like so many satyrs of the classic times, blinking their eyes and watching the little feast as if awaiting their time to be invited to join in.

"I say," said Pen suddenly, "that was very thoughtful and right of you, Punch, to cover over the muskets; but you had better put your jacket on again. These puffs of air that come down from the mountains blow very cold; when the fire flames up it seems to burn one cheek, while the wind blows on the other and feels quite icy. There's no chance of any damp making the locks rusty. Put on your jacket, lad; put on your jacket."

"That I don't," said the boy, in a half-whisper. "Who thought anything about dew or damp?"

"Why, you did."

"Not likely, with the guns so close to the fire. Did you think I meant that?"

"Why, of course."

"Nonsense! I didn't want these Spaniels to take notice of them."

"I don't understand you, Punch."

"Why, didn't you tell them we was English?"

"Of course."

"And at the same time," said Punch, "put a couple of French muskets down before them, and us with French belts and cartridge-boxes on us all the time?"

"Oh, they wouldn't have noticed that."

"I don't know," said Punch. "These are rough-looking chaps, but they are not fools; and the French have knocked them about so that they hate them and feel ready to give them the knife at the slightest chance."

"Well, there's no harm in being particular, Punch; but I don't think they will doubt us."

"Well, I don't doubt them," said Punch. "What a jolly supper! I feel just like a new man. But won't it be a pity to leave here and go on the march again? You know, I can't help it, comrade; I shall begin thinking about the wolves again as soon as we start off into the darkness. Hadn't we better lie down here and go to sleep till daylight?"

"I don't know," said Pen thoughtfully. "These men have been very friendly to us, but we are quite strangers, and if they doubt our being what we said ours would be a very awkward position if we went off to sleep. Could you go off to sleep and trust them?"

"Deal sooner trust them than the wolves, comrade," said Punch, yawning violently, an act which was so infectious that it made his companion yawn too.

"How tiresome!" he exclaimed, "You make me sleepy, and if we don't jump up and start at once we shall never get off."

"Well then, don't," said Punch appealingly. "Let's risk it, comrade. These two wouldn't be such brutes as to use their knives on us when we were asleep. Look here! What do they mean now?"

For the two goat-herds came and patted them on the shoulders and signed to them to get up and follow.

"Why, they want us to go along with them, comrade," said the boy, picking up the two muskets.

"Here, ketch hold, in case they mean mischief. Why, they don't want to take us into the dark so that the goats shouldn't see the murder, do they?"

"I am going to do what you suggested, Punch," replied Pen, "risk it," and he followed their two hosts to the rough-looking stone shelter which kept off the wind and reflected the warmth of the fire.

Here they drew out a couple of tightly rolled-up skin-rugs, and made signs that the lads should take them. No words were spoken, the men's intention was plainly enough expressed; and a very short time afterwards each lad was lying down in the angle of the rough wall, snugly rolled in his skin-rug, with a French musket for companion; and to both it seemed as if only a few minutes had elapsed before they were gazing across a beautiful valley where mists were rising, wreath after wreath of half-transparent vapour, shot with many colours by the rays of the rising sun.

Chapter Forty One
Boots or Booty?

"There, Punch," said Pen, rising; "you didn't dream, did you, that our friends crept up with their knives in the night to make an end of you?"

"No," cried the boy excitedly, as he turned to gaze after the men, who were some little distance away amongst the goats, "I didn't dream it. It was real. First one of them and then the other did come with his knife in his hand; but I cocked my musket, and they sneaked off again and pretended that they wanted to see to the fire."

"And what then?" said Pen.

"Well, there wasn't no what then," replied the boy, "and I must have gone to sleep."

"That was all a dream, I believe, Punch; and I suppose you had another dream or two about the wolves?"

"Yes, that was a dream. Yes, it must have been. No, it was more a bit of fancy, for I half-woke up and saw the fire shining on a whole drove of the savage beasts; but I soon made out that they weren't wolves, because wolves don't have horns. So it was the goats. I say, look here. Those two chaps have been milking. They don't mean it for us, do they?"

The coming of the two goat-herds soon proved that they were hospitably bent, and the lads agreed between themselves that there were far worse breakfasts than black-bread cake and warm goat's-milk.

This ended, a difficult task had to be mastered, and that was to try and obtain information such as would enable the two questioners to learn the whereabouts of the British troops.

But it proved to be easier than might have been supposed.

To Pen's surprise he learned all he wanted by the use of three words— *soldado, Francés,* and *Inglés*—with the addition of a good deal of gesticulation.

For, their breakfast ended, the two lads stood with their hosts, and Pen patted his own breast and that of his companion, and then touched their muskets and belts.

"*Soldado,*" he said. "*Soldado.*"

The fiercer-looking of the two goat-herds caught his meaning directly, and touched them both in turn upon the breast before repeating the word *soldado* (soldier).

"That's all right, Punch," said Pen. "I have made him understand that we are soldiers."

"Tchah!" said Punch scornfully. "These Spaniels ain't fools. They knowed that without you telling them."

"Never mind," said Pen. "Let me have my own way, unless you would like to do it."

"No, thank you," replied the boy, shrinking back, while Pen now turned and pointed in the direction where he believed the French troops lay.

"*Soldado Francés?*" he said in a questioning tone; and the man nodded quickly, caught hold of the lad's pointing arm, and pressed it a little to one side, as if to show him that he had not quite located their enemies correctly.

"*Soldado Francés!*" he said, showing his white teeth in a smile; and then his face changed and he drew his knife. "*Soldado Francés,*" he said fiercely.

Pen nodded, and signed to the man to replace his knife.

"So far, so good, Punch," said Pen. "I don't know how we are going to get on about the next question."

But again the task proved perfectly easy, for, laying his hand upon the goat-herd's arm, he repeated the words "*Soldado Inglés.*"

"*Si,*" said the man directly; and he patted the lad on his shoulder. "*Soldado Inglés.*"

"Yes, that's all right," said Pen; "but, now then, look here," And pointing with his hand to a spot higher up the mountain, he repeated the two Spanish words with a questioning tone: "*Soldado Inglés?*"

The man looked at him blankly, and Pen pointed in another direction, repeating his question, and then again away down a far-reaching valley lying westward of where they stood.

And now the Spaniard's face lit up as if he fully grasped the meaning of the question.

"*Si, si, si!*" he cried, nodding quickly and pointing right away into the distant valley. "*Soldado Inglés! Soldado Inglés!*" he cried. "*Muchos, muchos.*" And then, thoroughly following the meaning of the lad's questions, he cried excitedly, as he pointed away down the valley, where an occasional flash of light suggested the presence of a river, "*Soldado Inglés, muchos, muchos.*" And then he tapped the musket and belts and repeated his words again and again as he pointed away into the distance.

"*Bravo amigo!*" cried Pen.—"There, Punch, I don't think there's a doubt of it. The British forces lie somewhere over there."

"Then if the British forces lie over there," cried Punch, almost pompously, "that's where the —th lies, for they always go first. Why, we shall be at home again to-night if we have luck. My word, won't the chaps give us a hooroar when we march into camp? For, of course, they think we are dead! You listen what old O'Grady says. You see if he don't say, 'Well done, me boys! Ye are welkim as the flures of May.' I say, ask him how many miles it is to where our fellows lie."

"No, Punch, you do it."

"No, I ain't going to try."

"Well, look here; these men have been very good to us, and we ought to show that we are grateful. How is it to be done?"

"I don't know," said Punch. "We ain't got no money, have we?"

"Not a *peseta*, Punch. But I tell you what will please them. You must give them your knife."

"Give them my knife! Likely! Why, it's the best bit of stuff that was ever made. I wouldn't take a hundred pounds for it."

"Well, no one will offer it to you, Punch, and you are not asked to sell it. I ask you to give it to them to pay for what they have done for us."

"But give my knife! I wouldn't.—Oh, well, all right. You know best, and if you think we ought to give it to them, there you are.—Good-bye, old sharper! I am very sorry to part with you all the same."

"Never mind, Punch. I'll give you a better one some day."

"Some day never comes," said the boy grumpily. "But I know you will if you can."

Pen took the knife, and, eager to get the matter over, he stepped to where the bigger goat-herd stood watching them, and opened and shut the big clasp-knife, picked up a piece of wood, and showed how keen the blade was, the man watching him curiously the while; and then Pen closed it and placed it in the man's hand.

The Spaniard looked at him curiously for a moment, as if not quite grasping his meaning.

"*Por usted*," said Pen; and the man nodded and smiled, but shook his head and gave him the knife back.

"Hooroar! He won't have it," cried Punch.

Pen pressed it upon the man again, and Punch groaned; but the man rejected it, once more thrusting the knife back with both hands, and then laughingly pointed down to Pen's boots.

"What does he mean by that, Punch?" cried Pen.

"Haw, haw, haw, haw!" laughed the boy. "He wants you to give him your boots."

"Nonsense!"

"Here, give us hold of my knife. Hooroar! Sharper, I have got you again! But he sha'n't have your boots; he shall have mine, and welcome.—Look here, my cock Spaniel," continued the boy excitedly, as he pocketed his knife, and dropping himself on the ground he began to unfasten his boots. But the man shook his head and signed to him that they would not do, pointing again and again to Pen's. "No, no; you can't have them. These are better. You can have them and welcome."

But there was a difference of opinion, the Spaniard persisting in his demand for the pair that had taken his fancy.

"Here, I didn't think he was such a fool," cried Punch. "These are the best;" and the boy thrust off his boots and held them out to the man, who still shook his head violently.

"No, no, Punch," said Pen, who had quickly followed his companion's example; and he drew off his own boots and held them to the man, who seized them joyfully, showing them with a look of triumph to his fellow. "There, put yours on again, Punch."

"Not me," said the boy. "Think I'm going to tramp in boots and let you tramp over the rocks barefoot? Blest if I do; so there! Here, you put them on."

"Not I," said Pen. "I don't believe they would fit me."

"Yes, they would. I do know that. You are years older than I am, but my feet's quite as big as yours; so now then. I tried yours when you was asleep one night, and they fitted me exactly, so of course these 'ere will fit you. Here, catch hold."

Pen turned away so decisively that the boy stood scowling; but a thought struck him, and with a look of triumph he turned to the younger of the two goat-herds.

"Here you are, cocky," he cried; and to the man's keen delight Punch thrust the pair of boots into his hands and gave him a hearty slap on the back. "It's all right, comrade," cried the boy. "Foots soon gets hard when you ain't got no shoes. Nature soles and heels them with her own leather. Lots of our chaps have chucked their boots away, and don't mind a bit. There was plenty of foots in the world, me boy, before there was any brogues. I heered O'Grady say that one day to one of our chaps who had had his boots stolen. I say, what are they going to do?"

This soon became evident, for the elder goat-herd, on seeing that the lads were about to start in the direction of the valley, pressed upon Pen a goatskin-bag which he took from a corner of the shelter, its contents being a couple of bread-cakes, a piece of cheese like dried brown leather, about a dozen onions, and the horn of salt.

"Come along, Punch," cried Pen cheerily. "They have given us a *quid pro quo* at all events."

"Have they?" cried Punch eagerly. "Take care of it then. I have often longed for a bit when I felt so horribly hungry. Old O'Grady told me over and over again that a chew of 'bacco is splendid when you ain't got nothing to eat; so we will just try."

"What are you talking about?" said Pen, as they marched along the mountain-slope like some one of old who "went delicately," for the way was stony, and Nature had not had time to commence the promised soleing and heeling process.

"What was I talking about? You said they'd slipped some 'bacco into the bag."

"Nonsense!" cried Pen.

"I swear you did. You said quid something."

"I said a few Latin words that sounded like it."

"Well, look ye here, comrade; don't do it again. Latin was all very well for that old *padre*—good old chap! Bless his bald head! Regular trump he was! And parlyvooing was all very well for Mr Contrabando; but plain English for Bob Punchard, sivvy play, as we say in French."

Chapter Forty Two
Friend and Enemy

The two lads started off light-hearted and hopeful, for if they could trust the goat-herds, whose information seemed to be perfectly correct, a day's journey downward to the river in the valley, though seeming far distant, must bring them pretty near the goal they sought—in other words, the headquarters of the army that had crossed over from Portugal into Spain to drive back the French usurper, the task having been given to England's most trusted General, Wellesley, who was in time to come always to be better known as Wellington.

Thanks to the goat-herds, the lads were well provisioned for a day; but at the same time, and again thanks to their hosts of the past night, they were sadly crippled for their task.

It was not long before they began to feel how badly they were equipped, for the principal production of the part of the country they traversed seemed to be stones, from the smallest sharp-cornered pebble up to huge blocks half the size of a house. But for hours they trudged on sturdily, chatting cheerfully at first, then growing silent, and then making remarks which were started by Punch.

"Say, comrade," he said, "is Spain what they call a civilised country?"

"Yes, and one of the most famous in Europe; at least, it used to be."

"Ah, used to be!" said Punch sharply. "Used. 'Tain't now. I don't call a place civilised where they have got roads like this."

"Yes, it is rough," said Pen.

"Rough! Rough ain't the word for it," grumbled Punch. "If we go on much farther like this I shall wear my feet to the bone. Ain't it time we sat down and had a bit of dinner?"

"No," replied Pen. "We will sit down and rest if you like, but we must try and husband our provisions so as to make them last over till to-morrow night."

"What's to-morrow night got to do with it? We ought to be along with the British army by to-night; and what's husbands got to do with it? We are not going to share our prog with anybody else, and if it's husbands, how do we know they won't bring their wives? Bother! You will be telling me they are going to bring all their kids next."

"Is that meant for a joke, Punch? Let's go a little farther first. Come along, step out."

"Step out indeed!" grumbled the boy. "I stepped out first thing—right out of my boots. I say, comrade, oughtn't the soles of our feet to begin to get hard by now?"

"Don't talk about it, Punch."

"Oh, you can feel it too? If it's like this now, what's it going to be by to-night? I did not know that it was going to be so bad. If I had, blest if that goat-stalker should have had my boots! I'd have kept them, and shared them—one apiece—and every now and then we could have changed foots. It would have been better then, wouldn't it?"

"I don't know, Punch. Don't think about it. Let's go on till we get to the first spring, and then rest and bathe our feet."

"All right."

The boys kept on their painful walk for another hour; and then, the spring being found, they rested and bathed their tender soles, partook of a portion of their provisions, and went on again.

That night the river seemed to be as far off as ever, and as they settled upon a sheltered spot for their night's rest, and ate their spare supper, Punch hazarded the remark that they shouldn't overtake the army the next day. Pen was more hopeful, and that night they fell asleep directly, with Punch quite forgetful of the wolves.

The morning found the travellers better prepared for the continuance of their journey, and they toiled on painfully, slept for another night in a patch of forest, and started off at the first blink of dawn so as to reach the river, which was now flowing swiftly westward on their left.

Their provisions were finished, all but a scrap of the bread which was so hard that they were glad to soak it in the river; but in spite of their pain they walked on more bravely, their sufferings being alleviated by the water, which was now always on their left, and down to whose bubbling surface they descended from time to time.

"I say," said Punch, all at once, "I hope those chaps were right, because we have come a long way, and I can't see no sign of the army. You must have patience, Punch."

"All right; but it's nearly all used up. I say, look here, do you think the army will be this side of the river?"

"Can't say, Punch.—I hope so."

"But suppose it's the other side. How are you going to get across? Are we likely to come to a town and a bridge?"

"No; we are too far away up in the mountains. But I dare say we shall be able to find a ford where we can cross."

"Oh!" said Punch thoughtfully; and they journeyed on, beginning to suffer now from hunger in addition to weariness and pain; and just about midday, when the heat of the sun was beating down strongly in the river valley, Punch limped off painfully to where an oak-tree spread its shady boughs, and threw himself prone.

"It's all up, comrade," he said. "Can't go no farther."

"No, no; don't give way," said Pen, who felt painfully disposed to follow his companion's example. "Get well into the shade and have a few hours' sleep. It will be cooler by-and-by, and we shall get on better after a rest. There, try and go to sleep."

"Who's to sleep with a pair of red-hot feet and an empty cupboard? I can't," said Punch. And he took hold of his ankles, drew them up, and sat Chinese-tumbler fashion, rocking himself to and fro; while with a weary sigh Pen sank down beside him and sat gazing into the sunny distance.

"Couldn't we get over to the other side?" said Punch at last. "It's all rocks and stones and rough going this side, and all green and meadowlike over the other. Can you swim?"

"Yes, pretty well," said Pen; "but I should be too tired to try."

"So can I, pretty tidy. I am tired, but not too tired to try. Let's just rest a bit, and then swim across. It runs pretty fast, but 'tain't far, and if it carried us some way down, all the better."

"Very well, after a bit I don't mind if we try," said Pen; "but I must rest first."

Then the boys were silent for a time, for Punch, whose eyes were wandering as he scanned the distance of the verdant undulating slope on the other side of the river, suddenly burst out with: "Yes, we had better get across, for our chaps are sure to be on the other side of the river."

"Why?" said Pen drowsily.

"'Cause we are this. Soldiering always seems to be going by the rules of contrary; and—there!" cried the boy excitedly, "what did I tell you? There they are!"

"What, our men? Where?" cried Pen excitedly.

"Right over yonder, a mile away."

"I can see nothing."

"You don't half look," cried Punch angrily, bending forward, nursing his tender feet and staring wildly into the distance. "I ketched sight of a bit of scarlet ever so far off, and that must mean Bri'sh soldiers."

"No; it might be something painted red—or a patch of poppies perhaps."

"Oh, go it!" cried Punch angrily. "You will say next it is a jerrynium in a red pot, same as my mother always used to have in her window. It's redcoats, I tell you. There, can't you see them?"

"No."

"Tchah! You are not looking right. Look yonder—about a mile away from the top of that hill just to the right of that bit of a wood. Now, do you see?"

"No," said Pen slowly. "Yes, I do—men marching. Do you see that flash in the sunlight. Bayonets! Punch, you are right!"

"Ah!" said the boy. "Now then, what do you say to a swim across?"

"Yes, I am ready," said Pen. "How far is it, do you think?"

"About a hundred yards," replied the boy. "Oh, we ought to do that easy. You see, it will be only paddle at first, and then wade till you get up to your chest, and then swim. Perhaps we sha'n't have to swim at all. Rough rivers like this are always shallow. When you are ready I am. We sha'n't have to take off our shoes and stockings; and if we get very wet, well, we can wring our clothes, and they will soon dry in the sun. Look sharp and give the word. I am ready for anything with the British army in sight."

There was no hesitation now. The lads took the precaution of securing their cartouche-boxes between the muzzle of their pieces and the ramrod; and, keeping the muskets still slung so that at any moment they could let them drop loose to hang from the shoulder, they stepped carefully down amongst the stones until the pleasantly cool water began to foam above their feet, and then waded carefully on till they were knee-deep and began to feel the pressure of the water against their legs.

"Ain't going to be deep," said Punch cheerily. "Don't it feel nice to your toddlers? How fast it runs, though! Why, if it was deep enough to swim in it would carry you along faster than you could walk. It strikes me that we shall get across without having it up to one's waistbelt."

The boy seemed pretty correct in his judgment, for as they carefully waded on—carefully, for the bottom was very uneven—they were nearly half across, and still the water was not so deep as the boy had prophesied.

"There! What did I tell you?" he said; and then with his next step he caught at his companion's hand and went down to his chin.

The result was that Pen lost his balance, and the pair, half-struggling, half-swimming for about a dozen yards, were carried swiftly along to where a patch of rock showed itself in mid-stream with the water foaming all around.

They were swept right round against the rocks, and found bottom directly, struggling up, with the swift stream only now to their knees.

"What a hole!" cried Pen, panting a little with his exertions. "I say, you must take care, Punch."

"Oh yes, I will take care," said the boy, puffing and choking. "I don't know how much water I have swallowed. But it's all shallow now, and we are half-over. How about your cartridges? Mine's all wet."

"Then I suppose mine are too," said Pen.

"Never mind," cried Punch cheerfully. "Perhaps they will be all right if we lay them out to dry in the sun. Now then, are you ready? It looks as if it will be all shallow the rest of the way."

"I sha'n't trust it," said Pen, "so let's keep hold of hands."

They started again, yielding a little to the stream, and wading diagonally for the bank on Punch's left, but making very slow progress, for Pen noted that the water, which was rough and shallow where they were, seemed to flow calmly and swiftly onward a short distance away, and was evidently deep.

"Steady! Steady!" cried Pen, hanging away a little towards the bank from which they had started.

"All right; I am steady enough, only one can't do as one likes. It's just as if all the water was pushing behind. Ah! Look out, comrade!"

Pen was already looking out, and he had need, for once more his companion had stepped as it were off a shelf into deep water, and the next moment, still grasping Punch's hand with all his might, he was striking out; and then together they were being borne rapidly down by the stream.

Chapter Forty Three
Fresh Comrades

Pen never could quite settle in his own mind how it all happened. He was conscious of the rush of water and the foam bubbling against his lips, while he clung tightly to his companion till they were swept against rocks, borne into eddies, whirled round now beneath the surface, now gasping for breath as darkness was turned into light; then feeling as if they were being dragged over rough pieces of rock that were slimy with weed as he caught at them with one hand, and then, still clinging to Punch, who clung to him, they were being carried slowly over a shallow patch where the water raced beside their ears, till at last he struggled out, half-blind and dizzy, to find himself alone, with the sun beating hotly upon his head.

He was giddy, breathless, confused in his excitement, as he pressed the water from his eyes; and then he uttered a cry, for about twenty yards from where he stood, with the water barely up to his ankles, he could see Punch lying upon his face, gradually gliding away towards the spot where the stream was beginning to run smooth and deep.

He could recall this part of his adventure, though, well enough: how he staggered and splashed to the place, where he could catch hold of the boy, and turn him over before getting hold of his belt and dragging him right out of the river on to the sandy bank where it was hot and dry.

And then he could recall how a great despair came upon him, and he knelt helplessly gazing down at his comrade, with the horrible feeling upon him that he was dead.

Then all was misty again. The river was running onward with a swift rush towards its mouth, and he was conscious that he was safe upon the bank from which he had started. Then he knew that he must have swooned away, and lay, for how long he could not tell; but the next thing that he remembered clearly was that he opened his eyes to see Punch bending over him and rocking him to and fro according to the drill instructions they had both learned as to how to deal with a fellow-soldier who has been half-drowned.

"Oh, Punch," he cried, in a voice that sounded to him like a hoarse whisper, "I thought you were dead!"

The boy was blubbering as if his heart would break, and it was some moments before he half-sobbed and half-whimpered out, "Why, you couldn't have done that, because it's what I was thinking about you. But, I say, comrade, you are all right, aren't you?"

"I—I suppose so," gasped Pen.

"Oh, don't talk like that," sobbed the boy.

"This 'ere's the worst of all. Do say as you are coming round. Why, you must be, or else you couldn't talk. But, I say, did you save me, or did I save you? Blest if I know! And here we are on the wrong side after all! What's to be done now?"

"Wring our clothes, I suppose, Punch," said Pen wearily, "or lie down and rest without."

"Well, I feel as if I should like to do that," said Punch. "This 'ere sand is hot and dry enough to make us steam. I say, comrade," he continued, wiping his eyes and speaking in a piteous tone, "don't you take no notice of me and the water squeezing out of my eyes. I am so full of it that it's running out. But we are all right, comrade. I was beginning to think you had gone and left me all alone. But I say, this 'ere's a nice place, this Spain! Here, what's the matter with you?" continued Punch excitedly. "Don't turn like that, choking and pynting. Oh, this 'ere's worse still! He's in a blessed fit!"

He had seized Pen by the shoulders now, and began shaking him violently, till Pen began to struggle with him, forced him aside, and then pointing across the river, he gasped out, "Cavalry! Look, look!"

The boy swung himself round, one hand felt for his musket, the other at his belt, where the bayonet should have been, for the word cavalry suggested to him preparations for receiving a charge.

Then, following the direction of his companion's pointing hand, he fully grasped what was meant, for coming down the slope across the river were a couple of English light dragoons, who had caught sight of the two figures on the opposite bank.

The men were approaching cautiously, each with his carbine at the ready, and for the moment it seemed as if the vedette were about to place the lives of the two lads in fresh peril. But as they drew nearer the boys rose and shouted; though the rushing noise of the river drowned their words.

As the boys continued to gesticulate, the men began to grasp the fact that they had been in the water, and what they were, for one of them began pointing along the stream and waving his hand, as he shouted again and again.

"Can't—understand—what—you—say!" yelled Punch; and then putting his hand to his lips, he shouted with all his might, "English! Help!"

The word "help" evidently reached the ears of one of the dragoons, for, rising in his stirrups, he waved the hand that held his carbine and pointed downstream, yelling out something again.

"I don't know, comrade," cried Punch dolefully. "I think it was 'Come on!'"

"I know now," cried Pen. "It was 'ford.'"

Then the drenched, exhausted pair staggered on over the dry sand, which suggested that at times the river must be twice its present width; and the vedette guided their horses carefully on amongst the stones of the farther bank, till, a few hundred yards lower down, where the river was clear of obstructions and ran swiftly on in a regular ripple, the two horses turned right and paced gently down into the water, which, half-way to their knees, splashed up as they made for the opposite bank, which the lads reached at the same time as the vedette.

"Why, hallo, my lads! We couldn't make out what you were. The —th, aren't you?"

"Yes."

"What! Have you been in the river?"

"Yes, tried to cross—'most drowned," said Punch hoarsely.

"You should have come down to this ford. Where are you for?"

"Our corps, when we can find it," said Pen.

"Oh, that's all right; about two miles away. Come on."

"Not me!" said Punch sturdily. "I have had enough of it."

"What do you mean?" said the other dragoon who had not spoken. "Afraid to cross?"

"Yes, that's it," said Punch. "So would you be if you had had my dose. I'm nearly full of water now."

"Well, you look it," said the first dragoon, laughing. "Here, take hold of our stirrup-leathers. We will take you across all right."

Punch hesitated.

"Shall we risk it, comrade?" he said.

"Yes, of course."

And Punch limped painfully to the side of the second dragoon, while Pen took hold of the stirrup-leather of the first.

"Here, I say, this won't do," said the man, as their horses' hoofs sank in the hot, dry sand of the other side. "Why, you are both regularly knocked up.—Dismount!" he cried, and he and his companion dropped from their saddles. "There, my lads, mount. You can ride the rest of the way. Hallo! Limping?" he continued. "What does that mean? Footsore, or a wound?"

"Wound," said Pen quietly. "My comrade, there, has been worse than I. How far do you say it is to the camp?"

"A couple of miles; but we will see you there safe. How have you been off for rations?"

Pen told him, and an end was put to their famishing state by a surprise of the dragoons' haversacks.

About half an hour later the led horses entered the camp, and the boy's hearts were gladdened by the cheery notes of a cavalry call.

"Ah," whispered Punch, as he leaned over from his seat in the saddle to whisper to Pen, "that seems to do a fellow's heart good, comrade. But 'tain't so good as a bugle. If I could hear that again I should be just myself."

Chapter Forty Four
Before the Aquiline

Three days in the English camp, and the two lads had pretty well recovered; but they were greatly disappointed to find that during the absence of the dragoons on vedette duty the —th and another regiment had been despatched for a reconnoitring expedition, so that the lads had encountered no old friends.

"Well, I suppose we oughtn't to grumble, comrade," said Punch, "for every one makes no end of a fuss over us, and are always beginning to ask questions and set one telling them about all we did after we were left behind."

"Yes; I am rather tired of it," said Pen. "I shall be only too glad when we are able to join the regiment."

"Oh, I shall be glad enough," said Punch. "I want to see old O'Grady, me boy; and, I say, do you think, if I was to make a sort of petition like, the colonel would put me in one of the companies now? Of course I used to be proud enough of being bugler, but I want to be full private."

"Well, you have only got to wait till you get bigger," said Pen, smiling.

"Bother bigger!" cried the boy. "Why, I am growing fast, and last time I was measured I was only an inch shorter than the little chap we have got; and what difference does an inch make when a fellow can carry a rifle and can use it? You can't say that I ain't able, though it was only a musket."

"No, Punch; there isn't a man in the regiment could have done better than you did."

"There, then!" cried the boy, with his eyes sparkling. "Then I'm sure if you would speak up and say all that to the colonel he would let me go into one of the companies. I want to be in yours, but I would wait for my chance if they would only make me a full private at once."

The boys were sitting talking together when an infantry sergeant came up and said, "Here, youngsters, don't go away. Smarten yourselves up a bit. You are to come with me to the officers' tent. I will be back in about ten minutes."

The sergeant went off in his quick, business-like way, and Punch began to grumble.

"Who's to smarten himself up," he cried petulantly, "when his uniform is all nohow and he's got no proper boots? These old uns they've give me don't fit, and they will be all to pieces directly; and yours ain't much better. I suppose they are going to question us again about where we have been and what we have done."

"Yes," said Pen wearily, "and I am rather tired of it. It's like making a show of us."

"Oh, well, it don't hurt. They like to hear, and I dare say the officers will give orders that we are to have something to eat and drink."

"Punch, you think of nothing but eating and drinking," said Pen again.

"Well, after being starved as we have, ain't it enough to make anybody think that a little more wouldn't do them any harm? Hallo, he's soon back!" For he caught sight of the sergeant coming.

"Now, boys," he said, "ready?"

"Yes," said Pen; and the keen-looking non-com looked both of them over in turn.

"That the best you can do for yourselves?" he said sourly. "Well, I suppose it is. You are clean, and you look as if you had been at work. You, Punchard, can't you let those trousers down a little lower?"

"No, sir; I did try last night. They have run up through being in the river when we were half-drowned."

"Humph! Perhaps," said the sergeant. "I believe it was the growing so much."

Punch turned sharply to his comrade and gave him a wink, as much as to say, "Hear that?"

"Now then, forward!" said the sergeant. "And look here, put on your best manners, boys. You are going before some of the biggest officers, so mind your p's and q's."

A few minutes later the sergeant stopped short at the largest tent in the camp, stated his business to the sentry who was marching to and fro before a flag, and after waiting a few minutes a subaltern came out, spoke to the sergeant, and then told the boys to follow him.

Directly after, the pair were ushered into the presence of half-a-dozen officers in undress uniform, one of whom, a keen-looking, aquiline-nosed man, gave them in turn a sharp, searching look, which Punch afterwards said went right through him and came back again. He then turned to a grey-haired officer and said shortly, "Go on. I will listen."

The grey-haired officer nodded and then turned to the two lads.

"Look here, boys," he said, "we have heard something about your adventures while you were away from your regiment. Now, stories grow in telling, like snowballs. Do you understand?"

"Oh yes, sir," said Punch, "I know that;" and, apparently not in the slightest degree abashed by the presence in which he found himself, the boy eagerly scanned each officer in turn, before examining every item within the tent, and then letting his eyes wander out through the open doorway.

"And you, my lad?" continued the officer, for Pen had remained silent.

"Yes, sir," said the lad quietly.

"Well," said the officer, "we want the plain, simple account of where you have been, without any exaggeration, for I am afraid one of you—I don't know which, but I dare say I shall make a very shrewd guess before we have done—has been dressing up your adventures with rather a free hand."

"I beg your pardon, sir," said Pen quietly, "my comrade here, Punchard, has told nothing but the simple truth, and I have only answered questions without the slightest exaggeration."

"Without the slightest exaggeration?" said the officer, looking searchingly at Pen, and there was a touch of irony in his tone. "Well, that is what I want from you now."

Pen coloured and remained silent while the officer asked a question or two of Punch, but soon turned to the elder lad, who, warming as he went on, briefly and succinctly related the main points of what they had gone through.

"Very well said! Well spoken, my lad," said the aquiline-nosed officer; and Pen started, for, warming in his narration, Pen had almost forgotten his presence. "How long have you been a private in the —th?"

"A year, sir."

"Where were you before you enlisted?"

"At Blankton House School."

"Oh, I thought they called that College."

"Yes, sir, they do," said Pen, smiling; "but it is only a preparation place."

"Yes, for the sons of gentlemen making ready for the army?"

"Yes, sir."

"And how come you to be a private in his Majesty's Rifle-Regiment?"

Pen was silent.

"Speak out, comrade," put in Punch. "There ain't nothing to be ashamed of."

"Silence, sir!" cried the officer. "Let your comrade speak for himself." Then turning to Pen, "Your comrade says there was nothing to be ashamed of."

"There is not, sir," said Pen gravely.

"Well, then, keep nothing back."

"It was this way, sir," said Pen. "I was educated to be an officer, and then by a death in my family all my hopes were set aside, and I was placed in a lawyer's office to become a clerk. I couldn't bear it, sir."

"And you ran away?"

"No, sir. I appealed again and again for leave to return to my school and finish my education. My relative refused to listen to me, and I suppose I did wrong, for I went straight to where they were recruiting for the Rifle-Regiment, and the sergeant took me at once."

"H'm!" said the officer, looking searchingly in the lad's eyes. "How came you to join so quiet-looking a regiment?"

Pen smiled rather bitterly.

"It was because my relative, sir, always threw it in my teeth that it was for the sake of the scarlet uniform that I wanted to join the army."

"H'm!" said the officer. "Now, look here, my lad; I presume you have had your eyes about you during the time that you were a prisoner, when you were escaping, and when you were with the *contrabandista* and had that adventure with the Spanish gentleman whom you suppose to be the King. By the way, why did you suppose that he was the King?"

"From the behaviour of his followers, sir, and from what I learned from the smuggler chief."

"H'm. He was a Spaniard, of course?"

"Yes, sir."

"Do you speak Spanish?"

"No, sir. We conversed in French."

"Do you speak French fluently?"

"Pretty easily, sir; but I am afraid my accent is atrocious."

"But you should hear him talk Latin, sir!" cried Punch eagerly.

"Silence, boy!" snapped out the grey-haired officer; and the chief gave him a look and a smile.

"Well, he can, sir; that's quite true," cried Punch angrily. "He talked to the old father, the *padre*, who was a regular friend to us."

"Silence, boy!" said the aquiline-nosed officer sternly now. "Your comrade can say what he has to say modestly and well. That is a thing you cannot do, so do not interrupt again."

"All right, sir. No, sir; beg pardon," said Punch.

"Well," continued the officer, looking keenly and searchingly at Pen, "you should have been able to carry in your mind a pretty good idea of the country you have passed through."

"He can, sir," cried Punch. "He has got it all in his head like a map."

"My good boy," said the officer, biting his lip to add to the severity of his aspect, "if you interrupt again you will be placed under arrest."

Punch closed his lips so tightly that they formed a thin pink line right across the bottom of his face.

"Now, Private Gray, do you think that you do carry within your recollection a pretty good idea of the face of the country; or to put it more simply and plainly, do you think you could guide a regiment through the passes of this wild country and lead them safely to where you left the French encamped?"

"I have not a doubt but that I could, sir."

"In the dark?"

"It would be rather harder in the dark, sir," replied Pen, "but I feel confident that I could."

"May I take it that you are willing to try?"

"I am the King's servant, sir, and I will do my best."

"That's enough," said the chief. "You can return to your quarters and hold yourself in readiness to do what I propose, and if you do this successfully—"

The speaker stopped short, and Pen took a step towards him.

"What were you going to say?" said the officer.

"Let me try first, sir," said the lad, with his pale face, worn by what he had gone through of late, flushing up with excitement.

"That will do," said the officer, "only be ready for your duty at any moment.—Well, what do you wish to say?"

Pen stretched out his hand and laid it upon Punch's shoulder, for the boy had been moving his lips almost continuously during the latter part of the conversation, and in addition making hideous grimaces as if he were in pain.

"Only this, sir," said Pen; "my companion here went through all that I did. He was keenly observant, and would be of great assistance to me if at any turn I were in doubt."

"Then you would like to have him with you?"

"Yes, sir."

"And you feel that you could trust him?"

"Oh yes, sir," replied Pen. And the boys' eyes met—their hands too, for Punch with his lips still pressed together took a step forward and caught Pen by the hand and wrist.

"Take him with you, then," said the officer.

"Oh, thank— Hooray! hooray!" cried Punch, wildly excited now, for he had caught the tramp of men and seen that which made him dash towards the open tent-door.

"Bring back that boy!" cried the officer; and the sergeant, who was waiting outside, arrested Punch and brought him before the group of officers.

"How dare you, sir!" cried the chief wrathfully. "You are not to be trusted. I rescind that permission I was about to give."

"Oh, don't do that, sir! 'Tain't fair!" cried the boy. "I couldn't help it, sir. It was our fellows, sir, marching into camp—the —th, sir—Rifles, sir. Ain't seen them, sir, since I was shot down. Don't be hard on a fellow, sir! So glad to see them, sir. You might have done the same. I only wanted to give them a cheer."

"Then go out and cheer them, sir," said the officer, frowning severely, but with a twinkle of mirth in his eye.—"There, Pen Gray, you know your duty. It is an important one, and I have given it to you in the full belief that you will well serve your country and your King."

Chapter Forty Five
No more bugling

That same night not only a regiment but a very strong brigade of the British army marched upon the important service that was in hand.

They marched only by night, and under Pen's guidance the French forces that had been besieging the old mine were utterly routed. This happened at a time when provisions were failing, and the *contrabandista* captain saw nothing before him but surrender, for he had found to his dismay that the adit through which he had hoped to lead the Spanish monarch to safety had been blocked by the treacherous action of some follower—by whom, he could not tell, though he guessed that it was a question of bribery.

There was nothing for it but to die in defence of his monarch, and this they were prepared to do; but no further fierce fighting had taken place, for the French General, after securing every exit by the aid of his reinforcements, felt satisfied that he had only to wait for either surrender or the dash out by a forlorn hope, ready to die sword in hand.

Then came shortly what was to him a thorough surprise, and the routing of his forces by the British troops in an encounter which laid open a large tract of country and proved to be one of the greatest successes of Sir Arthur Wellesley's campaign.

The natural sequence was a meeting in the English General's tent, where the King was being entertained by the General himself. Here he expressed a desire to see again the brave young English youth to whom he owed so much, for he had learned the part Pen Gray had taken in his rescue.

It was one afternoon of such a day as well made the Peninsula deserve the name of Sunny Spain that the —th Rifles were on duty ready to perform their task of acting as escort to the dethroned Spanish monarch on his way back to his capital; and to the surprise of Pen a message was brought to him to come with his companion to the General's tent.

Here he was received by the King in person, and with a few earnest thanks for all he had done, the monarch presented him with a ring which he took from his finger. He followed this up by taking his watch and chain and presenting them to Punch, who took them in speechless wonder, looked from one to the other, and then whispered to Pen, "He means this for you."

The General heard his words, and said quietly, "No, my lad; keep your present. Your friend and companion has yet to be paid for the modest and brave way in which he performed his duties in guiding our force.—Private Gray, his Majesty here is in full agreement with that which I am about to do. It is this—which is quite within my powers as General of his Britannic Majesty's forces. In exceptional cases promotion is given to young soldiers for bravery in the field. I have great pleasure in presenting you with your commission. Ensign Gray, I hope that some day I may call you Captain. The way is open to you now. I wish you every success."

"Oh, I say!" cried Punch, as soon as they were alone.

The boy could say no more, for he was half-choking with emotion. But within an hour he was with Pen again bursting with news and ready to announce, "No more bugling! Hooray! I am the youngest full private in our corps!"